LAURA and TOM McNEAL

CROOKED

For Sam

Published by
Dell Laurel-Leaf
an imprint of
Random House Children's Books
a division of Random House, Inc.
1540 Broadway
New York, New York 10036

If you purchased this book without a cover you should be aware that this book is stolen property. It was reported as "unsold and destroyed" to the publisher and neither the author nor the publisher has received any payment for this "stripped book."

Copyright © 1999 by Laura McNeal and Tom McNeal
Cover photograph copyright © 1999 by CORBIS/Bettmann

All rights reserved. No part of this book may be reproduced or transmitted in any form or by any means, electronic or mechanical, including photocopying, recording, or by any information storage and retrieval system, without the written permission of the Publisher, except where permitted by law. For information address Alfred A. Knopf, a division of Random House, Inc., 1540 Broadway, New York, New York 10036.

The trademarks Laurel-Leaf Library® and Dell® are registered in the U.S. Patent and Trademark Office and in other countries.

Visit us on the Web! www.randomhouse.com/teens

Educators and librarians, for a variety of teaching tools, visit us at
www.randomhouse.com/teachers

ISBN: 0-440-22946-4

RL: 5.5

Reprinted by arrangement with Alfred A. Knopf
a division of Random House, Inc.

Printed in the United States of America

October 2002

10 9 8 7 6 5 4 3 2 1

OPM

If there are obstacles, the

shortest line between two points

may be the crooked one.

—Bertolt Brecht, from

The Life of Galileo

* * *

There was a crooked man,

And he walked a crooked mile.

He found a crooked sixpence

Against a crooked stile;

He bought a crooked cat,

Which caught a crooked mouse,

And they all lived together

In a little crooked house.

1

KEEPING THE LOCKS LOCKED

Before everything stopped being normal, the thing that Clara Wilson worried most about was her nose. It wasn't straight. The bridge began in a good downwardly vertical line, and then it just swooped off to the left. It was crooked even in her baby pictures. It looked as if someone—a doctor? a nurse? God in a mean mood?—had laid a finger at the side of her nose and pushed the straightness right out of it. The problem was, a crooked nose could make a whole face look crooked. Even when she was in a good mood and smiling, some little part of Clara was observing herself. *She smiled a crooked smile*, she would think. *She grinned a crooked grin. She walked a crooked mile.*

Her best friend, Gerri, whose nose was perfect, said Clara's nose wasn't *that* bad, but if it bothered her so much, why didn't she just get a nose job and forget about it?

That was Thursday lunch. Clara and Gerri were sitting alone at the farthest end of the cafeteria, at a table positioned under a big blue and black sign that read:

MELVILLE WHALERS
"WE GO GALE FORCE"

Gerri hated this table, but Clara liked it. It was away from all the din that carried from the more popular tables, which Gerri habitually watched over Clara's shoulder. It reminded Clara of how her father couldn't keep from sneaking glances at a televised football game in a restaurant. Clara said, "So how much does a nose job cost, innyhoo?"

Gerri shrugged. "Who knows? Just ask your dad for it." What things might cost was never a question Gerri had to worry about. She pulled out a file and began working her nails.

Clara had known Gerri for seven years, all the way back to second grade. Gerri's parents were definitely loaded. Clara's were definitely not. "I guess I could save up for it myself," she said, but her voice trailed off.

Gerri looked up from her fingernails. "Except you're already saving for that retardate horse camp."

Clara lowered her eyes. The horse camp wasn't for retardates. It was for girls who liked horses. And if Clara got to go to horse camp, Gerri had agreed to go, too, as long as Clara promised not to tell anybody. Though it was looking less and less like Clara would get to go. Her parents had said she would have to pay half. She'd saved $112 from her paper route, but half cost over $400.

"We're going skiing this weekend," Gerri said, without looking up from her fingernails. Gerri's family was always going somewhere weekends, and Gerri always invited Clara along. But today was slightly different. Today Gerri hesitated one long beat before saying, "You wanna come?"

Clara *did* want to come, in the worst way. But she hated asking her parents again for money. Lately, whenever Clara asked if she could go someplace with Gerri's family, her parents would glance at one another like something was wrong, and then her father would say, "Okay, but this is the last time for a while."

"Stowe or Killington?" Clara asked.

Gerri was working intently on a cuticle. "Stowe."

Stowe was the most expensive ski resort within five hundred miles.

Gerri glanced up. "You don't *have* to come or anything. I'm not begging."

Clara said, "No, I want to go, but…"

"But what?"

But I can't afford it, Clara thought. And so, without wanting to say it, Clara said she guessed she'd better not go this weekend because she had a World Cultures project due, and besides, she had her paper route. But that wasn't the worst of it. The worst of it was that Gerri looked almost relieved.

"Oh, that's okay," she said, staring past her to one of the popular tables. "We'll probably go again in a couple of weeks, and you can come with us then."

That night, while she was doing her homework, Clara suddenly changed her mind. She would spend some horse camp money for the ski weekend. But when she called Gerri to tell her the good news, Gerri said flatly, "What about your World Cultures project?"

"I got that mixed up. It's not due for another week."

There was an awkward silence, which Gerri finally ended. "Well, the thing is, when I thought you couldn't go, I asked somebody else," she said.

"Oh," Clara said. "Oh, that's okay. It's no big deal."

"I'm really sorry," Gerri said. "Next time for sure. Okay?"

"Sure."

The next day at school, Clara heard through Lisa Bates,

who'd heard through Melinda Sipp, that Gerri had asked Sands
Mandeville to go in her place. Sands Mandeville, who began life
as Sandra Ann, became Sandy by fifth grade, turned into Sondra
by seventh, and now was simply Sands. Sands, who'd been a
princess in the Color Day Court, who played on the girls' tennis
team, and who had the lead in the school play.

Friday afternoon, when Gerri was supposed to be at Clara's
locker, she wasn't. Instead she'd wedged a folded note into the
vents on the locker door. *Call ya 2nite from Stowesville*, it said.

I'll bet this is colder than Stowe, Clara thought as she threw *The
Jemison Star* that afternoon. Jemison was one of the minor towns
in wind-bitten, snow-buried upstate New York, and the bitter
February gusts made Clara's ears ache. Clara wore a green canvas
apron that slung over her shoulders, and Ham, her stout black
Labrador mix, carried a double-slung pouch of papers over his
back. She'd chosen Ham at the animal shelter on her tenth
birthday, and he'd been helping her walk her paper route ever
since. Ham always seemed to like the cold, whereas Clara did
not. The first thing she did when she came in on this Friday
night was go upstairs to her room, take off her clothes, and ease
herself into a tub of hot water. She read *TV Guide* and kept
adding hot water to keep the bath warm until her mother came
home, just before six.

"Clara?" she called from downstairs. "It's me! I'm home!"

It was her mother's good-mood voice, which, Clara thought,
was nice to hear for a change. When Clara dressed and went
downstairs, she found her mother busy and humming to herself.

"Tonight's the night, sweetie!" her mother said. Clara's father had been in Chicago on business all week, but was flying into Buffalo that night. He traveled all the time, but Clara's mother, to her surprise, was pulling out all the stops tonight for his homecoming. Over the next hour, Clara watched as her mother neatly filled a brand-new picnic basket with expensive deli food (including a bottle of fancy red wine), put on her silky black dinner-party pants, and spritzed on her best perfume (Chanel No. 5).

"These?" her mother asked, turning to Clara and holding up a long, dangly glass earring to one ear and then holding up a pearl earring to the other, "…or these?"

Clara said the pearl.

"That's you, Clara," her mother said, beaming out a smile that wrapped around Clara and pulled her in. "Class over flash."

Clara leaned down and gave Ham a two-handed scratch behind both ears. "Is that what I am, Hambone? Class over flash?" Ham seemed to smile back.

"You are also," her mother said cheerily, "a gal who likes to have the last word."

"I am?"

"Yes, you are."

"I think you're right," Clara said, in part playing along and in part because she really did like having the last word, whenever it was available.

Downstairs, after her mother had pulled on her long wool coat and checked her purse for keys, she invited Clara to come along to the airport, but only halfheartedly. And Clara said no, there was a movie on TV that she wanted to see, so she'd just stay home if that was okay.

Her mother winked and picked up the picnic basket. "Well," she said, doing a slow full turn. "How do I look?"

"Extremely *deluxe*," Clara said. This was something she'd heard Sands Mandeville say in the food court after a hunky lacrosse player had passed by. For this, Sands Mandeville had gotten a laugh from the circle of girls who always surrounded her, a circle that would never in a million years include Clara, with her crooked nose, but which might now include her best friend, Gerri.

"Clara?"

Clara blinked and refocused on her mother. "What?"

"I said keep the locks locked and don't wait up."

"Keep the locks locked" was what her mother always said when she was leaving Clara alone in the house. Her father always said, "Batten the hatches."

"I've got Ham to protect me," Clara said, which was what *she* always said on these occasions, and as she watched her mother walk off into the dark winter night, Clara knelt down and curled an arm around the Labrador's massive black head.

Clara Wilson lived with her mother and father in an old two-story house, loose-jointed and creaky. Usually she knew the whereabouts of others just by listening, and now, as she stood alone and still, the house seemed unnaturally quiet, as if it were holding its breath. Clara quickly went to the family room and turned on the TV. She ran through the channels, then wandered into the kitchen. She made popcorn, a bowl for herself and a bowl for Ham. She tried to read a book. To Ham, out loud, she said, "I wish I was in Stowe with Gerri."

Ham let his tail sweep the linoleum floor.

"Money," Clara said, and Ham lifted and cocked his head.

"Moola moola," she said, and Ham cocked his head the other way.

The telephone rang, but it wasn't Gerri. It was her father, wanting to know if her mother had left yet. His voice was edgy, a bad sign.

Clara said she had, ages ago. "Where are you? Is anything wrong?"

"Nothing serious. Just another communication glitch between your mother and me." Then, in a softer voice, he said, "But it's nothing for you to worry about, okay?"

"Okay."

"Are you all right, Polkadot?"

"Sure."

"And Hambone, too?"

"Yeah, he's fine, too, Dad."

"Okay, well, I better try to reach your mother at the airport. Have you battened the hatches?"

"Yeah," Clara said. And then, to make it easier for her father to get off the phone, she said, "And don't forget I have Ham for protection."

The minutes crept by: 7:43; 8:30; 9:12. Clara thumbed through her mother's *Vanity Fair*, glanced at the clock, then skimmed through a *Glamour*. She picked up and put down a *Good Housekeeping*. She got up and stared into the freezer. She had a bowl of her father's MochaHubba ice cream. She looked again at the clock.

10:15.

"Guess Gerri's not going to call," she said, and Ham, lying in the middle of the kitchen linoleum with his chin outstretched on his paws, rolled his eyes her way.

Clara went into the bathroom, pushed her nose straight, and held it there. She closed her eyes, counted to a hundred, then for good measure counted out another hundred, and then, when she released her hold, watched her nose default back to its swoop.

10:24.

Clara wandered up to her mother's room, which looked like some kind of neatness-free zone. Scarves and underwear and blouses were strewn everywhere. Since no one was home, Clara started snooping around the mess. In the drawer of her mother's nightstand, she found a book called *Saucy Monogamy*. Clara looked at the chapter headings. "Lotions & Notions." "32 Flavors." "Undressing for the Occasion." It made Clara a little queasy. She turned to a chapter called "The Heartpopping Homecoming," which suggested, among other things, taking a long oiled bath, putting on lacy underthings, and greeting the returning husband at the airport "in a slinky dress with an extravagant bottle of wine and a prepaid room key for a nearby Hilton."

Clara flipped to the cover. Just below *Saucy Monogamy* it read, *101 Ways to Put the Sass Back in the Married State*. How come her parents needed sass, anyway?

All of a sudden the sound of her mother's telephone went shooting through her. For one crazy moment, Clara felt as if she'd been caught at something. She let the phone ring twice.

"Hello?"

"*Cómo está, Senorita Clarita?*" It was Gerri's wooden Spanish. This was her customary greeting, only now she was whispering.

Clara laughed and said what she always said: "*Estoy okay.*"

"Really? Everything's okay?" This was Gerri's gentle voice, the nice one that made her feel like a good best friend.

"Yeah," Clara said, and was suddenly overcome with the need to make her evening sound interesting. "You should've seen my mom getting ready to pick up my dad at the airport. It was totally weird. It was like watching your own mother go off on a *date* or something. She was wearing black silk tap pants. And just a minute ago I figured out she's been reading this very scary book called *Saucy Monogamy*."

"Adult human beings," Gerri said conclusively after Clara had read off some of *Saucy Monogamy*'s juicier chapter titles. Whenever Gerri wanted to point out the complete weirdness of everyone over twenty-one, she used this phrase: *Adult human beings*.

But what had struck Clara was how strangely *un*adult and *un*motherlike her mother had seemed tonight. "I don't know," she said. "It's pretty weird watching your own mother get ready for a heartpopping homecoming with your own father."

Gerri made a muffled laugh.

Clara took a deep breath and said, "So how's Sands, inny-hoo?"

If Gerri thought this was a tender subject, she didn't show it. "Sands is unbelievable," she said. "She's an industrial-strength hunk magnet. We walked into this ski lodge tonight and the minute my folks turned the corner, guys were all over us."

Clara sat on the side of her parents' bed stroking Ham with her stocking feet and trying to imagine Gerri and Sands Mandeville surrounded by hunky guys. She knew she ought to say something nice, but all she could come up with was, "Well, Sands is that type."

Gerri took this as a compliment. "Yeah," she said, "and you can't believe the things guys have said to her on dates. Three different guys have asked her to marry them. And somebody she said I know offered her two hundred dollars for oral sex."

Clara didn't know what to say, so she said, "That seems like a lot of money."

Gerri laughed, and in a low, all-knowing voice that didn't sound like the old Gerri, she said, "Not enough, let me tell ya."

There was a short silence. Clara wondered where Sands Mandeville was while this telephone call was going on. "So where are you calling from, innyhoo?"

"The hotel. It's a cool hotel. Except I guess it's really a B and B. I'm in the bathroom. They've got a telephone in the bathroom and a cool itty-bitty color TV."

Clara was beginning to feel like she was about three squares behind. She didn't know what a B and B was, and she didn't want to ask. "So where's Sands now, innyhoo?"

There was a stiff pause. "She's sleeping in the next room. We're in twin beds." Another pause, then: "She kind of snores."

Clara had to laugh. "Sands Mandeville *snores?*" Clara said this with real gusto, but it became quickly clear that a little snoring wasn't something Gerri was willing to hold against her new friend Sands.

"Yeah, a little, but not much," Gerri said. "It's not that loud." Then, after a second, she said, "Hey, Clara, don't stick that *innyhoo* at the end of your sentences anymore, okay? It's kind of dinky and gets on my nerves."

Clara's body stiffened as if she'd been slapped. How many times had she said it? For a moment, she was actually incapable of speech. Then, when she could speak, she said, "Yeah, okay." A moment or two passed. "I guess sometimes I don't even know I'm doing it."

Neither of them said anything for a while. Because it was the worst phone call they'd ever had, it also seemed to Clara like the most important call they'd ever had. She didn't want it to end like this, but she also didn't know what to say. She was suddenly afraid of saying something Gerri wouldn't approve of. So she didn't say anything at all.

Finally Gerri did. She said, "Well, I better go now. When my dad sees this phone bill he'll have a whole herd of cows."

"Yeah, okay," Clara said in a flat voice. Then, trying to be nice, she said, "Have some fun." After putting the phone down, she thought how dinky that probably sounded, too.

Clara went to her room, stared out the window—a black night, patches of dirty snow in the yard, everything still and silent—then put on a flannel nightgown and got into bed. She closed her eyes and pictured herself in the Adirondacks on a strawberry roan—a horse the same color as her hair, like in her father's old bedtime stories. She pictured herself riding with a straight back and a straight hat and a straight nose. And then she thought of how Gerri's face always went kind of blank whenever she talked about horses or horse camp. Suddenly Clara knew Gerri would never go to horse camp with her, never in a million years, whether she kept it a secret or not.

Ham pulled himself onto the bed and nested beside her. Clara snuggled close and wrapped her arm around him. "You don't care about my nose, do you?" she whispered. "And you don't think my talking sounds dinky." When she started to massage the base of his ear, Ham began to murmur contentedly. Clara began to feel the calm of sleep coming over her. She glanced at the clock: 11:23.

When Clara next read the clock, it said 4:17 and something was wrong. It began with a haze of light in the hall and a scratchy dialogue that Clara finally realized was coming from her mother's TV.

"Ham?" she whispered.

Ham's black fur heaved a little at the foot of the bed, where he wasn't supposed to be sleeping, and he turned to look at her. Ham was good company, but at night he seemed to consider himself off-duty. Still, he followed Clara down the hall to the flickering light of her mother's room.

The door was half-open. What Clara saw, standing unseen just outside the room, was a surprise. Her mother lay propped in bed with the picnic basket beside her. There were foil and plastic wrappers on the bedspread. On the bedstand, next to a single wineglass, the fancy bottle of wine stood half-empty. Clara's father was nowhere in sight. Her mother picked up a tube of toffees and peeled one off. She was looking at the TV without really looking at it. She seemed about twenty years older than she had when she was getting ready to go to the airport ten hours ago.

"Hi, Mom," Clara said from the door in a small voice.

Clara's mother turned with a start. Her stretched-out face quickly collected into a false smile. "Oh, hi, sweetie," she said. "Did the movie wake you up?"

"Yeah, kinda. Where's Dad?"

Her mother made a dismissive gesture with her hand. "Some little problem. He couldn't come. But here *you* are!" She motioned Clara closer. "Come over here and keep me company."

Clara eased onto the bed. "How come you're watching TV so late?"

"It's a Humphrey Bogart film fest," her mother said, as if this explained something, though it didn't.

Clara glanced at the screen. The movie was one of those old ones, in black and white. Clara looked again at the scatter of food on the bed and bedstand. "Wasn't all this stuff kind of expensive for just eating alone?"

"Well, now I'm not alone," her mother said brightly. "Have a stuffed olive. It's good for your complexion."

But Clara knew her parents had money problems. "But where did you get the basket and all this stuff? Couldn't you have taken it back for a refund?"

Her mother's eyes seemed to glaze over. "I got all of it at Kaufmann's. And no, I couldn't take it back. Not after I told everybody and his brother that it was for a romantic picnic with your father."

"Oh," Clara said. Kaufmann's was the gigantic department store where her mother worked to help out with expenses.

"Humphrey Bogart is the man up in the rocks," her mother said now, pointing at the TV. "He's a fugitive."

Clara studied the man on the rocks, who was somehow smoking a cigarette while returning police fire. Close by, hiding behind the same boulder, a frightened woman clutched a frightened dog.

"Know what Humphrey Bogart said a while back?" Clara's mother asked. "He said, 'What kind of a sap would go up in those hills with a dog and a dame?'" Clara's mother let out a laugh, but it didn't sound very happy. "Know what *I* say? I say what kind of a dame would go up in the hills with a sap like that?" With a plastic fork, she speared an almond-stuffed olive from a narrow jar. "He's going to get it, by the way. You just watch. Bogart is not long for this world."

Clara hated it when her mother was in this kind of gloom-mood. It happened when her father had been out of town too long or when her mother had decided she would never learn fluent French or look like Candice Bergen or cook like Julia Child. Clara watched the screen with her mother, and it turned out she was right about Humphrey Bogart getting it. First one bullet and then another tore into him. It wasn't very realistic, though. They had better special effects in their own school play, Clara thought. In this old movie, it looked like the dying man was just having a hard time getting to sleep and then finally did.

When Clara turned, her mother had tears on her eyelashes. She glanced at Clara and tried to smile. "He was a jerk, but I guess he was a lovable jerk." She muted a commercial but continued to stare at the screen. "The next movie stars Bogart and Lauren Bacall, who glommed onto him when he was still married. Not that they cared."

Clara didn't know how to respond. After a second or two, she said, "In our school play—the one I told you about—we've got this stage gun that shoots paint balls, except we call them blood balls." She looked at her mother, who seemed not to be listening. "It makes it look like a death scene from hell."

Clara hoped the word *hell* might get her mother's attention. It didn't. "You know how late it is?" her mother asked, then seemed to lapse into herself.

Clara walked to the window, pulled the curtain aside, and saw that the sky was still black. She could see her face in the glass, and although her mother always made a big fuss about Clara's thick reddish hair and pale skin, Clara saw her nose and touched it automatically, as if perhaps it were clay she could push into a different shape. A truck with a huge, whining motor crinkled the ice in the street and *shush*ed to a stop. The milkman's boots crunched on the frozen yard. *Hello, Mr. MacKenzie*, Clara thought, and then, just as he looked up at her window, she remembered her nightgown and let the curtain fall back.

In an empty voice, Clara's mother said, "The milkman already. That's how late it is."

On the muted television screen, women with big hair were giving testimonials for a telephone psychic named Jacquelina Vital. Clara tipped the picnic basket and looked inside. Lying at the bottom was a handmade card. White stars stood out against a black sky. Below, it read: *Remember the stars over Penacook Falls?*

Clara inhaled. She told herself not to end with *innyhoo*. She said, "Mom, what happened to Dad?"

Instead of answering the question, her mother swept some crumbs into her hand.

"Was Dad's flight canceled or something?" Clara asked.

Her mother made an unhappy laugh. "You really do like the last word, don't you?" she said. She took in a long, tired breath. "No, your father's flight wasn't canceled. It turned out he had to stay a few more days in Chicago. Something occurred so late on Friday that he couldn't call and tell me about it before I drove off to the airport. Something compelling, I'm sure."

Oh, Clara thought. "He tried to call here after you left," she said.

Her mother clicked off the TV and sighed. She was wearing her peach chenille robe, the one Clara's father had given her a long time ago. It was dingy now at the cuffs and ragged at the hem, and it reminded Clara of how she used to sleep in her mother's bed when her father was out of town. She would put on her mother's robe and fall asleep with a pile of blankets, and then her mother wouldn't have the heart to move her.

Her mother tried to smile. "Want to sleep in here?" she asked.

"Sure," Clara said, even though she didn't really want to. She wasn't good at changing her mother's mood, though her mother could almost always change hers. Clara looked at the opened bottle of wine and the bits of foil that had peeled off the chocolate and stained the sheets. She felt like she had awakened to a terrible adult slumber party where the last, most lonely person to be awake was her mother.

At odd times—and this was one of them—Clara would wonder if her mother wasn't somehow like Mary Jemison, the town's namesake. Clara had heard Mary Jemison's story about a hundred times at the annual Mary Jemison Pageant. During the French and Indian War, the Jemison farm was raided by Seneca Indians. The Senecas killed Mary Jemison's parents, but they took Mary, who was fifteen, home to their village. They treated her kindly, and by the time the British came to rescue her, she was married to a Seneca, had a baby, and didn't want to be rescued. And so she stayed with the Senecas, raised five children, and lived to be ninety-one.

After the pageant last year, Clara's family had gone out to eat. Her mother poked at a salad while Clara and her father ate cheeseburgers and fries. Clara's father had a little dribble of catsup at the corner of his mouth. Her mother looked at him, then pushed away her salad and stared out the window. Finally, in a low voice, almost to herself, she said, "I wonder if Mary Jemison somehow knew she wasn't in the right place *before* she'd been kidnapped."

Now, in bed, Clara turned toward her mother. "Mom?"

"What, sweetie?"

"I don't always have to have the last word."

Her mother made a murmuring laugh. "You don't?"

"No."

"Okay," her mother said, and Clara had to stifle herself from adding a final *okay*.

In the morning, the picnic basket and fancy bottles were gone. So were the stockings and scarves that had spilled over the cedar chest and the dresser. So was *Saucy Monogamy*—the bedstand drawer was empty. When Clara opened the closet door, all the lingerie was folded and put away and the old chenille robe hung neatly from its hook. It was as if her mother had re-formed and then disappeared.

In the kitchen, Clara found a note from her mother that read:

> Sweetie, I'm at work until the normal time. There's oatmeal on the stove. I'll make you chicken potpie tonight unless an inheritance comes in the mail and then I'll take you out (Ha!).
>
> Love you, Mom

The oatmeal was gluey, but Clara ate most of it anyway and mixed the rest with Ham's kibble. Then she took a long hot bath and shaved her legs, following the advice in one of her mother's magazines. She hoped Gerri might call again but knew somehow that she wouldn't.

Clara looked out the window and tried to look forward to spring, and from there to summer, but what if, when summer finally came, Gerri wasn't her friend anymore and she couldn't go to horse camp? Five days at the Black Stallion cost $890, and she'd saved only a fourth of her part. Her paper route was fine, but it wasn't enough. She needed another source of income. She turned to Ham and in a playful voice said, "Maybe I should rent you out, Hambone!"

And that gave her an idea.

Girl for rent, she thought. She even said it aloud to Ham as she untangled his leash from the umbrella, walked him four blocks to Banner Variety, and looped his leash around a parking meter.

Inside, holding a little roll of her horse camp money, Clara started looking for inspiration in the sale bin. Dusty zippers, American flags on toothpicks, red and green crepe paper, a torn picture of Lincoln—nothing that suited her purposes. Finally Clara picked out some plain white stationery in a pale gray box. It wasn't in the sale bin. It looked like something you might use if you needed to write a thank-you letter to the Princess of Monaco, and was priced accordingly. But she remembered something her mother had liked to say when she was paying tuition when she went back to college. *Sometimes you have to spend money to make money.* Clara spent almost all the money she'd brought.

Then, when she was back outside, something bad happened.

It wouldn't have been bad if she'd had a tissue in her pocket, but she didn't. And she needed, all of a sudden, to blow her nose just as Amos MacKenzie stepped out of Value Village, the thrift store across the street.

Amos MacKenzie was in the ninth grade, like Clara, but he seemed older because he was smart and almost never said anything. He had light brown skin, blond hair, and dark brown eyes. It had occurred to Clara, watching him in History, that if he were a horse, he would be a palomino. It had also occurred to her that this was a weird way to think of boys. She had a picture of Amos hidden in her desk at home—last year's Christmas card from the Cosgrove Dairy, in which the whole MacKenzie family was standing beside the milk truck on a fall day.

Now, as Clara removed Ham's leash from the parking meter, Amos and his father were putting a used snow shovel into a rusty white Ford van. So they had money troubles, too. At least Clara's father didn't take her to Value Village.

Clara felt in her pockets for a tissue and came up with a ticket stub from going to the movies with Gerri. When she glanced at the rusty Ford van, Mr. MacKenzie seemed to be looking her way, but Amos was already seated and staring straight ahead. Then Mr. MacKenzie did a slow U-turn that brought them close to the curb. Clara sniffled, pulled on Ham's leash, and waved, which for some reason made Mr. MacKenzie pull over, lean past Amos, and roll down the window. "Hi," he said, and grinned. "I suspect you must be Miss Wilson."

Clara nodded uncertainly and even blushed a little. She hadn't ever been called Miss Wilson before.

"I know because that canine looks familiar," Mr. MacKenzie

said, nodding at Ham, who was happily straining at his leash. "Sometimes he says hello when I bring the milk."

"Yeah," Clara said, "he likes to check everybody out." She sniffled and brought her hand to the bridge of her nose at the same moment that Ham put his front feet on the van and began to pant in Amos's face. "Oh, no!" Clara said. She pulled Ham down and rubbed the side of the car for scratches.

Mr. MacKenzie laughed and in a half-comic voice said, "The value of this van, like all things important to me, goes way beyond surface beauty." He nodded at Amos, who was blushing. "My son isn't old enough to see things this way yet. Amos hopes this old boat goes to the junkyard before he gets his license."

"Oh," Clara said, and looked at Amos, who kept his eyes down. This didn't subdue Ham in any way. He wagged his tail and then lunged for the van again, which caused Clara to drop the Princess-of-Monaco stationery. Several sheets slid out of the box into the dirty slush of the street.

"How are your parents?" Mr. MacKenzie asked while she was steadying herself.

"Oh, they're fine," she said.

"I noticed people were up bright and early this morning," he said.

Clara wondered if Mr. MacKenzie had seen her standing at the window in her nightgown, and her face got hot. But Amos wasn't looking at her. He was now leaning out and petting Ham. "Like your dog," he said, glancing up at Clara. "What's her name?"

"Ham. She's a he."

"Oh," Amos said.

A car was approaching, and Clara sniffled as quietly and discreetly as she could. If there was anything in the world worse than a runny nose, she thought, it was a crooked runny nose.

"Well, Miss Wilson," Mr. MacKenzie said in his easy, familiar way, "we better get moving or the neighbors will talk," and then, with a saluting wave of the hand, which was accompanied by a stiff nod from Amos, he drove away.

2

TUMS

Amos MacKenzie slumped down in the car seat and tried to slow down his mind, which was bouncing around like a pinball. Ever since eighth grade, when she got pretty all of a sudden, Amos had sneakily paid attention to Clara Wilson. And just now, while they'd been talking, she had acted nervous. Did that mean she cared what he might think? And could that mean she might like him? A fine layer of sweat rose on the back of Amos's neck. Could she think he might like her? And why did that make him feel so weirdly happy? Most of the things that made Amos happy worked from the outside in—receiving an A on a test, say, or getting tickets to a World Series game, or eating his favorite German chocolate cake. But what he was feeling now was the opposite. It seemed to come from within him. It worked from the inside out.

Suddenly, without even meaning to, Amos found himself thinking of Clara Wilson's hair. In his mind, it was brown, but in the sunlight, it had looked almost red. It was so clean and soft-looking that he imagined himself gathering it into a ponytail with his hand, something his mother always did with his sister's hair when they were watching TV.

"Whatcha thinking, slugger?" his father said.

"Nothing."

Amos pretended he didn't notice his father smiling and glancing over at him. It was something his father did. Whenever

Amos's feelings went fluttering off in every direction, his father not only knew it but found it strangely entertaining. It was just one of about one million things annoying about his father.

Amos stared out the window and tried to be perfectly still so his father would decide he was mistaken this time. A few blocks passed. Then, on the sidewalk up ahead, Amos spotted a long-legged girl walking alone in tights, fuzzy sweater, long open coat—and with a shock realized it was Anne Barrineau, the Elusive One. At school, she smiled at almost everyone but talked to almost no one. She was smart, pretty, and remote. Rumors flew. *She doesn't date because she already has a boyfriend who goes to Jemison High.* Or: *Her parents are deaf-mutes, that's why she never talks.* As the van passed her by, Amos sneaked a glance back. Anne Barrineau, as always, was looking straight ahead, smiling.

Amos sat back in his seat and watched the stores pass: Pringle's Drugstore, where Bruce Crookshank had dared him to buy a pack of condoms; Doug May Sporting Goods, where he'd used his yard money for a Rawlins John Olerud–model first-baseman's glove; Carat's Clothes for Men, where just two months ago, Amos's mother had taken him for a suit to be baptized in, which was the strangest of the numerous strange ideas his mother had been coming up with lately.

Lately.

What was lately? *Lately*, he decided, was ever since his father had been going to that doctor. But whatever the doctor had been doing or saying to his father was some kind of big-deal secret. If Amos was home with his mother when his father came back from the doctor, his father would give a thumbs-up sign and say, "Tip-top. A-okay." And sometimes his mother and father would stop talking when Amos came into the room or make up new, cheery things to talk about, which got on Amos's nerves. He wasn't eight years old, he wasn't their delicate retardate child, so why couldn't they just keep on talking?

When his father turned the rusted-out Econoline onto Adams Avenue and there was no longer much to look at, Amos still slouched down, staring out.

"Pretty girl, don't you think?" his father said in that over-gentle voice he used when he was trying to get Amos to say things he didn't feel like saying.

"Who?" Amos said.

"Miss Wilson," his father said.

Amos didn't say anything.

"The girl who was flirting with you."

"Nobody was flirting with me," Amos said in a sulky voice. "Maybe she was flirting with you," he said.

"Well, now," his father said amiably. "That kind of shines a whole new light on things, doesn't it? This pretty thirteen-year-old flirting with a forty-two-year-old bald man."

"She's fourteen," Amos said. His skin was prickly with sudden heat.

"And how did you come by that information?" his father said, still smiling.

"Because she's in the ninth grade," he said, and stared out the window. He realized with regret that he'd opened the door to even more questioning from his father, but none came. Finally Amos turned to look at him, and what he saw was startling. There was a strange, contorted look on his father's face until he saw Amos looking, and then his father made a tightly constrained smile.

"Tums time," he said, and reached across Amos to the glove compartment, where, to Amos's surprise, there was a big twenty-four-count box of Tums tubes. His father unwound the wrapping from four tablets and began to chew them. For five or six blocks his expression didn't change, and then the strange distorted face relaxed and became his father's face again. When finally his father talked, his voice was relaxed, too. "Guess I ate one too many flapjacks for breakfast," he said.

Amos nodded, but it wasn't like his father had eaten a mountain of pancakes or anything. In fact, he hardly remembered his father eating anything at all.

A pickup truck splashed by to their right, spattering Amos's window with dirty water. "Moron," Amos said under his breath to the other driver. He waited. Sometimes his father, when provoked, would use one of his favorite dopey words. *Jackanapes*, or something like that. But today it was like his father didn't even notice. He just drove along in his own little world. Finally, about three blocks from home, he broke the silence.

"Amos," he said, "I want you to tell me something. If you could wish for one thing in the world, what would it be?"

Amos didn't know what to answer. He had the funny feeling he should give the answer that would have been true a few years ago, an answer that would be as comforting to his father as Tums. The truth was, Amos's wishes were different now. Now he wished he could walk over to the lunch table where Clara always sat with her friend Gerri and make some excuse to sit down. He wished he had his own car. He wished he didn't wish his father wasn't a lowly milkman whose big outings were twice-a-week Moose Lodge meetings and Thursday night bowling, but he did.

"To play first base for the Blue Jays," Amos said, and then, re-fining a little, "and to hit for higher average than Olerud and more homers than Carter."

And Amos was right. His father smiled and relaxed again in his seat.

3

EGYPTIANS

Clara's house had an attic. By parting the clothes in the upstairs hall closet and climbing the rungs of a permanent vertical ladder, you came to the trapdoor, which when pushed open allowed entry into the long empty room. "The schizophrenic attic," Clara's mother called it, because one side was so unlike the other. All of the junk had been pushed into a disorderly heap in one half of the room. The other half was severely neat. It was here that her mother had set up a desk and tried to complete her master's degree in something called Egyptology. All Clara knew about it was the strange flat eyes of Egyptian art, which faced toward you even though the faces were in profile.

But that was before the money troubles. The company that employed Clara's father sold top-of-the-line office furniture, but not much of it was selling right now. It had something to do with businesses failing and used furniture flooding the market—that's what Clara got out of it, anyhow. So that was the end of Egyptology. Her mother had failed to find a teaching job and had finally taken a job at Kaufmann's Department Store, folding towels and ringing up sheets.

Clara thought Kaufmann's was a nice place to work, and she thought her mother looked elegant leading customers through the rows of pillows and bright towels, but when her mother came home for dinner, she would complain to Clara's father

long-distance wherever he was and then talk to her sister—
Clara's aunt—in Dalton.

Clara could always tell who her mother was talking to just by
her tone of voice. With her father, her mother's voice was flat and
tired-sounding. "Fine," she would say when asked about her day,
and then they might talk about the latest storm front. "Well,
that's life in Jemison," Clara's mother would say in her weary
voice, "where the weather changes all the time, but the people
never do." But with Clara's aunt, her mother's voice grew bright
and alive with hopes and schemes. She talked about new possibilities for making money: catering, sewing, furniture refinishing,
anything. Lately, the big new idea was teaching abroad. "There
are jobs right now, as we speak, for someone with my credentials
in Kyoto and Provence," Clara heard her mother say one night to
her aunt. Clara was good at geography. She knew Kyoto was in
Japan and Provence was in France. Clara was amazed and a little
afraid. Why would her mother look for a job *there* when her family lived here?

Clara opened the gray box of Princess-of-Monaco stationery
on her mother's desk and considered her plan. If she was going to
put advertising flyers in the newspapers, she needed to get people's attention. She pulled out one of her mother's books and after
some practice made a drawing of an Egyptian girl pulling a huge
square stone across the page. Under that, she wrote: *Girl for rent!
Let me do your errands on snowy days. I'm fourteen and I can get your
groceries, your mail, or your hardware supplies, or walk your dog. Dependable and inexpensive! Call Clara at 543-4245.* At the last
minute, she found a copy of her mother's résumé on the desk, so
she added, *References upon request.*

Clara liked the way her advertisement looked, and carefully made fifteen more, enough to give to all the elderly people on her route. Then she thought of Amos MacKenzie and had another idea. The MacKenzies were on her route, too. It had always been her favorite part, in fact—approaching the MacKenzie house and throwing something toward Amos's front door. So maybe she would give them an advertisement, too, and add a note to Amos.

She opened a book that translated the tiny pictures that stood for letters in the Egyptian alphabet. She found the Egyptian symbols for Amos's name, and she drew them precisely at the very top of one of her advertisements: a forearm, then an owl, a quail chick, and a folded cloth. *Amos*, it spelled, but what it looked like was a pair of birds about to be caught and served for dinner. After looking at the symbols for a while, she decided to write the letters of his name underneath, and before it, *Hi!* She folded the paper, slid it into its immaculate envelope, and wrote his name on the outside. She slipped the flyers under the rubber bands when she folded her papers in the late afternoon, and she put the letter with Amos's name on it in the paper she would save for last.

It wasn't quite dark when she went outside with Ham sniffing and pulling on one hand and the canvas vest full of papers thudding against her chest. The canvas apron tended to push her bra sideways and up. She'd never expected a bra to pinch. She had assumed it would be like a shirt or underwear—something you never noticed you were wearing. And she hated to wear white shirts now because the bra was so distinct underneath, reminding everyone, she felt, how little she needed it.

Carrying the paper for Amos MacKenzie made her walk

faster. The whole evening seemed prettier and more mysterious, as though the lights in the windows were the lamps of happy people who were about to do exciting things. It was only much later that night, when she was lying on the couch near her mother and half listening to the TV and the low sounds of her father's voice coming through the phone, that Clara began to wonder if she'd done the right thing. And, lightning quick, she knew she hadn't. She'd done something stupid. Childish and stupid. She imagined people—especially Amos—dropping the expensive white paper into trash cans all through the neighborhood. He'd probably been totally repulsed by her runny nose. Her crooked runny nose.

"So you're coming home tomorrow for sure?" her mother said into the air above the telephone. She was doing a crossword puzzle, so she was using the speakerphone, which Clara knew her father disliked. He said he felt like he was doing a radio show.

From what seemed a great distance, her father said, "The flight's supposed to arrive at three-fifteen."

"I'll still be at work then," her mother said in her flat, distracted voice.

"That's fine," her father said, and because his voice was so thin as it came through the phone, Clara couldn't decide whether he really thought it was fine or not. "What time do you get off work?" he asked.

"Six or so," her mother said, filling in a long vertical word in her puzzle.

"Perfect. Maybe Clara and I will cook something," her father said. "We could have some Thai food ready when you get home."

Thai food was her mother's favorite, something Clara always

dreaded because she preferred plain rice with butter. But it seemed a very bad sign when her mother, putting down her pencil to pick up the receiver and cut off the speakerphone, said, "No, that's okay. You and Clara go ahead. I'll probably just have something before I leave the store." Instead of the usual exchange about missing him, she said a quick and wooden "Good night." And then, before going back to her crossword, her mother set the phone down so carefully she might have been putting a china cup on display at the store.

4

PRUSSIANS

While Clara was making up her flyers, Amos was lounging around his basement reading a book and trying to ignore his buddy Bruce Crookshank. Amos was sprawled on one of the five old sofas that had collected against the concrete walls. Bruce stood in the middle of the big room, under a single bare lightbulb that hung down from an unpainted beam.

Bruce was even taller than Amos, except he was already a little heavy in the middle, so that his body had a large, soft look to it. He wore a stretched-out sweatshirt, and his thick hair poked out at odd angles over his ears. Today Bruce was pretending, as he often did, to be pitching for the New York Yankees. He held a tennis ball in his mitt, stared at the imaginary catcher to get imaginary signals, then, winding up, went into the play-by-play. "Howe into his stretch...checks the runners...comes in with the fastball... *strike three called!* Oh, my! Did he paint the corner with that one, fans, and Molitor's caught looking with the bases loaded."

"Fat chance," Amos muttered.

"That's Molitor's third straight K, fans, and hey, take a listen, the crowd is going wild!" Bruce made a muffled moaning sound of distant crowd noise.

"Molitor's hitting over .340 lifetime against Steve Howe," Amos said matter-of-factly.

"Not in this league," Bruce said as he picked up a broomstick handle and took a couple of practice swings, then tapped at his shoe soles as if to knock mud from cleats. "Leading off the bottom of the ninth, the Yankee third baseman, Mike Pagliarulo, and let me tell ya, Pags is on a heckuva tear!" More crowd noise.

Amos preferred the Blue Jays, and the fact that in Bruce's imaginary league, the Yankees always came from behind to win in the bottom of the ninth got on his nerves.

"A lazy fly ball to left," Bruce was saying, "Carter settles under it and makes the...no...no...I don't believe it, fans, but I'm here to tell you! Carter drops the ball! The Yankees are still alive!"

The book Amos was reading was called *Mademoiselle Fifi*, a worn paperback he'd seen with his father at Value Village and gone back alone to buy, along with two more innocent-looking books. *No other woman in France would have yielded to his caresses!* it said on the cover, just below the picture of a Prussian officer in black boots seated in a velvet chair with a beautiful, mostly undressed woman sitting in his lap. The writer was a Frenchman named Guy de Maupassant, but the book was pretty disappointing, as far as Amos was concerned. To begin with, it wasn't a novel, it was a bunch of short stories. And although there was mention of an orgy, the author never said what exactly was going on at this orgy.

Bruce, in a world of his own, said, "Ground ball sharply to second...under Amaros's glove! under Amaros's glove!...Oh, my!...It went right through his legs, fans, and now the sacks are packed with pinstripes!"

"Hey, Crook," Amos said.

Bruce, swaggering like Jose Tartabull, the Yankees' cleanup hitter, took a few practice swings with his broomstick.

"Hey, Crook, listen to this. C'mon."

"We talking sex?" Bruce said, stepping back out of the imaginary batter's box.

Amos said, "Yeah. Well, sort of, anyway." He explained the situation. The Prussians in *Mademoiselle Fifi* had invaded France, and as the Prussian officers at the orgy got drunker and drunker, they made more and more insulting remarks to the French girls, who had been hired from something called a "house of public accommodation." Finally the main officer set a glass of champagne on the head of the nicest French girl and said, "All the women in France belong to us!"

"Any pictures?" Bruce asked.

Amos ignored the question. "So then, after this insult, the girl gets her composure and says, '*I?* I am not a woman. I am only a strumpet, and that is all that Prussians want.'"

Bruce looked at him blankly. "So?"

"Isn't that creepy? That she would have to say that about herself?"

Bruce stared at him for a while. "Maybe you're reading too much into it."

Amos kept thinking about it.

"I like that *strumpet* word, though," Bruce said. "Kind of sounds like a dessert for grownups." Besides his photographic memory of sports trivia, Bruce Crookshank had one other highly prized talent. He could imitate almost anyone's voice of either gender and any age. Now he threw his voice into the husky register of a male middle-aged New Yorker. "I'd like coffee, brandy, and a French strumpet, please."

Amos rolled his eyes. "Anyhow, the Prussian officer goes ballistic and slaps the woman, and, presto, she stabs him in the neck with a table knife."

"Now we're talking," Bruce said. "Read that part. Make it dramatic."

Upstairs the phone rang, and they could hear Amos's big sister crossing the dining room to get it.

Amos found his place. "'Something that the officer was going to say was cut short in his throat, and he sat there with his mouth half-open and a terrible look in his eyes.'"

When Amos looked up from the book, Bruce was slumped on the floor acting the part of the dead man.

"If you're dead, Crook, my prayers are answered."

A few seconds later, the door at the head of the basement stairs opened and Amos's sister, Liz, poked her head in and said, "That was your brother, Crooky-poo. He says the Judge is on the prowl, and if you're not home in fifteen minutes, your little dinger's in the wringer. Or words to that effect." She slammed the door before a rebuttal could be composed. The Judge was Bruce's father.

Bruce looked at Amos. "Guess your folks aren't home for her to talk like that."

"They're off at the doctor's," Amos said.

Bruce turned and yelled up through the floorboards. "Gives me goose bumps, Elizabeth, when you talk dirty like that!"

Amos tossed the book on the floor. "Hey, Crook, did I mention sighting the Elusive One walking on Banner Ave. today?"

Bruce wheeled around. "You sighted Anne Barrineau?"

Amos nodded. "The one and only."

"Specifics, please."

Amos smiled and stretched. Bruce, along with half the guys

at Melville, spent a lot of idle moments fantasizing about Anne Barrineau. "Okay, let's see," Amos said. "Walking alone. Headed due west. Approximately three miles per hour."

Bruce took this in slowly. "What was she wearing?"

"A sweater, tights, long coat, and, let's see, two matching shoes. Also, I imagine, underwear."

"Yeah," Bruce said, "I imagine, too."

Amos grinned. "Yeah, I imagine you do."

Amos stood, went over to the window, and stared out into the dusk. It was a view he liked, the window sunken into a light well at yard level so it was like you were lying on your stomach seeing things. He'd been staring out for a while before he realized that a girl was standing by the gate, very still and quiet, just staring up at the house. It was Clara Wilson. Amos instinctively stepped back. "Turn off the lights," he said in a tight whisper to Bruce.

"What?"

"The lights. I don't want her to see us."

The lights went off, and Amos edged back closer to the glass.

"Don't want *who* to see us?" Bruce said.

"Her." Amos stepped aside so Bruce could see, too.

"It's the Brainette," Bruce said, "Clara Something, the goofy newspaper girl. The one with the nose. And her best friend, Spot."

They both watched as Clara finally came to life. She tossed the MacKenzies' paper onto the porch—*plop*—and then she and her stout black dog walked on.

"God, Amos," Bruce said. "She was staring at your house. Do you think the Brainette wants to be your strumpet?"

It took Amos a second to turn around. Then he said, "Oh, yeah. That's likely."

In a girlish falsetto that grew breathier with each word, Bruce said, "Oh, Amos, Amos, sweetie, kiss me, kiss me, I know the capital of Sri Lanka."

Amos gave him a solid shoulder punch to snap him out of it. "Guess you forgot you're running late."

Amos hid *Mademoiselle Fifi* in his shirt and followed Bruce up the stairs and out into the freezing night. The newspaper lay where Clara had thrown it, the small bundle of newsprint bound in a blue rubber band and...

An envelope.

Amos stared at it, and Crook, sensing something, followed his gaze to the tidy white rectangle with the word AMOS on the front. They both grabbed for it at the same time, but Bruce had the angle. He plucked it neatly from its fastened place.

"Oh, my, fans, we've received a note," Bruce said, screening the envelope from Amos. He ripped it open, stared at its contents, and couldn't contain himself. "*Girl for rent! The Brainette does* want to be your strumpet!"

Amos, flushing, said, "What is it?"

Bruce grinned and went back to his falsetto. "Why, it's a special girl-for-rent note for you and only you, Amos, precious. It's got your very own name in extra-special cave drawings."

Amos grabbed the paper from Bruce's hands, and his eyes swam over the symbols and letters. He was stunned, embarrassed, and strangely pleased.

Bruce was already through the gate, making a point of laughing like a hyena, when Amos said, "It's not cave drawings, you moron. It's hieroglyphics."

"Love," Bruce sang back. "I call it love."

Amos stepped back into the house. Liz was frying hamburger meat and leaning into the living room, where *Love Connection* was on.

"How come you're cooking?" Amos asked. "Where's Mom and Dad?"

His sister didn't take her eyes from the TV screen. "They called. They're still at the clinic and are going to be late. You're getting hamburger and mushroom gravy. Except we're out of hamburger, so I'm using Tender Vittles."

"My sister, one of this nation's truly gifted comedians," Amos said, and moved on. He went into the backyard to check his pigeons' food and water, then, back inside, climbed the stairs to his room. He pulled out the shoe box hidden in the antique radio cabinet behind his stacks of old comic books. He slipped the letter inside *Mademoiselle Fifi* and put the book into the shoe box, next to his signed Paul Molitor baseball, the Dr. Reuben sex book, the switchblade he'd found at Monument Park, and the condoms he'd bought at Pringle's.

5

THE NAKED AMOS

On Sunday morning, Clara was awakened by the telephone. She let it ring because her mother was always up first, but when she didn't hear footsteps, she raced to the hallway and picked up the phone to hear an old woman ask for Clara Wilson.

"This is she," Clara said. In Civics, Mr. Duckworth made them answer roll call, *This is he* or *This is she*. But in real life, it sounded weird.

"Hello, this is Sylvia Harper on Kensington Avenue, and I received your notice in my paper last night."

"Oh," Clara said, picturing the old wrought-iron sign with two rusty squirrels, one holding up the address and the other holding up "Harper." Clara had always guessed that Mrs. Harper, a widow, was lonely. She tended to watch through her curtains for the newspaper, and when Clara came around to collect the money, she always had ready a white envelope with PAPER written in ballpoint pen on the outside. When it was cold and Clara stepped inside to write a receipt, Mrs. Harper's house smelled first like vanilla candles and then like the three yellow cats that sat staring at her from different chairs in the front room.

Now Mrs. Harper said, "I might need you to do a job for me, but I'd like to talk to your mother first. Is she there?"

"I think so," Clara said. "Just a minute and I'll bring her to the phone."

The bathroom was empty, though, and so was her mother's room. "Mom?" Clara yelled, hoping that Mrs. Harper couldn't hear. The need to explain her scheme fast enough to get permission made Clara feel slightly ill and excited, like when she'd auditioned for *The Smiling Gumshoe*.

"Mom?" she tried again from the kitchen, and then she could see her mother through the pantry window, a blue-coated figure stepping carefully across the snow that had fallen all night. Clara knocked on the window, and her mother turned around. She frowned when Clara motioned her back to the house, holding up the black kitchen phone and pointing at it.

Her mother stamped her feet on the mat, smelling of perfume and cold air. She wasn't wearing any makeup, but her earrings made it clear that she was dressed for work beneath her parka. She was holding an old photo album. "Morning, sweetie. Is that Dad on the phone?"

"No," Clara said, "it's Sylvia Harper. Our neighbor."

"I know who she is. But why is she on the phone?"

Clara explained. "She wants to know if I'm responsible. Say I am, okay?"

"You want me to lie?" her mother asked, raising one eyebrow in mock alarm.

"Hurry, Mom, okay? She's been waiting on the phone forever."

Clara's mother unwound her scarf and picked up the phone. "Hello, Sylvia? Yes, this is Angie."

Mrs. Harper began to talk at length. Clara petted Ham, who'd found a tennis ball somewhere and was now panting at her and begging her to throw it.

"Well," her mother said at last, "Clara's had her paper route for some time now with no complaints. I don't know how much time she's going to have when she starts rehearsals for the school play, but she's very responsible and dependable."

Mrs. Harper's voice started droning again, and Clara's mother had an amused look on her face, as though she and Clara had decided to make some prank calls together and were enjoying an especially good one. Her mother began to study her fingernails, which were peach this week, and then she nodded. "That sounds fine, Sylvia. I'm happy you can use Clara's help. I'll put her on."

As it turned out, Mrs. Harper needed Clara to do two things. She needed Clara to shovel snow and then to buy her some things at the market. She wanted Clara to come over at nine o'clock, and it was a little after eight when Clara hung up. The old brown photo album that her mother had carried in was now sitting on the kitchen table. "What's that album?" Clara asked her mother, who was adjusting the gas flame under a pan she'd greased with olive oil.

"Want a cooked tomato and some toast?" her mother asked. When Clara nodded, she said, "Your dad stored his old things out in the shed when we first moved in. They should be moved to the attic, where they'll stay dry."

To Clara, this had the feel of a half-truth instead of a whole truth, and she made a mental note to check out the album some time when no one was around. "Could we have hot chocolate with breakfast?" Clara asked.

"If you run upstairs and get dressed first. You should put on some layers if you're going to be shoveling and then running all over the place for Mrs. Harper. And I need you to do our driveway first. For free."

While Clara was standing in the upstairs hallway pulling a comb through wads of wet, snarled hair, the phone rang again. When the voice asking for Clara Wilson turned out to be male and young, a little vacuum opened up in her chest, a wide, sinking space that made it hard for her to say, in proper English, "This is she."

"Hello, this is Amos MacKenzie," the voice said. "And I'm naked as a jaybird."

"What?" Clara asked.

"Naked," the voice said again.

"That's disgusting," Clara said, and quickly replaced the phone.

"What's disgusting?" her mother asked. She'd come up the stairs with Ham and was looking through the linen cupboard. The linen cupboard was the one place in the house that had flourished in the past few years. The shelves overflowed with lacy bargains she brought home from Kaufmann's, and every time her mother felt depressed about a failed scheme for a more exciting job, she would bring home a new piece of cloth and say, "Isn't it splendid, Clara? It's the one good thing about my job, so I'd better take advantage of it."

"I just got a prank phone call," Clara said.

"What did they say?"

"It was just some kid at school. He called to say he was naked."

Her mother folded a burgundy plaid blanket into a tighter square. "Do you know who it was?"

"No." This was more or less the truth.

"Are you sure it was a boy, not an adult?"

"Yes," Clara said. In the back of her mind, she hoped it wasn't really Amos. She had no idea what his voice sounded like on the phone because she'd hardly spoken to him in person. It just didn't seem like something he would do, not unless he thought the note she'd left him was dumb and this nasty phone call was his way of saying, "Grow up. I'm too old for silly notes from girls I hardly know."

"If he calls again, hang up immediately, then call me at work and I'll call the phone company. Okay?"

Clara nodded.

"Okay, then. And when you get the groceries for Mrs. Harper, will you get some things for us?" her mother asked.

"For dinner, you mean?" Clara asked. "I thought you were going to eat at work."

"Well, I changed my mind. Here's some money and the list."

The list contained ingredients for the Thai supper, and Clara felt, as she read *cellophane noodles* and *coconut milk*, that she had never been so happy to see a list of foods she hated.

By the time Clara was heading off to Sylvia Harper's, her mother had brought a cup of coffee out to the living room, sat down on the couch, and begun turning through the black pages of the photo album, studying the pictures.

Mrs. Harper was watching from her curtains when Clara approached the square white house with the glass porch. To Clara's horror, Ham lifted his leg, aimed more or less at the front gatepost, and left a dizzy yellow pattern on the snow. In her mind, Clara said *damn* three times. Pulling Ham away from the snowdrift only widened the pattern he made, and beneath her heavy clothes, Clara felt herself begin to sweat. Mrs. Harper frowned through the curtains, but Clara finally managed to get Ham to follow her up the steps. A dusty Christmas wreath made of cinnamon sticks and pinecones was still on the door, and when Clara wiped off her feet, she could smell crushed cinnamon and cats.

"You brought that dog with you" was the first thing Mrs. Harper said when she opened the door. "I hope he won't chase my cats."

"He's not interested in cats," Clara said. She hoped this was true, and generally Ham did keep to himself. He was wagging his tail at Mrs. Harper now and looking anxiously around for something to present. He settled on a fake mouse in the corner and got it in his mouth.

"Is he hungry?" Mrs. Harper asked.

"No," Clara asked. "He just wanted to give you a present."

"Well, how polite," she said, and bent down to pat Ham on the head, prompting him to rear up and place both paws on her flowered dress.

"Down, Ham, down!" Clara yelled, and Mrs. Harper was already stepping back into the house, as if Ham were not Ham at all but some rabid animal. She looked down at her green-flowered house dress, where the combination of wet snow and a dirty front porch had produced a smear of paw prints. "What a mortifying dog," Mrs. Harper said—is that what she said?

This was off to a bad start. "I'm sorry," Clara said.

"But I suspect that creature is not," Mrs. Harper said, and it was true that instead of looking sorry, Ham looked like he wanted to jump up again and have his head properly stroked. Mrs. Harper stepped back, dug into the pocket of her dress, and brought out a folded envelope. "Here's the shopping list," she said, "and some money, and the shovel is right there." She pointed to a new shovel leaning against the glass wall of the porch. The white paper envelope was marked STORE. "There are some lunch ingredients in there, so try to be back by eleven if you can," she said, and after giving Ham another measured look, she went back in the house.

Clara was sweating by the time she finished half the driveway, so she took off her gloves. She took off her hat and scarf when she started on the sidewalk, and her coat when she got to the mailbox, trying all the time not to think of Amos sitting naked by the phone. Of all the people in the world to think of naked by the telephone, he was probably the least repulsive, but the problem was she couldn't think of a single person she'd *like* to see naked by a telephone. That was at least one of the important differences between males and females, she thought suddenly, because boys could probably name you ten girls in five seconds they would like to see naked by a telephone.

Up and down the street, people were throwing shovelfuls of snow onto high drifts, and the busy scraping sound of metal on concrete was pleasant under a blue sky. Now and then, Clara could see the curtains in Mrs. Harper's living room window ease back, and on those occasions, she made sure Ham was sticking close by. When she had just started pushing the shovel along the edge of the sidewalk to get a clean line, a car moved past her and she saw two boys in the back. Bruce Crookshank was one. Amos was the other. Bruce was pointing at her and holding Amos's coat by the shoulder so he couldn't slump down. "Hi, Clara!" Bruce shouted through the half-opened window. "Loved your note!" This was all that could be said before the car turned the corner and Clara was left, humiliated, on the wet sidewalk.

So Amos *had* shown her ridiculous message to his friends. Maybe he had really called her, then. Bruce was probably listening the whole time, egging him on, and they would laugh all day while she shoveled sidewalks and climbed through drifts to get to the grocery store. Clara turned around to see Mrs. Harper watching her. She waved, held up the white envelope, and attached Ham's leash for the suddenly tiresome walk to Dusty's Oldtowne Market. Halfway there, from a phone booth at the Conoco station, she dialed Gerri's number in hopes she was home by now, but she wasn't.

"Yo, it's me, Gerri. Speak at the beep and maybe I won't call back, but probably I will."

"It's me," Clara said a little forlornly. "Call me as soon as you get home, okay?"

6

A FRIEND LIKE CROOKSHANK

Amos, slumped down in the back of Crook's brother's Pontiac Bonneville, wanted to turn around to see Clara's face but didn't want Crook to know he cared that much.

Outside, all the tree limbs and fences and TV antennas were thick with snow. There were four of them in the car—Amos and Bruce in the back; Zeke, Bruce's older brother, at the wheel; and Zeke's friend Big Dave Pearse riding shotgun. They were heading up to the high school gym, where Zeke and Big Dave, because of their varsity status, were allowed to shoot around on weekends. Amos and Bruce were along because they hoped to find some pickup games in the warm gym afterward.

Before Bruce called, Amos was at church, the last place he wanted to be. His mother had bribed him and Liz with blueberry waffles, had ironed all their good clothes, and had, at the last moment, put on a hat. "It's not Easter, Mom," Liz had said. His mother, turning the rearview mirror toward herself, said, "When I was a little girl, women covered their heads in church."

During the hymns and the sermon, Amos wondered when his mother would get over this religion thing. He studied the backs of his hands, the leather of his shoes, the stained-glass windows, and the program. His mother had been religious before she got married, and she knew the words to all the songs without looking at the hymnal. She sang, she watched the reverend, she shut her eyes during the prayers, and—surprisingly—so did his father. He sang in a deep voice that sounded, Amos had to admit, pretty good. He also had to admit that his mother was the only woman in church wearing a hat.

On the far side of the backseat of the Bonneville, Bruce was suddenly going through his pockets as if he'd lost something important.

"What?" Amos said.

But Bruce kept fumbling through pockets until at last he came up with a copy of Clara's flyer. He tapped a telephone number on it and smirked.

"I thought I owed it to you to verify that this was in fact the Brainette's genuine number."

A bad feeling shot through Amos. "You called her up."

"That's correct. This very A.M."

"And?"

"And not much, really," Bruce said. "I say, 'Is this Clara Wilson?' and she goes, 'This is she,' like she's the receptionist at some kind of snooty office or something, and I say, 'Well, this is Amos MacKenzie, and I'm naked as a jaybird,' and then she said I was disgusting and hung up."

Up front, Zeke and Big Dave Pearse let out appreciative hoots.

Amos looked at his friend. "Swear, Crook?"

"On any book you like."

Amos stared out at the passing yards trying to decide whether Crook would've done something like that. The problem with a friend like Bruce was it was hard to imagine anything he *wouldn't* do. Amos turned and looked at him seriously, drilling his eyes into him until Bruce had to turn and look back.

"Question?" Bruce said.

In a low voice he hoped couldn't be heard up front, Amos said, "Did you really call her and say that?"

Bruce tried to look as if he actually felt bad about it. "Yeah, I did. I'm sorry. I don't know what got into me."

"You're such a troglodyte, Crook," Amos said in a tight, surprisingly high voice, and up front, Bruce's brother hooted and Big Dave Pearse, who'd been twirling a basketball on his index finger, palmed the ball and turned around with an ear-to-ear grin. "A deep dent, Crook, my man. A very deep dent."

Bruce, grinning himself, said, "I wouldn't know. So what does it mean, that I'm a troglodyte?"

"It means the things you do are troglodytic," Big Dave said, "and there's not much, if anything, lower. I'd make him take it back if I were you, though thank God I'm not."

Amos was surprised how much he liked that idea. "You should, Crook. You should try to make me take it back."

"Tell me what it is and then I'll probably have to."

Amos considered it. "A troglodyte is basically a cave dweller, a subhuman."

"And that's the most decent sort of troglodyte," said Big Dave over his shoulder. "That's a troglodyte from the better part of town."

Bruce leaned back amiably. "Oh, well, I thought maybe it was something bad. One of those guys who wear rubber undies or something."

At the gym, Bruce and Amos played five or six pickup games, half-court, two on two or three on three. Bruce, who was a half foot taller than everyone else, still preferred to stay outside the lane, looking for opportunities to bring his feet close together, bend the knees, and collect his long, segmented body into the gentle coil that preceded his set shot. Bruce had a nice touch—a calm eye, clean release, perfect backspin—and he was an optimist. He would watch the long arc of the ball while taking a step or two *back*, as if there were no reason in the world to follow it to the basket for a possible rebound.

Amos was the opposite. Though less hefty than Bruce, he liked working inside, and today, especially, he enjoyed the bumping and shoving that was going on beneath the basket. Amos felt a kind of meanness unfolding within him and was glad there was a way to use it. He leaned heavily into bigger opponents to screen them from the backboard; he crashed through screens that were set against him. It was a funny but good feeling, as if by playing hard enough, he could change the way the world felt about him. And after the last game, when it was just starting to get dark, it gave him a strange satisfaction to tell Crook he'd just walk home, that he didn't feel much like riding along with him right now.

7

THIEVING

Dusty's Oldtowne Market was crowded with people in wet snow boots, but shopping by herself made Clara forget about Amos a little. Mrs. Harper's list specified the cheapest brands, so Clara just looked for the bargains her mother usually chose.

It was while comparing generic oatmeal with the happy Quaker that Clara became uneasily aware of the Tripp brothers. Everyone knew Eddie and Charles Tripp. Even in elementary school, they had been pale and scary, and somehow they had learned early on to enjoy how much they scared people. They shaved their heads and gave themselves tattoos. No one wanted to touch them when learning the Virginia reel in gym, and Eddie started to smoke cigarettes the same year Clara got a pink bicycle. Charles was the older one, the hulking, big-headed, leering one, whose shaven scalp was his one truly revolting physical feature. Its whiteness was mapped with swollen blue veins. It was worse than unpleasant. And yet one day, through the public library shelves, Clara had glimpsed Charles's face from the forehead down and had been shocked at his rugged good looks. With the veiny scalp out of the picture, he looked almost like Patrick Swayze. So what was especially weird was that instead of letting his hair grow out to cover his grotesque scalp, Charles shaved it so that people would *have* to look at it. For Clara, who would've loved to disguise her crooked nose, this was beyond comprehension and made Charles seem not just scary but horrific.

Eddie, the little brother, was a foot and a half shorter than Charles. Eddie was compact and muscular, with close-set eyes of a shade of blue that made Clara think of swimming pools. Clara didn't think scariness came as naturally to Eddie, but he seemed willing to learn from his older brother. People said they both had high IQs, but they cut classes and repeated grades. Charles was a senior now, and Eddie was two years older than Clara but in her same grade. When they'd both been seventh graders at Melville, Eddie had started sitting behind Clara on the bus. He would be quiet for a long time. Then he would lean forward and say, "Are you a virgin?" Clara had stopped riding the bus.

Now, in the aisle of Dusty's Oldtowne Market, Clara turned slightly so that she could peer at the Tripp brothers over the oatmeal box. They both wore baggy military fatigues and expensive black Nikes. Eddie's head wasn't shaved anymore—he had tightly curled black hair. Charles's scalp was shaved clean, so clean that Clara wondered how he'd done it without cutting any of its protruding blue veins. Charles was even bigger now than he was last summer, when he used to lounge with Eddie in the bleachers at the high school and watch cheerleading practice, girls' track, and women pushing strollers, all the while making low comments audible only to Eddie, who would cackle with laughter.

The shopping cart the Tripp brothers were pushing had only a few things in it—some catsup, several cans of Red Dog beer, a small log of salami—and Charles was evidently looking for something in his coat because he kept unzipping it and checking out the lining. It was then that Eddie saw Clara.

Clara glanced away immediately, a sure giveaway that she'd been staring. While she pretended to study the oatmeal, she could see that the Tripps were moving out of her aisle, pushing the cart casually, and then they were gone.

Clara didn't give them another thought until she reached the checkout stand, where she realized that the two brothers were in the line to her left. What was strange was that none of the things she'd seen in their cart earlier were there now. Instead, there was only a bag of generic potato chips and a two-liter bottle of generic cola. Eddie had his wallet out and was studying its contents. Charles was turned toward Clara but not looking at her. He was staring in dull fascination at the rack with magazines and tabloids. As he leaned forward to pull out the *Enquirer* from the rack, his jacket fell open and Clara saw a bottle of catsup. From another pocket peered a can of Red Dog beer. Other pockets, too, seemed to be bulging, but her view was blocked when Charles spread open the tabloid in front of him.

When Charles put the newspaper back, Eddie's eyes fell on Clara. They were the same pale glassy blue that made him almost handsome. She *had* thought he was handsome, in fact, before he started asking if she was a virgin.

"Hey, Clara," he said now, moving so that he stood in front of his brother's jacket. "Haven't seen you much since your daddy started taking you to school." He tried his best to smile.

Clara didn't know what to say. Eddie Tripp seemed creepy to her, but not completely creepy. She decided to try being nice. "That was a long time ago," she said, shrugging and smiling. "So how do you like it at Melville? I hardly ever see you now."

Eddie grinned. "Yeah, well, you're in those bright-child

classes"—he grinned wider—"whereas the shrewd observers have got me pegged as the vocational type."

Charles, after throwing a quick look toward Clara, gave his little brother a sharp push from the back. Eddie put the generic cola and chips on the counter.

In her aisle, the conveyor belt suddenly moved and her checker was talking. "How are you? Do you have a Dusty's card? Cash, check, or credit? Paper or plastic?"

When Clara next looked their way, Charles and Eddie Tripp were leaving. As Charles pushed and herded Eddie ahead of him, Eddie smiled back at Clara. It was a nice smile. "Maybe our paths will cross again, hey?"

Clara, feeling color rise in her cheeks and thinking of her crooked nose, lowered her face and didn't say anything. She supposed she hoped their paths would never cross again, but the way Eddie paid attention just now wasn't so horrible. After a second or two, she glanced up and saw Charles departing, his pockets jammed, herding Eddie ahead of him. The doors, as if at Charles's command, swung open before them.

8

SNOW PEOPLE

Outside the high school gymnasium, Amos MacKenzie stood tugging his hooded sweatshirt tight against the cold. He snugged his black and blue ski cap over his hood, looked out at the warm yellow lights of houses coming to life in the early minutes of evening, and began to regret declining a ride home in Zeke's car. It was cold.

Amos began to run on the downhill descent and then just kept running. He ran and ran, easy loping strides, the cold biting deep into his lungs but his body sweating and warm. It was simple and easy, moving along like this, through the dusk, under the streetlights, the rhythmic squeak of his shoes on the packed snow, and pretty soon, everything in the world—not just running— seemed simple and easy. He would go home and write Clara Wilson a letter telling her he hadn't been the one who'd called her this morning, that it had been his so-called friend Crookshank, who had perhaps been dropped as an infant but who in any case had certain mental deficiencies, and that he, Amos, hoped that...

Up ahead, in the thick dusk, a solid clanking sound. Two dark moving forms, some low talk, and then another thunderous *clank*. Sometimes a porch light came on, but not until the two forms had moved on. Following behind in the shadowy light, Amos could see a crushed mailbox and, up ahead, another.

Amos couldn't help himself. He began to follow the dark forms, slowly and quietly, pulled along by a strange combination of fear and curiosity. Amos slowed and stopped. Something had changed. There was a new silence. The clanking had stopped.

As they turned south on Adams Street, Amos's street, the forms—one large and hulking, the other short and compact—seemed vaguely familiar to Amos. The bat that one of them carried was aluminum, and he began tapping it on anything metal—the parking signs, a fire hydrant, a light pole—but gently, making only a muted clink, as if stealth was now part of their strategy.

Then, as the forms passed through the circle of yellow light, they became the two people Amos hoped they weren't. They became Charles and Eddie Tripp.

A queasy feeling rose in Amos. He knew the Tripp brothers, or at least he knew everything he needed to know. One day after school, Eddie Tripp had taken Amos and Bruce and some others to watch his brother feed their snake. When they got to the Tripp brothers' house, a small crowd of boys was already clustered around a large glass terrarium. The snake was a boa constrictor. The food was a live kitten. Amos was never sure what made him despise the Tripp brothers more, the fact that they'd be merciless to a small live animal or the fact that they'd led the hoots and laughter when Amos and Bruce, seeing what was about to happen, walked away from the proceedings.

Tonight, as they clinked and loitered along Adams Street, the Tripp brothers came to a stop and huddled. Their voices were hushed and tight. They were standing in front of the Goddard place, staring at a snowman with a scarf and a tennis racket on one side of a tennis net, and a snow woman with a racket and a scarf on the other side. The Goddards were childless, middle-aged, and, Amos thought, a little nutty. They were famous in the neighborhood for their elaborate snow scenes, and Amos's father always liked to drive the family by the Goddards' house after a snowfall to see what was new.

Charles looked around, and Amos instinctively stepped back into shadow. "Okay, this is it," Charles said in a hissing whisper that carried through the cold air. His smaller brother pushed open the gate and drew close to the snow people. Charles took something out of his jacket—Amos couldn't see what—and went off looking around on the ground until he found what looked like a stick and then came back to the figures. He did something with whatever he found, and Eddie laughed, a sharp cackling laugh that, to Amos, sounded weirdly made up, the same way Eddie had laughed when Amos and Bruce had left the feeding of the snake. Charles walked around the figures again, this time closer, doing something Amos didn't want to guess at, and Eddie laughed again, the same fake-sounding laughter. Charles laughed, too, but his laugh was deep and full, as if it came from his darkest center and was completely his own. "Off with their heads," Charles said in a laughing voice, and Eddie stepped forward and cocked the bat behind his right shoulder.

No was the word that popped into Amos's head, but what popped out of his mouth wasn't a word at all. It was more of a muffled, foolish-sounding grunt. It sounded a little like *"numph."* It sounded nothing at all like his own voice.

Still, it was enough.

Charles, after stilling himself for half an instant, spun menacingly toward Amos, who stood frozen in his tracks. Before yelling, Amos had felt hidden and safe. Now, after opening his mouth and letting loose this funny, unfamiliar voice, he felt a sudden, complete, and paralyzing fear.

Eddie, who seemed oblivious to Amos's presence, swung the bat, decapitated the snow woman, and let out another harsh laugh.

A porch light blazed on.

Charles glanced wildly at Amos, then grabbed the bat, leaped up the steps of the Goddards' porch, and knocked the light fixture into pieces. It was dark again. Amos heard footsteps crunching through the iced snow. They were growing louder. In the dark, Charles had again become a ghostly form, except now it was moving toward him. Amos again tried to yell, but this time nothing at all came out. He stood completely mute, frozen there, while, within his motionless body, his heart pounded furiously. The footsteps stopped. Amos's heart kept pounding. The ghostly form drew close and stopped. For a moment, Amos thought Charles might turn away. Then he heard a peculiar whirring sound as the bat took flight toward him.

9

GOING

There were no more requests for deliveries when Clara came home with fifteen dollars in pay that afternoon. This just barely paid for the stationery, and she'd forgotten to clean their own driveway, a fact she realized when she saw that her mother had dug out the car, stuck the shovel into a drift by the driveway, and left. Probably she'd been late and would be mad when she came home. Clara checked for messages from Gerri—none—then went in to set the ingredients for Thai food on the counter. If they all had a nice dinner, maybe her mom wouldn't care about the shoveling.

First Clara set the table with their best tablecloth and the good china. The pale pink tablecloth, still tagged with a Kaufmann's label marked down three times, had to be ironed, and the china had been sitting so long in the cupboard that gnats had died in the cups.

When all the dishes lay gleaming on the table, Clara built a fire that went out, then another, and when that also failed, she took Ham and the electric heater up to her room, where she stashed her money and stared at her old copies of *Misty of Chincoteague* and *Stormy: Misty's Foal*, horse books she'd read at least five times each. Clara didn't open them. In fact, her heart sunk a little just looking at them. When she'd first started at Melville, she'd brought these and similar books to school with her to read at free moments, but after a while, whenever she brought one of them out of her backpack, someone would make the low shuddery neighing sounds of a cartoon horse, which made everybody laugh. Then one afternoon, standing beside Clara's locker, Gerri nodded at her horse books and said, "Maybe you shouldn't bring those baby books to school anymore, you know?"

Clara fell asleep, and when she woke up to the heater whirring into bright orange again, it was nearly five. Wasn't her father supposed to be home by now? She went to the window and saw no car in the driveway, just wet pines and snow.

The phone rang repeatedly after that, and later, when she thought of that day, she remembered the empty china plates and the sound of the phone, the extended, ominous ring that it had when the house was closed up against darkness and cold. The first call was from her father at the airport, very cheerful, saying he'd be home within the hour. "Just called to see if I should bring anything from the store," he said. "Is your mother home yet?"

"Not yet," Clara said. "I bought everything for dinner, though. And the table's all set."

"Good girl! We'll have a great time. Have you got your homework finished so we can go out for an ice cream afterward?"

"I was just about to start," Clara said.

"Well, see how much you can do and I'll help you while I cook. How's that?"

Clara had done six algebra problems when the phone rang again.

"Clara?" a voice said. It was a boy, but Clara could tell, with a rise and then a plummet of hope, that it wasn't Amos calling to apologize.

"This is Bruce Crookshank," he said. "Remember me?"

"Sure do," Clara said. Then there was a silence.

"I'm calling on behalf of Amos MacKenzie," Bruce said.

"Then forget it," Clara said. "I'm busy."

"Well, I've got to tell you something."

"Does it involve nudity?"

"Nudity is something I—"

Clara cut him off by hanging up and was surprised at how pleased it made her feel. It was like getting the last word, only better. She got some Oreos out of the pantry and sat back down to her algebra. She was drawing lines and exponents, x's and division brackets when the telephone rang again.

"May I speak to Clara Wilson?" an adult voice asked.

"Speaking," Clara said. Suddenly she was afraid that her father's cab had spun off the road, or that her mother had been in an accident.

"This is Butch MacKenzie, Amos's father," the voice said, and when Clara, a little uncertain of the voice she was hearing, said nothing, he continued: "I wouldn't be calling except that there's been an accident and I believe you could be of help."

"Accident?" Clara asked. She began to cough from swallowing an Oreo almost whole. "What kind of accident?"

"A quite serious accident," the voice said so gravely that Clara pictured Mr. MacKenzie with a pipe in his hand.

"Was somebody hurt?" Clara asked. She had begun to feel like a movie character, and the question sounded false, almost eager, when in fact she felt a measure of panic, like she did whenever she heard an ambulance on the road.

"I'm afraid it's our boy, Amos," the voice said.

"Amos?"

"He has been struck by a baseball bat."

For some reason, this statement had a ring of truth that the voice didn't have. For all its drama and strangeness (Mr. MacKenzie wouldn't say "our boy," would he?), the conversation began to seem urgent in some way.

"Who would do that?"

"We don't know yet. A vandal of some sort. The main thing is that we'd like you to visit him tomorrow if you can."

"Me?"

"He *asked* for you, actually. He said your name and mumbled something."

"Well," Clara said, "I could come after school. Where is he?"

"St. Stephen's Hospital. Room 623. Let's say three-thirty sharp."

Clara's father came home shortly thereafter, complaining about the roads, wondering about Clara's mother's whereabouts, and acting generally distracted. Clara usually felt proud of the way her father looked and dressed. He almost always wore nice leather deck shoes, khaki pants, and a solid Ivy League shirt in pale blue, pink, or yellow—Clara called it his uniform. But tonight her father looked rumpled and worn down.

To cheer him up, Clara told her father about Mrs. Harper, but he hardly listened. She didn't mention Amos MacKenzie. She thought her father might disapprove of her going to the hospital or think the whole thing was strange, which it was, but somehow it was hers, personally. "Mrs. Harper said she'd hire me again," Clara said. "She paid me fifteen dollars."

"That's good," her father said, as if he were thinking about something else. He shuffled through the stack of mail on the kitchen table, then tied an apron over his blue shirt and diced vegetables while the rice slowly popped its lid up and down. The kitchen windows steamed over, the smells of coconut and garlic steeped sharply into everything, but her mother didn't come home.

Finally, when everything was not just ready but growing cold, her father called Kaufmann's. When he identified himself, he waited while he was transferred to someone else. Several minutes passed. Her father's body seemed to be slowly going limp. Then suddenly he snapped to. "Yes, this is Thurmond Wilson. I'm trying to find out if my wife, Angelica, is still at the store."

What followed was short periods of her father listening and saying nothing except "What?" and, once, "Now wait a minute." He was quiet for another few moments before he said, "And that was it? She didn't say anything to anyone?"

He glanced at Clara, who lowered her eyes.

Then her father stood listening for an even longer time, and when he next spoke, it was in a tired voice. "And you say she left the store at two this afternoon?" He waited, listened, and said, "Well, I appreciate your candor. And I understand"—her father hesitated, and Clara knew he was suddenly aware of her standing behind him, listening—"your position regarding her continued employment."

After he hung up, there was a long, still moment before he turned to Clara. His face had changed. It looked gray and waxy, like Clara's grandfather had looked in his coffin. "She hasn't been at the store since two o'clock," her father said. "Your mother just walked off."

Clara glanced at the kitchen clock: 8:35. "Are you going to call the police?" she said. "Maybe there's been an accident."

Her father, almost more to himself than to her, said, "I think I'll call her sister first." But he didn't call from the kitchen. He went upstairs to his office and closed the door. Almost an hour passed before he came back down. He was still wearing the apron over his shirt, and his face still looked deathly gray.

"Your mother is going to stay at Aunt Marie's for a while," he said.

A store of thoughts Clara didn't even know she had came flooding out of her. "So she's really going to do it. She's going to leave us here and run off to that teaching job in France." She felt her face twisting up as if she were going to cry.

Her father stared at Clara closely. "What teaching job?"

Clara managed to clamp back the tears. She narrowed her eyes. "In France. Or Japan. Aunt Marie knows all about it. Mom talks about it with her all the time."

Her father tried to act like this wasn't news to him, but Clara could tell it was. "Look, Clara, your mother's not running off to France or Japan or anywhere else. She's upset right now, but she isn't abandoning you."

Clara expected him to add, "or me," but he didn't.

As she was scraping the uneaten food down the disposal, Clara remembered her mother conversing with audiocassettes in the living room. "*Ça va?*" the tape said. "*Ça va,*" her mother replied cheerfully. This was, Clara knew, the French way of asking how things were with you, and it meant, in literal translation, "It goes."

There was a gloomier phrase Clara wondered about. It was the French way of saying, "She went."

10

DREAMLAND

Room 623 of St. Stephen's Hospital. Amos was twitching in his sleep. His eyes were swollen and yellowish black. Above his forehead, there was a long rectangle of shaved scalp where the doctors had stitched together a two-inch gash.

Amos was dreaming of Charles and Eddie Tripp. In this dream, Amos is strapped into a chair watching Eddie Tripp eating something that Charles hands him one at a time. The food looks like Tater Tots, except Amos knows they aren't. They are something else. Wooden-faced boys stand nearby and laugh each time Eddie licks his lips, pops one of the Tot-like objects into his mouth, and extends his hand toward Charles for another. While he watches, Amos's feet feel cold. Finally he looks down. His feet are bare and have only two toes. The others have been cut off. With a sickening sensation, he knows what Eddie Tripp has been eating.

"Amos?" Someone was tugging at his toes. "Amos? Are you off in dreamland?"

With difficulty, Amos opened his eyes. It was his nurse. It was always his nurse. The protocol was that the nurse would awaken him every two hours, ask him a few questions to make sure he was lucid, and then move on. "What city are you in?" she might ask. "What's seven times nine?" Today, after Amos had answered several such questions, she'd said, "A hundred percent! A+! Top marks!"

"I'm deeply relieved," Amos said in a groggy voice, and the nurse departed.

Left to himself, Amos began again to think of the Tripp brothers. Amos hadn't told anyone that it was Charles Tripp who'd knocked him gaga with a baseball bat. He hadn't told the doctor, the police, or his parents. He knew in his heart he *should* say it was the Tripps, but he knew in his gut he wouldn't. If he did, the Tripps would eventually come looking for him. So he'd said it was too dark, he couldn't see faces. But somehow the police had suspected the Tripp brothers anyway. The investigator had shown him photographs of Charles Tripp, huge and smirking with his tongue poking his cheek out from inside his mouth, and little curly-headed Eddie, looking blank and almost confused. Amos had waited a long time—too long, he thought later—before saying, No, he couldn't be certain it was either of them.

Amos closed his eyes and was just beginning to slip back into sleep when Bruce popped through the door. "Big news," he said. "Absolutely jumbo."

"How jumbo?" Amos said in a slow, thick voice. He was so sleepy. He was so sleepy and so tired of being poked awake every two hours by nurses. He'd been here two days. He wanted to go home.

Bruce had visited Amos before. He'd seen the injuries. He called it Amos's slash-and-gash look. "Jumbo squared," Bruce said. "Jumbo cubed." He folded his big body into the chair near Amos's bed and sat for a moment savoring the information he was about to reveal. Then he leaned forward and said, "Jay Foley came to school with pictures of Anne Barrineau naked."

Pictures of Anne Barrineau naked *were* big news, and Amos

knew he ought to be more interested than he was. It was just that
he was so sleepy.

"Foley got 'em with his telephoto Sunday afternoon through
her bathroom window right out of the shower," Bruce said. He sat
back. "So, anyway, I figured I owed you one for me calling Clara
and saying I was the naked you, so I explained to Foley that you'd
acted heroically in defense of a snowman, and after some serious
negotiation, I have brought you the photos in question."

These words registered slowly. Amos turned in disbelief.
From an interior pocket, Bruce withdrew a plastic bag containing
a batch of photos, which he fanned out like a card hand, face sides
down. "Pick a card, any card," he said.

As Amos examined first one picture and then another, he
began to feel funny about it. What had Anne Barrineau done to
deserve Jay Foley taking pictures of her in her own bathroom and
then showing them around at school?

"So whattaya think?" Bruce said. "Is it A. Barrineau au na-
turel or not?"

Amos handed them back and touched his closed right eyelid,
which hurt so much that he felt a little sick. "Maybe. But you
can't really see her face."

Bruce set the photos in a row at the foot of Amos's bed and
was studying them closely. Suddenly he slid them together. "It's
her all right. I've got a very strong feeling about this." He put the
photos into the Ziploc bag and slipped the bag into the lining of
his coat. He looked around the room. The boy with the ruptured
spleen who'd been in the other bed yesterday was gone this afternoon. "Where's the spleenbuster?" Bruce asked, nodding toward
the empty bed.

"Went home," Amos said, and thought about it. "Lu[...] him." He closed his eyes. "See you later, Crook. I'm asleep. I'm sleeping boy."

Amos thought he heard Bruce leaving but didn't open his eyes. He felt suddenly lazy and serene, and then he was actually asleep, dreaming first of Anne Barrineau coming to a window and staring out, and then of Clara Wilson coming forward and saying, "Amos, it's me, Clara." In his dream, Amos was nodding. "Can you hear me, Amos?" she asked. "Amos, it's me, Clara," she said again, and this time Amos felt himself reach out in his sleep to touch one of her breasts, at which point, to his complete surprise, he heard Clara Wilson scream.

11

RENDEZVOUS

"Where's Mr. MacKenzie?" Clara asked in a sharp voice, stepping back and staring at Bruce Crookshank, who was standing at the hospital room door laughing his fool head off.

"Who?" Bruce asked when he'd regained a portion of his composure.

"Mr. MacKenzie," Clara said. "Amos's father." She felt as if she were surrounded by lunatics. "Amos's father said I should come and visit Amos."

"I'm sure he'll be back directly. Our boy has a steady stream of visitors."

"No, I don't," Amos said weakly, but Clara ignored him because the second that Bruce said *our boy*, she knew that the reason Mr. MacKenzie's voice had sounded strange on the phone was that it hadn't been Mr. MacKenzie at all. It had been Bruce Crookshank.

"And *you*—" she began in an even sharper tone, turning to Amos. But then she broke off. He looked too pale and shocked and uncertain to be yelled at right now. He had two black eyes and a partly shaved head. And the thin nightgown he was wearing made him look about ten. In a miserable, confused-sounding voice, he said, "I don't know how what happened happened."

"Yeah, right."

"No, I mean it."

But she didn't believe it. He had to have been a part of
embarrassing prank, had possibly even been the brains behind
and just so they could make her the butt of their awful joke. Sh
stepped toward the door and stared hard at Bruce until he stepped
aside. Before leaving, she turned back for a moment. "Just so you'll
know. I don't think any of this was even the tiniest bit funny."

Clara walked down the corridor on legs that hardly felt her
own. Cool beads of sweat coursed along her rib cage. She
thought of Amos playing this joke on her and her mother leaving home, and suddenly Clara's face was gathering around her
mouth in the way it did when she felt like she might cry against
her will. She heard tennis shoes squeaking behind her and
glanced back. It was Bruce.

Clara kept walking, but he caught up to her by the elevator,
where a trembling man in pajamas stood braced by a walker. The
walls were pink and lavender, like the floor. Clara looked at the
man's red corduroy slippers while Bruce's words streamed past her.
"Hey," he said, "what happened wasn't Amos's fault. That wasn't
our Amos. Listen to me. He wasn't trying to do that."

Clara ignored him. The elevator opened, and the trembling
man started to move uncertainly forward behind his walker. To
Clara's surprise, Bruce held the elevator open for him. The trembling man inched his way inside and nodded at Bruce, and Clara
stepped in, but Bruce still kept his hand on the door.

"It wasn't Amos's fault," he said. "It musta been the drugs that
made him do that. Or maybe the anesthetic."

"Oh, piddle!" Clara said, stealing a phrase from her mother,
then flushed to hear how silly it sounded, which annoyed her
even more. She slapped Bruce's hands from the door and pushed

rst-floor button. The doors closed like a curtain, and Bruce gone.

The trembling man in the elevator didn't say anything. reathing took his attention instead, and the glow of the lighted numbers as the car went downward. A smell of disinfectant filled up the elevator car, and when the doors finally slid open, Clara gasped for air before turning back to help the man to a bench in the lobby. It was he who smelled of Lysol. That was one surprise. Another was the sight of Eddie Tripp sitting in the lobby with a magazine open on his lap, his face turned toward the television screen.

When he glanced her way, his expression jumped from boredom to real interest. "What are you doing here?" he asked after what felt like a full ten seconds of staring, during which time Clara became keenly aware of her nose. (*She stared crookedly*, she thought. *She smiled lamely but crookedly*.)

"Nothing," she said. "What are you doing here?"

Eddie's grin had a sneering aspect to it. "They get more cable channels here," he said, pointing toward the TV.

Clara understood this was a joke, but she was too uncomfortable to laugh. In the next moment, Eddie was standing up and putting his hands in his pockets. "Hey, you want a Philly cheese steak?" he asked. "I know a place where they make a great Philly cheese steak, and I got a car."

"You drive?"

Eddie grinned. "Yeah, I'm sixteen, remember? The oldest kid at Melville." His grin stretched wider. "I flunked kindergarten a couple times." A pause. "So how about it? Can I talk you into a Philly cheese steak?"

"I'm not that hungry," Clara said, uneasy with his asking and yet weirdly flattered, as she had been the first time Eddie Tripp took the seat in front of her on the bus and fixed his light blue eyes on her face. "I can't," Clara said.

Eddie smiled. "'I can't' is what a girl who doesn't want to start living her life would say, but the truth is, you can. It's as simple as saying, 'Sure. Why not?'"

Clara ignored this. Eddie kept walking beside her as she went past the emergency room. It seemed funny, walking with somebody and not saying anything, so Clara said, "How come you're at the hospital?"

Eddie's eyes shifted slightly. "To see my grandma."

"Your grandma," Clara said doubtfully.

"Yeah, she's got Wilkinson disease, but don't ask me what it is."

"And that's why you're here?"

Eddie's grin turned somehow cockier. "That's my story and I'm sticking to it." They walked a few more paces. "How about you? Why're you here?"

"I came to see a friend. Who got a concussion."

Eddie's pace slowed so slightly that it was almost unnoticeable, but not quite. Clara noticed it. "A friend?" Eddie said.

"Maybe an ex-friend," Clara said. "Or maybe never a friend to begin with."

"What's his name?" Eddie said.

Clara stopped short. "I just said a friend. How did you know it was a boy?"

Again the slight shift in Eddie's blue eyes. "Guess it was the way you said it."

Clara didn't believe this. She continued walking. "His name's Amos MacKenzie," she said.

Eddie took this in without any visible change in expression. "How'd he get the concussion?"

Bruce, impersonating Amos's father, had told her a vandal had hit Amos with a baseball bat, but that might or might not be true, so Clara said, "I don't know."

"You don't know? He didn't tell you?"

"No, he didn't. We hardly talked." Clara didn't like having to answer Eddie's prying questions. And why was he so interested in Amos anyhow? She decided to turn the tables. "So where's your big brother? How come he's not visiting this grandma, too?"

"Charles never comes." A pause. "He makes me come instead."

"How does he make you come?"

Eddie actually snorted. "Charles? Charles could write a book on making people do things."

"Well," Clara said, "why doesn't your dad make Charles visit this grandma?"

"My dad's long gone." An odd, awkward pause. "In a way it's good, though, because my mom's tired of us and next week we're going to move into a place of our own. Charles and me."

All of this was interesting and even sad, if it could be believed. But that was the hitch—if it could be believed. "So how was your grandmother?" Clara asked, and at that moment, over Eddie's shoulder, she saw Bruce Crookshank appear at the far end of a long corridor, look around, and head her way.

"Haven't seen her yet," Eddie Tripp said. He flashed his grin. "They told me they were dressing her wounds."

"You have to dress wounds for Atkinson's disease?"

Eddie kept his cocky grin. "*Wilkinson* disease," he said. His grin softened to what looked like a genuine smile. "I was serious about the Philly cheese steak, you know. I'd buy you one if you want. All you have to do is say yes."

"I have to get home," Clara said, just as Bruce Crookshank caught up with them. He kept a certain respectful distance from Eddie, but when he made eye contact with Clara, he said, "I kind of need to talk to you."

Clara glanced toward Eddie. A tight scowl had come into his face, and when he spoke, it was with the hard edge he'd used long ago on the school bus. "Looks like you're already dating one of the mental patients," he said. "So let's just forget I asked." He turned around and walked off toward the waiting room.

"Asked what?" Bruce said to Clara.

"Nothing," she said, and they walked down the hospital steps toward the bus stop. It was a windy, bitter day, and the gray plastic sides of the bus stop, marked with spray paint and penknives, bubbled out like full sails.

"You're taking the bus?" Bruce said.

Clara turned toward him. "You're a regular Sherlock Holmes." She gave him the chilliest look she could make. She wasn't going to say anything more, but couldn't help herself. "My father doesn't like me riding the city bus. But I rode it down here, and now I'm riding it back. You know why? Because I thought my coming here was *important*."

Bruce looked slightly embarrassed. "I'll ride with you—you mind if I ride with you?"

"I do, very much," Clara said without looking at him.

The bus door squealed open, and the driver sat in the humming bus, waiting for her to climb in. "Bye," Clara said firmly, but Bruce stepped in behind her.

Clara dropped her coins into the chute and sat down in the nearest empty seat. Up front, only a few yards away, Bruce was frantically going through his pockets, looking for money, muttering, going through his pockets again. He unzipped an interior pocket of his coat and, drawing his hand out, inadvertently pulled out a plastic bag with it. The bag flipped to the floor of the bus and lay there for just an instant. There were photographs inside it, Clara saw—but of what? somebody? somebody *naked?*—before Bruce snatched them back up.

The passengers in the bus were so annoyed with the delay that Clara could feel them pulsing with impatience. The bus driver said, "I have to get on with the route, pal. Pay up or step off."

Clara came forward and dropped in enough change for Bruce, then sat back down. He sat directly across the aisle. The bus hummed along, and its warmth worked slowly into Clara. She looked out at the dirty snow piled along the street, the long icy teeth hanging from eaves. She wondered what her mother was doing right now, whether she was warm, whether she was sad, whether she missed being home.

"Thanks."

Clara turned around.

"Thanks," Bruce said again. "I owe you one." He had a sheepish look, but Clara reminded herself how good he was at acting.

"Those pictures that fell out," she said sharply. "Who are those pictures of?"

The question seemed actually to catch Bruce off guard. His face pinkened. "Nobody," he said.

"How can you have naked pictures of nobody?"

The shade of Bruce's face moved toward red. "Who said they were naked pictures?"

"I do. Because I saw."

A moment passed. "Well, if you saw, then you don't have to ask who."

Something flashed in Clara. "I don't know why I thought I could talk to you."

Bruce opened his mouth to speak.

"Don't say anything else," Clara said. She stood up and moved five rows back and sat next to a window, but a few seconds later, she felt the heavy depression of the seat as he sat down next to her.

"Here," he said. His breath was surprisingly sweet. He was offering her a cherry candy from a little round tin. She took one and popped it in her mouth. The top of the tin said *Rendezvous*, and all at once it put Clara in mind of her mother's crazy plan to go to France.

"I know you don't like me," Bruce said, "but I have to say three things to you."

Clara stared fixedly out the window.

Bruce pressed on. "The first thing I need to say is that I'm the one who called and said I was the naked Amos. It wasn't Amos. And I was wearing all my clothes, just so you'll know. The second thing is that I saw the note you put in the paper that day for Amos and grabbed it before he could. Or maybe that's the first bad thing, and the other one came second. Third, I only pretended to be Mr. MacKenzie because you wouldn't listen to me when I said I was Bruce. He *had* said your name in his sleep, but he didn't try to get you to his sickbed to make a pass at you. Amos wasn't in on it." Clara glanced at Bruce, who shrugged. "That's not Amos's style." He slouched back in his seat. "That's it," he said, "that's all I wanted to say."

Clara was surprised at how much she wanted to believe what Bruce was saying, and the moment she realized that in her heart she *did* believe him, she was struck by the fear that he was duping her again.

The bus was rolling north on Genesee toward her stop. She reached up and pulled the cord so the driver would pull over, and then she peered through the grainy veil of salt and snow that had dried on the windows. Her house was visible, but it was dark; the porch light was the only one on, which meant her father hadn't come home yet. Or her mother.

The bus eased to a stop. The driver pulled a lever, and the back door jerked open with an enormous hydraulic breath, illuminating the curb, the sidewalk, and some shards of black snow. "I'm getting off here," she said to Bruce.

"But what are you going to do?" Bruce asked, following her off. "Will you give Amos a call?"

Clara wheeled around and looked at him. She wasn't mad anymore. She was just tired. The bus pulled away, billowing diesel fumes. Clara waited for the noise to pass, then said, "You and your friend Amos made a fool of me once, but that's all you get. Find somebody else to make fun of."

When she walked away from him this time, Bruce didn't follow and he didn't call after her. The red taillights of the bus receded, and all Clara could hear was her own footsteps as she crunched through the ice to her house.

Nobody was home except Ham, but there were two messages on the answering machine, both from her mother. "Hi, sweetie, it's me. I'm at Aunt Marie's and I need to talk to you." The next one said, "Hi, sweetie, me again. I guess you're not home yet and Marie and I are going to be out tonight. I just wanted to let you know how much I miss you. I'll be here awhile longer, but I miss you so much. Bye."

Out loud, to the machine, Clara said, "If you miss me so much, why don't you come back, then?"

There were no messages from Gerri. Clara dialed her number, but when the answering machine came on—"Yo, it's me, Gerri"—Clara hung up.

She went to her father's study and pulled out his enormous medical dictionary. There was no such thing as Wilkinson disease.

A half hour later, in her room with a bowl of soup, Clara was surprised to look out and see Bruce still at the bus stop down the street. He was standing in the cold wearing nothing but his light coat and baggy cotton pants. As the cars passed, the headlights threw a gleam on his face and his crossed arms. Clara began to wonder where he lived and who was waiting for him at home. Maybe his father was the kind who was always working late, or his mother didn't live with him at all. Maybe he had a dog and maybe he didn't. Maybe he had a normal life or maybe not.

She set her soup bowl on the floor for Ham to finish, something she could never have done while her mother was home. When he was done, he laid his big head on her knee. They sat like that for a while, in the dark room of the empty house, perfectly still, Clara at her window watching Bruce Crookshank stomp his feet and cross his arms against the cold until finally he gave up on the bus and started walking, his breath rising above his head in a cold, miserable fog.

12

AN APOLOGY

Amos touched his shaved head and winced. It was Wednesday, and he was home. He could smell pancakes and bacon and wondered if his mother would bring them to his bedside, or if he would be allowed to walk to the table. It was possible to imagine the rustling of his father's newspaper, or maybe he could actually hear it. Maybe the whack in the head had affected his hearing as well as his sight, which seemed painfully acute just now, making sunlight hard to bear. Maybe he was turning into a superhero and would be able to see through walls, hear baseball games without a radio, and telepathically tell Clara that Bruce was a subhuman for setting her and Amos up the way he had.

"Hey, slugger," his father said, easing into the room with a yellow-flowered tray, "don't know how you rate it, but what we've got here is room service."

"What time is it?" Amos asked. It seemed strange to have his father home at breakfast time. Usually he was on his route until much later in the morning.

"It's ten-thirty, you slugabed." Then, more seriously, "How're you feeling?"

"Okay. Fine, I think."

His father's face visibly relaxed. "So nothing feels different?"

Amos thought about it. "I kind of feel a little stupid about everything."

"Really? About what, for example?"

"I don't know. About everything, I guess." He took a gulp of orange juice. "So, can I go back to school tomorrow? I have a test in physical science."

"Possibly. Possibly not. Depends on the patient's progress."

"So how do you feel, Dad?"

"Me? Not bad. Good enough, and bound to improve." He seemed about to say more on the subject, but didn't. Instead he talked about Amos's pigeons, how Liz had been feeding them faithfully and changing their water while Amos was gone. "I suspect she thinks you owe her big for this, slugger," he said, smiling.

Amos's mother stepped into the room. She looked like she'd been crying, but Amos couldn't be sure. Maybe she'd slept badly worrying about him. "Hey, Mom," Amos said, "thanks for the pancakes."

"They're blueberry," she said. "But don't think we're going to spoil you forever. By Monday, dumpling, you'll be back to oatmeal."

"I'm not a dumpling," Amos said, and his father, trying to keep the mood light, said to his mother, "He's not a dumpling, dumpling."

When Amos had eaten four and a half pancakes and five slices of bacon and gulped down all the milk and orange juice, he realized suddenly that he had eaten way too much and might be sick any minute. He lay back on the bed and tried to think of his stomach expanding comfortably to accommodate this great mass of food. He'd read that you could visualize things in your body and think positive, healing thoughts about the sick parts. These thoughts supposedly acted on the body parts and made them do what you hoped they'd do. He had read this in a book he'd found next to his father's chair. Since then, he'd imagined his father devoting each night to a train of healing thoughts while he pretended to watch TV. Only what parts, exactly, were sick in his father's body? Where did the Tums figure in? If Amos directed his own thoughts in the same direction, would that help?

Amos still felt woozy. He closed his eyes and laid a towel over his face to shut out the light that seemed to blast through the curtains. He was trying to imagine his stomach as a placid, shallow basin in which the water level had only temporarily risen when he heard heavy footsteps in the hall and then, close by, Bruce Crookshank saying, "Amos, my man, you're finally out of stir!"

Hearing Bruce's voice made Amos realize that he wasn't even close to forgiving Crook for making him look like a fool with Clara Wilson. Without lifting the towel, Amos said, "I'm sick, Crook, and you sure aren't the cure. Why don't you do the honorable thing and leave?"

Through the towel, Amos heard what sounded like receding footsteps, then silence. He waited a minute, then a minute more. He lifted the towel and peered out. To his surprise, Bruce was actually gone.

Amos pulled the towel back over his head and toyed with the idea of calling Clara after school. Or maybe he should write to her, since she would probably hang up the second she heard his voice. He lifted his head, decided the pancakes were going to stay put, and found a spiral notebook in his bag beside the bed.

Dear Clara, he wrote, then crossed out the *Dear* because it sounded too sappy.

> I just wanted you to know that I didn't call
> you up and say I was naked. That was somebody
> else and I didn't know about it. Also, I thought
> your card in the newspaper was nice. Bruce saw
> it because he was at my house that night. I'm
> sorry about what happened at the hospital, but I
> was asleep and pretty confused.

Amos stopped there and put his hand over his eyes. That last part was a problem. He couldn't exactly say he'd been dreaming about girls' breasts and so in his sleep had just naturally reached out to touch hers. Even mentioning the word *breasts* would just give her more reason to think he was some kind of a pervert, and maybe he was. Maybe he was no different from Crook and Jay Foley. Maybe the only difference was that they were more honest about it.

> I don't know how to explain it except that it
> was a mistake and I was actually asleep, not just
> faking it. Anyhow, I promise to leave you alone.
> I just wanted to explain my side.

Amos reread the letter, which suddenly seemed as stupid and puny as his own stupid, puny life. Then, just to get it over with, he signed his name, folded the letter into an envelope, and sealed it.

13

ENDANGERED SPECIES

Gerri hadn't called since returning three days earlier from Stowe, and it seemed clear she was avoiding Clara at school, taking different routes to classes and going off campus for lunch. Clara's mother called Clara twice more, both times in the morning before school. Each time, after saying she was fine, Clara stood at the kitchen phone and said, "You want to talk to Dad?" but her mother said, "No, sweetie, I just want to talk to you and find out how you're doing and tell you how much I miss you."

The third time her mother had said that, Clara said, "Then why don't you just come home? Then you can stop missing me because you'll be here."

A second passed before her mother spoke. "The *why* of it is very complicated, sweetie, and it runs pretty deep." She spoke in her most adult voice, which to Clara was her most annoying voice of all, because it always seemed to say, "I'm an adult and you're not, which is why I understand these things and you don't."

"I'd better go or I'll be late for school," Clara said, and her mother, in her normal voice, in her sweet sad normal voice, said, "Okay. *Au revoir*, sweetie."

Clara hated it when her mother used French words, but this time it reminded her of a fight between her parents that had ended in reconciliation. It was last summer, and her father had been reading in his chair while her mother watched a French lesson on one of the educational channels. Verbs conjugated themselves on a blue background, followed by scenes in which Parisian students ordered *limon pressé* at sidewalk cafés.

"Oh, Thurm," her mother said, "just look at that street. Don't you wish sometimes we'd gone to live abroad the way we planned?"

Her father glanced briefly at the screen and said nothing. A few minutes later, he said, "I'm going out," and out he went, the screen door banging shut behind him. Clara watched her father walk down the drive, stand at the end of it, and stare at the traffic with his hands in his pockets. If he put his hands on his hips, Clara thought, he would look more decisive.

"Dad's standing on the driveway," Clara said.

Her mother turned around and parted the curtains. He was still standing there with his hands in his pockets.

"He looks sad," Clara said. "Maybe you should go out there."

For some reason, this worked. Her mother switched off the TV, stepped into her shoes, and joined him. After a few minutes, her mother took her father's hand and they went for a walk.

This was what Clara thought about while she walked to Mrs. Harper's house on Tuesday afternoon. She had to think of a way to do that again. Her mother might be living in Dalton, and her father might be willing to wait with his hands in his pockets, but maybe if Clara said the right thing, a meeting would occur and her mother would come home.

Clara changed the cat litter and dusted under Mrs. Harper's figurines. Then she gently wiped cobwebs off the lampshades. She had the feeling Mrs. Harper was testing her for regular work. If she didn't break any knickknacks, if she cleaned things she wasn't specifically asked to clean, if she left Ham at home, where he couldn't threaten the cats, she would be given more work, and her camp fund—now up to $140—would rise accordingly. Except that maybe instead of horse camp, she could use the money to take her parents on vacation.

But Mrs. Harper's house was the wrong place to feel hopeful about her mother. It was lonely there, and the heat was on too high. The air smelled musty, like a house preserved by the historical society. It was as if Mrs. Harper had ceased to exist once her husband died but someone had to keep house in his memory.

Clara's house felt a little that way with her mother gone. She still found herself obeying her mother's rules: *Don't cut paper with the sewing scissors. Don't leave the dishrag wadded up in the sink. Don't cut meat on the bread board.* When Clara came home from Mrs. Harper's, she started to cut newspaper with the sewing scissors and stopped short. Maybe this was a test—like the princess and the pea. Maybe if she kept things the same and remembered all the rules, her mother would come back for her things, see how careful Clara had been, and decide to stay home. Clara went to the kitchen for the old paper-cutting scissors.

The newspaper article she was cutting out was about the juvenile offender who'd vandalized private property and assaulted Amos. *So at least that much of what Bruce Crookshank had said was true*, she thought. The offender's name wasn't given because he was a minor, but Clara, like everyone else at school, knew it was Charles Tripp. This made her wonder about Eddie Tripp, too. Had he been at the hospital to try to find out about Amos—and to find out what he was telling people? According to the news story, the damage to postboxes and lights was estimated at $1,566. It said that Amos MacKenzie, who had interceded to stop the vandalism, had been hospitalized but was recovering quickly.

Clara put the clipping in her desk drawer with her camp fund and the Christmas card showing the MacKenzies beside the milk truck. Amos stared back at her, uncomfortable as always, one arm behind his back. He didn't *look* like a jerk. But, as her mother liked to say, jerks don't always wear an identification label.

Gerri dodged her all day Thursday, and that afternoon, after throwing her papers and before her father came home, Clara dialed her on the telephone. Her little brother, Kendrick, answered the phone. "It's me, Clara. Who's this?"

"It's me, Kendrick, the King of All Revolting Noises, do you doubt it?"

Clara knew better than to say she did. "Not for a second," she said. "Is your sister there?"

Clara heard the clunk of the receiver being laid down and Kendrick's voice yelling, "Ger-ri! Ger-ri Erickson! Call for Gerri, the Hairiest Hairy One!"

Seconds passed. Nearly a minute. Finally Kendrick came back on the line. In a careful voice, he said, "She's not in at this moment."

Clara knew what this meant. She had seen Gerri use this trick on James Martinson when she didn't want to talk to him.

Gerri would go out on the front porch and tell Kendrick to tell James Martinson that she wasn't in at this moment.

"Okay," Clara said. "But could you tell Gerri that I really need to talk to her? And that it will only take a second?"

"Roger," Kendrick said. "Over and out."

Clara set the phone down. She only had one real question for Gerri, but it was probably the only one she could never ask and Gerri would never answer. It was, What did I *do?*

It was Friday when the letter from Amos arrived. She and Ham had finished their paper route and had just returned home with their empty canvas pouches. It was full dusk. Her father wasn't home yet, so Clara checked the mailbox on her way by. She was hoping for a letter from her mother or maybe even Gerri when the smudgy envelope from Amos, with its serious, formal hand-writing, came out of the box with two bills from credit card companies. Amos had neatly printed his return address in the corner. There was an oily, dime-sized stain near the bottom left-hand corner, and Amos had drawn an arrow toward it and writ-ten, *Oops!* Then, under that, he'd written: *Neat's-foot Oil. (Nothing gross.)*

Feeling a little stunned, like she had when she was chosen for her little part in the school play, Clara carefully opened the envelope. She read the letter once fast and then again slowly. So it *had* all been a misunderstanding, then, and it confirmed what Bruce had been trying to tell her that day on the bus. Which meant that Amos might be as nice as she hoped after all.

Clara was still sitting in the living room staring at Amos's neat handwriting when her father came in wearing gloves and his heavy winter coat.

"That from your mom?" he asked, nodding at the letter in her hand.

"No," Clara said. She felt herself blush. But her father didn't seem to notice. Once she'd said it wasn't from her mother, he turned away and hung up his coat.

"It's from Amos MacKenzie," Clara said.

"Amos MacKenzie," her father repeated. "Do I know Amos MacKenzie?"

"His father's the milkman."

"Oh, right. Another of our endangered species. Men in white uniforms, milk in glass bottles." He took off his gloves and picked up the two bills.

Clara didn't like it when her father was in the mood to make everything seem useless. "Well, his son, Amos, was hit with a bat."

Her father mumbled, "Uh-huh" and opened the first bill.

"Some vandals threw the bat at Amos when he stopped them from doing more vandalism," Clara said. "Amos got a concussion."

"Hmm," her father said while staring at the bill.

"It was really the oldest Tripp brother who did it," Clara said. "That wasn't in the paper, but someone told me about it at school."

For the first time, her father paid attention. "Well, I wouldn't believe all the gossip," her father said. "Remember, 'Just the facts, ma'am. We only need the facts.'"

Clara thought about telling her father that it was a fact that she'd seen Eddie and Charles Tripp together just a little while before the vandalism and assault, but she didn't. Clara didn't know why, but she didn't want to think that Eddie had been involved. So she said, "Well, the facts are that Charles Tripp was arrested and hasn't been at school."

Her father nodded, but he'd opened the other bill and his attention was elsewhere.

"I have play practice tonight," Clara said, remembering suddenly that she also had five chapters to read for English by Monday. And math homework.

Her father didn't look up from the bills. "What time?"

"Seven to nine."

"Well, I'm thinking of going to Dalton tonight. Do you think you'll be okay walking to the school?"

Going to Dalton. To see her mother. This was even better than a note from Amos. "Sure," she said. She waited until her father had put the credit card bills back into their envelopes. "Are you going to bring Mom home?"

"I don't know, Polkadot. That's up to your mother. She wanted me to take her some clothes and books, and then we'll just have to see about the rest."

That night, at play practice, they were just blocking their moves on the stage and getting measured for costumes. But it was pleasant in the little auditorium with the warm lights, the wooden floor, the Roaring Twenties set, and Mrs. Van Riper's voice sailing musically over the din. "People! People! Opening night approaches and we are far far from ready!" Backstage was a bustle of clothes and good cheer, and for the first time in days, it seemed to Clara, life was a warmer, cheerier place. Gerri was still being horrible, but she'd gotten the letter from Amos, and her father was off in Dalton, maybe sitting in Aunt Marie's guest room right now, at this very moment, listening to her mother confess that she'd made a mistake and wanted to come home and straighten everything out with everybody. That could happen. *That*, Clara thought, standing in front of a large cardboard speakeasy, *could very easily happen.*

14

CHINESE CHECKERS

It was the longest weekend Amos could remember. After Amos had sent him off, Bruce hadn't stopped by or even called, and although Amos knew he had no right to hope that Clara Wilson might call him over the weekend, he'd hoped it anyway and been disappointed.

Amos lay on the sofa and did his makeup homework, but only halfheartedly. He watched sports events on ESPN that he could not have cared less about, and then fought with his sister when she wanted to turn the channel to some Saturday afternoon dance show. He just felt lazier and lazier and crankier and crankier. He wasn't hungry, so he hardly ate. Even Saturday night, when his mother made pork chops and applesauce especially for him, he just picked at it. His father tried to perk him up by advising him that the Blue Jays were leading the Grapefruit League, and Amos said, "That's only spring training, Dad. Everybody knows spring training standings don't mean anything." Worse, even though he knew he might've hurt his father's feelings, Amos couldn't break out of his mood enough to care.

On Sunday nights, the whole family usually watched a Perry Mason rerun and ate cheeseburgers with milk shakes, but the doctor was going to do some kind of procedure on Amos's father the following day, and this meant that all day Sunday, his father had to drink some kind of mineral oil that cleaned out his whole body.

So Liz and Amos had cheeseburgers while their mother went upstairs with their father, who'd gone to lie down. Amos turned the
TV to Perry Mason at seven o'clock, but no one came into the
living room until almost eight, when his mother sat down to read
one of her new religious books and his father carefully laid out a
board game on the coffee table in front of Amos's sofa. Amos let
him. Amos waited until he was completely done laying it out
with like-colored marbles in all their colored holes. Then he said,
"Dad, don't you think I'm a little too old for a game like Chinese
checkers?"

Amos knew at once that he shouldn't have said it. It was
rude, and he expected his father to say something sharp about his
rudeness. But what happened was far worse. His father's face
turned suddenly pink, as if he'd just been slapped, and then just
as suddenly it lost all its color. His father looked almost tearful,
but surely that couldn't be. He looked completely defeated, as
though he had just realized something final and irreversible. Just
as soon as this look came over him, his father straightened himself and walked from the room with as much dignity as he could.

All at once his mother was putting down her book, hurrying
from the room, and saying, "Shame on you. Shame on you, Amos
Thomas MacKenzie."

15

SWALLOWED BY A WHALE

Clara's weekend had been no better. On Friday night, she waited up after play practice for her father. She took a quilt with her to the couch and curled up where she could see the hall light shining. On the hope that her mother might be with her father when he returned, Clara made Ham stay on the floor, and she made sure that all the dishes were done before she lay down with her homework.

It was hard to do homework so late at night, and Clara kept popping up to do one more thing that would make the house look inviting to her mother: hanging her coat in the closet, scrubbing the kitchen sink with cleanser, dusting the mantel. Then she would do a math problem and hear a car that seemed to be slowing down outside the driveway. But the car always turned at the next street instead.

She couldn't believe all this huge stuff was happening and she couldn't even tell Gerri. During the course of the evening, Clara called Gerri's number three or four times, but on all but one occasion, she hung up when the machine came on. The other time she waited for the beep and in a small voice said, "Hi, it's me, Clara." She waited for a few seconds, but nobody picked up. Which meant Gerri either had gone for the weekend or was out doing something with other friends or was at home not wanting to talk to Clara.

When it was almost ten and she'd finished the last five math problems, Clara pulled out the reading she was supposed to do for English. They were reading *Great Expectations*, and the words were so difficult that she had to have a dictionary nearby. Tonight she was too tired to get the dictionary, and it was a chapter where Pip went to an old woman's house and was asked to lead her around and around a rotten wedding cake. On and on they circled the old cake, and when Clara woke up, her father was trying to lift her off the couch.

"Did Mom come with you?" Clara asked.

"Not this time," he said. He sounded tired. "She's having a good time visiting with her sister, and now they won't have to call each other every day."

"Oh, Dad, you didn't fight about the phone bill again, did you? Is that why she wouldn't come?"

"No, Polkadot," he said in a weary voice. "We didn't fight about anything."

Clara wrapped the quilt around her arms and allowed herself to be steered toward the stairs. "She's already been gone for six days," she said miserably, almost to herself. How could her mother stay gone like that when her father wasn't even out of town? She always complained about her father's long trips, and now she was doing the same thing. What if she didn't come back to see Clara in the school play?

She didn't even know about Amos's wonderful letter.

The worst part about going to bed every night since her mother had left was passing her parents' bedroom. Since her mother had cleaned up after the midnight picnic and swept everything into hiding, and since her father had come home and left his suitcases standing half-emptied by the bed, it looked more like a motel room.

"Sing that song, Dad," Clara said as she entered her own bedroom and dropped onto the bed. "The one about the teacup and the whale."

> *Sit up to the breakfast table*
> *And cry about your troubles.*
> *Let your tears fall in a teacup*
> *That flows into the ocean,*
> *Where they're swallowed by a whale.*

He sang for a little while, and she pretended to fall asleep, thinking about the time she and her parents had gone to Washington, D.C., on vacation. They had driven until late into the night, and her mother had fallen asleep in the front seat while Clara slept in the back, waking only once to hear her father singing that song to himself, driving the three of them safely and snugly through the night.

In the morning, things didn't seem snug at all, even though her father turned up the heat. He built a fire, too, and then sat in front of it without a book or any music on. Even Ham sat at a distance from his chair. It was an overcast Saturday outside, the kind of day when the clouds seemed to reach all the way down to the ground, to be everywhere and nowhere.

"You want to read your book, Dad?" Clara asked. "It's right here." She held up the book about the French Revolution that he'd been reading since Christmas.

"Sure," he said, and took it from her. He opened to his book-mark, but when Clara came back to the living room dressed for play practice, he wasn't reading.

"I'm off to play practice," she said. "I'll be back around noon."

"Sure," he said. "Noon. And what else are you doing today?"

"My papers and some errands for Mrs. Harper." She had also thought about writing back to Amos, but she wasn't sure. She couldn't call him. Her mother said that if someone sent you a let-ter, you should write back immediately, not call, especially if they sent you a present as well. But did that rule apply to anyone be-sides grandparents? Did it apply to boys you didn't know very well?

Her father looked over his book to the fireplace. The fire he'd built was consuming itself as it collapsed and hissed. A horn sounded outside, and Clara could see the headlights of a car shin-ing weakly into the fog.

Clara's father glanced at her and gave her a quick nod that meant, You'd better get going. Then he looked down at his book, adjusted his glasses, and lifted one page with his index finger.

"Bye, Dad," Clara said, and the horn beeped again outside.

"So long," her father said, and methodically turned the page.

When she came home later, Clara noted what page he was on, and though her father again seemed to be reading the book by the fire Saturday night and Sunday morning, when Clara checked his bookmark Sunday night, it hadn't moved a page.

Living among kids wasn't that great, Clara thought, but liv-ing among the adult human beings was worse.

16

SUFFER NO FOOLS

Monday morning, 7:15. Amos's mother, as if totally distracted, hadn't said a word to Amos or Liz over breakfast, which in itself seemed more than a little bit weird. No "How do you feel?" or "Are you sure you feel well enough to go to school?" In fact, she spoke only when Amos's father entered the kitchen carrying a small overnight bag. "Got everything?" Her voice sounded hollow and almost afraid.

"Got everything for what?" Amos said, and was embarrassed when his father said, "Oh, this little procedure they're doing today." Which was something Amos should've remembered. "What exactly are they doing?" he said.

Amos's father smiled. "First they starve you, then they put you under, and then they poke and prod. Doctors have a strange idea of fun."

Amos glanced at Liz, who was reading the paper and didn't look up.

"And when they're done," his father said, grinning, "I'm going to have me a big ol' steak and a big ol' baked potato."

He said this so much like he'd say any everyday thing that it satisfied Amos that it *was* just an everyday thing, and before he could have second thoughts, his mother was telling him to bring his plate to the sink, get his coat on, and get moving, or he was going to be late.

His father pushed a worn leather glasses case across the table toward Amos. "Found these in a snowbank a few weeks ago while I was on my route. Thought you could use them."

Inside the case were a pair of Carrera black aviator sunglasses.

Amos wasn't at all sure about them, but Liz, after dipping her newspaper to glance at them, said, "Hey, cool," so Amos decided to try them on.

"A scarf and some stubble and we'll start calling you Ace," his sister said good-naturedly and went back to her reading.

"I just thought it might save some questions about the shiners," his father said. "I know how kids can be at that age."

Amos doubted that very much, but he sort of liked the glasses.

"We called the principal. He said you could wear the glasses and your hat during class for the first few days." The hat, which his father now presented, was a new Blue Jays hat meant to hide Amos's stitches and shaved scalp. Amos turned the cap in his hands. It looked stiff and brand-new. He wasn't that crazy about it.

He suddenly became aware that his father was staring at him. "Thanks, Dad," Amos said, and his father broke his gaze and stood up.

"Okay, we better scoot," he said to Amos's mother, but then, before leaving, he did something else weird. He put two fingers under Liz's chin, tilting her head slightly so that he could give her a gentle kiss on the forehead. "Be good, Liz," he said in an odd, tight voice, and then hurried out.

After their parents had gone, Liz gave Amos a look. "And they say we're strange," she said.

Amos pulled on his cap and coat, then, outside on the front walk, stood for a moment wrapping his scarf tight to his neck. It was funny to think he'd been away from school for a week and yet had heard nothing at all about it. No gossip, no test scores, no jokes. No half-court basketball in the gym, no girls to sneak looks at. It was almost as if school had for a time ceased to exist. The nervousness reminded Amos of how the first day of school felt when you were about to enter a new grade.

The sun was out, but you couldn't feel it. Just snowy glare and wind. Amos, on his way to school, turned onto Teal Street just in time to see the Number Five school bus lumber away from the curb a half block ahead. Reflexively, Amos sprinted a few yards, but the aviator glasses bounced loosely on his nose and Amos saw that running was futile anyhow. He pulled up and began the long walk.

It was, as always, cold—the kind of cold that clothes just couldn't keep out. And right now, Amos thought, baseball players were running around in shirtsleeves under a bright sun in Florida and California and Arizona. Amos turned the corner onto Ellis and was passing the Goddards' house before he knew it. He stopped. The snow-covered yard was vacant. Where the snow people had held their tennis rackets, there were now just chunky mounds of snow.

"Sad sight, wouldn't you say?"

Amos looked up. It was Mr. Goddard standing behind the screen door in a yellow parka.

"Did you take them down?" Amos asked.

"What was left of them."

Amos stepped into the yard, hoping Mr. Goddard would come out onto the porch, but he didn't. "I'm Amos MacKenzie. I live just over on Adams Street."

"You the boy that tried to run those hoodlums off?"

This sudden recognition surprised Amos. "Not really. I just made a grunting sound, and then one of them conked me with a bat." Amos took off his dark glasses to reveal his black eyes.

"So you're the boy," Mr. Goddard said, and stepped out on the porch. Mr. Goddard was older than Amos's father. His skin hung looser, his hair was a woolly white, and there was a milky brown look to his eyes.

"I was just wondering what those guys had been doing to the snowmen when I came up on them," Amos said. "I couldn't see what they were doing exactly."

The question made Mr. Goddard's eyes turn dead. "They're gone," he said. "The wife and I decided it that very night. Those were the last of our snow people."

Amos wasn't certain what Mr. Goddard was saying. "Well, I hope not," he said, but Mr. Goddard didn't reply. Mr. Goddard just stood there looking a little lost on his own porch.

Amos waited a second, then said he guessed he'd better go now.

"I'm sorry Mrs. Goddard wasn't here to see you," Mr. Goddard said, and his voice and eyes drifted again. "She's at the library. She's just a volunteer now."

There was another awkward silence, which Amos broke by saying, "Miss Martin'll kill me if I'm any later to my first-period class."

Mr. Goddard seemed not to hear.

"Well, thanks," Amos said, backing down the steps.

"No," Mr. Goddard said. "Thank *you*. And I'll tell Mrs. Goddard you stopped in. She'll scold me for not providing refreshments."

Out on the street again, Amos began noticing the mailboxes

the Tripps had been beating that night. Most of the boxes had been reconnected in their dented state, a few had been replaced with new boxes, and one or two still stood loosely attached to their leaning posts.

"Hey, Hero!"

A Jeep full of high school jocks had pulled alongside Amos, and peering from the lowered passenger-side window was Big Dave Pearse, grinning hugely. "Heroes don't walk, kiddo. Heroes ride first class."

Amos had the vague idea he was being made fun of, and kept walking. The Jeep pulled ahead, and Big Dave jumped out. He held the door open for Amos. "Step in, my man. We'll get you to your institution of lower learning in style." Then, sensing Amos's uncertainty, he said, "I mean it. We're giving you a lift."

Amos squeezed in between Big Dave and the driver, whom he didn't know. He didn't know the guys in the back, either, although they both wore letterman jackets and one of them was from the high school basketball team. Big Dave wrapped an arm around Amos and said, "Guys, this is my main man. A freshman phenom." He stretched his grin wider. "And let me remind you gents that I knew him when he was just one of the little people. Before he was what he is today."

Amos felt at once incredibly embarrassed and incredibly happy.

From the backseat, one of the varsity guys said, "You the kid Charles Tripp took a bat to?"

Amos didn't say anything. It *had* been Charles Tripp, but he wasn't telling anyone that. Still, everybody somehow seemed to know.

"Affirmative," Big Dave said.

In a lower voice, one of the guys in the backseat said, "Well, the kid's got more balls than I do. Charles Tripp is one twisted individual."

Amos cleared his throat. "So what did those guys actually do to the snowmen?"

The driver of the Jeep sniggered and said, "Go ahead, Pearse. Explain to your main man what the Tripps did."

"Amos, my man," Big Dave said, "the Tripp boys were, shall we say, *indelicate* in their approach to the snowy tableau."

"Try it in English, Pearse," the driver said.

"Okay. Here's what they did. They made Mr. Snowman anatomically correct with a tree branch, and they sullied Miss Snowman's reputation."

Amos was trying to make sense of this when a voice from the back said, "In other words, they marked their territory with Tripp brother urine."

After a few seconds, Big Dave said without his usual bluster, "You can't see it in them *physically*, but Charles and Eddie are cripples."

"Charles and Eddie are assholes," the driver said.

Someone in the backseat said, "Too bad they didn't nail both of them, instead of just Charles. Charles is always covering for his slimy little sibling."

A minute or two later, an old Beatles song came on the radio, and one of the guys in the back said to turn it up. The driver did.

"Louder."

When it was loud enough, a couple of them, Big Dave included, were singing along, and in the backseat the basketball player had pulled out a couple of drumsticks and begun tapping out rhythm on the window pane. A happy energy filled the Jeep, loud enough to get lost in.

The Jeep moved smoothly through the slush and traffic. Amos had never been in a car that girls repeatedly stared into. Big Dave and the others seemed to take these looks as a matter of course, but Amos didn't. He felt funny about it. He wasn't one of these high school jocks. He was just a junior high bozo who happened to be along for the ride. Still, when clusters of his classmates turned to stare as the Jeep pulled up in front of Herman Melville Junior High, Amos was aglow with foolish pride. As Amos walked away from the Jeep, Big Dave leaned out the window. "Amos, my man, keep the powder dry and suffer no fools!"

Amos had no idea what this meant but nodded as if he did. Then, as he strode up the wide stairs to the main entrance of Melville, Amos felt the eyes of the parting students fixed on him in a way he didn't understand. When he'd reached the top step, a familiar face stepped up from the rear of the crowd. It was Eddie Tripp. He stood and waited for Amos to draw close. He was wearing a composed, contemptuous smile. In a low voice—almost a whisper—he said, "Hello, Milkboy."

And then Amos was past him, sliding along in the current of the crowded hallway.

The shape of school society was, in Amos's mind, a kind of pyramid. If you were good-looking or cool or athletic or wild or rich or experienced in sexual matters, the mob pushed you toward the top of the pyramid. If you had bad teeth, bad acne, or weird clothes, if you had a potbelly like Crook or a voice that cracked when you had to read out loud in class, the mob stepped aside and watched while you slid down to the base of the pyramid, where hardly anybody would talk to you and where it was best to act like you wouldn't want to be up toward the top even if you could.

Amos knew this from experience. His first year at Melville, he had noticed people sneaking glances at him and snickering. When he sat down in homeroom, somebody said, "It's Amos the famous!" which provoked mean laughter, and somebody else said, "Hey, Amos, where's your truck?" Amos had felt sweat pop from what seemed like every pore of his body. It was after homeroom that he understood the source of the joking. Taped to his locker was an enlarged color Xerox of the card his father had left for his customers that Christmas. That year, his father had made Amos wear a stupid Santa's cap and sit on the fender of the truck looking like a moron. On the copy, somebody had written: AMOS THE FAMOUS MILKBOY!!!

What Amos wasn't prepared for was the pleasure of being pushed up the pyramid. And this was exactly what now occurred. During his absence, rumors about Amos had spread through Melville. Amos MacKenzie had taken on the Tripp brothers. Amos MacKenzie had two black eyes and a cracked skull. Amos MacKenzie had brain damage. Amos MacKenzie might not live. And today, there was more news. Amos MacKenzie was escorted to school by bodyguards, high school football players, linebackers mostly, mean mothers.

All this was unknown to Amos, so in the halls between first and second periods, it was a surprise to have people he hardly knew greeting him, to have acquaintances punching him in the arm like friends, to have friends catching up to him in the halls, squeezing between others to be the first to pass on the gossip to Amos.

"Anne Barrineau's parents got her transferred to Eliot," said the first boy.

"They got Crook with the pictures," said the second.

It wasn't until the second-period late bell rang that Amos, seated in Mr. Farmer's class, realized with a start that the desk two rows over, where his buddy Crook normally sat, was empty.

Suspended. Crook had been suspended. Jay Foley himself told Amos about it during Nutrition. The rumors of the photographs had finally gotten back to Laurie Lee Caton, who broke the news to Anne Barrineau, who called her mother to take her home. "The next day, her parents went to the principal," Jay Foley said, "and the principal set loose the dogs. Guys were grilled left and right." Eventually people who weren't willing to squeal on Foley (who had high pyramid status) *were* willing to squeal on Bruce (who didn't). The boys' dean himself had searched Bruce's locker, then his person. In a zippered interior coat pocket, the boys' dean had found a plastic bag containing just one picture of Anne Barrineau, with her clothes still on. Bruce was escorted to the office. He said he hadn't snapped the photographs. He said he'd found them. He'd destroyed the ones of her naked, out of respect, he said. That was his story. The boys' dean kept increasing the days of his suspension, but Bruce didn't change his tune. He'd found the photographs near the gym in a bag. He didn't know where they came from. He hadn't shown them to anybody. He'd destroyed all but one of them and he wished he had destroyed that one, too, but he hadn't, so he would take his punishment.

Jay Foley, smiling, shook his head. "I underestimated Bruce. I surely did."

"One picture is all he had, though?" Amos said.

Foley shrugged. "Yeah, I don't get that, either. There were fourteen total. Believe me, I counted them." Foley started to veer toward the west wing but turned back. "Hey, you tell Crookshank I'm a big fan."

"Hey, Amos!"

Amos turned and nodded at someone he'd never before spoken to. A few seconds later, someone passing by grabbed his hand and pressed a note into it. He whirled around to see a retreating girl he didn't know. He unfolded the note in Civics.

> Hi, I'm glad you're alive and back in school. I always liked you, but now because you almost died I'm just going ahead and saying so.
>
> Deanna Adkins

Deanna Adkins? Had he even had a class with Deanna Adkins? Amos was thinking how much he might've liked a note just like this one if it had been written by Clara Wilson, when Mr. Duckworth, his Civics teacher, appeared suddenly in the aisle beside Amos and plucked the note from his hands.

The classroom fell quiet. Mr. Duckworth had a deep, resonant voice, and his custom was to read captured notes aloud.

A look of amusement formed on Mr. Duckworth's face as he read the note to himself. Then, after a moment of theatrical deliberation, he smiled down on the class. "Allow me to share," he said, his rich voice caressing the room. He let his gaze settle on the note. "My dearest dearest Amos dear," he proclaimed, as if reading from it. "I have always liked you, but now, to be quaintly inarticulate, I like you even more. Yours very hormonally et cetera et cetera et cetera."

This drew laughter from the class, and embarrassment from Amos, but not entirely. Part of him was pleased, too, that he'd received a note like this and that the rest of the class should know it.

When Amos sat down at an empty lunch table, the chairs around him slowly filled with boys who wanted to see his black eyes (Amos would briefly lower his Carreras) and his stitched scalp (he would for a moment doff his Blue Jays cap). They also wanted to hear what happened, and Amos told them, more or less. "I was too stupid to be afraid," he said, hoping this would sound modest. He never said the Tripp name, but the other boys did, which made Amos nervous. "Taking on the Tripp brothers solo," one of the louder boys said. "That's more than slightly awesome."

When Amos looked at this boy, he happened to glance beyond him. Off at the edges of the lunch area, leaning against a post, Eddie Tripp stood staring at him.

At the beginning of fifth period, Amos asked for permission to go to the bathroom. He didn't like using the west-wing bathroom, but sometimes it was unavoidable, and this was one of those times. To his relief, the bathroom was smoky but unoccupied. Amos was at the urinal when the door swung open and someone walked over to the sink and began running water. When Amos turned around while buttoning up, he saw that it was Eddie

Tripp. He was wetting his hair and reworking a curl over his fore-head until it was just so. Amos, feeling real fear, headed for the door, but Eddie wheeled neatly and blocked his path.

"Ain't you gonna wash up?" he said, and made his sneering grin.

Eddie was actually smaller than Amos, but Eddie's menace made it seem the other way around. Amos went over, turned on the water, and wet his hands. He pumped the soap dispenser, which he knew was foolish—there was never soap in the soap dispenser, just as there were never paper towels in the towel dispenser. Amos washed without soap and was wiping his hands on his pants when Eddie Tripp smiled scornfully and said, "So every-body's calling the Milkboy a hero."

After a moment, Amos said, "I wouldn't know about that."

Eddie was shaking his head slowly, as if thinking of something sorrowful. "Everybody's so happy to have Charles and Eddie Tripp get caught at something, they'll turn something as pathetic as you into a hero over it." He smiled unhappily at Amos. "That's how much people despise the Tripp brothers."

Amos was still wearing his Carrera glasses, but Eddie asked him now to remove them. "It's not polite," Eddie said, "talking indoors with dark glasses on."

Amos removed the glasses and held them in his hand.

"Yikes!" Eddie Tripp said in mock surprise when he saw Amos's eyes. "Couple of real serious shiners you got there."

Amos nodded.

"How'd you get 'em?" Eddie said.

In a low, sullen voice, Amos said, "How do you think I got them?"

"Well, I'm asking in order to find out what you'll answer." Eddie grinned and fixed his eyes evenly on Amos. Without looking away from Amos, he reached into a pocket of his fatigue jacket and withdrew a metal object that Amos recognized as the kind of utility knife painters use to scrape windows. When Eddie depressed a latch with his thumb and pushed it forward, a razor blade slid out from its metal sheath.

"I didn't tell anybody anything," Amos said.

Eddie finally broke his gaze from Amos. He looked down at the razor blade. Inscribed in the metal were the words *Use Extreme Caution*. "Well, somebody told somebody something," Eddie said with a restraint that made his face seem brittle, as if it might break at any moment and turn into something monstrous.

A student—nobody Amos knew—opened the door to the bathroom, took one look at Eddie Tripp's expression, and turned right around and went out.

Amos said, "Look, Eddie, I'm telling the truth. I didn't tell anyone anything."

Eddie smiled. He pushed up his jacket sleeve and began slowly combing the edge of the razor blade back and forth along the length of his bare arm, pushing the nap of his black arm hair first one direction, then the other, *shhhh shhhh shhhh*. "The po-lice were smug when they got hold of us," Eddie said. "Smugger even than normal. They said they had a positive eyewitness ID on Charles and a close approximation on me. That's what the po-lice called it, a close approximation. They had my mom all weeping. So Charles tells them I wasn't there and if everybody'll accept that, he'd have something to say. They went for it, of course, and now he's in juvie spending his time thinking about Amos MacKenzie."

"But I didn't—"

Eddie cut him off. "Oh, I know. You didn't say a word, you didn't name a name." Eddie's scornful smile widened to a scornful grin. "So what you're trying to tell me is that the po-lice had no positive eyewitness ID, had nada, nothing, and we folded to their bluff." His eyes flew up so quickly it startled Amos.

"I didn't say—"

"You know what?" Eddie said, staring hard at Amos. "What I'm learning here is how little I like the sound of your voice. You know how that is? How sometimes somebody's voice just begins to get on your nerves, and pretty soon you think you're just going to have to do something about it?"

Amos understood this was not a question he was meant to answer.

Then Eddie did a strange thing. He turned the edge of the razor blade and drew it quickly and cleanly across his forearm. It made a thin line on his skin, a line that widened as blood rose. He watched it for a second and then looked up smiling at Amos.

"I'll take those fancy sunglasses now," he said.

First Amos tightened his grip on the sunglasses, then loosened it again. The sunglasses dropped to the floor.

Something tightened in Eddie's face. "Now you need to pick them up."

Amos did.

"And wash them off."

Amos was holding them under the faucet when the bathroom door swung open again. It was two teachers, who immediately broke off their conversation. "What's going on here?" one of them asked.

Amos glanced at Eddie, who'd somehow hidden his utility

knife and was now leaning close to the mirror and combing his hair with elaborate casualness. He'd pulled down his jacket sleeve to keep the bloody cut on his arm out of view. "Nothing," Eddie said, and Amos, sliding behind the teachers and heading for the door, said he was just cleaning his glasses and needed to get back to World History.

"Well, then, git," one of the teachers said, and the other one, turning toward Eddie, said, "And as for you, Mr. Tripp, where do you rightfully belong at this hour?"

Amos was gone so fast he didn't hear Eddie's reply. Amos almost ran back to class.

By the end of the period, not only was Amos's heart beating normally again, but he was beginning to think he'd cheated Eddie Tripp out of some satisfaction. When, between classes, another boy asked why Amos had looked so freaked out when he came back to fifth period, Amos said, "Eddie Tripp paid me a visit in the west-wing head. He told me he wanted my Carreras." Amos smiled and tapped his sunglasses meaningfully, as if to say, "And look who's still got 'em."

But even while he spoke, Amos was keeping an eye out for Eddie.

Amos hadn't seen Clara all day. Hour upon hour, while teachers droned on about circumference and tangents, tobacco and respiratory tract cancer, Muslims in Pakistan and Hindus in India, Amos imagined what Clara Wilson would think if she heard that Amos MacKenzie had been driven to school by high school jocks. And maybe someone would've told her about the note Mr.

Duckworth had read and she'd see that he wasn't such a bad catch after all.

When Amos opened his locker after last period and found an envelope with his name written on it in Clara's handwriting, he felt his heart break into a gallop. He glanced around for Eddie, then opened the envelope with an air of extreme casualness, leaving his aviator sunglasses on, which made reading more difficult. The note was written on white stationery. The date and Clara's address were at the top, as though she were writing to a pen pal in a distant country. But the message was shockingly brief. *Thank you for your letter,* it said in rushed pencil. *I believe you, not that it matters now. Clara Wilson.* Without thinking, Amos took off his sunglasses, and as he read the note again, he began at the same moment to feel both hot and foolish. He felt his face reddening, put on his sunglasses, and, ignoring first one, then another student who called out his name, made for the front door and descended the long set of steps to the street.

A horn was honking.

Buses filled the air with the smell of diesel fuel, kids yelled and skuttered here and there, and the sun's reflection off the snow was sharp, almost blinding.

The horn honked again. "Amos, you little jerk! Don't pretend you don't see me!"

It was his sister, Liz, double-parked in the rusted-out Econoline their father had bought for $200 from the dairy. Beneath a thin application of white paint, it was still possible to read the words *Cosgrove Dairy—We Still Deliver!* It seemed to Amos that all activity around him had abruptly stopped when Liz had called out to him, that every set of eyes now followed him as he walked down the grade toward the old van. Curbside, he slipped for just an instant on the ice, and though he caught himself, Amos thought he heard someone snicker.

"Just get in," his sister said. "I don't like driving this thing in public either."

Amos slouched a little and made a point of looking away from the school grounds. "What's going on?" he said when Melville was safely behind them.

"Oh, Mom's in hyperspace. She called me out of school and told me to pick you up so we can visit Dad in the hospital. Which, considering the fact that he's supposed to come home tonight, seems pretty mongoloid, but there you are."

They rode along in silence, Amos staring out at the dirty snow and ice through his Carrera sunglasses. He felt in his pocket for Clara's note and fingered its edges. He wanted in the worst way to take it out and try to make some sense of it, but he didn't want his sister to see him do it.

"So I heard they got the guy who hit you with the bat," Liz said.

Amos nodded and looked away.

"Charles Tripp," Liz said. "The usual suspect." She shot Amos a look. "Was he the guy who did it?"

"I guess so," Amos said in a low voice. "If that's what the police say."

"What do *you* say?"

"I don't. It was too dark to tell." Then, "I guess it could've been the Tripps."

Liz turned sharply. "The *Tripps*. Plural?"

Amos shrugged. "Maybe."

A block passed before Liz spoke. "Well, if it was Eddie, too, you should tell the police. He might not be quite the convict his brother is, but give him time and he will be."

Amos stared ahead. A few minutes passed in silence. Then, after the Econoline backfired three times coming to a stop, Liz said, "You'd think Dad would at least get the muffler fixed."

Amos didn't speak. Whatever it was that had pumped him up and floated him through the school day had leaked out and left him completely flat.

Liz, glancing to her left at a stoplight, looked suddenly stricken. "Oh, God, there's Eric Bradstreet," she said, and Amos, peering around her, saw the very Jeep he himself had ridden to school in that morning, driven by the same handsome, thick-haired boy who owned it. Before he knew it, Amos ducked back, too, and, like his sister, stared frozenly ahead.

St. Stephen's Hospital was situated on the floor of Jemison Valley, and most of it was already shadowed by the hills behind it. Only the uppermost stories of the main building still caught the late-afternoon light, which gave the white walls a comforting, buttery color.

Inside, however, the lobby was anything but comforting. It made Amos think of an airport in bad weather—a lot of tired people sitting around waiting for announcements they feared would be bad. It took two different people at the reception desk to even determine their father's room, and another twenty minutes before someone from another floor telephoned to say that their mother would be down in a few minutes.

Amos and his sister gravitated toward a lounge area that had televisions mounted on three walls, each of them showing some-thing different. Almost nobody was watching them. Amos sat down and flipped through a *Jemison Star*, but the sports page was missing. His sister picked up a *People* magazine and, to nobody in particular, said, "Who cares how many hats celebrity moms have to wear?" Nearly an hour passed before a nun approached them and explained that their mother would be detained a few more minutes yet.

"Fine," Liz said. "Not a problem."

Amos knew she thought it really was a problem, but he was glad she wasn't showing it. Or maybe she'd caught on to some-thing Amos was still missing. He watched her closely, but she seemed unanxious. She glanced at a couple more magazines, stood up, and, while stretching, cast an eye around for boys. Then, finding no one of interest, she settled back into her chair, stretched her legs onto the coffee table, and fell asleep.

Amos pulled the note from his pocket. *Thank you for your let-ter. I believe you, not that it matters now.* He read it four or five times, then folded it back up and slipped it back into his pocket. It was icy, barely civil. It was not a good sign.

Amos was seized by sudden remorse. It was like sometimes in the middle of the night, when he was wide awake and all he could think about was the many little unkind things he'd done to people. Why hadn't he worried about his father all day instead of acting like some kind of fathead hero? Had he thought of his father even once? Amos went back through his day. No. Not once. Had he spent one minute worrying about Crook? The Goddards? His mother at the hospital? No.

Amos walked over to the row of telephone booths and dialed Bruce's number. Nobody answered, but he didn't hang up. It was still ringing when he saw the elevator doors open on the other side of the lobby. A lone woman walked out wearing a familiar navy blue dress and carrying a familiar brown purse. It took Amos a full second to realize it was his mother. Yet it was not quite his mother. She seemed like a foreigner. Later, this would seem to Amos like the moment he should have known something was wrong. A nun came over and held his mother's elbow and pointed toward Liz, still asleep in her chair.

Amos hung up and walked across the lobby. His sister was standing up now, wide-awake. "What?" she said.

Their mother seemed in some sort of daze. "He can't see you tonight. They're keeping him and we can't see him tonight. Where's the car?" She looked around the lobby as if she expected to see it there.

"Are you okay?" Liz asked.

"Yes," Amos's mother said, and looked around again.

"We could take the van," Amos said.

His mother nodded.

She didn't button her coat against the cold as they walked toward the door, didn't look around, didn't say a word until Liz began shaking her purse looking for the keys. Then Amos's mother said, "I'll drive."

She started the van, looked over her shoulder past Amos, and, hitting the gas, drove *forward*. The van jumped the restraining bumper and rammed a concrete post. Glass tinkled. The motor stalled. Amos's mother sat there looking confused. The van was so cold that Amos could still see his breath. Something had gone wrong with his dad. He felt it in his bones.

"I'll drive, Mom, if you want," Liz said in a soft voice. She got out and came around. Their mother slid over, rubbed her forehead, and then decisively opened the passenger door. "I've changed my mind," she said. "I can't leave. You go home and I'll call you in a couple of hours."

"Maybe we should come with you," Liz said.

"No, you go ahead. I just have to get back inside right now."

Amos leaned forward from the backseat and knew he ought to say something, but he wasn't sure what, and so was relieved when Liz asked, "What happened, Mom? Did something go wrong with Dad's surgery?"

Mrs. MacKenzie didn't answer. She was standing by the van in the full dusk. A line of taillights stretched out below the hospital. A car leaving the parking lot fishtailed slightly, then recovered.

"Mom?" Liz asked.

"Something went wrong," their mother said in a dull voice, "but everything will be okay." She shut the door. They could barely hear her through the windows as she said it again. "Everything will be fine."

17

AN EMPTY HOUSE

Clara, home after delivering newspapers, thought she smelled baked potatoes. When she opened the oven, there were two brown potatoes on the rack, looking wrinkled and forlorn. Her father's idea of dinner, she supposed. She climbed upstairs, where the door to the study was wide open and the computer made a slight ticking noise as a spray of animated snow fluttered across the light blue screen, followed at last by a red snowplow. "Dad?" she called. Tax forms were spread over the table, and a cup stained with coffee sat on a coaster, proof that her father had also not given up her mother's rules.

Thurmond L. and Angelica W. Wilson was written at the top of one of the forms; *Husband and Wife.* These people, with their formal-seeming names, were the ones who were married. Monty and Angie, Clara's mom and dad, were also married, but only barely. Thurmond. Her father's friends called him Monty, but her mother always called him Thurm.

"Dad?" Clara called again, but no one answered.

Ham was also gone, and the gleam from the lamps showed a fine layer of dust on the computer screen, the glass face of the clock, and the shelves in her father's office. Clara opened a drawer and found her father's stash of Good & Plentys. Clara chewed a couple. They were worse than chocolate but better than, say, taffy.

On the edge of the desk, under a shuffle of papers, Clara spotted the photo album her mother had brought from the shed. She opened it and looked at the photos of thin men in very thin ties, girls in taffeta, athletes in peculiar shorts.

Clara was studying a pair of girls who were kissing her father on the cheek when the telephone rang. She located the phone beneath a pile of receipts, and her mother said, "Hi, sweetie. It's me. Your mother."

Clara felt mixed up. The last time she'd talked to her mother was nearly five days earlier, on Thursday before school. So she was relieved to hear her mother's voice, but she was also angry that she hadn't called sooner and was still gone. In a low, hollow voice, she said, "Oh, it's you."

"I left you messages," her mother said. "Did you get my messages?"

"No," Clara said. "I didn't. When did you leave them?"

"Well, maybe your father erased them," her mother said. Then, trying to sound cheery, she said, "Or maybe that machine ate them."

"Maybe," Clara said.

A pause. Then her mother said, "I guess you're mad at your mom, huh?"

Clara, to indicate this was true, said nothing at all.

After a moment, her mother said, "How's play practice going? What's it called again?"

"*The Smiling Gumshoe*," she said in her low, bland voice. "It's going fine."

This time the silence on the line stretched longer. Finally her mother said, "What're you thinking, sweetie?"

Clara deliberated. Then, in her stony voice, she said, "You've been gone eight days. Eight days is a long time."

Her mother's voice softened. "I know, sweetie. It's an awfully long time."

"So when are you coming home, inny..."—she corrected herself—"anyhow?"

Another long pause. "I'm not sure. I know it's hard for you to understand, but I'm not sure of anything right now. Except how much I love you."

Her mother's voice had cracked as she said this, and Clara said in a soft voice, "I love you, too, Mom."

For a time, her mother said nothing, but from the other end of the line, the faraway Dalton end of the line, Clara could hear snuffling. When her mother finally spoke again, she was more composed. "How's our old Hambone?"

"He's fine."

"And Gerri?"

Clara considered telling a white lie but decided against it. "She took a new friend skiing with her last weekend, and now she's avoiding me."

"Oh, honey, I'm sorry."

Clara again decided to be truthful. "Me, too."

"What else is new, then?"

Clara thought at once of Amos, of the nice letter he'd written, but it was better to tell things as they happened, before the first impression had worn off. Now it was old news, and Amos had been so cocky at school, wearing super-expensive sunglasses and acting like a fathead. She'd hardly wanted to give him any message at all, and the first letter she'd written seemed too gushy, so she'd torn it up and scribbled something during history. Thinking of all this made the world seem small and mean, and all of a sudden she said to her mother, "I don't like school very much anymore."

This, as she expected, got her mother's attention. "What do you mean?"

"I don't know. It's just like all the subjects and assignments that used to seem important just don't seem important anymore."

"Oh, sweetie. It *is* important. It's *so* important. It's what will give you all the opportunities and choices to make the kind of adult life you want and deserve."

Clara said nothing. Among the adult human beings, she thought. She would *never* live among the adult human beings. She would simply refuse, like Peter Pan.

"Clara?"

"How come you left Kaufmann's that day?" Clara said without thinking. It was just what came sourly to mind.

Her mother took a second to respond. "I don't know. I'd just finished folding a whole display of designer towels—all in shades of white—and a man on the other side of the table waited until I was done and then came around to the table I'd just neatened. He reached in and unfolded one towel, and then another, and then another. And then he left them there in a mess and walked away."

Clara didn't get it. "And that was it?"

"Yeah, that was it. But if it hadn't been that, it would've been something else just as tiny. It was just that I didn't feel that my life was mine anymore, sweetie."

Clara looked out the window into the darkness. Downstairs, the front screen door squeaked open.

"I heard the door. It must be Dad. You want to talk to him?"

"No, not right now, sweetie."

Clara thought, She's avoiding him just like Gerri's avoiding me. She listened for other sounds downstairs. There were none. There had been only the screen door, and then nothing.

"Maybe next weekend you can come visit me here in Dalton," her mother was saying.

Clara doubted it. "Maybe," she said, and then, "I better go downstairs and help Dad with dinner."

But when she reached the bottom of the stairs, she saw that Amos MacKenzie, not her father, was standing between the open screen door and the glassed front door, his face looking as surprised as her own.

18

LOST

Amos watched numbly as Clara Wilson approached. Only when her arm extended for the doorknob did he instinctively step back. The screen door slipped and banged shut, but Amos hardly heard it. He kept staring blankly at the door while backing away from it until finally the porch gave way and he went tumbling into a snowdrift. Amos didn't feel the fall. He didn't feel the cold. He stood up and looked around. From above him, a pleasant, tinkling laughter spilled into the cold night, but when he turned, the sound ceased. Clara Wilson stood on the porch covering her mouth, trying not to laugh anymore.

"Whoops," she said, remembering too late that in the hospital, his head had been in a bandage. He still had black eyes, too. Maybe she was laughing when she should be calling an ambulance.

"Sorry," Amos heard himself say, and when she saw he wasn't laughing, Clara's face turned serious. She carefully descended the slick steps.

The sweetness of Clara's breath—of licorice or black jelly beans, Amos thought—hung in the freezing air. He wasn't even sure what she'd said. She seemed to expect an answer. He nodded very slightly.

Before he knew it, she'd escorted him inside and he'd taken his coat off and seated himself on a sofa in the living room. Clara was talking, but Amos hardly heard. She offered him hot cider twice before he nodded yes.

After Clara went off to the kitchen, Amos's eyes settled on the cold fireplace. A couple of charred logs lay almost whole on the andirons. When Clara returned, she carried a tray with cookies and two cups of hot apple cider, a cinnamon stick poking out of each. Amos wrapped his cold hands around the cup and kept sipping until Clara set hers down. "So, how come you're here?" she said.

"I don't know," Amos said. He turned his eyes from her and said, "I was supposed to find my sister, Liz." He tried to take another sip of cider and was surprised to find he'd already finished it all. "Around eight o'clock, my mother called from the hospital and told me to find Liz, even though I told her I didn't know where she was or even who she was with." He glanced up. "She was with some boy I'd never seen before. Anyway, all I knew was they were going driving and would probably go to Bing's for fries and stuff, so I went down to Bing's."

"You walked from your house all the way to Bing's?"

Amos nodded. "She wasn't there, though. So then I thought, what if she's really doing what she always pretends to do? I went up to the library, but of course she wasn't there, and then on the way home, I saw Genesee Street." He looked down at his hands. "Just wanted to see what your house looked like, I guess." He gazed around the room. "It's a really nice house," he said.

Clara looked around, too, and was glad somebody besides herself thought it was nice. Her parents seemed to think that it had once been nice and might someday again be nice, but that it wasn't very nice now. Then she remembered something about Amos's story. "What were you supposed to tell your sister?"

Amos, as if just poked by something, turned his head sharply away. He said something in a low, muddy voice that she couldn't understand.

"What?" she asked.

He kept his eyes averted but spoke up now in a strange, formal voice. "I was supposed to tell her that they lost our father."

A light swept across the room as a car turned into the Wilson driveway. "That's my dad," Clara said almost to herself, then turned back to Amos. "What does that mean, 'they lost your father'?"

Amos set his cup down. He stood up and was pulling on his coat. "I need to go now. Thanks for the apple juice. I'm sorry about coming to the door like that."

And moments before Clara's father entered through the back door, Amos exited from the front.

19

LO SIENTO

When he walked in, Clara's father was carrying a paper bag in one hand and Ham's leash in the other. An untethered Ham trailed happily behind.

"Dad, could we give someone a ride home?"

Her father set the bag down and looked around. "Is there someone here?"

"There was. A friend from school. He lives on my paper route, and I think he's walking home now."

"*He*? So it was a *male* friend?" Her father winked. "Now that's interesting."

But her father didn't seem anxious to go out again. From the bag he withdrew potato toppings—scallions and plum tomatoes for him and sour cream for her. Clara said, "What does *lost* mean when it's in a sentence like *We lost our grandfather*?"

Her father said, "Well, you could literally lose him, in the woods, say, or at Disney World. Or..." His face became suddenly serious. "Why do you ask?"

Clara wanted to explain that Amos had said he'd just lost his father, but it seemed too startling to be possible. It didn't make sense that Mr. MacKenzie could be dead, and yet what else could Amos have meant?

"The boy who was here was Amos MacKenzie. His father's Mr. MacKenzie, the one who delivers our milk. Except Mr.

MacKenzie was in the hospital today and I think something bad happened to him."

Her father had gotten his serious face. He felt in his coat for his car keys.

While they were getting in the car, Clara told her father where Amos lived and wondered what it would be like to get a phone call saying your father was dead. It would be like her mother being gone, only permanent. Immediately, Clara had a thought she knew was terrible. *At least then you'd know your mother or your father didn't want to leave you.* Still, Clara didn't want her mother to die.

Her father drove slowly and studied the sidewalk on his side of the car. Clara could hear the crunch of snow beneath their slowly revolving tires while she peered out and tried to see footprints. The trouble was that paths had been made in the snow already and then frozen there.

"What exactly did the MacKenzie boy say?" her father asked.

"He said he was looking for his sister because his mother called from the hospital and said they lost his father."

"Oh," her father said in a soft voice, and Clara knew she was right about *lost* referring to the worst possible thing. "Was he sick?" her father asked, and then, as they approached the intersection, "Which way?"

Clara pointed and said she didn't know if he'd been sick. It was strange driving in the dark like this on a route she knew by foot. The road had still been faintly light as she did her route. Now, from her father's warm car, she saw lamps in windows, chain-link fences, and broken porch rails, but Amos was nowhere to be seen. *He must have cut through an alley*, she thought, *or gone another direction to find his sister.*

Her father let the car idle in front of the MacKenzies' house. It was dark. "Well, shall we go back home, or do you know where else to look?" he asked.

The MacKenzies' house was more than dark. It reminded Clara of a TV screen that had been playing a sitcom full of laughs but then had been suddenly switched off right in the middle of things. "I don't know anywhere else," Clara said.

The next day, Clara's fears were confirmed. No sooner had she gotten to her locker than Eddie Tripp materialized behind her. "Guess who croaked?" he said.

Clara turned away and began pulling out the books she needed.

Eddie said, "Your little boyfriend's old man."

Clara, flushing with confusion and anger, turned and looked steadily into Eddie's eyes. "I don't have a boyfriend," she said.

Grinning now, Eddie said, "Well, that's good. I was a little afraid you did."

"And I'm not looking for one," Clara said.

Eddie nodded slowly. "Well, if you ever do, it'd be pretty disappointing if you picked out somebody who was not only a smudge but a stoolie."

"Who's a stoolie?"

"Well, *you* weren't one the day you caught us hooking goods at the market." Eddie's face relaxed and became almost handsome. "That was pretty cool of you."

Clara flushed at the compliment even while wanting to dispute it. "I wasn't sure what I saw that day. That's the only reason I didn't say anything."

Eddie shrugged, smiling.

"So I repeat. Who's a stoolie?"

Another shrug. "Ask around. Start with the Milkboy. Everybody's hero."

Eddie tugged on an earlobe, smiled, and shambled off. When he'd pulled on his ear, his sleeve had ridden up and exposed a fine linear scab on his arm.

Clara would've liked to talk to Amos about all this, but because of a "death in the family," as her homeroom teacher put it, he wasn't in school at all that day.

That night, when Clara couldn't concentrate on her homework, she wanted in the worst way to call Gerri or Amos but knew she needed to wait until they called her. Finally she went to her father's study, where he sat in front of his computer. Slim columns of figures filled the screen. Her father peered down at the papers on his desk through his glasses, his hand on the back of his neck.

Clara noticed something. The photo album was not in the same place she'd set it the night before. Which meant he'd probably been looking through it. Clara looked over her father's shoulder, then began leafing through the album while he continued to work. "Weird clothes," Clara said, and her father, chuckling but not looking up, said, "We didn't think so at the time."

Then Clara said, "Do you still see any of the people in these pictures?"

A strange look seemed to come and go on her father's face. He considered his answer. "Rarely, if that often," he said. Then, "Why do you ask, Polkadot?"

"Oh, I just wondered what they look like now."

Her father chuckled. "Not much like they did then," he said. He stretched and yawned. "Hey, don't you have some homework to do?"

She did, but she didn't care. Still, she couldn't say that to her father. She was back in her room reading an old *Mademoiselle* when the phone rang. Clara, hoping it was Amos or Gerri, waited for her father to call her to the phone, but he didn't, not right away. But ten minutes later, he appeared in the door of her room.

"It's your mother," he said in a stiff voice. "She wants to talk to you."

The serious way he said this made Clara's heart pound.

"Hello?" she said into the receiver, and after that, she hardly talked. She just listened.

Her mother was calling to say she'd just accepted a teaching job in Spain.

Spain? Her mother was going to Spain? Clara looked at the calendar on the wall and read the numbers like some sort of code. 26. *Your mother's leaving*. 27. *Your mother's gone*.

"Sweetie?" her mother said.

"You don't even speak Spanish," Clara blurted, and began to cry, but it was no use. Her mother was speaking in the calm, steady voice she used when she described things that had become fact.

"This is just something your mother feels she owes it to herself to do," her mother said.

Why was she calling herself "your mother," as if she were delivering this news on behalf of someone else? "Well, what about what my mother owes *me*?" Clara said, but as soon as she said it, she knew it hadn't come out right. It made Clara sound like the selfish one.

"*Lo siento,*" her mother said. "In Spanish, that's *I'm sorry.* It's the one phrase I already know." There was a silence. "I'll call, sweetie. I'm hoping you'll come visit me in Spain. You could even go to school there if your father agreed."

Without another word, Clara put the phone down and raced down the hallway. She was headed for the attic, and when she got to the top of the ladder, she slammed the trapdoor and stood perfectly still in the dark. She hated the school in Spain for wanting someone who would only speak English in the classroom, and she hated her mother for staying calm and not crying even when Clara did.

She turned on the light that illuminated the shelves of her mother's books: *The Art of Egypt, A Picture Book of France, The Culture of Ancient Egypt, Conversational French, In the Louvre,* and on and on. There were volumes about Russia, too, and medieval Europe, but not a single book about Spain. She stared at the books and kept hearing her mother say, "You could even go to school there."

She would never go to school there.

Clara, crying, began pulling the books down from the shelves one at a time, letting each one lie where it fell. When she got to the last book, she opened it in her hands and began tearing out pages, one by one.

She heard her father push up through the trapdoor, and she wiped her face with one sleeve. "Clara?" he said. He pulled himself up into the room. He was still wearing his reading glasses, and his hair looked very short. He had such a serious face, and he suddenly looked much older, more like the photographs of his own father. He didn't say anything else to her, and somehow that made it possible for her to walk toward him when he held out his hand to her. Once he had her against his shirt, he touched the top of her head and said, "It's not you that she needs to leave for a while, Clara," he said. "It's your father she's leaving, and that's hard, too, but you'll have to suspend your judgment for a few years, okay? When all the facts are in, when you're married, too, then you can decide. But for now, we're just going to try and be a family anyway."

20

MORE SNOW

On the morning of his father's funeral, Amos had gotten up around five A.M. and pulled open the curtains of his bedroom window and stared out. It was a day he dreaded and wanted behind him. Ever since his father's death, the house seemed to have fallen under some strange kind of siege. Relatives and friends of his parents kept dropping by with covered dishes. Sometimes they came and went in short order, which was fine by Amos, but usually they stuck around, speaking in low voices. Amos's mother and—a surprise—his sister, too, had somehow gotten used to conversing in these hushed voices, explaining the specifics of the failed operation, saying the same things over and over, but Amos just wanted everyone gone. He wanted the house back. He wanted to walk around in torn pants and his favorite T-shirt, drink milk out of the bottle, watch some TV, sit outside watching his pigeons. He didn't expect the house to be the same with his father gone, but it would be more the same when the intruders left.

Last night, when there were again guests in the den and his aunt Amelia came looking for him, Amos had ducked into his parents' bedroom and eased the door shut. He stood there in the dark, absolutely still, listening to his aunt softly calling his name and cracking open the door to his room and finally moving back down the hall—Amos knew the map of its creaks and groans—

and saying to somebody, "I don't know where he's gone, unless he's down in the basement."

Amos switched on the light near his parents' bed. The room looked the same, but it was changed. He could feel it. It was as if the walls had changed color, not much but maybe one shade, or maybe all the windows had been moved half an inch to the left. He went to the dresser and picked up and held in his hand the coins on the counter that his father had emptied from his pockets the day before the operation. He stared at his parents' wedding picture—his mother shy and uncertain, his father brash and broad-smiling. He quietly opened drawers. When he found his father's V-necked T-shirts, he held one to his face to inhale the faint scent of his father. It was the shirt at the top of the stack, the next one his father would have pulled from the drawer if…if what? If this cancer had just chosen some other stomach to grow in? Without really knowing why, Amos refolded the V-necked undershirt and gathered up a pair of his father's gray socks and a pair of his father's striped boxer shorts and took them all back to his room.

Now, on the morning of the funeral, Amos showered, straightened his bed, and laid out the clothes his mother had bought for his baptism—black shoes, gray coat, gray pants. Next to them, he laid out what he intended to wear beneath all that—his father's white V-necked undershirt, his father's gray socks, his father's striped boxer shorts. He stood in front of the full-length mirror on his closet door, and then he pulled on boxers, undershirt, socks. What surprised him was that they more or less fit. Still, they were his father's clothes, a man's clothes, and Amos felt like a kid trying to play an adult in a school play.

A tap on the window and Amos turned, startled. Looming there on the roof, smiling wide, was Bruce's face.

Amos wound open the window, reached through, and gave Bruce a quick Dutch rub. "Hey, Crook, am I glad to see you."

"You are?" Bruce seemed genuinely relieved to hear it. "I didn't know if I ought to come by or not." He seemed abashed and stared down at his boots. "I don't know anything about this stuff. I've never even had a pet die." Then he quickly added, "Not that this is anything like having a pet die."

Amos didn't know what to say, either. He didn't know how to describe what he was feeling. It was just this awful dark feeling that went from dull-achy to sharp-achy, depending on the freshness of whatever little reminder you'd just run into. "It's weird," he said to Bruce. "Friends and relatives coming into the house, pretending they're not watching you while they do." Then he said, "Besides, you had your mom die."

Bruce shrugged. "I was like ten months old. I don't remember the specifics."

"No. I guess not."

Another silence. Finally Bruce glanced pointedly at Amos's underclothes and said, "So what are you doing in the weird underwear?"

Amos looked down at himself and felt his face redden. "Trying on clothes for the funeral."

"Never seen you in boxer shorts before."

"Yeah, well."

Bruce stood there in the cold grinning at him. "I say stick with the jockey shorts. The gals like to know what you've got to offer."

Amos laughed. It felt good having Bruce there, saying stupid things. "It occurs to me the gals might be happier not knowing what you've got to offer."

"Maybe in your case," Bruce said.

Amos laughed again. "So, you got any money?"

"Why is it you ask?"

"I was thinking maybe we'd go out for breakfast."

"McBreakfast? I could absorb a McBreakfast."

Amos threw on some heavy clothes, then he and Bruce ducked through the window, edged out to the eaves, and plumped into the snow. Amos stood there exhilarated, brushing himself off, taking the raw cold into his lungs.

"Stuffy in there, huh?" Bruce said.

"Sort of, yeah. I guess I just don't know how to do things the way adults do."

"Who does?" Bruce thought about it. "Who would want to?"

They ducked through the side yard, behind the cars lining the driveway, and turned up the street, Amos leading the way. Neither of them said anything for a time while they walked. Then Bruce said, "Well, anyway, I'm sorry about your dad."

Amos felt the achy feeling suddenly sharpen. He said nothing and kept walking.

"The thing about your dad was you were always glad to run into him, you know? He always made you feel smarter or funnier than you thought you were. Or something like that."

Amos took a deep breath of cold air. "Yeah."

There was a short silence. Then Bruce said, "The strange thing is, I keep thinking I'll just turn a corner and run into him again." He paused. "I guess it's because it all happened so fast."

Amos kept striding ahead, trying to beat the achy feeling back into dullness. The bad part, the really awful part, was that when his father was there, Amos hardly ever gave him a thought, and when he did give him a thought, it was usually negative. He'd been embarrassed by the clothes he wore, the corny jokes he told, the job he had, the Moose Lodge meetings he went to. Things that, he knew now, didn't matter one little bit. *The things that matter to me go way beyond surface beauty.* Wasn't that what his dad had said that day to Clara?

Ten minutes later, they stopped off at McDonald's for turnovers and hot chocolate. It was warm inside, and un-crowded—a businessman reading the sports page, a couple with a road map spread on the table in front of them, two older guys in black leather jackets, who gave Amos and Bruce a fractional glance before dismissing them. Bruce finished off his hot chocolate and began idly ripping the paper cup into narrow strips. "I've been in Iowa, in case you were wondering."

"Iowa? I thought you were suspended."

"I was. But the Judge didn't want me home unsupervised because he was afraid I'd find his hooch or something, so he shipped me off to my uncle's outside Council Bluffs. They have a farm. It's calving season. All night long, they get up every two hours to check to see if any of those moonfaced heifers need help giving birth to moonfaced calves. My father gave my uncle orders that I had to make all those rounds with him so I'd begin to appreciate the life I lead here in Gemstone. It worked, by the way. I got to drive my uncle's truck some, which was fun, but otherwise it was one l-o-n-g week, partner. I was dying to come back. I wouldn't be here today except my uncle thought my suspension only went through yesterday instead of the rest of the week. So here I am, back on holiday."

"That was pretty good you didn't give them Foley's name."

"Yeah. I don't know what got into me."

"What'd you do with the other pictures?"

"Destroyed 'em. Just like I told them."

"How come?"

Bruce folded his empty chocolate cup into itself. "I just started thinking it wasn't that fair to Anne Barrineau to have her pictures flying all over the place. I mean, Foley was passing them out like party favors." He looked up, ready to change the subject. "So you go and look at your dad's body beforehand, that's what my brother told me."

"Yeah, we did that last night."

"What did he look like?"

Amos considered it. "Like a wax dummy of my father except whiter and smaller."

"You didn't touch him or anything?"

Amos shook his head, but the truth was he had. He'd lagged behind his mother and sister and gone back. First he touched the suit. Then he touched his face. It didn't feel like skin. He didn't know what it felt like, but it didn't feel like skin. Amos had looked at the body and said good-bye out loud. Now, to Bruce, Amos said, "I was mean to my dad the night before he died." Amos thought of the Chinese checkers, and the sharp-achy feeling came rushing back. He fell silent.

Bruce started to say something but held back. Finally he said, "We all screw up sometime, Amos."

Amos stared out the window. "It'll snow," he said. He wondered what Clara was doing right now. He'd decided that after showing up and acting like a zombie the other night, he would have to call her and try to act completely normal, but he knew he should wait until after the funeral.

"Want to head back?" Bruce said.

"Naw. Not yet. Besides, there's something I want to check out."

They hiked up the old school hill, then, following Amos's lead, swung left on Adamson.

"What's the destination?" Bruce asked, and was ignored. They walked another three blocks, and Bruce said, "Well, then, how about the estimated time of arrival?"

"Thirty minutes."

When they got to Foothill Park, Bruce stopped to watch some girls sledding in stretch pants, but Amos kept walking until he reached the farthest soccer field. Foothill Park adjoined and overlooked Fairhaven Cemetery. From the last soccer field, Amos stared down at the cemetery layered by snow, the headstones stark and gray, the trees bare. Perhaps a hundred yards beyond the woody lilac hedge, near the grave sites of Amos's grandparents, a large yellow backhoe was droning and clanking. The huge toothed bucket bit into the frozen earth, turned stiffly, dropped the dirt into a growing pile to the side. Another worker stood near the hole holding a Styrofoam coffee cup and smoking a cigarette and glancing up at the sky as the snow began. Amos watched the grave digging for a while, for a longer time and more intently than he realized, because when he finally turned around, he was surprised to find that Bruce was standing silently behind him, watching, too.

It was a dry snow, large flakes floating through the stillness.

Bruce stared at Amos for a moment, his face full of awkward misery, and then, suddenly, Bruce tilted his head toward the sky and, closing his eyes while opening his mouth wide, let the snow fall into it.

21

CONTACT

Clara added Mr. MacKenzie's obituary to the envelope containing the newspaper clipping about Amos's head injury. The photograph of Mr. MacKenzie was not at all like the navy portrait of her own father, whose face at twenty-two seemed to be frozen in some perfect light. Mr. MacKenzie's face was blurred, as though the picture had been snapped at some happy, crowded event in color, not black and white. He was smiling, looking off to the side, and his collar wasn't buttoned up. His age at the time of death was forty-four, the obituary said. A memorial service would be held Thursday morning at ten A.M. at Burke's Mortuary.

Maybe she would go. And then, a second later, she thought, *Yes, I will*.

Thursday morning, as she put on her black tights and black skirt, Clara wondered if she would tell her father she was going to the funeral. She knew she should, because she needed a note from him to excuse her absence. But she wasn't sure she would.

Clara didn't have a black blouse, so she settled on the plain white one she'd worn in chorus. Her black shoes had grown tight since she wore them to the ballet with her mother in the fall. Looking in the mirror and trying hard to retract her toes, Clara felt something was missing. She looked like a housemaid, she decided, a housemaid with a crooked nose. For the millionth time, she wondered how much too much a nose operation would cost. Then she went downstairs.

Beneath the oversized barbecuing apron he was wearing, her father was ready for work—beige pants, blue Ivy League shirt, maroon tie. Eggs and sausage sizzled in a black skillet. English muffins lay hot with tiny pools of melted butter. Since Clara's mother had announced her departure for Spain, her father had turned into Mr. Mom. He wasn't a very good cook, but Clara didn't mind.

"Good morning," he said when Clara turned the corner. He eyed her attire and asked, "Singing in the chorus today?"

Clara tried to think how she should present her plan. To stall for a minute, she just said, "No, I'm not in chorus this year." Now was the time to say she was dressed for a funeral and needed him to write a note, but she didn't.

"Milk, orange juice, or both?" her father asked from the refrigerator.

"Milk."

The bus was the problem. To get to the funeral, she had to take the city bus, and her father thought the city bus was dangerous.

Toward the end of breakfast, after a long sip of coffee, her father said, "Do you want a ride to school?"

Now, Clara told herself. *Explain.* But she didn't explain. She sat slicing her last sausage, wondering if her father could see her cheeks flush, but when she looked up, he was busily gathering up dirty dishes. "No," she said, choosing her words to make them slightly less a lie, "I'll probably just walk."

The bus trip was a nightmare. The transfer bus she was supposed to catch was early, and her own was late, so the place where they should have intersected—a blue bus sign beside a Frostee Cone and You Bet Dry Cleaning—was deserted. The next bus wasn't due for forty minutes. While she waited, little wispy flakes of snow blew down, the stoplights changed from crimson to green a hundred times, and behind all the approaching headlights were the faces of strangers who seemed to view her—if they saw her at all—with the same suspicion: Why wasn't she in school? She kept expecting her father to drive by, to stare at her in disbelief that would turn to anger when he realized she'd lied to him and skipped school.

When at last the city bus approached, she was so grateful that she thought she would cry with relief, and hardly cared that her watch showed ten-fifteen. The funeral had already started. The bus was warm and nearly empty, but it wound so slowly down so many strange avenues that when it finally stopped one block from the mortuary, it was a quarter to eleven.

The service was over, but people were still milling around outside the mortuary. Clara stepped into the lobby in her wet, pinching shoes, and there, beside clusters of adults in nice clothes, was Amos. He was standing with his back to her, looking at an oil painting on the wall with his hands in his pockets. The adults were talking in low voices. When someone laughed, it was subdued laughter. From behind the closed chapel doors, an organ was playing. Amos looked so formal standing before the painting that Clara had the impulse, for a moment, to walk back out. Instead, she walked up and stood beside him. "Hey," she said in a low voice.

When Amos turned, she saw that his eyes were still dark around the edges and a little puffy. He smiled awkwardly. "Didn't expect to see you here."

"I meant to be here for the service," Clara said. "I missed the bus somehow."

"It's nice you came," Amos said, looking down again. The stitches were out on his forehead, but the incision line was still visible.

"I wanted to," Clara said. She shook her coat to let some of the water run off. Her feet were freezing.

Neither of them said anything for a time, then Amos said, "Aren't you missing a big test today in Duckworth's class?"

"Yeah." She shrugged. "Sometimes he's nice if you explain things."

"Sometimes he isn't," Amos said a little glumly.

Clara nodded at the painting behind Amos, a shaft of light breaking through clouds to illuminate the open sea. "Were you looking at that because you liked it?"

"Not really. I was just looking at it so I wouldn't have to talk to anybody else." He regarded the painting. "I think it's meant to calm you down, but instead it's just kind of sappy."

Clara smiled. "Yeah, it kind of is." She looked around at the hovering adults, most of them in groups. "Lots of people," she said.

Amos nodded and quickly scanned the room. "What's weird is, I really didn't know my dad had so many friends."

After a second or two, Clara said, "So what happens now?"

"Oh, there's a smaller graveside deal."

At that moment, Bruce stuck in his head from a side door. "Hey, Amos, they're waiting on you."

Amos turned to Clara. "I know this isn't the greatest field trip of all time, but do you want to come? We'd just ride with my mother and sister. And Crook. They already said I could bring Crook along."

Clara didn't know. "I really should get back to school."

Amos moved toward the door, but he was still talking. "The graveside service is supposed to be short." When he got to the door, he stopped, turned, and suddenly waved her over. His tense, expectant expression made the gesture seem urgent.

There was a long moment during which Clara understood that she was choosing between the pleasure of sitting beside Amos in a car and the safety of not going. By the time she'd gotten to the end of this thought, her pinched, cold feet were already moving in Amos's direction.

She slid into the backseat between Bruce and Amos, everyone careful not to press into one another. She was introduced to Amos's mother, whose skin looked actually gray, and to Amos's sister. Clara had never seen Liz MacKenzie up close before, and if she hadn't nodded so understandingly, Clara would have been intimidated. She was a pretty, dark-haired version of Amos, busty and dressed in what Clara knew were the right clothes for a funeral: a dark wool jacket with a lot of buttons, a plain dark skirt, a velvet hair band instead of a hat.

At the grave site, Clara stood with Amos, who stood behind everyone else in the family. After Mr. MacKenzie's minister spoke about his recent baptism into the church, others were invited to step forward and speak. Three or four people from his new church did, saying how happy they were that Mr. MacKenzie had committed to God before going to serve him. Amos was fidgety during these little speeches, and that made Clara fidgety, too.

At that moment, though Clara didn't mean to, her hand

touched Amos's. She thought he'd be startled and pull away, but he didn't. He took hold of her hand quickly, as if he'd been waiting for it and wasn't going to let it get away. A strange and wonderful feeling flooded through her. It was as if all of her senses were driven from their normal places and were now transmitting and receiving everything through her left hand, the one that was holding Amos's right.

On the ride back to the MacKenzies' house, Clara sat between Amos and Bruce, who stared silently out the window. Clara felt her arm rest against Amos's. The sensation reminded her of science films in which molecules were animated to show how they bumped against each other in a liquid and then in a gas.

Inside Amos's house, she felt less at ease. "This is my friend Clara," Amos said to a man who had been gazing out the window. "Clara, this is my favorite uncle, Uncle Bub." He shook Clara's hand, and Clara realized he was an older version of Amos's father and that this was the funeral of his younger brother.

Amos led Clara and Bruce out the back door toward his pigeon coop, a wood-and-wire structure that housed twelve pairs of birds; these birds sat on boxes or perches and made a pleasant chorus of throaty gurgling. Toward the top of the coop, there was a landing and opening, with thin metal bars hanging in front of it. "What's that?"

"A one-way opening." He demonstrated with his hand. "They can use it to come in, but they can't get out." He grinned. "I mean, they *could* if they were smarter, but they're not."

"They are in fact birdbrained," Bruce offered, which made Clara laugh.

"So you let them out?" Clara asked. "And then they come back?"

"Yeah. They're racers. You let them out from greater and greater distances and see how long it takes to come back." He shrugged. "Mine aren't that fast."

Clara pondered this process. What if her mother were just like a racing pigeon let out at the farthest possible distance and now Clara would just have to see how long it would take for her to come back?

"See that reddish one?" Amos said, pointing.

In one corner nest, among all the gray and black and blue, a large, beautiful red-tinged racer sat, and perched nearby was an even bigger gray bird, who, Amos explained, was her mate. "That's Ruby and Hurricane," he said. Ruby was the only reddish pigeon in the coop. Amos stepped into the pen. He slowly approached her, saying her name in a low croon. Then he laid his hand gently over her back. The beautiful red pigeon blinked and stepped easily into his other hand, and Amos began to stroke the bird's smooth reddish blue head.

Once Ruby hadn't come home from a 300-mile drop, Amos told Clara, not for days and days, and Hurricane flew nervously around the pen, stopped eating, and started to molt prematurely. Amos found himself watching the skies from the schoolyard, looking for a huge reddish pigeon who might be disoriented. There had been severe storms, and according to other members of the racing club, nearly 60 percent of the birds hadn't returned from this drop. That was a lot. Amos had begun force-feeding Hurricane. The bird didn't like it and would struggle in Amos's hands, shaking his beak to keep him from inserting the syringe. Each day, he seemed to grow lighter and bonier. Then one day after school, while Amos was feeding him, he heard the shuffle of wings and the soft landing of a newly arrived bird. He turned. There on the perch, pacing in front of the one-way bars, was Ruby. "She was pretty ragged," Amos said now as he stroked the bird's head, "but she was home."

"What brought her back?" Clara asked, and didn't mind when Amos just shrugged, because Clara already knew. Love brought her back. Maybe some weird and instinctive and, well, *birdy* kind of love, but still, it was love.

"Food!" Liz called out from the back door.

They slid through the adults and stole up to Amos's room with dishes of chicken potpie. Clara was so jittery that she couldn't eat, but Bruce sat on the floor with his plate on his knees and ate ravenously. Amos sat on the edge of the bed and ate only the carrots, then only the peas, then only the crust. "I don't know," he said when Clara asked why he didn't eat the chicken. "I guess sometimes it just reminds me too much of pigeon."

When they finished eating, Amos spread an old army blanket on the bed and counted out pennies from a tobacco tin, and they all three began to play penny blackjack. Amos and Bruce coached her through a few hands, and then she played on her own—very casually, barely counting up the cards in her hand, but she kept winning pennies. "Good thing this ain't strip poker," Bruce said. "I'd be down to my jockeys." He cast a glance at Amos. "Whereas Amos would be down to his boxers."

It was odd how the grief was impossible to sustain. Clara was glad to laugh, glad even to be embarrassed. "You guys are just letting me win," she said.

"Bingo," Bruce said. "So as to suck you into a higher-stakes game."

"No," Amos said, sending a shock of pleasure through Clara merely by smiling at her, "you're just getting good cards."

During a shuffle, Clara got up and walked around Amos's room, peering into his closet (a mess), checking out the view from the window (a line of bare trees behind the weathered pigeon coop), looking at the posters on his wall (baseball players, mostly). To the side of his desk was a corkboard she hadn't noticed before, with photographs and tickets and programs pinned to it. She read them aloud and Amos responded. "Nineteen ninety-two World Series, Game Three, Blue Jays v. Braves."

"Yep. My dad and I went and it was pretty cool. Blue Jays won it in the bottom of the ninth."

"*Ten Little Indians*," Clara read from a play program.

"My sister was in it." He grinned. "It was pretty good anyway."

Clara thought of telling them about her part in the upcoming school play, but decided it would sound stupid, with her having only one line in it anyway.

At the bottom of the corkboard, a rusty tack pierced an envelope. Someone had typed MR. AMOS on the front and then folded the envelope four times for transporting. "What's this?" she said.

"What's what?"

"The envelope with your name on it."

Amos gave her a blank look.

"Right here," Clara said, pointing.

Amos stood and came over. He pulled out the tack, opened the pleated envelope, and read the letter. Confusion rose in his eyes, then his face stiffened.

"What's the matter?" Clara asked.

When Amos said nothing, she turned to Bruce, who had also grown oddly still.

"What?" Clara asked, feeling suddenly scared.

Amos extended the letter toward her. She read it once and then twice and still didn't know what it meant. It was typewritten in all caps:

> DEAR MR. AMOS,
>
> DATES AND TIMES OF FUENRALS ARE EASY TO GET AND I'VE HEARD OF BAD THINGS HAPPENING SO I DECIDED TO WATCH OVER THINGS WHILE YOU WERE OUT.
>
> SIGNED YOUR VERY OWN GARDIAN ANGLE.
>
> P.S. I MISPLACED SOMETHING WHILE I WAS POKING AROUND, IF YOU FIND IT JUST LET IT GO.

"Creepy," Bruce said. "Also, your guardian angel can't spell."

"Neither can Eddie Tripp," Amos said.

"You think?" Bruce said. "I mean, *they* cracked *your* head with a bat. You owe them one, not vice versa."

"Yeah, but you're thinking like a human being, which the Tripps aren't," Amos said. "They think I ratted on Charles. They think I put him in juvenile hall."

"Did you?" Clara said. She'd remembered her conversation with Eddie in front of her locker—the part where he'd said somebody was a smudge and a stoolie.

"No," Amos said. "I *should've*, but I didn't. I said it was too dark to tell."

The room was quiet while this sank in. Then Clara spoke. "So how come you didn't identify them?" she said, stopping herself from adding "innyhoo."

"Don't know." Then: "Actually I do. I was afraid what the Tripps would do if I ratted on them." Amos smiled unhappily. "Now I'm finding out what they would do if I didn't."

Bruce, after staring at the note for a few moments, straightened himself and went into his Rod Serling/*Twilight Zone* voice: "Presenting for your consideration, a note from the great devoid." Then, in his normal voice, Bruce said, "Well, I guess we'd better look around for whatever it is your guardian angel left behind."

They proceeded gingerly, looking under the bed, in corners, under cushions. Clara didn't know about Amos and Crookshank, but she hoped very much that she wouldn't find anything. She had just gotten up her courage to look behind the window curtains when the door swung open behind them.

Liz stood in the doorway looking more furious than Clara had ever seen a girl look in real life. In her hand was a Tupperware container.

"What do you know about this?" she asked in a shaky voice. Her face looked not so much white as simply without color.

"About what?" Amos said.

"About somebody's sick trick, and I'm telling you, Amos, if this is your doing, or yours and your pals'"—here she let her eyes swipe past Bruce—"there are going to be real consequences."

Even while listening to Liz, Clara couldn't take her eyes off the closed plastic container Liz held in her hand. Suddenly Clara heard herself say, "What's in the Tupperware?"

Liz turned toward Clara, then looked down at the plastic container. She peeled back its beige lid and tilted the container forward for Clara to see.

It had been a dessert, some sort of frozen lemon or pineapple custard, Clara guessed. But now, frozen on top, in a neat coil, was the pencil-thin body of a small red snake.

22

A SHORT VISIT FROM DETECTIVE O'HEARN

The next morning, Amos rode with Liz down to the police substation. This wasn't his idea. Once he'd mentioned to Liz that
Eddie Tripp might be responsible for the frozen snake, she'd in-
sisted that the police should be told. Amos wasn't so sure. Things
were bad enough without upping the ante. Maybe the Tripps had
had their fun, he thought. Maybe they were through now. Maybe
they would go away.

"The police?" Amos said. "What can the police do?"

"Something," Liz said. "It's their job to figure out what."

The police substation was housed in four prefabricated units
that had been rolled into the parking lot of the A&P and then
bolted together to make one huge but flimsy room. The floor was
covered with cheap carpet and linoleum blackened with cigarette
burns. It was, Amos thought, the last place you'd want to be in bare
feet. "My enthusiasm wanes," he said as they stepped inside, but Liz
charged ahead. They worked their way toward what seemed like a
reception area, where two policewomen, crisp and trim in full blue
uniforms, ignored Liz and Amos completely. Finally Liz cleared her
voice and said she needed to talk to someone about a crime.

The younger of the two women looked up, split a glance between Liz and Amos, and said, "Somebody beat up on the boy?"

"No," Liz began, "somebody broke into our house." After about
two more sentences, the policewoman's face went bland with

disinterest and she began looking around the room for someone to pass Amos and Liz on to. "There," she said, interrupting Liz, "see the large gentleman over there?—blue shirt and red tie?—that's Detective Lucian O'Hearn. He's the one you'll want to talk to."

Amos would've guessed it was impossible, but Detective O'Hearn seemed even less interested in Liz's story than the policewoman. While Liz spoke, he gazed at her with a glazed half smile. He seemed not to have noticed Amos at all, but when Liz finished talking, the detective blinked slowly and suddenly redirected his gaze toward Amos. "Where'd you get those shiners, son?"

Amos was caught off guard, but Liz jumped in. "Somebody hit him with a baseball bat!" she said. "The older brother of the one who broke into our house yesterday!"

Detective O'Hearn nodded seriously. "So what would you like me to do, miss?"

"Arrest Eddie Tripp."

Detective Lucian O'Hearn had a large, perfectly bald head. He tilted back in his chair, stretched, and then folded his hands serenely on his ample stomach. He looked benign, imperturbable, and he was wearing a gun. He turned his calm smile back to Liz. "Did you say what kind of dessert it was that was decorated with the reptile?"

Amos wanted to leave. The man was making fun of them. Amos hardly ever felt sorry for Liz, but he felt sorry for her when she said in an earnest voice, "My mother calls it pineapple icebox dessert."

"Pineapple icebox dessert," Detective O'Hearn repeated. He seemed to be suppressing a great laugh, the kind of laugh that might make his whole stomach shake like a Jell-O mold. But he kept his benign official smile. "And tell me again what this criminal stole from you?"

Liz looked suddenly confused. "Well, he didn't steal anything. But—"

The large detective steered his smile to Amos. "Look, son, you're at an age where buddies play tricks. Sometimes they get a little carried away. Sometimes they do things that aren't in the very best taste."

Liz stood abruptly and in a snappish voice said, "I want to file a report."

Detective O'Hearn smiled and shrugged. "Suit yourself, miss." He nodded back toward the bored policewoman at the desk. "Officer Evans will take a report."

As they were heading back toward Officer Evans, the large detective said, "Say, Miss MacKenzie, give me the suspect's name again."

"Edward Tripp," Liz said. "Two *p*'s."

"Two *p*'s," the detective said amiably, and went away.

Officer Evans, when advised that Liz and Amos wanted to file a breaking-and-entering report, told them to take a seat and she'd get to them as soon as she could.

Twenty minutes passed, and Liz went back to the desk to ask how much longer it would be. Without looking up, Officer Evans said that was impossible to say.

"Well, then, maybe we'll go back where we came from," Liz said.

Officer Evans just kept staring at the computer screen in front of her. She didn't seem to mind if Liz and Amos went away mad, as long as they went away.

"C'mon, Amos, this is hopeless," Liz said.

But as they were leaving, the floor began to tremble slightly. It was Detective O'Hearn, lumbering their way. He motioned them back to his office, where he said in a quiet voice, "Okay, just so you'll know. Edward Tripp has no record at all. None. I'm not saying he's a Boy Scout poster child or anything, but most kids who dabble at crime finally get caught at it. Now his brother, Charles, is another story. Juvenile detention is his home away from home. It's also his alibi, in this case. He's been in juvenile detention since"—Detective O'Hearn peered down at his notes—"the third, and he won't be sprung for another ten days."

Ten days. Amos could hardly believe it. Charles Tripp was only in J.D. for ten more days? "What happens after he's out of juvenile detention?" Amos asked.

The big detective shrugged amiably. "A free man till he makes his next mistake."

Amos stood silent, taking this all in. He didn't like what he was hearing. He didn't like it at all. He guessed it must've shown on his face, because Detective O'Hearn said, "Tell you what. Once Charles is sprung, I'll visit him and Eddie and see if I can't get their attention."

"Thanks," Liz said, as if she meant it. Amos thanked the detective, too, but insincerely. What he really wished was that Detective O'Hearn would leave the Tripps alone so maybe they'd do the same for him, Amos, the milkboy hero.

23

DISCONNECTION

A few days later, Clara and her father were driving to the airport to see her mother off to Madrid. Clara and her father rode in silence. The fields they passed were frozen on top. The cattle and horses seemed neither to move or to breathe. *Madrid*, Clara thought. Her only images of Madrid were from the reassuring black-ink drawings of a children's book, where a peaceful bull named Ferdinand slept under a cork tree. It was a book she had loved, and now she wished she'd never seen it. Finally Clara said, "Isn't March a funny time for Mom to start a teaching job?"

Her father kept staring at the highway ahead. "Somebody quit," he said. "They needed someone right away to finish the term."

They fell into another silence; then Clara said, "Okay if I turn on the radio?"

"Sure," her father said vaguely.

Clara worked her way through the stations—news, talk radio, country and western, farm reports, commercials. Before she could change the channel, they listened to a woman gush over the linens at Kaufmann's Department Store. Clara glanced up at her father, but he didn't say anything. How odd to think that your own mother had run away. *Run, run, just as fast as you can*, Clara thought. *You can't catch me, I'm the Gingerbread Man.* Clara felt like running or shouting, but all she could make her body do was curl up tighter. She put her feet on the dashboard, which was forbidden. She was almost relieved when her father said, as he always had in the past, "No feet on the dash, please." He didn't say it in his usual funny way, but at least he still said it. She put her feet, which felt tense and cold, back on the floor.

When they got to the airport, Clara was surprised to find that her father wasn't going into the terminal with her. "I've already said good-bye," he told Clara. "This is your chance. Just go straight to gate 24a. She'll be waiting for you."

Clara nodded dumbly and walked off. But instead of going to gate 24a, she went through the security gates and into the ladies' lounge. She went to the mirrors and applied lip balm. She pushed her nose straight for a moment. She combed her hair, and then combed it again with water. She always had static in the winter. Twice she went into a toilet stall, closed the door, and just stared at the floor.

She could hear the flights being called: *Flight 1201 to Dallas, Flight 331 to Edinburgh, Flight 609 to Atlanta.* It was a woman's voice, then a man's, impersonal and automatic like the faucets that came on when you waved your hands under them. She felt like she was in a tunnel, a shiny white tunnel at the center of the earth.

While she sat in one of the stalls, Clara began rummaging through her purse for nothing in particular. She examined paper-sleeved toothpicks, splayed barrettes, and finally a matchbook that read in gold letters, THE TIFFIN ROOM. The paper corners had been rubbed into softness by her purse, but the words were still legible. SERVING JEMISON SINCE 1942.

The Tiffin Room was a restaurant in the same downtown area

as Kaufmann's, and sometimes on Saturdays, Clara would meet her mother for lunch during her mother's break. "Wherever you want," her mother said. Clara loved these lunches. When they met at the Tiffin Room (and at first, Clara never chose anywhere else), they each arrived independently with their purses and nice clothes, and it was as if Clara were not a child anymore. The Tiffin Room was all dark wood and maroon leather, the kind of place that served veal cutlets, meat loaf, chow mein, shrimp cocktail, and club sandwiches. The waitresses were all older and called Clara "love" or "hon." They had hair like lacquered pinecones and wore short beige dressy uniforms with white aprons.

While they ate, her mother would talk to her almost as if she were an adult—a daughter, say, who was home from college. Her mother would talk about the funny customers who'd been in that day, and she'd talk about this coworker, who was especially nice, and that coworker, who was not.

Outside the stall, two stewardesses were talking and the bathroom was loud with swirling, plummeting water. *Run, run, just as fast as you can*, Clara thought again, picturing the cookie arms and legs in motion, running headlong to the river. Clara flipped the matchbook in the toilet. *I don't care*, she thought suddenly, and it was true, she didn't. She didn't care that Mr. Duckworth had given her an F for missing the exam without an excuse note. She didn't care that her math homework wasn't done, that her history homework wasn't done, and that she didn't know this week's vocabulary words. And she didn't care that her mother was going to Spain.

When Clara left the bathroom, she found herself under a sign pointing to gates 14 to 24.

Flight 1755 to JFK, with connecting flights to Madrid and Helsinki, is now boarding at gate 24a.

Clara walked into a magazine shop on her left. It was just the first call. She had plenty of time. She picked up *Cosmopolitan* and flipped around until she found an article that gave pointers for saving your marriage after your husband had had an affair. "Don't use the other woman as a cudgel to punish him. Slipping her name into conversation will only drive you farther apart." *Don't use the other woman as a cudgel?* Clara was thinking.

Final boarding of Flight 1755 to JFK at gate 24a.

Clara, turning, saw a man and woman trotting down the corridor, baggage slung over their shoulders. Clara put the *Cosmopolitan* back in the rack and walked slowly toward gate 24a. Up ahead, the trotting man and woman were waved through a door and up the enclosed ramp. Standing beside the door, looking distractedly around, was her mother. Clara stepped back behind an awning stretched from a fancy coffee-and-pastry wagon, where she could watch her mother unobserved. A stewardess was talking to her mother, but Clara's mother kept looking over the stewardess's shoulder, frantically scanning the path that led to the waiting area. The stewardess firmly took hold of her mother's arm with one hand and motioned toward the ramp with the other. Even as she began to move up the ramp toward the plane, her mother kept looking back.

Clara bolted from her hiding spot and ran toward the door, but her mother had disappeared up the ramp. A male steward closed the door securely. From one of the floor-to-ceiling windows, Clara peered out at the enormous jet. There seemed to be hundreds of windows on the side of the plane. There were faces at all of them, strange faces heading for strange cities.

Clara raised her hand and waved it slowly. "Bye, Mom," she said.

"How did it go?" Clara's father asked when she got back to the car.

"Not that great," Clara said. "I got mixed up and got there just as the last passengers were loading."

Her father took this in slowly. "You mean you *didn't* say goodbye?" He stared at Clara while she stared out the window. Finally he said, "Do you feel bad you missed her?"

Clara thought about it. "A little bit," she said.

"But not a lot?"

Clara didn't answer.

"Did you dawdle on purpose because you're mad at your mother, Clara?"

Clara thought about how angry her father would be if she lied. "Maybe," she said. "I don't see what difference it makes. Aren't you mad at her?"

Her father started the engine and merged with the lines of departing cars, the cars of people who were not going anywhere or who had for some reason chosen cold upstate New York as their destination.

"I'm sad she's leaving," her father said at last. "I'm a little mad at myself for the mistakes I've made along the way. But no, I'm not really mad at your mother."

Clara thought about something her mother had said in their last phone call: "The only thing I completely, totally, 110 percent regret is leaving you," her mother had told her. Why didn't her mother regret leaving her father, too?

Clara and her father fell silent. Perhaps ten minutes passed. The highway cut through frozen farmland. "Is she going to call?" Clara asked.

"Yes."

"Are you going to talk to her?"

Her father seemed thrown off by the question. "Well," he said carefully, "I told her it wouldn't be a good idea for her and me to talk while she was in Spain, but we both agreed that it would be good for her to talk to you."

Clara looked out at a boy about her age chipping ice from a stock watering tank. She said, "If Mom calls, I don't want to talk to her."

Her father let the car decelerate ever so slightly. "Polkadot..."

"No," Clara said. "I really don't want to. It'll just make me more upset." She thought about it. "Anyhow, she made her decisions about what was best for her, and now I'm making my decision about what's best for me."

"You should sleep on this, Polkadot. It's not right to make a decision when you're in this kind of mood."

Clara stared out the window. "I'll sleep on it," she said. "But I won't change my mind."

It was true. She didn't. The next morning, while she and her father were having breakfast, the telephone rang. "You get it," her father said casually, but Clara wouldn't. The answering machine was off. The telephone rang and rang.

"Clara, pick up the phone," her father said.

Clara stepped close, but she didn't pick up the phone. It kept ringing.

"It's probably Gerri or the MacKenzie boy," her father said.

Clara raised the receiver to her ear.

"Hello?" It was her mother. Her voice sounded close by, like she still might be at Aunt Marie's in Dalton. "Hello? Clara? Monty?"

Clara said nothing.

"Sweetie?" her mother said in a hopeful tone. "Is that you, sweetie? It's me, Mom, and I'm in Valencia, Spain, in a beautiful old hotel that was a convent two hundred years ago. Are you there, sweetie?"

Clara didn't answer. She didn't care if it was cruel or childish. She set the receiver down hard in its cradle.

24

BETRAYAL

"Any more notes from the great devoid?" Bruce asked one afternoon a week later while shooting baskets with Amos at the old gym. They were playing horse. Bruce, who couldn't miss, was winning big.

"Nope," Amos said, "no more notes." He wheeled for a long arcing eighteen-footer. It rattled like a pinball on the rim, seemed about to be swallowed into the net, and then somehow jumped back out for a miss. Just as he expected.

Bruce laughed and, in his sports announcer's voice, said, "Oh, my, fans, MacKenzie just can't *buy* a bucket," then tossed up a no-look hook, which swished.

"Eddie's always watching me, though," Amos said. "That's creepy enough." Even more creepy, though he didn't say so, was the fact that on Friday Charles Tripp would be out of juvenile detention. Amos casually positioned himself to duplicate Bruce's no-look hook and tossed up an air ball. The game was over. He drifted to the sidelines to pick up his coat and books.

Bruce, still on the court, was back into announcer mode: "Okay, fans, Celtics down by two, three seconds to play. Inbound to Bird. Jukes left, pulls up, lets fly for a three"—Bruce's shot floated through the air—"and oh, my, fans, he gets nothing but net! Nothing but net! Celts win by one!"

"See ya, Crook," Amos said.

Bruce turned suddenly, as if just remembering something. "Hey, did you ask the Brainette out yet?"

Amos shook his head no. He wished he'd never told Bruce he was thinking about asking Clara out. The problem was, the mere thought of asking her to do something with him made his skin pricklish with fear. And the longer he waited, the bigger his fear grew. At the gym door, Amos said, "Coming by tonight?"

Bruce shrugged. "If the Judge is on a toot." Bruce's term for one of his father's drinking binges.

Amos nodded, said, "Exit Amos," and left. This was a term he'd gotten from Clara when they talked at night on the telephone. She'd told him everything about *The Smiling Gumshoe* (she was the props manager, as well as having a small part), and at the end of their conversations, instead of saying goodbye, Clara would say, "Exit Clara" and Amos would say, "Exit Amos."

When he got to his own front gate, Amos regarded his house. It looked more or less the same as it had when his father was alive, but it was like taxidermy—it sort of resembled the living thing, but not very much. And it had the same creepy effect.

The house was quiet when Amos unlocked the door. Amos's mother had always loved music in the house when she was cooking or reading, but now she never turned the radio on. She didn't go near the TV. She hardly talked. She read books in silence, not the Agatha Christie mystery books she used to read, but serious books: *The Confessions* of St. Augustine and the poems of John Donne. When either he or Liz watched a sitcom, she would ask them to turn it down—she said she couldn't stand the laugh tracks. Liz went out with boys more. Amos spent hours at a time sitting on a wooden box pulled up close to his pigeon coop, watching the birds swoop and glide as they had always swooped and glided, listening to them click and coo as they had always clicked and cooed.

Tonight he made a sandwich, put his coat on, took the cordless phone out to the pigeon coop, and called Clara, who answered after he spoke into the machine.

"Enter Clara," she said in a playful voice.

Amos felt his whole body relax. "I was hoping you'd be there."

She laughed. "I was hoping you'd call."

"Still screening so you won't have to talk to your mom, huh?"

"Yeah," Clara said quietly.

Amos bit into his sandwich, chewed, and waited. He knew she would've been thinking about it and would want to say what she'd been thinking, and she did. She said, "It's just that she's got what she wants, which *excludes* me, except she wants to tell me how much she misses me and loves me so she can tell herself she's doing everything she can to *include* me." Then, in a softer voice, "So what're you doing?"

"Watching the pigeons."

"Describe," Clara said, and he did, between bites, and then they talked as usual about almost anything—her ex–best friend, Gerri, Bruce's obsession with Anne Barrineau, Clara's parents, Amos's mother and sister—until Amos began to feel a kind of calm overtake him, and then a tiredness, and he knew finally he could go upstairs, crawl into bed, and fall asleep.

* * *

At school, Amos was cooler than ever. News of his father's death seemed only to jack up his status. Boys still collected around him, still wanted to check out his scalp (stitches out; bristly blond hair filling in) and talk about the weird things Eddie Tripp was saying to people ("Tell the milkboy hero I love his Carreras," or "Tell the milkboy hero that Chaz is *at large* as of Friday"). As Charles Tripp's release date got closer and closer, Amos got more and more uneasy. But then, when that fateful Friday finally did arrive, nothing happened, or so it seemed.

Amos was so relieved at not seeing the Tripps all day that the first thing he did when he got home from school was call Clara. Then, before he had time to think about it, he asked her out. "Want to do something Sunday night?" he said, figuring that Sunday would seem less big-deal than Friday or Saturday. "Maybe just walk somewhere and get pizza," he added.

But Clara didn't say yes. "I can't," she said finally. "It's my dad's rule. I can't date till I'm sixteen."

"It's not really a date," Amos said. "We'd just be getting pizza."

After a moment's deliberation, Clara said, "Well, it wouldn't be a date if you were to come over and have pizza here at my house."

"No," Amos said, his spirits lifting again. "No, it really wouldn't."

"Oh, but I can't this Sunday," Clara said. "I've got to help Mrs. Harper clean out her attic." But then her voice brightened again. "I could next Sunday, though."

After he'd hung up, Amos sat on his box by the pigeon coop, feeling better than he'd felt since before his father had died.

Pizza. Pizza with Clara.

Amos was floating along on this happy prospect when the phone in his hand rang again. He expected it to be Clara, but it wasn't.

It was Sands Mandeville and Sophie Whitaker, calling from Sands's house, each on a separate extension. Amos had never talked on the telephone to either of them—he'd hardly even said hi to them at school—but like everyone else, he'd regularly seen their pictures in *The Leviathan* and watched them holding court on campus.

"What're you doing?" Sands said, as if she and Amos talked all the time.

Amos felt a little tongue-tied. "Watching my pigeons," he said, and both the girls laughed. Sophie said, "Are they doing it or something?" and without waiting for an answer, both the girls laughed again. Amos laughed feebly, too.

"Okay, Amos-poo, here's the deal," Sands said, and explained that she and Sophie were going to be at her house tonight, watching a video on her giant-screen TV, and they wondered if he wanted to come by. Before Amos could say anything, Sophie said that Sands's folks were off in Barbados for the week and they had a whole bunch of R-rated videos in their video library.

An evening with Sands Mandeville and Sophie Whitaker?

Amos couldn't help himself. He was both excited by the prospect and a little afraid. "Naw, I don't think so," he said.

"You won't be alone," Sands said, or maybe it was Sophie. Amos was having a hard time telling who was who. "We aren't going to pounce on you or anything. Dave Pearse is coming, too. In fact, we told him to come by and pick you up around seven."

Dave Pearse? Big Dave was going to give him a ride? It was almost too crazy to consider. "Look," Amos said, "why don't you just give me the address and then if I can make it, I'll just walk."

"He said seven," Sands said, "but he's always late. I'd plan on seven-fifteen."

Amos didn't say anything.

"And wear that flannel shirt you wore today at school, okay?"

To his own surprise, Amos heard himself say, "Okay. Okay, sure."

At seven-twenty, Big Dave Pearse elbowed his car horn and Amos went walking out to meet him. Even though he'd put on the green shirt, he thought he was going to tell Big Dave that he couldn't go after all, that something had come up, but as he approached, Big Dave leaned over, swung open the passenger-side door, and said, "Hop in, Hero," and Amos's idea of not going somehow vanished.

It was warm in the car, and full of loud music. Two blocks along, Big Dave turned down the volume. "So I guess you won the Sands Mandeville lottery. Which would make you just about the youngest contestant ever."

"I don't know about that," Amos said, and he didn't. He didn't even know that it was Sands Mandeville who was inviting him tonight.

"Yeah, well, I do. I keep hoping my number'll come up, but it doesn't. Not that I mind Sophie, but Mandeville—Mandeville's got the major Sigourneys."

They pulled up to a stoplight, and Amos said, *"Cigorneeze?"*

"Sigourneys," Big Dave said. "As in Sigourney Weaver." He cast Amos a quick glance and laughed. "As in Olympian mammary glands."

"Oh."

"Hey, don't pretend you haven't noticed Mandeville's northern territory." Big Dave grinned again. "Even amateur explorers admire the Tetons."

Amos *had* noticed Sands Mandeville, of course. But now, to think Sands Mandeville might actually be interested in him, Amos MacKenzie—it was a thought that frightened and exhilarated him.

"So what do I do?" Amos said.

Big Dave laughed. "Nothing. Just follow along. Mandeville likes to lead."

It was a cold, clear night with enough moon to illuminate the pitted snowbanks and rutted streets. These were houses, Amos knew, where his father used to deliver milk. In his father's route book, there were always particular instructions as to where the milk should be left—front porch, back porch, or even, in a few cases, the customer's refrigerator (his father had his own keys for those houses). Watching the yards go by, Amos realized that one year ago to the day, his father had probably seen these same nighttime houses under the same thin moon.

To Amos's surprise, Big Dave swung onto Genesee, Clara Wilson's street.

"Where're you going?" Amos asked.

"Shortcut up to Bandy Ridge. Mandeville's in the high-rent district."

Clara Wilson's house approached on the left. Amos scooched down a bit but kept a line of sight on the house, and especially the second story, where he believed Clara's bedroom must be. But he saw nothing. An upstairs light turned the empty pane yellow. Amos sat back up. He thought of asking Big Dave to let him out, so he could walk back and see if Clara was home, but he didn't. The car hooked left, onto Walnut, and began the ascent to Bandy Ridge, Jemison's most exclusive neighborhood. As they climbed, expansive views of the lighted city opened below them. When they turned a corner near the top of the ridge, Big Dave pointed past a sign that read: DEAD END, NO OUTLET. "Actually, there's a bike path through there, and it takes you right down to the South Face Mall and the Kensington District." He smiled. "You can walk to the mall almost as fast as you can drive, not that walking's anything anybody up in this district would ever do."

The Mandeville house stood at the end of a cobblestone lane that curved through a wide, rolling lawn. Big Dave parked under a portico (that, anyhow, was what Big Dave called it; to Amos it looked like an elaborate, columned carport). Inside the house, the girls were in high spirits. They had dressed almost identically, in Levi's and soft sweaters—Sands in lavender, Sophie in beige—and both came to the door in stocking feet.

"Well, well," Sands Mandeville said, smiling at Amos while Sophie took their scarves and coats, "we finally got the famous Amos out into society."

Amos blushed deeply, felt sweat gloss his upper lip. They were standing in an entryway that felt like a fancy movie lobby. The floor was marble. Beyond Sands, in a recessed alcove, there stood a black marble statue of a naked woman.

"C'mon, Mandeville," Big Dave said, "give the youth some breathing room."

Sands Mandeville laughed and swiveled. "We're in here," she said, and led the way. The house itself was enormous and high-ceilinged, with glass chandeliers, smooth-plaster archways, and wood-framed modern paintings. It was the kind of house Amos had seen only in movies and magazines, and glancing into an enormous kitchen, Amos wondered whether the Mandevilles drank Cosgrove milk.

Finally Sands led Amos and the others to a room that had a vast TV at one end, encircled first by thick carpeting and large lounging pillows, and then by a second circle of curving leather sofas. "I guess this is the breathing room," Amos said, and everyone laughed, even Big Dave Pearse.

To Amos, Sophie Whitaker was a darker version of Sands—brown eyes instead of blue, brown hair instead of blond, and, it seemed to Amos, hardness instead of softness. "Well, David," she said in a commanding voice to Big Dave, "what spirits did you bring?" and Big Dave, drawing pint bottles of brandy from each interior jacket pocket, said, "Two flavors—peach and blackberry."

"Yum," Sands Mandeville said. "Amos and I'll split the blackberry." This worried Amos. He and Bruce had once tasted some of the Judge's bourbon and had hated it.

Sophie said, "Okay, you chose the brandy, David and I choose the movie."

"Got anything with Sigourney Weaver in it?" Big Dave said, and flashed at Amos a grin that made him feel suddenly inside of all this. It was enough of a good feeling that the blackberry brandy seemed to taste better than he'd feared. After a gulp or two, it seemed even to taste good, in fact.

The foursome settled on a video called *Half Moon Street*, with the sound off and some classical music that Sands liked tinkling away instead, something by Debussy. She asked Amos if he liked Debussy.

Amos decided to tell the truth. "Never heard of the guy."

Sophie chortled. "Join the club. Mandeville's gone highbrow on us because she's got this new piano teacher she thinks is a big dreamboat."

Sands Mandeville shrugged and in a matter-of-fact voice said, "You have to admit, for a piano teacher, he's pretty deluxe."

Amos, imagining the deluxe piano teacher, felt the need to say something. "I listened to Edvard Grieg one day. I was sick, and before my mom went out, she put it on and left it on replay. I was too sleepy to get up and change it. Every time I'd fall asleep, I'd wake up and hear all these maniac kettledrums and I'd be in the hall of the mountain king, and then a little while later, the record started again with this soft song about morning, and I'd get drowsy again."

Sophie stared at him blankly.

"Amos, my man," Big Dave said, "that is what we in the story-telling business would call boring."

"I thought it was a sweet story," Sands Mandeville said, and took another sip or two of blackberry brandy. Amos already felt a little disconnected from his skin, and he hadn't drunk a third of what Sands had. He found himself staring happily at a lighted display case of small porcelain figures, pale girls whose arms were thin and long and glossy.

"Too *bright* in here," Sophie said, and switched the lights off so that the room swam in the fitful bluish light of the huge TV, where Sigourney Weaver, in preparation for what evidently was a date, sat in an old-fashioned bathtub.

"I *love* those Sigourneys," Big Dave said.

"Actually, her real name is Susan Weaver."

"Well, then," Big Dave said, "I *love* those Susans!"

Sands Mandeville, who had the blackberry brandy in one hand, poked Amos with her other. "We're in the company of sick individuals. Let's go way over there to the other side of the room, where we can't even hear them. To another locale where they don't even exist." Her voice sounded melodic and dreamlike. She led him closer to the long-limbed porcelain girls in their long dresses.

"To another country," Amos heard himself say, which made Sands laugh.

"To another planet," Sands said.

Such was Amos's present state that when Sands Mandeville told him to take off his beautiful shirt so she could scratch his back, it seemed perfectly normal to him, though he left on his black T-shirt underneath. They stayed like that for a time, Amos stretched out on the floor and propped up on an expansive pillow, watching Sigourney Weaver in various states of undress, while Sands Mandeville, the maybe third or fourth most popular girl at Melville Junior High, scratched his back. She only paused from time to time to take another swallow of blackberry brandy, after which she would always murmur, "*Yum.*"

What Sophie and Big Dave were doing Amos couldn't tell. It was quiet over there, and mysterious. After one especially long period of speechlessness, Sophie left the room and was several minutes in reappearing. "Hey," she called out from her side of the room.

"Hey," Sands Mandeville answered.

"Let's play dinks. One a thousand, two a thousand..."

"Kathy Andrews," Sands Mandeville said. "One a thousand..."

"Tim Brewer," Sophie said.

"Johnec Clouse."

They continued. The game, as Big Dave explained to Amos, was to name somebody they considered a dink in alphabetical order in less than three seconds. The winner got to choose something from the loser's clothes closet.

"James Martinson."

Sands Mandeville laughed, then got right back to business. "Bob Nesbitt."

It went on. Amos, uneasy, stared at the polished cherrywood cabinet, at the expensive porcelain girls with fixed half smiles on their smooth creamy faces.

"Shelly Vineyard. One a thousand, two a thousand..."

It was Sands Mandeville's turn. She said, "Misty AKA-the-Nose Wilson."

Sophie groaned. "Tie," she said.

Amos, who had a bad feeling in his stomach, said, "What about X, Y, and Z?"

Big Dave said, "They only play through W. It's a queer rule, but then it's a queer game."

Sands Mandeville, who'd stopped scratching Amos's back during the game, peeled up his T-shirt so his back was bare and resumed scratching, except now she used only her fingertips instead of her nails. Amos had never felt anything quite like it. The last thing he wanted was for her to stop. Still, he had a question.

"Who's Misty Wilson?"

"Misty AKA-the-Nose?" Sands Mandeville stopped to finish off the rest of the blackberry brandy— "*yum*"—then said, "She's this girl who's doing props in the play Sophie and I're practicing for right now."

"Clara Wilson?" Amos said.

"Yeah, that's her."

Amos knew what AKA-the-Nose meant. *Also known as the Nose.* "Where does the Misty part come from?" Amos asked.

"Oh, she used to bring these lame horse books to school. Her personal fave was *Misty of the Chicateaparty*, or something like that." Sands went back to her massage. Amos tucked the big pillow tighter under his chest. When Sands leaned forward, Amos could feel her sweater press against his bare back.

Amos thought about it a long time. Finally, in a quiet voice, he said, "I don't think Clara Wilson's a dink."

Sands Mandeville burst out laughing, a harsh, loud crackling laugh.

"What?" Sophie said from the other side of the room.

"The famous Amos doesn't think Misty AKA-the-Nose is a dink."

"Oh, Misty's a dink, all right," Sophie said. "She's got the nose, for one thing, and for another, her mother dresses her funny."

"That was before her mother vamoosed," Sands Mandeville said. "Now Misty dresses herself funny."

After the girls' laughter died down, Sophie said, "And you should've seen her when in addition to props she got a part in the play," Sophie said. "It was *the* teeniest part. One line. But she almost cried, she was so happy."

"Maybe it's a great line," Big Dave said.

"Not exactly. She says, 'I guess you know I can't keep this to myself,' and then she gets shot with this gun that makes this cool-looking blood stuff, and that's it, she's dead. Twenty seconds onstage, max, which is a blessing, let me tell you."

More whoops and raucous laughter.

Finally there was a silence. Finally they were done. For a few seconds, Amos said nothing, and was afraid he would continue to say nothing. At last he said, "Yeah, but I'll bet if you got to know her, you'd see she's pretty cool."

"A dink!" Sophie whooped. "That's what you'd find out she is."

Sands Mandeville chuckled. "It's true. Lowercase *d*, dink. Ver-ry dinky."

She turned around and stared at Amos in the flickering light. She had a soft, foolish grin on her face. She leaned forward and kissed Amos's ear, then spoke into it two words that shot down his spine. "Say it," she whispered.

"Say what?'

"Say 'Clara Wilson's a dink.'"

Amos drew slightly away.

Sands Mandeville took his hand and slid it under her sweater, moving it slowly up her stomach, and then stopped.

"Say it," she whispered.

Amos didn't speak.

She nudged his hand slightly upward, and Amos suddenly realized that Sands Mandeville was not wearing a bra. She *had* been, he was pretty sure of that, but it was clear she wasn't now.

"Say it," she whispered again.

"Clara Wilson's a dink," Amos mumbled quickly.

"What?"

"Clara Wilson's a dink," Amos said more distinctly, and Sands Mandeville's lips curled into a satisfied half smile. For one fleeting moment, Amos's hand covered her breast, taking quick, greedy impressions. But Sands, whose whole body had felt loose-jointed and lazy, suddenly stiffened. "Wait," she said.

"What?"

She sat bolt upright. "Wait," she said again. She pulled her lavender sweater down and woozily stood. "Bathroom," she said, and then was gone.

She didn't get to the bathroom. Halfway down the marbled hallway, Sands Mandeville stopped, pulled her hair back, bent forward, and threw up.

"Welcome to the exotic City of Upchuck," Big Dave said.

Sophie was laughing.

Amos asked where the mop and stuff were, but Sands had disappeared into the bathroom. "She wouldn't know anyway," Sophie said. "They have *help*, you know?"

Amos stared at her and wondered if *help* just meant housekeepers and cooks, or would it include other people, like the milkman? While the others stood around, Amos found a mop and some sponges in the pantry. He did most of the cleanup. It looked like Sands had dined chiefly on tomatoes, cottage cheese, and carrot sticks.

While he was finishing up, Sands emerged from the bathroom looking surprisingly refreshed. She grinned as if nothing had happened. "What's next?" she said.

Amos, turning, whacked the mop handle into the cherry-and-beveled glass display case behind him. Inside the case, one of the pale, half-smiling, long-limbed porcelain girls rocked and fell forward. The umbrella she held snapped and shattered. Amos, staring down at the broken figurine, said, "I'll pay for it."

From behind him, Sands laughed. "Not unless your father left you a sizable inheritance." She stepped forward and started cleaning up the glass shards. "We'll just throw her away and space the others out and they'll never miss her." Sands grinned. "Or if they do, they'll blame it on the help." She was close to him now. Just behind the mouthwash she'd rinsed with, he detected the sour smell of vomit.

Amos took the pail out to the kitchen to get clean water. While he was there, he noticed that his coat was thrown over one of the chairs. He didn't know why he did what he did next. He walked over to the refrigerator—its front door was wood-paneled just like the rest of the kitchen cabinets—and pulled it open. Inside, it looked like an expensive deli case with all sorts of cheeses and olives and fancy sliced meats. And there, lined up in a neat row along one side, were several glass quarts of milk from Cosgrove Dairy.

Amos pulled one out. The date on the foiled lid was too recent. His father was already dead when the bottle made its way here in someone else's truck. No, that wasn't right. In his father's truck, driven by someone else. Amos looked at the pail in the sink. He looked at his coat slung over the chair, and he looked at the door that led from the kitchen into the backyard. In the backyard, there was a gate. Through the gate was the long cobblestoned driveway. Down the driveway was the street, the everyday, ordinary street that led back to the everyday, ordinary world.

25

AMOS ACCOSTED

Amos pulled his jacket collar snug and headed back home the way he came. It could've been worse, he decided. It could've been colder tonight. He could've been walking uphill instead of down. He could've been the one to unload his dinner instead of Sands Mandeville. Still, it was all pretty disappointing. And—a real surprise—although he'd had his hand around Sands Mandeville's breast, he couldn't remember exactly what it felt like, and if you couldn't remember the particulars and, worse, wound up feeling grimy besides, how big an achievement could it be?

He turned right on Genesee and checked his pace as he approached Clara Wilson's house. Clara Wilson, whom he had betrayed, out loud and in public. There was a light in an upstairs bedroom, slight shadowy movement on the ceiling. Probably it was Clara's room and Clara's shadow. Amos looked around. On the dirty sidewalk, there were wet pebbles of just the right size to tap at her window without breaking it. But what would he say even if he got her attention? "Hi, I was just walking by after feeling up Sands Mandeville and calling you a dink"?

Amos walked on. He was tired and cold and miserable. He wanted nothing now except to be home, to talk to no one, to crawl into bed and stay there for about a year. Most of the houses he passed were dark or had just a single light on in some dim room. Only an occasional car would pass, its tires hissing on the wet pavement. A lighted bus droned by, carrying a single rider. When a car slowed alongside him, Amos had the fleeting fantastic thought that it was his father, smiling, alive, coming to pick him up in the old Econoline, to give him a warm ride back to a warm, normal life, and so Amos turned with a kind of pleasant expectancy.

It wasn't his father's Econoline, of course.

It was half car, half truck. The front portion contained two seats and looked like a large sedan; the rear had been fitted out with pickup bed and lockbox. There were three people in the front seat. The passenger-side window went zipping down. The driver leaned past the passenger and spoke in a soft crooning voice. "Hello, Hero."

Amos stopped, completely dumbfounded. And then, trying for nonchalance, he lifted his chin and said, "Hello, Eddie."

Eddie was leaning forward and grinning past a girl in the middle of the seat and, on the far end of the seat, his brother, Charles, who was paying little attention to the girl and even less to Amos, or so it seemed. Charles stared straight ahead. In profile, Amos could clearly see the strange veiny contours of his shaved scalp. He said something under his breath, and the girl let out a raucous laugh. Charles smiled thinly and let the girl tangle herself more tightly into him. Eddie ignored them. "C'mon over closer," he said to Amos. "I don't like to yell."

Eddie was acting more normal than the time Amos had seen him in the west-wing bathroom. He stepped closer to the car, but not too close. Charles was now turned away from Amos, whispering to the girl, who kept laughing moronically. Amos could see her legs. They were parted and bare. Eddie, still leaning past the occupied couple, gave Amos a friendly grin and waved him closer.

Amos took one more half step, and while he was leaning close and glancing at the girl's bare legs, Charles Tripp's long arm flashed out, caught Amos's belt buckle, and yanked him close enough that he could get his other hand on Amos's jacket collar. In another second, Amos's head had been pulled into the car and Charles had raised the window until the glass bit into Amos's Adam's apple.

"There," Eddie said in a soft voice. "We've been meaning to speak to you, and now we can."

Charles made a murmuring sound. The girl dipped her head and grinned at Amos. She wore heavy black and white makeup; when she playfully wagged her tongue at him, he saw at least two silver studs.

Eddie idly massaged his own neck and let a pleasant smile stretch across his face. "Where ya been? Up at Clara Wilson's? Is that where you were, Hero?"

This reminded Amos of how you feel when the dentist asks you questions while he's got two different sharp tools in your mouth. Amos tried to roll his eyes toward the dashboard but couldn't see much. All he was really aware of was the girl's bare legs, a thick smell of tortilla chips, and, when Charles Tripp belched, the sour smell of beer. "Can't talk," Amos said in a strangled voice.

Charles lowered the window fractionally.

"Now," Eddie said soothingly, "what were you doing at Clara Wilson's house?"

"Walking by it," Amos said. "I was coming home from some-where else."

The girl laughed derisively, then her hand disappeared inside Charles's clothes. Charles smiled and stared straight ahead, looking at nobody.

"You might've gone home a different way, though," Eddie said.

"I guess so, yeah."

"And I suppose the next time you would?"

Eddie Tripp was jealous about Clara Wilson? But Amos played with this strange notion a half second too long. Charles cranked the window until it clamped into Amos's throat. *"Mmmf"* was the sound Amos made.

Eddie, in his smooth voice, said, "I take that as an affirmative, right?"

"Mmmf."

Hard laughter spilled out from the girl's lips and, right behind it, the stale smell of beer.

"Okay, change of subjects," Eddie said. "Our real reason for speaking with you is that we've been wanting to thank you for putting us on notice. Charles and me moved into our new place today, and whattaya know? We haven't even got the beer into the fridge when we have a visit from a Detective Obese. A nice guy, Detective Obese. He said you'd had some trouble at the house. We told Detective Obese we were sorry to hear it. We told him our rule is not to screw with the rules. We told him we're not the problem. The problem is that the rule guys like to make up a special set of rules for Charles and me." Eddie's eyes drilled into Amos. "So we're not too happy when some little dickhead milkboy sics the rule guys on us with their special set of rules. *Comprende,* Hero?"

"Mmmf," Amos said. Then, when Charles slightly lowered the window, Amos said, "Yeah, sure. I understand."

"Loud and clear?"

"Loud and clear," Amos said.

Charles said nothing. He continued to stare straight ahead. The girl was running her tongue along a bulging blue vein on Charles's scalp, and Amos didn't look where her hand was. Eddie said, "What I'm telling you, free of charge, is that you're in control of your own fate here. If you make trouble for us, what can we do except add a little helping to it and send it right back at you?"

Amos said nothing. Eddie studied the road in front of him. Then he eased off the brake and the car lurched a foot or two forward. Amos, his throat vised by the window, stumbled ahead. The car stopped.

"It's up to you," Eddie said, letting his close-set eyes bore into Amos before glancing up at his brother. "Any words of advice for our young friend, Charles?"

Charles stared silently forward for a long enough time that Amos thought he hadn't heard the question. Then he said, "Just this," and Amos felt the window again raised tight into his throat, tighter than before.

The girl let out another hard laugh.

Charles made a flicking-forward motion with his chin, and Eddie again eased off the brake. The car rolled ahead. Amos, panicked, tried to yell and keep up with the car at the same time. A few yards more, and the car stopped.

Eddie Tripp shrugged and smiled broadly at Amos. "Oops," he said. Charles lowered the window, and Amos pulled free of the car. He didn't want to rub his neck in front of them, but he couldn't help it.

"You okay, Hero?" Eddie said with exaggerated concern.

"Yeah," Amos said.

"Excellent," Eddie said. "And thanks again for sending out the nice fat man. We enjoyed making his acquaintance. But do yourself a favor and make sure he doesn't visit again."

When Eddie stopped talking, Amos stood frozen. He didn't know what to do next. He didn't know what Eddie and Charles would *let* him do next.

Eddie grinned past Charles and the girl. In a mocking voice, he said, "You want to run along now, or would you like to stay and keep chatting?"

The girl laughed one last raucous laugh, and Amos, stinging with humiliation, turned and started walking. The dark half car, half truck pulled away slowly, unhurriedly, so that Amos could watch its taillights for a long while before they dissolved into the black winter night.

When he got home, his mother was sitting in the front room with her back to Amos, reading a book called *Major Biblical Prophecies*. The week before, she'd taken a waitressing job (at Bing's, of all places, where everyone went). She'd told Amos and Liz that she just needed something to do and that she'd always actually liked waitressing, but Liz had told Amos that she needed the job to help make ends meet. Tonight, while she read, Mrs. MacKenzie was still dressed in her green-and-tan waitressing uniform. Amos stood in the doorway for a while, but his mother didn't turn. "I'm back," he said.

She didn't move.

"Mom?" Amos—and this would later shame him—almost didn't want to touch her. Finally, though, he did, laying his hand on her shoulder and giving it a little shake. "Mom?"

Her eyelids rose heavily. She stared blankly at Amos. "Oh, hi, dumpling," she said in a thick, slurry voice. "I'm sleeping."

"I know," Amos said, "but it's late. Don't you want to go upstairs to bed?"

His mother's half-opened eyes shifted toward the general direction of her upstairs bedroom. "I guess so," she said.

Amos went to the kitchen table to check for messages. There were three, scribbled on a used napkin by Liz. *Crook called. Clara called. Somebody named Sands called and said you should call her tonight whenever you get in no matter how late (what is she, your FIANCEE?) 654-9868.*

Amos went outside, checked his pigeons, then came back in and called the number. "It's me," he said to the female voice that answered, "Amos MacKenzie."

"It's me, Sands Mandeville." She laughed. "So how come you left? It was no big deal about the Lladro."

"The what?"

"The thing that broke."

"Oh. Well, I thought I'd better leave before I got the help in more trouble."

There was a silence.

Sands said, "You left your shirt here."

Amos wanted the shirt back, but he didn't really want to have to go through Sands Mandeville to get it. "Why don't you just keep it," he said.

Something brisk and bitter came into Sands Mandeville's

voice. "Okay, fine by me," she said, and then she said, "See you around."

She hung up.

Amos went upstairs and, lying on his bed fully clothed, tried to fall asleep but couldn't. He had a gnawing thought. He got up and checked his bulletin board to see if there might be some further message from the Tripps tacked to it. There wasn't. There was just the *Ten Little Indians* program and other souvenirs, including the World Series ticket stubs. He unpinned them and held them in his hand. The tickets had been the highest prize in a Cosgrove Dairy sales contest, and Amos's father had been determined to win them, which had struck Amos as strange, since his father wasn't a baseball fan. But day after day, weekend after weekend, his father had gone door to door signing up new customers, and then one night at the dinner table, he laid in front of Amos an envelope that contained two box seat tickets for Game Three of the World Series. Amos could hardly believe it.

The afternoon before the game, Amos and his father drove north and stayed in a motel about fifty miles from Toronto. Game day was cold, windy, and rainy, but inside the SkyDome, where the game was played, it was a perfect day for baseball. What Amos remembered most about the game was how, when anything good would happen on the field—when Devon White made his circus catch in the fourth inning, say, or when Candy Maldonado drove in the winning run in the ninth—he would feel his father looking not toward the field but toward him, and when Amos turned, he would just grin and say, "Some play, huh?" or "Some hit."

That, Amos suddenly thought, was what his father enjoyed—
not the game itself, but Amos's enjoyment of it. Then he wondered
a strange thing. He wondered if his father was still watching him.
He hoped he hadn't been watching when he was at Sands's house,
but he hoped he might be watching from now on. Amos went over
to the window curtains and opened them wide. Moonlight filtered
into the room.

26

HEARSAY

Saturday, after lunch with her father (soup, sandwich, and salad—"all the important food groups," he'd said of his menu), Clara declined his invitation to ride along on his errands. "I've got homework to do," she said, not that she intended to do it. "And then I've got play practice at three. Could you pick me up at six?"

After her father had gone out, Clara changed into loose-fitting work clothes. What she intended to do was clean up the house for Amos's visit in two phases, deep cleaning this weekend, surface stuff the next. For the following few hours, tapping some strange source of energy, Clara cleaned between the dirty shoulders of faucets, around the little plugs that seemed to screw the toilets to the floor, beneath the kitchen cupboards where bits of cereal had skipped away from her all winter. The only time she stopped was when she screened telephone messages.

Beep: "Hello, sweetie, are you there? It's your mother, sweetie." Silence. "These calls are costing me a fortune, Clara—couldn't you just please pick up and say hello?" Long silence. *Click.*

Clara stared at the machine, then sprayed Lemon Pledge into her folded dustrag. Well, why don't you just spend your money on a plane ticket home, then?

Beep: A light musical laugh. "Thurmond Wilson, it's Lydia Upchurch Elgin with unbelievable news. I've been transferred to

Jemison. We're neighbors again! I'd love to get caught up and maybe meet your daughter. Whatsay, Thurmondo? Here's my new number. Call anytime. You won't wake me."

This was a voice Clara didn't like. This voice was more than friendly. It was flirtatious. Clara sat down in her father's chair. She turned on the desk lamp, and it made a fuzzy circle of light on the leather photo album. It was an old album with square black-and-white photos secured at each corner by slotted black triangles. Names were neatly printed beneath. Clara liked the photographs. Everyone seemed young and happy and carefree, as if they'd just been given good news, and then, suddenly, toward the back of the album, Clara turned a page and found herself staring at the name *Lydia Upchurch*.

Clara studied the photograph. Lydia Upchurch wore jeans and a short-sleeved sweater, and she stood smiling from a bridge. The wind blew her blond hair off her neck. Lydia Upchurch was beautiful, more beautiful even than Sands Mandeville. More beautiful than Clara's mother, even when she was young.

Whatsay, Thurmondo.

Clara closed the photo album. To Ham, lying nearby, she said, "I don't think I like Lydia Upchurch Elgin so very much."

Ham wagged his tail approvingly.

"In fact, I think maybe I want her to have a massive stroke."

Ham intensified his tail wagging.

Clara went over to the machine and erased Lydia Upchurch Elgin's message. "Whoops," she said, and once again Ham wagged his tail mightily.

Clara was standing on a chair cleaning the living room chandelier when the phone rang again.

Beep: "Yo, Clarita, it's me, Gerri. Dial me up. I heard something weird today that might grab you big-time. Are you there? Hello, hello, hello? Testing, one, two, three, four..."

At first Clara thought she must be mistaken. Gerri never called anymore. Still, feeling a pleasant little zing of hope, Clara jumped down from the chair and ran for the receiver. "Gerri, hi. It's me. I just got in."

"From where?" Gerri said. She sounded exactly the same as she used to, even though they hadn't talked for three weeks, even though she'd avoided Clara in the halls.

"I mean, I just got into this room. Where the machine is. I was downstairs."

"What's the matter with that phone?"

Clara thought of explaining what had happened with her mother—three weeks ago, Gerri would've been the first person she would've wanted to tell—but now she didn't feel like going into it. "There've been some weirdo calls, so now I screen them," Clara said.

Gerri didn't seem to be listening. With her mouth away from the receiver, she was whispering to someone and then suddenly yelling at her little brother. "You do, Kendrick, and your ass is grass!" she yelled at him.

Clara waited.

"You there?" Gerri said presently in her normal telephone voice.

"Yeah. Still here."

"You're *extremely* lucky you don't have a retardate brother," Gerri said. Then, "So what've you been doing, reading your horse books?" Before Clara could answer, Gerri said,

"Anyway, I heard the weirdest thing today about Amos MacKenzie and I went, Isn't Clarita hanging with him? so I thought I'd go straight to, you know, the horse's mouth and check it out with you."

"Check what out with me?" Clara said.

A pause. "It's probably not true," Gerri said.

"What's probably not true?"

"Well, I heard that Amos and Dave Pearse and Sophie Whitaker were over at Sands's having one of their brandy parties when her parents were out of town."

Clara almost laughed. Amos at Sands Mandeville's? "I doubt it."

"You do?"

"Yeah, I do. Very much."

"So to this rumor you'd say nay?" Gerri said this in a strange voice, almost coy.

"Yeah, I would," Clara said.

A moment or two passed. Then Gerri said, "There was other stuff, too." Pause. "Really weird stuff." Pause. "Some of it was about you."

Suddenly and with absolute clarity, Clara thought, *Gerri Erickson is not my friend anymore*.

"You want to hear the rest of it?" Gerri was saying.

"No," Clara said, "I really don't."

"To that question you'd also say nay?"

From the other end of the line, from somewhere near Gerri, but not from Gerri herself, came the muffled sounds of suppressed female laughter.

"Bye, Gerri," Clara said, and hung up the phone.

* * *

Clara had thought about skipping play practice. Except for her one line, she was just the prop person—they could get along without her. But in the end, Clara went to practice for a surprising reason. She wanted to see Sands Mandeville and Sophie Whitaker, to look at them in this new light, as possible friends of Amos MacKenzie. She wanted to see if it could feel true to her.

Only a week of rehearsals remained before the opening night of *The Smiling Gumshoe*, and the closer the play got, the more irritable Mrs. Van Riper, the faculty director, had become. When Clara had let herself in through the back door last night, she'd heard Mrs. Van Riper telling Bill Spender in a sharp voice to put more duct tape on the microphone wire. This afternoon, as Clara arrived, she saw Mrs. Van Riper briskly leading two of the stagehands off to the main building, turning once to say, "C'mon, c'mon. Light a little fire!"

Just inside the door, Clara took off her shoes. They weren't supposed to track mud on the stage, and socks kept the noise down behind the curtains. The flaps of black velvet were parted enough to reveal a slice of the stage, where much of the cast was crowded around Sands Mandeville and Sophie Whitaker, who were looking at themselves in handheld mirrors while Candi Allen, the makeup person, fussed with their moll outfits. Being a moll meant stockings with seams, peignoirs with matching boas (aqua in Sophie's case and apricot in Sands's), and little satin mules that Sands and Sophie had bought at Victoria's Secret. What was awful about the moll costumes, as far as Clara was concerned, was that Sands and Sophie looked great in boas and mules, and knew it.

As Clara set her bag down under the prop table, voices slid through the nearby curtain. "Then what?" said Jason Jackson, who played the smiling gumshoe and was already dressed in his trench coat and felt porkpie hat.

Sands laughed. "Well, by now Amos thinks he's going to get somewhere. He isn't, of course, but he doesn't know that. He's been lamely defending his little horse friend, so I go, 'Before further exploration, you need to admit she's a dink.'"

"And?"

"He did. Once in a whisper, and once, upon request, at higher volume."

The smiling gumshoe laughed. So did the others.

Clara wanted to slip away from the curtain, to step back to some point where she couldn't see them and couldn't hear them. But she was frozen. She couldn't move. On the other side of the curtain, Sophie leaned forward to examine the colors in Candi Allen's makeup box. Clara could see the peculiar glitter of face powder on Sophie's illuminated, high forehead. "Where's the black stuff?" Sophie asked. "My eyes don't feel mollish yet. That's not the best part of the story anyway," she said. "Tell them what happened when Gerri Erickson called Clara to tell her about it."

"Oh," Sands said. "Gerri calls and she goes, 'Hi, Clara, reading your horse books?' and of course she denies it, and then when Gerri tells her about Amos, she won't believe it, and Gerri goes, 'So to this rumor you would say *naaaaaaay?*'" Sands stretched this into the long and prolonged cry of a comic horse, and the others broke into laughter.

Suddenly Mrs. Van Riper's voice, aided by the popping microphone, snapped everyone to attention. "Okay, ladies, this is a dress rehearsal, not a coffee klatch. Get to your places and let's go through the first scene."

Clara receded. She put her finger over the tape recorder that would play first a doorbell and then a ringing phone. When someone passed by, she pretended to examine the tape recorder buttons.

"Clara, are you back there?" Mrs. Van Riper called out.

Clara poked her head out and made a small wave.

"Excellent! And don't forget the gun now."

Part of Clara's responsibility as prop person was to take the stage gun from a safe in Mrs. Van Riper's office before practice and return it to the safe when practice was over. The stage gun was used for her own stage murder. It was perfectly harmless, but it didn't *look* harmless, so Mrs. Van Riper had entrusted it to Clara and the safe.

Onstage, the lights went up. Clara started the tape—*dingdong*—then slipped out the side door and, circling to the back of the auditorium, approached Mrs. Van Riper from behind. "Key," Clara whispered.

While staring intently at the stage and actors before her, Mrs. Van Riper picked through the contents of her purse. She found the key and handed it to Clara. She turned quickly. "Thanks, sweetie," she said, smiling, then turned back to the stage. The fact that Mrs. Van Riper called a lot of her students *sweetie* was one of the reasons Clara liked her. It reminded Clara of her mother.

She went to the safe, which operated with both a combination and a key. As she spun the dial—left 33, right two to 41, left to 25—Clara thought it was a funny word. Safe. Because who was? Nobody.

When it was Clara's turn to go onstage, she had to say her line over and over again while she practiced falling. First Sean Brickman, holding the stage gun in his hand, said, "What now, doll-face?" and then Clara said, "I guess you know I can't keep this to myself." Then the shot was fired and she fell. She'd fallen four, five, six times, and still Mrs. Van Riper wasn't satisfied. "And again," she would say, and they would do it again, ending with Clara crumpling to the floor, dead.

It was nearly six. The cast was tired. Everyone wanted to go. "And again," Mrs. Van Riper said.

But this time, just before Clara was to fall dead to the floor, someone from behind the curtain issued a long, low reverberant *naaaaa*y. First one, then another of the cast broke into laughter. It was like an epidemic. Soon everyone everywhere seemed to be laughing, except Clara and Mrs. Van Riper, who came marching up to the stage. The laughter quieted.

"I have no idea what's going on here," Mrs. Van Riper said in a sharp, serious voice. "But I can tell you two things. One, cruelty is not funny. It's a weakness, possibly the worst. And two, if you people don't get focused, it will be *you* up onstage making asses of yourselves. *You*. Not me, and not Mr. Ed back there. *You*." She slowly scanned the whole cast, then turned and left without another word.

Clara bolted for the back door. It was cold outside, cold

enough to refreeze the snowbanks and puddles of snow melt. Her father wasn't there yet. Clara rushed around the corner and stood in the deep shadow of a street tree. Every now and then, the clang of the auditorium door echoed across the dark quad. Voices carried.

"Where'd she go?"

"She's gone. She must've gotten a ride."

"*Naaaaay.*"

Laughter in the dark, male at first, but girls, too.

Clara stood in the shadow thinking. When she got home, she would tear Amos's picture into tiny pieces and flush them down the toilet. She would take her horse camp money to a doctor who would pity her and straighten her nose with a complicated operation at reduced prices. The operation would leave her pale but beautiful. Still, she would begin to waste away. The doctor would fall in love with her, her mother would have to come back from Spain, and she would marry the doctor in a secret ceremony to which her mother and Amos MacKenzie and Gerri Erickson would not be invited.

"Hi, Polkadot!"

Clara hoped Ham would be in the car with her father, but it was just her father alone. Usually by this time of night, he looked tired and even a little sad, but tonight his face seemed strangely animated, as if he'd just heard good news.

"So how'd you do, Doodlebug?" he asked, looking not at her but at the blank space behind the car as he tried to back out of an iced pothole.

"Fine," Clara said.

In the heat of the car, she let herself shrink down so that her coat collar brushed her ears and her chin rested on the cold teeth of her zipper. It was a little like the way she crumpled to the floor when the fake pistol sent a fake bullet to her heart. "How come you're late?" she said.

Her father actually laughed. "The strangest thing. A phone call." He smiled and shook his head to himself. "From an old friend I haven't seen in a while." He glanced at Clara. "We just got to talking, and I guess I lost track of time."

A faint rain misted the windshield. Clara began distractedly to push against the curve of her nose. "An old friend of yours, or of yours and Mom's?"

Clara could feel her father choosing his words. "A friend of mine. But one of the reasons she called was in hopes of meeting my family." The rain was turning sleety. Her father leaned forward to turn on the wipers. Then, in an elaborately casual voice, he said, "She said she left a message earlier today, by the way."

"It's possible," Clara said. "There was a bunch of messages for me. I might've erased hers by mistake. What was her name?"

"Lydia. Lydia Upchurch." Pause. "Only now it's Lydia Elgin."

Clara couldn't help herself. "She's married, then?"

It took a moment for the question to register with her father, whose mind seemed to be elsewhere. "Oh. No. She used to be, but she's not anymore."

Clara fell silent. *Naaaaay*, she thought. She never again wanted to go to play practice, where Sands and Sophie were, or to school, where Gerri and Amos were, or to her own home, where her mother wasn't. Clara's face suddenly contorted. Tears welled and slid from her eyes, but her father didn't notice. He was concentrating on his driving. The stoplights made neon streamers on the wet roads, sending a green light across the car as they turned onto Genesee, where the streets had begun to whiten. In Jemison, it was starting to snow again.

27

ALL THE LITTLE DETAILS

The following week felt like a year to Clara. It went on and on. First, her aunt and uncle brought her mother's car back from Dalton. For one thrilling moment, Clara thought her mother had changed her mind and come home, but when Clara rushed inside and said, "Mom?" it was her aunt Marie who stepped out of the kitchen.

There was no more neighing at play practice, but Clara didn't feel like talking to anyone, even when they tried to be nice to her. Being the butt of a joke was the worst, she decided, but being the object of pity wasn't much better.

She avoided Amos. She didn't call him. She wished she'd never met him. Twice, when her father tapped on her bedroom door to say Amos was on the phone, she called out that she was doing her homework and couldn't talk right then.

If Clara had told her mother to say something like that, she would've come in and asked some gentle questions and gotten to the bottom of things, which was what Clara really wanted. But her father wasn't her mother. He just said, "How about if I tell him you'll call him when you're done with your homework?"

Clara had begun to think of her father as twins—Old Dad and New Dad. Two nights that week, New Dad went out after supper. He'd prepared them a full meal and, while cleaning up, had begun to sing some old romantic song about moonlight.

When he went out, New Dad didn't say where he was going. He just said he'd be home by eleven, and he was, right on the dot, to check that Clara was safe and in bed.

Thursday, the day before *The Smiling Gumshoe* opened, was dress rehearsal day. The cast practiced twice, once in the morning (mediocre performance) and once that afternoon (worse). "Well," Mrs. Van Riper said, trying not to sound discouraged, "it could've been better, and I'll bet tomorrow night it will be." During the practices, Clara looked at no one and spoke to no one, except to deliver her one line.

Between practices, Clara worked at Mrs. Harper's. She did all of her shopping now and cleaned once a week. In recent weeks, Clara had noticed some pleasant changes at Sylvia Harper's house. For one thing, she had a beau. That's what Mrs. Harper called him. They'd met at a mutual friend's house while playing duplicate bridge. Harold Onken was not a young man, but Mrs. Harper liked to point out that he was spry for his age. He drove a long bronze station wagon and often picked up Mrs. Harper about the time Clara did her afternoon paper route, and on these occasions, Mrs. Harper looked thrilled, her makeup fresh, her jewelry thick on the wrists and around the neck, her skirts and jackets obviously new. "Hello, Clara!" she always called. "Mr. Onken and I are off to dine!"

Another change that had occurred was in Mrs. Harper's attitude toward Clara. She was nicer to her. Often, between one chore and another, she would call Clara in to sit down and talk. One or two times, Mrs. Harper even brought out tea and ginger cookies to share while they talked. She would ask Clara questions about school and the play, and once she'd found out about Amos, she always asked about him, too. It was odd. Mrs. Harper seemed to want the real answers, not just the quick, polite ones older people usually wanted. She would listen to something Clara said—about Amos, for example—and then she would say, "Well, how do you feel about that?"

When Mrs. Harper asked this question after Clara had told her about Amos's evening with Sands Mandeville and the subsequent neighing episode, Clara thought about it awhile and then said, "Empty."

"Oh, I know," Mrs. Harper said, and somehow, Clara believed she did.

But today something occurred that shined a strange light on these question-and-answer sessions. Clara was dusting the nooks and crannies of Mrs. Harper's upright, fold-out antique desk when she came across an envelope that had notes scribbled on the back of it. *Milkman's funeral*, it said in ballpoint. *Boy's name—Amos*. Clara pushed through the little pile of notes. *$200 for horse camp. The Smiling Gumshoe. One line and death scene.* And *Father not usual self—"new dad" and "old dad."* And *Amos MacKenzie, same grade, "tall, shy, kind of cute."*

Clara stared in disbelief. She remembered Mrs. Harper pressing for details about Amos, and she remembered finally saying that he was tall and shy and kind of cute. But why would Mrs. Harper write that down? So she would remember Amos when they next talked? It must be the way old people kept their lives straight. It was like putting money in envelopes marked "Paper" or "Milk."

An hour later, after Clara had watered Mrs. Harper's plants and picked up two bags of groceries at Dusty's Oldtowne Market, Mrs. Harper appeared in the kitchen doorway, wearing a housedress and holding a black sweater. "What do you think, Clara? Can a dotty old matron carry off a black sweater with spangles?"

It *did* have spangles, and plenty of them—pearly spangles around the neck. "It's beautiful," Clara said, and it was. "Where are you going to wear it?"

"Well, I was thinking I *might* talk Mr. Onken into taking me up to the school to see *The Smiling Gumshoe* one of these nights." Mrs. Harper smiled mischievously. "Do you think it's worth seeing?"

Clara felt her face get hot. "I doubt it," she said. "I mean, compared to professionals, we're pretty lame. And I only have one line, so I hope you wouldn't be going on my account."

"No, I want to see you, of course, but I've always loved school productions." She looked down at the sweater, which she now held loosely draped over her arm. "It's just been a while since I've thought of going." She turned to Clara and smiled. "That's the thing, Clara. We're like vessels, or jars. I know you feel empty right now. After Mr. Harper died, I thought I would never, ever fill up again. But I have, a little, and you will, too."

There was a still moment in the room, and then suddenly Mrs. Harper had laid the sweater carefully over the back of a chair and was helping Clara put the rest of the groceries away. Afterward, she put water on the stove for tea and set out ginger crisps and two cups and saucers.

28

THE DREADS

For Amos, school had taken another turn, this one for the worse. He had a whole group of nasty concerns that he lumped together as *the dreads*. He dreaded seeing Sands or Sophie, and it seemed as if they were everywhere, smiling and reminding him of his deficiencies. He dreaded seeing Eddie Tripp, who seemed to be everywhere but nowhere, watching from some unseen vantage point. He looked forward to seeing Clara, but she was never in any of her usual places, and he dreaded the reason she might be avoiding him. In his spiral notebook, with a ballpoint pen, Amos wrote *dread* again and again and again.

The days dragged on. Bruce had found something new to occupy himself. He called it the Barrineau Project. "Presenting for your consideration one Anne Alexis Barrineau," he said in his Rod Serling voice, "the cosmo-ultimate example of all that might be hoped for in the female persuasion." Anne Barrineau had transferred to Eliot, but Bruce had started going to the library where Anne Barrineau studied, walking the routes Anne Barrineau walked, shopping the market that Anne Barrineau shopped. "We're not that different," he told Amos. "She likes peanut butter crackers and diet Dr Pepper just like I do."

"Two regular peas in a pod," Amos said, going for irony.

"Yeah," Bruce said, grinning. "Maybe we are."

"So when are you going to make actual contact, Crook?"

Merely thinking of it made Bruce's face turn pink. "Me? Talk to the Big A? Maybe in some alternate universe."

The Barrineau Project meant Bruce was around less, and Amos's house felt more empty than ever. Amos felt as if he and Liz and his mother rattled around inside its big hollow shell. His father's white milkman clothes still hung in the closet, his tools still hung on the garage wall, his goofy country-and-western cassettes still lay near the stereo. At first, it had felt as if his father's being gone for good and forever, his actual permanent *deadness*, couldn't be true. Now, knowing that it *was* true, that it *had* to be true, Amos had become angry at the unfairness of it, but it was a vague kind of anger—there was no one to get mad at. And now that everything was messed up with Clara, there was nobody to talk to about it.

Wednesday night, when no one was home, Amos walked from quiet room to quiet room. Finally he picked up the telephone and called Clara's machine. "Hi, it's me," he said in a low voice. "Are you in there? Maybe you're at play practice. Okay, bye." Wednesday. And he hadn't talked to her since Saturday. Something was wrong. Something was definitely wrong. He dialed Bruce's number and got his father, whose *hello* was slurred.

"Hi, Mr. Crookshank. It's me, Amos."

"Who?" Judge Crookshank said in his thick voice.

"Amos MacKenzie. I'm calling for Bruce."

"Who?" Near the phone Amos could hear the tinkling of ice cubes.

"I'll call back," Amos said, and went out to sit with the pigeons. He lifted Ruby from her nest, held her close to his chest, and thumbed her smooth, small head. Once, after a long, pleasant telephone talk with Clara, he'd held Ruby like this and whispered, "Know why I like you best? Because you're as close to a redhead as a pigeon can get." But tonight Amos said something else. He said, "Know what I'd like to do? I'd like to just flap my wings and fly away." He made an unhappy laugh and kept stroking the bird's head.

Friday morning, Amos slid a note into Clara's locker. As he turned away, his eyes were drawn to the stairwell across the corridor. On the third step, standing perfectly still, watching Amos with a half smile on his face, was Eddie Tripp.

Amos's note to Clara said, *Are we still on for pizza Sunday at your house?*

He heard nothing all day, but after last period, while he was picking up his books, he found a return note in his own locker. *Why wouldn't we be?* it said.

There was something about this question that seemed less simple than it sounded, and Amos realized that one of the many things he'd come to dread—Clara's finding out what he'd done at Sands Mandeville's—might well have come true.

29

LONG DISTANCE

Are we still on?

Clara had been shocked to find Amos's note. She'd presumed that by now, he'd've figured out that she'd heard the Clara-Wilson-is-a-dink story and never wanted to see him again. But Clara's feelings, raw and sensitive six days before, had now boiled down to something hard and salty. So, as she considered it during her classes all day Friday, she decided to have him come on Sunday if he wanted. He could try to defend himself. She could watch him squirm. She'd tried several different responses until she'd found the one she wanted, one that could be understood in at least two different ways.

Why wouldn't we be?

That night, the play opened and was better than they'd ever rehearsed it. From the wings, Clara could see it happening before her very eyes. The students had begun believing they *were* other people, and it was almost possible to imagine they were the molls and gunsels and private investigators they were playing. When Clara said her line and was shot, she actually imagined she could feel herself being shot, and grimaced and contorted and fell as she never had before. When the play was over and she came out to take her curtain call, the level of applause actually rose slightly, and Clara's spirits rose with it.

Backstage, Mrs. Van Riper caught up with Clara and threw her arms around her. "Oh, sweetie, you were so terrific!" she said. Then she released Clara and looked her in the eye. "You know how good you were? For a split second, I thought, *Oh my God, she's been shot by a real gun!*" Mrs. Van Riper broke out laughing. After she went on to talk to the other actors, Jason Jackson, the smiling gumshoe, came up in his trench coat and porkpie hat. "I just wanted to tell you, you were awesome tonight. You totally had me scared there." Behind him, Sean Brickman was nodding and grinning broadly. "Me, too. I thought I'd somehow used live ammunition. How'd you do that, anyhow? Make it look so totally real?"

And there was something else, an image Clara would replay with pleasure: twenty feet beyond Jason and Sean, with her head turned in an attitude of listening and her face slightly stiffened with jealousy, was Sands Mandeville.

It took Clara hours to fall asleep Friday night, and she was awakened the next morning by her father carrying the telephone in to her. "It's Mrs. Harper," he said. He was dressed in jogging clothes, which was news. He hadn't been jogging in years. He winked and waved, and as he left, Clara noticed the sweats were a little tight on him. This was definitely New Dad stuff.

"Hello?" Clara said into the telephone, trying not to sound sleepy.

"Oh, Clara," Mrs. Harper said, "I'm awfully sorry to wake you." She sounded far away, and there was highway noise in the background.

"It's okay," Clara said. "Where are you?"

"With Mr. Onken," Mrs. Harper said brightly. "We're on one of our little road trips. All he told me when we left is that he was taking me to see the ballplayers. What he meant was that we're going to Cooperstown to see the baseball museum."

"That sounds like fun," Clara said, even though it didn't.

"But I'm afraid I did something terribly stupid," Mrs. Harper said. "I think I went off and left the iron on. Would you be a sweetheart and go by and see if I did?"

Clara said she'd be glad to.

"And could you feed the cats?" Mrs. Harper said. "And the newspaper wasn't there by the time we left—could you bring that in, too?"

"Sure, no problem," Clara said.

"Oh, and your play!" Mrs. Harper said. "It was splendid! Mr. Onken and I both believed your wound was mortal! And I believe I saw your beau in attendance, in the back, sitting alone."

"I don't think so," Clara said. She'd peeked out at the audience before the play, and hadn't seen Amos.

"Oh, yes. We exchanged waves. He cuts *quite* a handsome figure!"

Well, if Amos came to the play Clara thought after hanging up the telephone, it was probably to see Sands and Sophie.

When Clara opened the door to Mrs. Harper's house, the first thing she heard was the ringing telephone. She left the door ajar and told Ham to stay. Clara laid the newspaper on the kitchen table, then went to the laundry porch to check the iron (it was already unplugged). The phone was still ringing. When it stopped, the house felt suddenly too quiet and a little bit spooky.

Clara moved quickly from the pantry to the garage to feed the cats, who were happy to see her. They scissored through Clara's legs, then went to work on the dish of tuna Clara put before them. Then, turning to go, Clara saw something she wished she didn't. Ham sat wagging his tail and staring happily at Clara. Behind him, leading from the front door across the hallway and kitchen, was a line of mud-colored paw prints. "Oh, no," Clara said out loud, and for a moment wanted to cry. It all felt like too much. But then she took a deep breath and went to the laundry porch for a bucket and rag.

She had just begun the cleaning when the phone started ringing again. It rang and rang and rang. *What if it's Mrs. Harper,* Clara wondered, *and she wants to tell me something else to do?*

The telephone kept ringing.

Clara, suddenly exasperated, grabbed for the receiver. "Hello?"

There was a short silence from the other end of the line. "Clara?"

It was a woman's voice, but it wasn't Mrs. Harper's. "Mom?"

"Sweetie?"

"Yeah, it's me. Clara."

Clara was confused, and her mother seemed confused, too. "You're at Sylvia's on a Saturday?" her mother asked.

"Yeah, just for a couple of minutes. Mrs. Harper's gone. I'm just feeding the cats and stuff. Except Ham snuck in and tracked mud all over the place."

Her mother chuckled. Then, after a moment, she said, "Oh, sweetie, it's just so absolutely wonderful to hear your voice." Another silence. Then her mother, trying too hard to be cheerful, said, "How *is* old Ham, anyhow?"

Clara knew that if she was going to keep her vow of silence with her mother, she was going to have to get off the line now, but she couldn't think of any way that wouldn't be awful, and besides, she didn't really want to hang up. "Ham's fine," she said. She looked down at him. "Except he tracks mud and sheds hair everywhere. When I get home after this, I've got to sweep and vacuum everything because I think this boy may be coming over for pizza tomorrow night, maybe."

Her mother laughed. "Amos may be coming over, maybe?"

Clara laughed, too, but then something suddenly struck her. "How did you know his name?"

A pause; then, "Oh, I think you must've mentioned him before I left."

Clara hadn't. She knew she hadn't. But because she wanted to so much, Clara went ahead and told her everything she could think of about Amos, even the part about his being at Sands Mandeville's and calling her a dink.

"I guess *dink* is a pejorative term, huh?" her mother said.

"It means they think I'm stupid."

"Well, your friend Amos lapsed, and a lapse might be a look into his real personality or might just be a lapse." A moment passed. "Even the best people do a bad thing every now and then, sweetie."

"Umm," Clara said, meaning *yes*, only she wasn't so sure she felt as forgiving as her mother seemed to think she should be.

"Whereas those girls are making snobbiness a way of life," her mother went on. "Those girls are horrible, and they'll grow up to be unhappy women."

This was difficult to picture. "Yeah, I guess," Clara said. Then, brightening, she said, "Anyhow, I got almost as much applause after the play as Sands Mandeville."

Her mother laughed, but it dissipated quickly. Clara wondered if it was because her mother realized she wasn't going to see Clara in her first play. Or maybe it was just because she was worried how much this phone call was costing. Still, there was one more thing Clara wanted to ask. "Mom?"

"What, sweetie?"

"How come you were calling Mrs. Harper?"

Clara thought she heard her mother inhaling. "Oh, all these weeks I just couldn't stand not knowing what you were doing, and your father wouldn't talk to me and you wouldn't talk to me, so…" Her voice trailed off for a moment. "So Sylvia was nice enough to tell me what you've been doing." She paused. "Perhaps now I could just deal with you direct?"

"Yeah," Clara said. "Maybe that would be better." But she had to hand it to Mrs. Harper, who'd been pretty good at digging up the facts. "What time is it over there?"

"Just past seven. At night. It's dark out."

In Jemison, it was still bright and sunny. In Spain, it was already night. It was like a different universe, Clara thought. She didn't know what to say, and pretty soon her mother was saying how much she loved Clara, and Clara knew it was time to get off the phone. "Are you ever coming back home?" she asked.

"Well, I won't stay here forever, sweetie, but I'm going to finish out the school year, I know that. I like it here. If you were here, too, it'd be heaven."

When her mother said this, something small and hard in

Clara made her say, "Someone named Lydia's been calling Dad up. Lydia Upchurch Elgin."

There was a short pause. "Yes, she'd called a couple of times before I left."

"Well, Dad seems kind of hyped about it. He's out jogging right now, trying to get himself in shape."

Another pause. "Your father and I are legally separated now, sweetie. So I guess we shouldn't be surprised if he begins to get out a little bit."

Legally separated. Clara stared out Mrs. Harper's kitchen window and imagined a thick wall of law books with her parents sitting quietly on either side.

Her mother tried to sound cheerful when she told Clara she would call soon, but Clara could tell she was not cheerful. She wasn't cheerful at all.

30

WOULD-BE BOYFRIENDS

Saturday night, Amos's mother was working at Bing's, Liz was out with friends, and Bruce had to go somewhere with his father. Amos, without really planning to, walked to the school, arrived a few minutes early for *The Smiling Gumshoe*, and slipped into one of the vacant seats in the last row. He knew the plot now, since he'd come the night before. Last night, when he'd seated himself, he'd had the definite sensation that he was being looked at. He'd scanned the theater, fearing he would see Eddie Tripp. But there, two rows ahead, smiling demurely back at him, had been an old lady in a black spangly sweater. She'd actually waved, and Amos, not knowing what to do, had waved uncertainly back.

The houselights dimmed. *The Smiling Gumshoe* was a murder mystery. People were dropping like flies, but these early deaths were loud, bloodless, and clearly faked. Then Clara came on, delivered her line (pretty well, Amos thought), and was shot dead. This time, however, unlike earlier deaths in the play, blood appeared. All the actors stiffened and stood frozen for a moment in what seemed like genuine shock; then, breaking character, they rushed for Clara's bloody body. Mrs. Van Riper, in one of her familiar school dresses, ran onto the stage and began shouting frantic instructions. "Lock the doors!" she yelled. "Nobody leaves! Call for an ambulance! Bring out the prop man!" Mr. Duckworth, also in normal school attire, appeared and carried Clara off the stage. Sands Mandeville, who'd been sent for the prop man, came back alone. She looked pale and scared. "The prop man's dead," she said, and then, while all the actors, as well as Mrs. Van Riper, turned to her in stunned silence, the curtains swept closed.

Immediately two students dressed as cigarette girls—pillbox hats, high heels, satin shorts, and cropped jackets—passed in front of the curtain carrying a banner suspended from a rod that rested on their shoulders. *End of Act I*, the banner read. The audience relaxed as one and broke into murmurs, mild laughter, and applause.

After intermission, the final act of the play concerned itself with finding the student who'd supposedly replaced the blank with live ammunition. It turned out to be a boy in the Clara character's social studies class. "A would-be boyfriend," the smiling gumshoe character said, putting his feet up on his desk and leaning back in his swivel chair, and the Sands Mandeville character, wearing a soft sweater and sitting on his desk, yawned and stretched in a way that showed her figure to advantage before the curtain fell on the final act.

When Clara came out and, smiling uncertainly, took a quick bow, Amos clapped so hard that a stinging lingered in his hands after he stopped. After the curtain closed for the final time, Amos drifted outside and into the shadows of the tennis courts, where he could watch for Clara while avoiding Sands and Sophie. He'd done this the night before, too, but Clara had somehow eluded him.

And she seemed to have eluded him again tonight. He'd left the courts and was just turning the corner when he heard Clara's voice and instinctively stepped back. "No, really, I can't," she was saying. She was talking to someone in a big sedan that had pulled over. Only it wasn't just a sedan. It was the half car, half truck Eddie Tripp had been driving the night he and Charles had accosted Amos. Tonight Eddie was alone. Amos could see his profile leaning from the driver's side toward the passenger window. Amos couldn't make out Eddie's words or Clara's. She'd leaned close to the window but now straightened up as a pair of headlights fell on her and the half-sedan. "There he is now. So thanks anyhow."

Clara jumped into her father's car, which slowly drove away. Eddie's sedan sat idling for a moment or two, then followed along behind. Amos, in the dark, stood watching both vehicles go.

31

PRIVATE INVESTIGATION

The next morning, Clara's father came in panting, with Ham trailing behind him. "Whew," her father said, catching his breath. He was wearing his jogging outfit and carrying the Sunday paper, which he unbanded and glanced at before going to the refrigerator.

"How about poached eggs and fat-free sausage for breakfast?" he said, peering in. This was another aspect of New Dad—he counted fat grams.

"And baked tomatoes?" Clara said. Her mother had liked to bake tomatoes.

"Yuck," her father said cheerfully, but pulled two tomatoes out of the fruit bin. He began whistling the old moonlight song, and Clara saw that this was a New Dad kind of day. Her father ate heartily, read the paper, and, after cleaning up with Clara, went up to shower. Clara could hear his singing through three walls. When he came downstairs, he was wearing a new shirt and his favorite khaki pants, fresh from the dry cleaner. When he passed by her, Clara caught the faint scent of New Dad cologne. "Okay, I'm off, Polkadot."

"Where to?"

A funny expression came and went in her father's face. "No place special. Just getting together with some friends. How about you? What's on your agenda?"

"Nothing. Homework maybe." Then, remembering, "Except that boy, Amos? He might come over for pizza tonight around six."

"Great," her father said, jangling his keys. He seemed anxious to leave.

"And I was thinking Appleby's pizza."

Her father nodded. His hand was on the doorknob now.

"But they don't deliver. So could you bring some home?"

"Sure," her father said. "I should be home by four." And then he was gone.

Clara had thought she would do the surface cleaning of the house this week, but now she didn't feel like it. Having a clean house for Amos, if he showed up, was just one more thing she didn't care about. She stood at the window thinking about all the things she might do that day but didn't really feel like doing. Finally she turned on the TV and ate ice cream and fell into a deep sleep on the sofa.

In her dream, Clara was in Spain in a big apartment overlooking the ocean. Everything was white and warm. Clara and her mother had been happy, playing cards and drinking iced sodas, but then an insect had gotten into the room, an invisible insect that made a strange, persistent tapping noise. It was driving her mother crazy, and it bothered Clara, too, because you could hear it but not see it.

When Clara opened her eyes, the tapping noise didn't go away. It grew louder. It was Eddie Tripp, staring through the living room window, tapping on the glass with a car key. When he saw she was awake, he waved her over.

It was hot in the front room. Clara, in a kind of sleep daze, came over and raised the window. Cool air rushed in. It felt good.

"Hey," he said, smiling a pleasant smile. His eyes in this light were a startling, opalescent blue.

"What are you doing here?" she said.

He laughed. "Watching Sleeping Beauty."

Clara blushed, then tried to keep the tone severe. "There's a name for people who peep through windows."

"I wasn't peeping." He grinned. "I was tapping."

"Worse," Clara said, but she felt something inside her giving way.

Eddie, still grinning, rubbed his chin and then seemed somehow to redirect his playfulness into his eyes, which he held steadily on Clara's before saying, "Wanna crawl out your window?"

The suggestion was so weird that Clara laughed. But she didn't say no. She said, "Why would I want to?"

"To say you did." Eddie stretched his grin. "And to go for a Sunday drive. And to have the best Philly cheese steak in Jemison."

Her mother was gone. Her father was gone. She didn't trust Eddie Tripp completely, but if Amos could hang out with Sands Mandeville and Gerri could find new friends, why couldn't she take one little ride with Eddie Tripp? She'd never been out for a go-anywhere drive with a boy before. She checked the time: two o'clock. "Could we be back by three?" she said.

At first, it was fun, in an uneasy kind of way. Once she'd slid into the front seat, Eddie said, "There's just one thing. The car

battery's dead, so I've gotta be careful not to let the engine die."
This made things interesting. "Wouldn't want to die here," he
said, grinning, while making a left turn in the middle of a busy
intersection or while slowing in front of the police station.
Eddie had let her choose the radio stations, and they had eaten
their sandwiches in the parking lot in the half-sedan, which he
said they called a *seduck*. "Can you guess why?" he said, and for
the first time, an actual chill coursed through Clara.

"No, why?"

"C'mon, you should guess. *Seduck*. You're one of the smart
girls. Where would that word come from?"

Clara didn't like this. "What time is it, anyway?" she said.

"Early," Eddie said. He turned the rearview mirror so he could
see his face, then wiped his mouth with a paper napkin. "It comes
from sedan and truck." He turned his cocky grin toward Clara.
"Put 'em together and what've you got? *Seduck*." He winked, then
let the car coast downhill out of the parking lot. He popped the
clutch, and the car engine jolted alive.

Clara said, "I would've called it *minotaur* or *satyr*, because
that's what it seems like — half man and half beast."

Eddie seemed to like the idea. "Is that what those are? Half
man, half beast?"

"Yeah. They're from Greek mythology." Then she said, "Why
do you need a car-and-truck like this? I mean, why not just get
one or the other?"

"It was Charles's big idea. He wanted two seats, so he could
ride in the back while I drove him around like a chauffeur. And
he needed the covered truck bed."

"What for?"

Eddie laughed. "Charles is often hauling things from one place to another."

Clara, to her own surprise, said, "Does Charles steal things?"

Again Eddie laughed. "Charles wouldn't call it that. Charles calls himself an appropriations man."

"And how about you? Do you steal things?"

Eddie's expression was momentarily serious, then returned to his characteristic grin. He shrugged. "Gotta pay the rent," he said.

Clara wondered why this answer didn't bother her more than it did. She leaned forward and ran through the radio stations until she got to an old Billy Joel song she liked.

Eddie rolled his eyes and in a pleasant voice said, "Yikes." When the song was over, Eddie said, "You're friends with Amos MacKenzie, right?"

Clara considered it. "Yeah. We're sort of friends."

Eddie slid her a glance. "Sort of?"

"Well, we were starting to be friends, but now I'm not so sure."

Eddie slowed to stare at a girl standing at a corner staring back, then resumed speed. "Isn't Amos the one who called you a dink in order to feel up Sands Mandeville?"

Clara sat back in the seat. "I guess so. That's what everybody says."

A block passed in silence, then Eddie said, "Snap quiz. Say the first thing that pops into your head. Okay: the nicest thing about Amos MacKenzie is...?"

"How much he likes his pigeons," Clara said without thinking.

Eddie turned in surprise. "*Pigeons?* What kind of pigeons?"

Clara told him about Amos's racing pigeons, and then she told him the story of Hurricane and Ruby. "Ruby's this really beautiful reddish pigeon, and I guess that's the reason she's his favorite," Clara said. "That and the fact that she came back after so long." Clara fell silent then. She was thinking of her mother again.

At Broadway, instead of turning left, toward Clara's house, Eddie turned right.

From a church clock, Clara saw that it was almost three. "I should go home now," she said.

Eddie said nothing, just kept smiling and driving. After several signals, the pavement narrowed and the car began to climb a winding road that led into the hills overlooking Jemison Valley.

"Eddie, I need to get back."

Eddie merely smiled and drove on. When he turned off the two-lane road onto a wooded and muddy dirt lane, Clara said, "What are you doing?"

"I'm going to show you something." He drove slowly, winding the truck between rocky outcroppings. The woods on each side of the road were dense. They were green and black. There was almost no sunlight here.

"What time is it?" Clara said, a kind of panic beginning to come over her.

Eddie didn't speak. He was leaning forward over the steering wheel, assessing the rocks and mud in front of him. Once, when the rear wheels began to spin, he accelerated steadily. After fishtailing, the car continued moving forward. Finally the woods became less dark and gave way to a wide flat area that overlooked the entire valley. Off to the right was another car, a red coupe, but Clara couldn't see who was inside. Its raised windows were covered with steam.

"Pretty cool, huh?" Eddie said, pulling up and leaving the

motor running. He leaned back and looked out. "It's like my favorite place."

Clara wasn't in the mood for scenic overlooks. "I've got to go now, Eddie. I really have to go."

Eddie seemed not to have heard. He just stared serenely out at the vista before him. The car engine hummed. Eddie glanced at the dark woods surrounding the clearing. In a low, joking voice, he said, "Now *this* would be a bad place to die."

A funny sickening sensation worked in Clara's stomach.

Eddie, with his gaze and grin fixed on Clara, reached forward with his left hand and switched off the engine. "Oops," he said in a low, calm voice.

It seemed suddenly very quiet. "This isn't funny, Eddie," Clara said.

Eddie kept his voice calm. He continued to smile. "No, it's really not," he said.

Clara turned away and glared out.

"You should come closer," he said. His voice was coaxing. He leaned toward her. His breath smelled minty. "It's getting cold, and now the heater won't work."

Clara sat rigidly, one hand frozen to the handle of the door.

"I'm not going to do anything," Eddie said. Then, after a little silence, he pulled back and straightened himself. "My brother used to make me drive him and his girlfriend here." A pause. "Usually they made me wait outside, but when it was real cold, they'd let me sit in the front seat and listen to the radio."

Clara didn't speak or look at him. Two forms had risen behind the fogged windows of the other car. From inside, a hand was wiping moisture from the windshield.

"Remember when I asked you whether you were a virgin?" Eddie said.

Clara felt her stomach fist. Some kind of bile shot into her throat.

The other car engine started. It began a three-point turn-around.

Clara abruptly swung her gaze toward Eddie. "Eddie, let's ask them for help. Maybe they have jumper cables. Let's ask them right now, before they leave."

Eddie seemed to be considering this.

Jump out, Clara told herself. Jump out and run over to the red car.

"They probably don't have cables," Eddie said. In the dimness, Clara felt his grin more than saw it. "And besides," he said, "we're not quite through here yet."

It seemed to take forever for Clara to jump out and run over to the other car. The driver, a boy with a flushed face, lowered his window only partway. Across the way, Eddie swung open his car door. His body rose above the roof of the half-sedan. "Hey," he called out. "What's wrong?"

"I need a ride," Clara said to the driver of the red car. "*Please*. I need a ride."

The boy didn't speak, but the girl beside him did. "Let's go, Leo." She stared straight ahead. "Let's *go*, Leo! This isn't our problem."

As Clara reached for the door handle, the boy punched the accelerator. The back wheels spun, then grabbed. The car shot forward. Clara watched it disappear down the muddy lane into the woods. She turned around. Eddie still stood beside his seduck. She could tell he was grinning.

"It's cold out here," he said in his sweet, coaxing voice. "Why don't you come on back?"

When he started to move toward her, Clara pried up a rock from the mud. "Don't," she said.

Eddie grinned and raised his hands in mock horror. "Hey, hold on, sister. Can't we work this out in some neighborly way? You be nice to me and it'll help my powers of concentration and I'll figure out some way to start the car."

Clara, still holding the rock, turned her back on him and began to walk down the muddy lane.

"Hey, c'mon!" Eddie called out. "What's wrong?"

Clara kept walking. She wanted to run but had the feeling it might arouse some chasing instinct in Eddie, so she just walked slowly, one rubbery step after another.

"Hey!" Eddie called again. This time there was something plaintive in his voice.

A few seconds later, from behind her, the engine roared alive. She looked back. The sedan was in motion, turning around. So there was nothing wrong with the battery—he'd only *told* her it was dead. It was like the running-out-of-gas thing you saw in stupid movies, only this wasn't a stupid movie. This was Eddie Tripp. Clara ran to a bend in the lane, then ducked into the woods and lay flat behind a fallen tree, blackened by lightning. The half-sedan rolled slowly along the lane, passed by, and then backed up and stopped. "Clara?"

Clara stayed low and squeezed shut her eyes. There was the sound of twigs breaking underfoot, and then stillness.

"Clara? It's me, Eddie." He was closer, maybe thirty feet away. "That was just a joke back there. A bad joke, one I kind of learned from my brother, but still just a joke. The battery's fine. If you come out, I'll take you home now."

A steady cold wind made a low, scary Coke bottle whistling in the trees. Otherwise, it was quiet. Clara was frozen in place. She could hardly breathe.

"I'm sorry," Eddie called out finally. A long second passed. "I can't leave you up here." Another second. "You could get hurt or sick up here and I'll get in lots of trouble." Then: "I promise I won't touch you. I mean it. You have my promise."

Please, God, make it be true, Clara thought before she rose and walked toward the car. She got into the backseat and squeezed herself against the right rear door, as far as she could get from Eddie, who quietly drove her home, as promised.

Only when he pulled up in front of Clara's house did he turn to speak. A hint of his cocky expression had returned to his face. "Well," he said, "you can't say it wasn't interesting."

"That *what* wasn't interesting?" Clara said.

"You know." Eddie grinned. "Our little adventure."

"I'll *tell* you what I know," Clara said in an icy voice, trying to make herself believe it. "I know that this afternoon with you never ever happened."

The house was dark. It was after five and her father still wasn't home. In her father's study, the message light flashed on the answering machine.

"Hi, it's me, Amos. I'm still coming tonight. It's kind of weird we haven't talked for so long, but I'm coming anyway. At six, right? Okay, bye."

Everything seemed wrong to Clara. The house was dark, her father wasn't home, and she felt horrible. It wasn't just that her clothes were smudged with soot from the blackened log she'd hid behind, it seemed as if she *herself* were smudged. She sat on the floor and began to cry and didn't stop until Ham came up to her and started licking her salty cheeks. She snuffled and wiped her nose. She turned on a light. The clock said five twenty-five. Where was her father? He was supposed to be home by four. He should be home, she thought, and the more she thought it, the madder she got. He should be home now, and he should've been home when Eddie came tapping.

In the drawer of her father's desk, in her father's address book, there was nothing under the name *Lydia* or *Elgin*. But under *Upchurch* she found a number along with the notation *Elgin/divorced*. Clara dialed the number.

A woman said hello after the eighth ring.

Clara said nothing.

"Hello?" the woman said again.

"Oh, hi," Clara said in a kind of blurt. "This is Clara Wilson and I need to talk to my father."

A moment passed before the woman said, "Hold on a second."

While the phone was down, Clara could hear music in the background. It sounded like Frank Sinatra or somebody old-fashioned and romantic like that.

Then her father said, "Hi, Polkadot. Is something wrong?" He was trying to sound casual, but there was strain and surprise in his voice.

"You were going to be home at four and get pizza."

"Oh, my gosh. I'm sorry. I just completely forgot." His voice sounded kind of caved-in, but then, recovering, he said, "If I pick up the pizza on the way home, I can still make it by a little after six. Will that be okay?"

Clara held out for a moment or two before saying, "I guess it'll have to be."

A silence followed. Clara realized that the volume of the Frank Sinatra music in the background must've been lowered, because now she could hardly hear it.

In a careful voice, her father said, "Did I give you this phone number? Because I knew I meant to, but I thought I went off and forgot it."

"Yeah, I think you forgot. But I kind of knew where to get hold of you."

Her father chuckled uneasily. "Well, Doodlebug, if you ever give up on medicine or the law, you could always make a career of private investigation."

But later, while standing in the shower trying to get herself clean, Clara decided the last thing in the world she wanted to be was a private investigator, because it seemed like the more you looked and the deeper you dug, the more you found stuff you never really wanted to find.

32

IMPERSONATIONS

The doorbell rang while Clara was on her knees in the bedroom, fully dressed except for shoes, which she was sorting through in hopes of finding a pair she had forgotten but really liked, sort of like finding a stray five-dollar bill in last winter's coat.

Clara dropped the cranberry pumps she was considering (too enthusiastic) and walked downstairs in her stocking feet. Carrying from the front porch were two voices—Amos's and Bruce's—and then, bursting through those voices, came the slamming sound of her father's car door. Greetings followed. *Bruce?* What was Bruce doing here? When Clara realized her hand was pushing at the swoop of her nose, she made herself stop. She took a deep breath and walked out.

Ham had already jumped up on Amos and Bruce by the time Clara reached the entryway. Amos was holding a pumpkin pie, and Bruce was holding a can of whipping cream. Her father held the pizza, and for a moment, Clara couldn't tell why he looked kind of kidlike himself. But it was because his hair was mussed and his shirt was wrinkled. He seemed hurried and uneasy. She could tell he was about to say something embarrassing, but Amos spoke first.

"My sister made pies today and she said I could bring one." He turned his eyes on Clara. "It's pumpkin."

Clara's plan had been to act a little icy, at least at first, but now she felt shy when she looked at Amos's hair, which had been wet-combed very carefully to the side. He looked tense and shy himself.

Clara's father broke into the awkward silence. "Well, I love a pumpkin pie, so you're at least scoring points with the elder Wilson." He nodded at the Reddi Wip Bruce was holding. "And today your sister made cans of whipping cream?"

Clara was about to interrupt and say that Bruce didn't have a sister when Bruce, quick on the uptake, said, "Yep, she's quite a gal. She just *loves* to can."

Clara's father laughed a deep-from-the-belly laugh, which bothered Clara, in part because she was hearing it as if through Amos's ears and in part because it seemed like a New Dad kind of laugh.

"You didn't say you were having *two* boys over for pizza," her father said.

"She might not have known," Bruce said. "I sort of invited myself."

But having Bruce there, Clara decided, was not so bad. He was at ease and able to talk when neither Amos nor Clara could, at least not with comfort, and then, when he heard Clara's father poking around the kitchen, he went out to give a hand. This left Amos and Clara alone.

Amos sat on the arm of the sofa and looked uncomfortable. Clara knew she ought to say something nice and hostess-like but didn't. Finally Amos said, "I tried to find you at school all week, and I tried to call on the phone a bunch of times. After a while, I decided you didn't want to talk to me."

"Why wouldn't I want to talk to you?" Clara said.

Amos stayed on the arm of the sofa and looked at his fingers.

Finally Clara said, "You can go ahead and sit all the way down if you want."

Amos did, but still didn't speak.

"So why wouldn't I have wanted to talk to you?"

"Well," he said finally, still looking down, "I guess you must know what happened." He glanced up—Clara did nothing to suggest this wasn't true—and looked again at his hands. "What I did was really bad, and I still can't figure out how I could've done it. But if you could possibly just not ask me any more about it…" He stopped. His face had turned red. "I mean, at least not until you have a chance to know me better and maybe have other things to weigh it against." He looked up at her with eyes that seemed, oddly, both earnest and frightened. Even while Clara was wondering whether she ought to give in, she knew she already had.

From the kitchen, Clara's father said, "We're dressing the salads. If you don't want blue cheese, speak now or forever…"

Clara raised her eyebrows in a question at Amos, who shrugged. "Blue cheese is fine!" she called back.

"I went to the play both nights," Amos said. "I liked it. You were really good, and the play was a lot better than I expected."

Clara was pleased, but she couldn't keep herself from wondering if he hadn't chiefly come to see Sands Mandeville. "You could've come backstage afterward and said hello."

Amos looked her in the eye. "Well, you might not believe this, but I didn't want to come backstage because I was afraid I'd run into Sands or Sophie."

Suddenly, without warning, a pleasant warmth flooded

through Clara. So maybe Amos actually had come to the play to see her. And he'd thought she was good.

At that moment, Bruce appeared with a tray of salads, which he set on the coffee table in front of the sofa. "Scooch," he said, and Amos moved over toward Clara so that Bruce could sit, too.

"Yeah," Amos said, "I thought you really had been shot."

Though secretly pleased, Clara said, "That's probably more of a compliment to the stage gun. According to Mrs. Van Riper, it's the same kind they use on Broadway."

Amos was smiling, Clara was smiling, and suddenly, somehow, the evening had broken free. While they ate, she sat next to Amos on the couch, but Bruce was also on the couch, so she didn't feel she had to worry all the time about how close Amos was, or whether that was Ham on the stairs or her father. And it seemed as if she really *could* forget that her afternoon with Eddie Tripp had ever happened.

They found a movie on TV and started watching it, but when Clara said one of the characters reminded her of Mr. Mueller, their U.S. history teacher from the year before, Amos said, "Hey, Crook, do Mueller."

Clara had no idea what this meant, but after some prodding, Bruce stood and, shoving his hands into his pockets and thrusting out his chest, did his impersonation of Mr. Mueller, which was remarkably like the real Mueller, only funnier. Bruce pointed his jaw sharply as he loudly and lengthily cleared his throat, then peered down, as if over reading glasses, to address Clara and Amos. "You may well wonder about Lewis and Clark. These were not merely cartographers, children! These were men of vision and men of genius! Mapping with only the aid of the stars and a sextant! And no women! Not for months and not for miles! You talk about hormonal yearning, and don't shake your heads, children, I know you do!" He paused and let his voice settle to a calmer register. "But these men! This Lewis and this Clark! They pressed northward, hormones or no!"

"Who wants root beer?" Clara said, jumping up, afraid not so much that Bruce's comments might stray too far as that her father might overhear them. Still, in the kitchen, cracking ice from the tray, it was a surprise to her that somebody as goofy as Bruce Crookshank should have this impressive comic talent. And to her surprise, part of what she felt was envy—Bruce was probably one of those kids who got decent grades without ever seeming to study.

From the entry, Clara heard the sound of the front door opening and closing. When she turned around, Amos was standing there. "Don't bother getting anything for Crook. He took off."

"For where? And how come?"

"Well, for one thing, the reason he came along in the first place was his father was in one of his moods." Amos shrugged. "His father drinks and gets real cranky until he falls asleep listening to Mozart in his chair. And the other reason was he'd heard that Anne Barrineau was going skating with a bunch of girls at the Ice Ranch and he wanted to go by there on the way home to see if he could see her."

"Bruce knows Anne Barrineau?"

Amos shook his head. "Only from afar. He won't even go into the Ice Ranch. He'll just look in through those viewing windows they have."

Clara thought about it—going by the Ice Ranch to sneak a

look at a girl who doesn't know you exist and then going home on the hope that your father's passed out so he won't bother you. "Bruce isn't so bad."

"Yeah." He sipped from his root beer. "He calls following Anne around the Barrineau Project."

Clara thought about it. "If it were somebody else, it'd be creepy."

Neither of them said anything for a few seconds. From overhead, the tinny sounds of TV voices drifted down—Clara's father was watching a movie. Suddenly, from his coiled sleep in the middle of the room, Ham blinked open his eyes, alertly raised his head, and let out a low, apprehensive growl, as if he'd heard a prowler.

Clara rose and pulled the curtain on the picture window behind the sofa. "It's not that we need privacy or anything," she said so Amos wouldn't misunderstand. "But sometimes I get the creepy feeling somebody's out there looking in."

After a second, Amos said, "Yeah, that's the feeling I get at school sometimes, and usually it's nobody, but sometimes it isn't. Sometimes it's Eddie Tripp."

Clara thought of talking about her terrible afternoon with Eddie Tripp but didn't. She said nothing.

After a few seconds, Amos said, "Do you still have that blue-and-white dress that looks kind of like a sailor dress?"

Clara laughed. "The sailor dress? My mom made that for me last year. I think it's kind of awful." The truth was, she hadn't thought the dress was awful until she'd worn it to school one day and Gerri had said, "Chip, chip, ahoy!"

"I like it," Amos said. "Or *liked* it. You hardly wear it anymore."

Clara shrugged and smiled. "My mom made it. It reminds me of when my mom was still here and trying to do nice things for me." After a second or two, she explained to Amos about Old Dad and New Dad, and how she was beginning to think it was also Old Mom and New Mom.

"Yeah," Amos said, "my mom's definitely different now, too." He turned his empty glass on the coffee table. "It used to be that on Sunday nights, my father always made cheeseburgers and chocolate milk shakes, but he'd always make a little extra chocolate shake that we'd save. After we ate the hamburgers, we'd all go into the family room at seven sharp and watch an old *Perry Mason* show. It's pretty lame, in black-and-white and everything, but I got to like it. It's a one-hour show, and after forty-five minutes, we'd each write down on a secret ballot who we thought the killer was, and whoever got it right got the leftover milk shake." Amos paused. "Since my dad died, nobody knows what to do, and my mom just goes off to the little den and reads religious stuff. So last Sunday night, we tried to do the old routine. Liz cooked the burgers and I made the shakes and we all tried to watch Perry Mason, but after about ten minutes, my mom started crying in this real quiet way, and pretty soon she had to leave the room. Liz turned the TV off, and we just sat there in the den with the TV off, not saying anything."

Upstairs, Clara's father could be heard walking from the bedroom to the bathroom. The toilet flushed, the water ran, and then he returned to his TV show.

Clara said, "We used to have a Saturday night thing where my mom would make breakfast for dinner, usually waffles, then we'd work on a jigsaw puzzle. My mother always picked ones of exotic foreign places." She made a faint smile and looked at Amos. "I guess that should've been a clue."

They fell silent, but to Clara, it didn't feel like an uneasy silence. Eventually Amos said, "What jigsaws did you pick when you got to choose?"

"Horses," Clara said, laughing. "Horses of every which kind. Wild horses, racehorses, draft horses." She laughed again. "Everything but a zedonk."

"A what?"

"When a zebra and a donkey mate," Clara said, "they have little zedonks." As she said this, without wanting to, she thought of the word *seduck*.

Amos was chuckling. "That's what the Tripp brothers are, a couple of zedonks."

Clara felt her face flush but said nothing.

Amos said, "I saw Eddie last night. Cruising around after the play."

Again Clara felt her face get hot. This time she said, "Eddie offered me a ride home." She looked straight at Amos. "It was pretty nice of him actually."

"Maybe," Amos said, but he sounded doubtful. He told Clara about the Tripps feeding a kitten to a boa constrictor and then about the episode with Eddie in the west-wing bathroom. "He just held out his arm and calmly sliced himself with that razor," Amos said. "I call that more than a little weird."

Clara nodded. It *was* weird. Eddie was weird. But he wasn't totally bad. He'd kept his promise to bring her safely home this afternoon, for example. Clara said, "Next Friday, maybe you could meet me after the play and we could walk home together? That way I wouldn't have to depend on New Dad—or anybody else."

Amos broke into a grin. "Sure," he said. "You can count on it."

When Clara's father came downstairs to get his vitamins—part of his New Dad pre-bedtime routine—Clara was shocked at how late it was. Her father was making a lot of obvious noise in the kitchen. "I guess you'd better go now," Clara said to Amos.

At the door, Amos said, "Thanks for being so nice to Crook." He looked down. "And also so nice to me."

A laugh slipped from Clara. "It wasn't so hard being nice to either one of you."

Amos looked into her eyes. "Well, okay," he said—with respect, it seemed, less to what she'd just said than to what he was about to do. He leaned forward and kissed Clara on the mouth. It was so sudden she barely remembered in time to close her eyes. She took in his soapy smell and held it. When she opened her eyes, he was beaming, happier than she'd ever seen him, and she knew that she looked the same.

"Exit Amos," she said in a quiet, happy voice, and then he was gone.

33

ANOTHER NOTE FROM THE GREAT DEVOID

When he arrived home, Amos could hardly remember how he got there. It was as if he'd moved through the crisp clear night without quite knowing how. It was a new, genial world, seen through new eyes, sensed with a new body. The sidewalk seemed to carry him forward on its own. The lighted homes seemed snug, the yards threw a wide welcome, the trees swept him along.

It was a surprise, then, when Amos found himself at home so soon. The gate had been left open, which was just like Liz, especially when she was hurrying off on a date. Only one room within the house was lighted, and that was the room that always seemed now to be lighted at all hours of the night. It was the small reading den off the kitchen. The lights always seemed to be on because his mother always seemed to be up. Even after a full shift at Bing's, she had a hard time sleeping, and her new way of filling the hours was to listen to the Bible, with commentary, on tape. A church friend had lent her a reel-to-reel tape deck along with the huge earphones that plugged into it. "The stone age of audio," Amos had said upon first viewing the huge apparatus.

Tonight Amos just glanced at his mother—she had her back to him, but the tape was slowly sliding through the two plastic spools—and walked on past without interrupting her. He was too jittery to sleep, so he took a root beer and sandwich out to his pigeon coop. It was quiet there, except for the throaty cooing of some of the birds at his arrival. From the house he heard the front door open and close; then the upstairs lights went on, first in Liz's room, then in the bathroom. So Liz was home from her date. Amos finished his sandwich and went inside.

Liz was still in the bathroom when he got upstairs. He knocked heavily on the door and said, "I need to get in there. As in *urgently*."

From within the bathroom, Liz said nothing.

"Okay," Amos said. "Thirty seconds and I'm coming in."

"I'm reeling with fear," Liz said.

"Twenty seconds."

From within, Liz said, "I'm quaking in my mules."

"Ten seconds."

As Amos raised his fist to pound again, the lock turned and the door opened. Liz, her dark eyes staring out from behind a creamy mask of white face-saver, gave him a mocking, older-sister smile. "So how do I look?"

"Better than normal," Amos said. This banter with his sister was reassuring to Amos. But Liz had changed since the funeral. She cooked when their mother was at the restaurant, she did her homework, she was looking for part-time work. She was never even late from her dates. It was as if she'd turned into an adult overnight. Exchanging insults was for old times' sake. "So how was your big date?" Liz said now, from behind her oily white mask.

"Wasn't a date," Amos said, already feeling his skin prickle.

"Ah," Liz said thoughtfully. "And did you meet this member of the opposite sex at an appointed time?"

Amos saw the trap and said nothing.

"Because if you did," Liz continued, "it was definitely a date." She gently took hold of his arm, then released it. "So how did it go?"

Almost before he could think, Amos said, "It was a lot of fun. I mean, we didn't really do anything. Mostly we just talked. But..." His voice trailed off.

"But what?"

"Well, I never knew talking could be that nice."

Liz was smiling. "Lucky you," she said, and then, giving his arm another squeeze, "Lucky her."

In the bathroom, Amos studied his image in the mirror, turning this way and that, trying to see himself as Clara Wilson might have seen him. He did this for quite a while, and then finally he went to his room, turned off the light, and slid into bed.

But as Amos slipped his hand under his pillow, his fingers brushed something foreign. It was paper, a packet, a packet that contained something. Amos sat up and turned on the bedside light. What he found under his pillow was a small paper folder. MR. AMOS was typed on the front. Inside the jacket were three color Polaroids. The first was blurry and distant, but under the light, Amos could see that it was a shot of him and Crook being greeted by Clara's father under the porch light. The next one was of Amos's mother, from the back, with her earphones on her head, which meant it was taken from within the house. The last Polaroid was of a bed. This one, evidently taken with a flash, was perfectly clear. The soft surface was a bedspread. It was chenille. It was exactly like the one on Liz's bed. Laid on top of the bed was a pair of girls' white briefs. A typed note read:

MACAMOS, MACMOM, AND MACLUSCIOUS—ALL
WORTH WATCHING.

P.S. YOU HAVEN'T BEEN ACTING RIGHT. IF YOU
WOULD JUST ACT RIGHT NOTHING WOULD
HAPPEN. SIGNED, YOUR GAURDIAN ANGLE

Amos pulled on his pants and crossed the hall. A band of
light shone at the base of Liz's bedroom door. "It's me," he said,
knocking lightly.

"It's open," Liz said.

She was sitting up in bed reading *Mirabella*, which she now
folded over her hand. "So?"

He handed the photographs and the note to Liz, whose face
grew wooden as she looked at them. "Who took these?"

"The Tripps come to mind," Amos said. He nodded toward the
photograph of the bed and briefs. "I suppose that's your underwear."

Liz got up and pulled open her underwear drawer. Everything
was in order. All the briefs and bras and slips were carefully
folded into neat rows. The briefs that had been photographed
were on top, carefully folded. Thinking of someone sneaking
into Liz's room and taking pictures of her briefs and then folding
them and putting them back sent a sickening wave of revulsion
through Amos.

Liz collapsed back on the bed. "This smells like the Tripps."
She exhaled tiredly. "Well, tomorrow we'll go see O'Hearn."

But Amos was hesitant. "I don't know about that," he said,
and then described how the Tripps had accosted him after Detective O'Hearn's last visit with them.

"But then we're letting *them* dictate to *us*," Liz said.

Amos looked down at his bare feet.

Liz rattled the note. "What's the business about 'acting right'?"

Amos shrugged. "I know Eddie Tripp didn't like my, you know, hero status. But I think he's also not that happy about my being friends with Clara Wilson."

Liz's face stiffened. "So what're you going to do, let them tell you who you can be friends with?"

Amos averted his eyes.

"Amos?"

"Look," Amos said finally, "it's not that simple. These guys are truly creepy." He wanted to say more, but had the feeling nothing would help. Liz was staring at him. Her disappointment in him seemed total.

Dad would've known the right thing to do, Amos thought as he lay down at last in his narrow bed and stared out his window into the moonless dark. *And I never will*.

Hardly aware that he was doing it, Amos pulled the bedcovers tightly over his head, just as he had used to do when he was still afraid of the dark.

34

TRUTHS AND LIES

"Amos!"

It was Monday morning, between second and third periods.

"Hey, Amos!" Clara called again.

Amos turned but barely waited for her to catch up. "Can't talk," he said. His eyes looked jittery and unfocused. They shifted to either side of her face, as if looking for someone over her shoulder. "We can talk on the phone, but not at school."

Clara felt all her good spirits draining away. "What do you mean?"

"I'll explain later. I'll call tonight." He turned quickly and became part of the stream of students flowing away from her.

Why wouldn't he want to talk to her at school when they had just had such a good time last night? Had he decided it was a big mistake? Was he embarrassed by her now? Unconsciously, she touched her hand to the side of her nose.

Out of nowhere, a nearby voice said, "I like your nose."

Clara, startled, stopped and turned.

Eddie Tripp stood grinning, just staring and looking directly into her eyes, and then, right in the middle of the hallway, he leaned close and touched the top of her nose and ran his fingertip down the curved bridge and would, she supposed, have touched her lips if she hadn't turned her face.

"I like that swoop in your nose," Eddie said in almost a whisper. "It makes you prettier."

"I'm late for World Cultures," Clara said. "I've got to go." And she did go, but not to World Cultures. She sneaked into the library and sat at a remote corner table staring at a book and wondering what it meant that, as Eddie Tripp had smoothed the tip of his finger along the crooked line of her nose, an actual and pleasant tingling sensation had run through her entire body, top to bottom, A to Z.

Sands Mandeville had receded from Clara's mind. This was in part because of the passage of time, and in part because Sands had clearly resented Clara's small success in *The Smiling Gumshoe*. But one of the things Clara was learning this year was that when it came to hurtful human behavior, almost nobody should be underestimated. And Sands Mandeville was no exception.

In leaving the library at the end of third period, Clara turned a corner and saw Sands Mandeville approaching from the other end of the corridor. It was the usual Mandeville—she walked down the hallway like she owned it. She called out to people, she smiled, she laughed, she knew she looked good. She was wearing black jeans with a green shirt, tails out. As she approached, Clara stared at the shirt with greater and greater disbelief. It was long-sleeved, flannel, and green. It was Amos's shirt. Clara knew this not just from the shirt itself but also from the cocked cold smile Sands Mandeville pointed fixedly at Clara as she passed. *Bang-bang*, the smile said. *Bang-bang*, you're dead.

* * *

White roses were sitting on Clara's front porch when she got home from her paper route that night. TO CLARA, the typed enclosure read. SORRY. There was no signature. They could have come from Amos, or they could even have come from Eddie. She told herself that she hoped the roses and apology were from Amos, either for not talking to her at school or for Sands having worn his shirt to school, and by the time her mother called from Spain a half hour later, Clara had converted this fainthearted supposition to fact. "It was so much fun," she said of her Sunday night pizza with Amos and Bruce. "We just talked and joked and had the best time." A long moment passed before Clara heard herself say, "And then this afternoon, Amos gave me six white roses."

Her mother's delighted laugh sailed across one ocean and two continents. "*Well*," she said, "it sounds like somebody besides Sylvia Harper's got a new beau."

Yeah, Clara thought. I just don't know who he is.

After dinner that night, Clara's father stayed seated. And when Clara rose to help clear the dishes, he said, "Let that go for a few minutes, Clara. We need to talk."

Clara. Not *Polkadot* or *Doodlebug*.

Clara sat back down. What did he know? That she'd gone riding with Eddie? That she'd let Amos kiss her? That she was messing up at school?

"Well, as you know, my job has always required me to travel, and I guess you've noticed that ever since your mother left, I haven't traveled at all. The company has allowed that. But they can't allow it forever because I can't do my job without servicing accounts. And the accounts are in many different cities."

Clara stared and waited.

"They've come up with a smaller territory, which means less travel. But not *no* travel."

Clara looked down at her dirty plate. They'd had a tuna casserole with no-fat cheese that wouldn't melt and tasted awful and now lay piled to one side of her plate.

"I'm going to have to make a quick trip this Thursday."

Clara looked up. Her father gave her a reassuring smile. "I'll be back Tuesday," he said. "I checked with Sylvia Harper, and she said you could stay those days with her. Or you could just line it up and stay with Gerri."

Clara hadn't told her father that she and Gerri were no longer friends. She'd presumed he must've noticed that Gerri never called or came around anymore, but now she realized he hadn't noticed at all. "Okay," she said, "I'll talk to Gerri."

This was a lie, of course, and it was also a lie when she told her father later that night that she had a headache and couldn't talk to Amos, who had telephoned. *Tell him that I'll have him paged at school tomorrow,* she thought. *Tell him to call Sands Mandeville if he needs someone to chat with.* "Tell him I have a terrible headache," she said.

Her father seemed concerned. "Oh, Polkadot. Have you taken aspirin?"

Clara nodded and refined the lie. "Tylenol," she said.

One lie after another. But after her father went away to carry her fib back to Amos, Clara sat on the floor with Ham's head in her lap and was shocked to find that telling these lies didn't bother

her, not at all. What bothered her was the *truths* she *hadn't* told her mother or her father or anyone else. That she'd gone off in a car with Eddie Tripp, or that she'd felt strange and happy not just when Amos had kissed her on the mouth but also when Eddie had stopped her in the hall and smoothed his finger along her nose, or that some part of her was glad her father was going away for a few days and she would have the house to herself.

Maybe that's just one more of the awful signs of growing up, Clara thought. When the unspoken truths are more bothersome than the say-out-loud lies.

35

INTRODUCING TRENT DeMILLE

The strange thing Amos had wondered about Monday night was the same thing he woke up wondering Tuesday morning. Why wouldn't Clara want to talk to him on the phone? Because she had a headache? But that wouldn't have kept her from at least saying hello. Because he couldn't talk to her the day before in the hall? But he'd said he would call and explain that.

During sixth period Tuesday, he wrote a note on lined paper: *Hope your headache went away. I'll call tonight.* But when he approached her locker to slip it inside, he saw Eddie Tripp standing in his overlook position on the stairs. Eddie's eyes were locked on Amos. On his lips was what looked like a smirk. Amos walked past Clara's locker as if he didn't know it was there.

When he looked back, Eddie was trailing a little ways behind, still smirking.

Amos ducked into the principal's office and asked some lame questions about an Honor Society field trip, checking over his shoulder to see if Eddie had walked on past. He hadn't. He lingered outside for almost ten minutes before leaving, a long enough time that Amos missed his bus.

"You, too?" Bruce yelled as Amos descended Melville's front steps.

Amos turned and waited for Bruce to catch up. "Yeah, I was

hiding from Eddie Tripp." He made a kind of apologetic shrug. "Some hero, huh?"

"Hey, Eddie's a damaged unit. You messed with him once. Nobody said you had to make it your full-time job."

They'd begun walking. Amos told Bruce about the pictures he'd found under his pillow Sunday night. Bruce let out a low whistle. "They really do come from the great devoid."

"The notes or the Tripp brothers?"

Bruce seemed to be thinking it over. "Both," he said finally.

While they waited for the traffic signal at Stanhope Boulevard, Amos changed arms with his books and said, "So how goes the Barrineau Project? Did you see her the other night at the Ice Ranch?"

Bruce's face brightened. "I did. She was in a short black skirt." He turned to Amos and wagged his eyebrows.

"And did you exchange a few words?"

Amos expected this to take the wind out of Crook's sails, but it didn't.

"Not that night, no."

Amos turned. "What's that supposed to mean? That you did some time later?"

Bruce nodded solemnly. "That would be partially correct."

"You can't partially talk to people, Crook. Either you do or you don't."

They waited for a bus to make a wide sweeping turn in front of them at the corner of Avenue C. "I spoke to her," Bruce said when the noise receded. He let this assertion hang in the air for a while with the bus's pungent fumes. Then he said, "She, however, believed she was talking to someone else."

Amos let out a hooting laugh. "Someday I'm going to read about you in a psychology book, Crook. Under *Adolescents, stunted*." In his mind Amos wondered how far that would be from *Adolescents, cowardly*. "So who does Anne Barrineau think she was talking to?"

Bruce turned on Amos a smile of extreme self-satisfaction. "Trent deMille."

"Trent deMille?" Amos said. "You called up and said you were Trent deMille?"

"I was going to call him Trent deVille, but I didn't want to push my luck."

Amos stared at Bruce in disbelief. This seemed to please Bruce, who said, "Trent deMille skis at Stowe and goes to a private boarding school. He drives a cool old pickup truck that's been featured more than once as a backdrop for J. Crew catalogues. He plans to go to medical school, and he captains his rugby team. Last year, because it was the state championship final, he played with a separated shoulder." Bruce grinned broadly at Amos. "Trent is a stud."

"And Anne Barrineau thinks this guy just called up out of the blue?"

Bruce kept his sunny grin. "Not exactly. I happened to notice our A. Barrineau watching some preppy guy at the ice rink when he wasn't looking. Once they actually skated into each other— something I believe she engineered, by the way—and she laughed and smiled encouragingly while he was helping her up, but he retreated quickly to the safety of his preppy friends."

"And?"

"And nothing. The preps went home. A. Barrineau and

friends went home. And then, last night, to her very great surprise, who should call but the boy who'd run into her last night at the Ice Ranch. He introduced himself as Trent deMille."

Amos considered this. "And what if she'd known the actual name of the actual preppy she'd run into?"

Bruce grinned sunnily. "I would've hung up promptly."

"Yo, Amos!" It was a classmate with his head out the back window of his mother's car as they passed by.

"So then what?" Amos said to Bruce.

"Well, she said she was very glad that Trent had called. We went on from there. We talked for some little while."

"No, you didn't," Amos said. "It was *Trent* and Anne Barrineau who talked for some little while."

"And they have a date to talk again tonight."

"But talk's all you can do! And only on the phone, as Trent the prep stud!"

Bruce shrugged. "I can do a lot worse than talking to her. I mean, I really enjoyed it, feeling like I was, you know, *somebody*, hearing Anne Barrineau laugh at Trent's little jokes, having her ask about his exciting life, listening to her talk about her own life."

"It's like Cyrano. Except you're your own Cyrano."

Bruce smiled serenely at Amos. "I didn't memorize twenty lines of that play for nothing." They walked a block in silence, then Bruce said, "What else should I have Trent do? I was thinking of having him fly to L.A. to take a screen test."

"God, Crook. Why don't you move in exactly the opposite direction? Make him a little more human, a little more like you, and then she won't be in for such a disappointment. She might even wind up liking *you*, though I doubt it."

Bruce seemed to be considering this idea seriously, but without much conviction. "Maybe, but I don't know," he said, and then, with a quick "Later," split off at Omaha Road and headed toward home.

A few minutes later, Amos turned the corner of his block and stopped short. Parked in front of his house was a black-and-white police cruiser.

36

OTHER POSSIBILITIES

Inside the house, standing in the kitchen while Liz sat in a chair at the table, was Detective Lucian O'Hearn. He turned when Amos stepped into the room.

"So your guardian angel is also part tooth fairy, eh?" the big man said.

Amos looked at him with blank confusion.

The detective nodded toward a set of photographs that lay on the table in front of Liz. "You found those under your pillow, didn't you?"

"Oh. Yeah. Yeah, I did."

"How come you didn't bring them to police attention?"

"I was going to," Amos said, and hated how lame it sounded. He shot a look at Liz for bringing the police into this.

Detective O'Hearn picked up the photographs and went through them one by one. Then he tucked them into an interior pocket of his coat. "Okay, here's the deal." He gave Amos and Liz a frank look. "Probably this is just more of the same. An extended prank. But we need to pay attention here because there are also other"—he searched for the word—"possibilities."

To Amos, this didn't seem like late-breaking news. He glanced outside and saw that the driveway was empty. "Mom still at work?" he said.

Liz nodded without looking at Amos. She was staring at Detective O'Hearn. "So what can you do?" she said.

"Well, what *you* can do is take normal healthy precautions. Lock the doors, keep the lights on, go nowhere alone. As for your police department, we can't *officially* do anything without more evidence than we have in hand, but unofficially, maybe we can scare up a little surveillance and make our presence felt."

As Detective O'Hearn was leaving, the kitchen floor gave perceptibly under his weight. At the door, he turned and looked evenly at Amos and Liz. "I'll stop by and talk to your mother at her work. But if you folks just keep your rear ends covered, we'll handle the rest."

Amos tried to smile while he nodded at Detective O'Hearn. After he'd gone, Amos, as much to himself as to Liz, said, "The last time our big detective made his presence felt, the Tripp brothers came out of their cave looking for me."

That night, when he telephoned Clara's number, Clara herself answered the phone. "Oh, hi," she said in a toneless voice. She sounded as if she were hoping it was someone else.

"I guess your headache's gone," Amos said.

"I didn't really have one," Clara said, and nothing else.

"You just didn't want to talk?"

A silence, then Clara said, "I wasn't the first not to want to talk."

"I couldn't talk in the halls. I mean, I *could've*, but Eddie was right there."

"And you can't talk to me if Eddie Tripp's around?"

Amos told her about the pictures he'd found under his pillow when he'd gotten home from her house Sunday night, but Clara seemed unimpressed.

"That could've been anyone," she said. "In fact, it sounds as much like Jay Foley or Bruce as Eddie Tripp."

"Crook? Jeez, Clara, give me a break."

But Clara said nothing.

"So was that why you wouldn't talk to me last night?"

"That was part of it."

"What was the other part?"

A few seconds passed before Clara told him about Sands wearing his shirt. "It was like she was rubbing my face in it, you know?"

"Rubbing your face in what?" Amos said, and knew at once it was a mistake. They were in cross-examination, and Amos knew from watching a lot of *Perry Mason* that you never asked a witness a question you didn't know the answer to.

In a cold, steady voice, Clara said, "In the fact that you called me a dink just so you could cop a cheap feel off of Sands Mandeville."

After a second or two, Amos said, "It wasn't that simple."

"Oh, yeah? It *sounds* pretty simple."

Amos didn't say anything. A solid minute passed in silence.

"So how'd she get your shirt?" Clara asked finally.

Amos took a deep breath. "Look, Clara, I screwed up. I admit it. I went over to Sands's and we watched a movie and drank some kind of sweet brandy and sort of made out for about two seconds before she gave me a lesson in projectile vomiting, which I had to clean up. I left my shirt there. She told me I could have it back, but by then I didn't want anything to do with her, so instead of going back over there for it, I just told her she could keep it."

"So she could wear it to school and wave it in my face."

Another silence. Finally Amos said, "I didn't think she'd do that. I'm sorry."

"Yeah, that's what the roses said."

This threw Amos. "What roses?" he said.

This time it was Clara who held the silence for a long time before finally releasing it. "The roses I guess you didn't send," she said.

Amos didn't understand this, but his footing was so slippery here he didn't pursue it. After a few moments, he said, "Do you still want me to walk you home after the play Friday?"

What Amos would remember most of this conversation was all the stony silences. Another one stretched out now. Then, in an unenthusiastic voice, Clara said, "My dad's going to be out of town on business. Which means I won't have a ride. So, yeah, I guess you'd better."

Well, I hope you can contain your enthusiasm, Amos thought, but then he decided that this was one of those goes-around, comes-around things. He'd hurt her feelings and now it was her turn to hurt his. "Yeah, okay," he said. "I'll be there."

37

PARTY OF ONE

When Clara came downstairs Thursday morning, the house seemed quieter than ever. Her father had left early to catch his flight. On the table he left a note:

> Morning, Doodlebug.
>
> Here's money in case you need it and also my itinerary with all the numbers where I can be reached. Be good.
>
> Love, Dad

She was holding this note when the telephone rang. It was her mother.

"Oh, hi," Clara said.

"Well, that's what I call a warm reception!" her mother said cheerily. "Is something the matter?"

There wasn't, not really. "No, nothing's the matter. It's just that I'm supposed to be getting ready for school."

"Okay, I won't talk long. But tell me what you're doing this weekend."

"Dad's on a business trip," she said, and then, thinking she needed to keep her story straight, she said, "So I'm going to be staying at Gerri's."

"You patched things up with Gerri?"

"Yeah," Clara lied. Then, foreseeing her mother calling the Erickson house over the weekend to check up, Clara added another lie. "Gerri and her family are going to Canandaigua for the weekend. I'm going with them."

"What about your paper route? And the play?"

Without hesitation, Clara said, "I found somebody to do my papers for me, and our Saturday performance was switched to tonight because of some conflict in the auditorium." This sounded pretty good. Clara thought she was getting better and better at lying, but it was sort of like getting better and better at digging your own grave.

Before hanging up, the last thing her mother said to Clara was, "I love you. Be good."

"Okay, Mom," Clara said, which was not quite the same as saying, "I will."

Clara's interior clock, which usually zipped along on school mornings, began to slow down. Clara lingered over her breakfast, had a second bowl of Cocoa Puffs, then read every one of the funnies. She went to the living room window. The streets were dry, but the ground was dark and damp. Sitting in front of the house, looking deserted and forlorn, was her mother's old Buick LeSabre. In both the front and the back windows were large *For Sale* signs, with all the specifics. In the car's layer of grime, someone had written, *Wash Me*, but Clara was afraid that would make the car more attractive and she preferred that it go unsold. Sell the car and you had one less thing for her mother to come back to.

Clara looked at the clock, and then, instead of going upstairs to shower and dress, she turned on the TV.

The Brady Bunch.

I Dream of Jeannie.

When she looked up at the clock, it said 8:59. School had already started. She looked down at Ham, who lay sleeping near the sofa. "Wanna play hooky?" she said, and Ham's tail swished approvingly.

The Monkees.

Laverne and Shirley.

Clara went to her father's office and read in their insurance booklet that cosmetic surgery was not covered. She called a doctor specializing in ears, noses, and throats, and the receptionist told her, "We don't do nose jobs, miss."

Embarrassed, Clara hung up.

At 10:45, she showered, put on nice clothes, and, after taking the bus to town, walked to Kaufmann's Department Store. She looked at the girls' clothes and then for a while at the boys', trying to imagine what might look good on Eddie (almost anything in black or white) and on Amos (blues, browns, and greens). Eventually she found herself upstairs, in linens.

"Can I help you?" It was an elderly woman with stiff blue hair. From her tone of voice, it was clear that she thought she couldn't help Clara, and in fact regarded Clara's presence in her department as something of an intrusion.

"I don't know," Clara said. "The last time I was in, I got some help from a nice woman. I was getting 300-count pima cotton sheets." Clara wasn't sure what 300-count pima cotton sheets were—she'd just heard her mother talking about them with her aunt Marie.

"The sheets are that way," the blue-haired woman said, and gave a vague nod in a vague direction.

"That woman was quite tall, with reddish-brown hair like mine. Does she still work there?" Clara knew, of course, that her mother didn't still work here, but she was hoping the woman might say something to explain why.

"I'm the only sales associate on the floor now," the woman said, and, curtly turning her back on Clara, began to refold a stack of oversized bath towels.

Outside Kaufmann's, Clara began to walk without conscious destination, so that when suddenly she caught sight of the Tiffin Room, it came almost as a surprise. She hadn't realized how tense she had been until, slipping into this warm room of dark wood, maroon leather, and soft music, her whole body began to relax.

"Party of one?" the hostess said, and after Clara nodded, asked, "Booth or counter?"

Clara slid into a booth and slipped the plastic-covered menu from its chrome holder. Meat loaf, chow mein, club sandwiches. The same specials, the same dishes, and—Clara looked around—the same waitresses. It was strangely reassuring.

A familiar waitress approached the table, pulling a pad from the pocket of her white apron. "Let's see, now," she said. "A Reuben with extra mustard and a strawberry shake."

Clara looked up in surprise. This waitress had always remembered her order, but it had been a long time since she'd been in. "You've got a good memory," she said.

The waitress shrugged. "In this business, it doesn't hurt." She finished writing in her pad. "So how's your mom doing?"

Clara's expression shrank slightly. "Fine."

The waitress nodded, taking this in. "Yeah, she just kind of stopped coming in here."

"She moved," Clara said. "To Spain."

The waitress nodded again. "And today—what?—you must be playing hooky?"

Clara felt her face getting hot.

The waitress laughed. "Well, there's kind of an art to it, and the first thing you've got to learn is how not to blush. I personally got real good at playing hooky, which is one reason I'm a forty-nine-year-old waitress." She laughed again. "I'll be right back with your shake."

The same songs played on the Tiffin Room jukebox, old singers her mother had taught her to recognize—Dinah Washington, Julie London, Billie Holiday—and all at once, for the first time all day, Clara was truly glad she'd played hooky. She liked it here. That was part of it. But there was something else. This was a place her mother had outgrown, but Clara knew that she herself never would, never in a million years. And she also knew that if she ever came here some Saturday with Eddie Tripp, he would make fun of the weird music and the waitresses' big hair, whereas Amos wouldn't. Amos would like it, and would sit within its warm influence and have interesting things to ask and interesting things to tell. Suddenly, thinking of Amos standing by his rickety pigeon coop on the day of his father's funeral and telling the story about Ruby and Hurricane, a kind of dam gave way within Clara, and a whole rush of good feeling for him went flooding through her.

But later that afternoon, after throwing her paper route, after going upstairs to her room, Clara saw something she could hardly believe. It was a note taped to the outside of the window facing in, so that it could be read from inside the room. In big typed letters, it said, DOLLFACE IS AN 11 ON A SCALE OF 1 TO 10. A faint thrill of exhilaration moved through Clara's body. Dollface was what Clara's character in the play was called. She rolled open the casement window, pulled the taped note from the window, then glanced down. Whoever had put the note in her window had climbed the rose trellis, then braved the steepest part of the slick slate roof. Whoever had put the note up was reckless and possibly fearless. And with absolute certainty, Clara knew who'd put the note there. It was Eddie.

38

THE PRISONER

"Uh-oh." It was the boy across the lunch table from Amos. They'd all been talking noisily. But now, seeing Eddie Tripp moving their way, the whole table fell quiet.

When he drew close, Eddie leaned back and squinted exaggeratedly at the edge of the table. "My, my, I thought that's what it said there in the fine print." He looked up and beamed a broad grin from face to face to face, stopping finally at Amos. "What do you suppose it says?"

Nobody spoke.

Eddie squinted at the imaginary spot again. "It says, *This table reserved exclusively for dinks.*"

Eddie directed his grin evenly at Amos. The silence at the table deepened. "You believe me, don't you, Hero?"

Amos looked down.

Eddie smiled mildly. "You're kind of a low talker, Hero. You're going to have to speak up."

In a brittle voice, Amos said, "Yes, I believe you."

"Why don't you come over here and read it for yourself."

Amos rose and came over. He felt like a robot on low batteries.

"Read it," Eddie said mildly.

Amos looked at the blank spot.

"Read it." This time there was a hint of the real Eddie in the voice.

Again Amos looked at the blank spot. Then, in an automatic voice, he said, "This table reserved for dinks."

Eddie grinned. "*Exclusively*. This table reserved *exclusively* for dinks."

Amos said it.

"Louder."

Amos said it louder. "This table reserved exclusively for dinks."

"Now kindly be seated," Eddie said, and Amos sat. The whole table was not only soundless but motionless. No one looked at Eddie. No one looked at Amos. No one looked at anybody. "Okay, at ease, dinks," Eddie said, but still no one moved, not until Eddie had come up behind Amos and whispered something in his ear before sauntering away.

Amos noticed two things when Eddie whispered something in his ear. One was that the menace he'd kept out of his voice for the other boys had returned in his whisper. The other was that his breath was minty.

"What'd he say?" the others asked after Eddie left. "What'd he say?"

Amos looked up at the last boy who had asked the question. "He said, 'Sometimes you don't look like such a hero to me.'"

The others at the table believed this lie because it didn't sound like one. They sat back in silence. Then, sneakily, one after another, they looked at Amos in this new light.

What Eddie had actually said was, "Your fat man paid us a visit, and I wish that he hadn't."

* * *

After school, Amos stood at the door of Big Dave Pearse's house. He knocked lightly, not quite sure whether he wanted to be heard or not. But within seconds, the door swung open and Big Dave's face broke into a wide grin. "Amos, my man! To what do we owe this unexpected surprise?"

"I'm not sure," Amos said, which was the truth.

"Okay," Big Dave said. "Multiple choice. A, money and sex. B, girls and sex. C, cars and sex. Or D, all of the above."

Amos chuckled uneasily. Big Dave stepped back, waving Amos in. He followed Big Dave through a TV room (where two other jocks lazed on old sofas watching ESPN), through the kitchen (where Big Dave dipped into the fridge and pantry for two Cokes and a bag of pretzels), to a large screened porch containing lawn furniture and a Ping-Pong table (homemade, freshly painted). It was quiet here. Big Dave expertly cracked the Cokes and opened the bag of pretzels.

"Okay," he said. "Out with it."

"Well, it's this guy," Amos began, and proceeded to tell Big Dave everything about Eddie Tripp, including his interest in Clara. Big Dave listened attentively, interrupting only to ask for clarification. When Amos was finished, Big Dave said, "Fear and loathing. That's what I left out of my multiple choice. Fear and loathing."

He took a long swig of cola, then leaned forward. "Okay, here's the deal. The first thing is, don't worry about this Clara girl. She's not the problem. She's just a symptom. When you solve the problem, everything will probably be okay with her. And believe it or not, Eddie's not the problem. Fear is the problem." He thought for a moment. "There's some Indian tribe that has this theory that if you have a significant enemy, you have to dream about him, and instead of running, you have to turn to confront him, and then—presto—he vanishes. Except in your case, it isn't a dream. You have to turn and confront the actual significant enemy." Big Dave's smile grew huge, as if he were spreading God's happy news. "Amos, my man, what you've got to do is take the bull by the horns."

Amos nodded. The reason, he supposed, it seemed easy to Big Dave was because taking the bull by the horns probably *was* easy for Big Dave. But for Amos, it seemed all but impossible. "I'll give it a try," he lied.

"Hey," Big Dave said, laughing, "either the Tripps'll kill you or they won't." His laughter tapered to a smile. "Either way, it'll set you free."

Bing's was bustling when Amos stepped in from the dusky cold and took a table in his mother's station. His mother's waitressing was depressing to Amos. He didn't like watching her write down other people's orders and hurry here and there with other people's food, having to be patient with cranky old people and smart-mouthed college boys. But his mother always put a good face on it. Tonight, as she slid Amos's chicken club onto the Formica tabletop, she said, "Already got two five-dollar tips tonight, dumpling!"

Amos wished his mother would stop calling him *dumpling* altogether, but he especially wished she'd stop calling him *dumpling* when other people were around. "That's good," he said.

Amos had just started his sandwich when, through a narrow line of sight between other customers, he saw Bruce's large form working his way.

"Hey," Bruce said as he took a seat.

"Hey."

"Where'd you go, anyhow?" Bruce said. "I waited after sixth period."

"I wanted to stop by Big Dave's."

"Really? Big Dave's? What for?"

Amos shrugged. He didn't want to talk about it. He took a big bite and through food said, "So how goes the Barrineau Project?"

"Nicely, nicely, thank you."

Amos kept chewing. "What does that mean?"

Bruce turned his fork thoughtfully. "It means that A. Barrineau looks forward to her nightly chats with Trent deMille." Bruce grinned. "These chats have become *quite* intimate."

"The details of which I trust I'll be spared," Amos said.

Bruce shrugged as if to say, *Whatever*.

"And she doesn't want to meet Trent deMille?" Amos said.

"Oh, she does," Bruce said. "But I'm afraid she'll have to wait."

"Why's that, Crook?"

"Trent's been grounded for falling under a four-point."

Amos groaned. "And what did she say to that?"

Bruce made a waggish grin. "She said we could sneak out late at night." He laughed and nodded at the same time. "I'm telling you, there's a whole 'nother world out there. It's where the Anne Barrineaus go to meet the Trent deMilles."

"You're going to meet her, then?" Amos asked.

Bruce gave him an are-you-crazy look. "Talk's better than nothing. I mean, I go around all day just replaying conversations we had, word by word. And you know what? She's got these *standards*. Like she decided to stop being friends with Roberta Quinn because she kept telling these classless jokes about Puerto Ricans."

Bruce kept talking, but Amos was no longer listening. He'd caught sight of Sands Mandeville coming into the restaurant with Sophie Whitaker and Gerri Erickson. As Sands began to scan the crowded restaurant, Amos slouched to the side, out of view. When he looked again, they were being led toward a booth that, Amos suddenly realized, he would have to pass on his way out. And the last thing he wanted was a tableside chat with Sands Mandeville.

"What?" Bruce said.

"Oh, nothing. Except I've just become a prisoner."

"Of what?"

"Of Sands Mandeville" was one answer. "Of cowardice" was another. But then something lucky happened. Sands Mandeville rose from her booth and strolled off toward the bathrooms. This was Amos's chance, and he knew it. "See ya, Crook," he said, and hurried to the cash register, but another customer stepped in front of him, and this customer had a disagreement over his charge for a second coffee. Amos considered walking out without paying but was afraid it might get his mother fired.

"Look! It's the famous Amos!"

It was Sophie's voice, sliding between customers. Amos pretended not to hear.

"Amos the famous Amos!" she called again, sharper this time, louder. It seemed to freeze one whole area of the restaurant. Amos turned and saw the falsely radiant smiles of Sophie and Gerri. Sophie waved him over.

Amos showed them his palms and shrugged. "Can't," he mouthed without really speaking. "I'm late."

But at that moment, Amos glanced up the aisle to see Sands Mandeville, a wide smile stretched across her face, striding his way.

"Hey, Amos," she said in her freewheeling way. "How're they hanging?"

Somehow Gerri and Sophie had materialized beside Amos. He was surrounded. "Okay, I guess."

"You guess? Well, if you don't know, I'm sure we don't," Sands said, which drew sly laughs from both Sophie and Gerri. But Sands kept her false smile steadily fixed on Amos. "Doesn't your mom work here?" she asked in her sweetest voice.

Sweat broke from what seemed like every pore of Amos's body. He felt his face flooding with color. "No," he blurted. "No, she doesn't."

"She doesn't? Somebody told me she did." Sands pretended to be thinking. "Not Melanie Smith, but *somebody*. Somebody told me she was a waitress here."

Amos shook his head and shrugged, trying to act mystified.

"I'll check my sources," Sands said demurely. "I'll get to the bottom of it."

Amos was backing away. He gave a meek wave to Sands and the others, then turned and was almost out the door when his mother's voice sang out. "Are you leaving, dumpling?" she called, and Amos, after the very slightest hesitation, pretended he didn't hear and with burning cheeks walked out into the cool night air.

Amos stopped at his front gate and stood where he'd first seen Clara Wilson standing in the snow with her dog staring at his house. It was not that long ago, but it felt like a previous lifetime, before he'd run into the Tripps, before his father had died, before his mother worked as a waitress, before his sister had suddenly grown up and Amos had grown into a coward.

Amos set the gate behind him. He was nearly to the steps when he spotted the square edge of a paper envelope peeking from beneath the front door mat. Initially, and without reason, Amos's hopes leaped toward the notion that it was a letter from Clara. It wasn't. MR. AMOS was typed on the front of the envelope, but inside was a blank note card, absolutely blank, no picture, no inscription, nothing.

Amos went room to room, turning on lights. Nothing seemed wrong, nothing seemed disturbed. He was standing in the kitchen wondering where to look next when a bad feeling took hold of him. He walked to the rear of the house, flipped on the backyard light, and headed for the pigeon coop.

The pigeons were acting strange, flying from one side of the coop to the other, and none were acting stranger than Hurricane. The big gray pigeon flew frantically from one side of the coop to the other, setting down in places where there was no purchase, slipping and flapping and flying again. The one pigeon that wasn't unsettled was Ruby. Ruby lay in a dim corner of her box. Amos entered the coop and came close. The beautiful red bird lay on her side with her beak open.

She was dead. She was without question dead.

"No," Amos said, low and disbelieving. "No, no, no."

He stood in the coop holding the bird in his hands. He held her a long time. At first she was still warm, but as he held her, she began to stiffen. Eventually he laid her back in her nest and brought a shovel from the shed. He slowly began digging a hole in the dirt in the center of the coop. She was going to lie as close to Hurricane as he could make it. He dug steadily, rhythmically in the fertile damp earth. The other pigeons had begun to settle. They resumed their soft cooing and gurgling. Amos dug the hole deep. Finally he wrapped the pigeon he'd called Ruby in an old towel and set the towel into a little wooden box, which he laid into the ground and began to cover with dirt.

Behind him, he heard the back door open and close. Amos, turning, saw Liz standing on the back stoop. "What're you doing?" she said.

Amos felt like he was swimming against a terrible current. "A pigeon died. I buried her."

Liz peered across the yard. "An old one?"

"Yeah."

"Not Hurricane or Ruby?"

After a second's hesitation, Amos decided to lie. "No."

Liz seemed relieved to hear this. "Need any help?"

"No."

When he was done burying the bird, Amos sat on his box inside the coop, holding Hurricane in the palm of his hand, settling the bird, stroking his broad head, saying, "It's okay. It's going to be okay." Finally the bird grew still and Amos stopped talking. But he didn't leave. He stayed there so long that another of the pigeons flew down with a quick shuffle of wings and landed on his shoulder, and then another followed, so that at last there Amos was, a boy with one pigeon in his hands and two more roosting on his shoulders while he sat, not moving, not talking, just wondering what in the world to do next.

39

TWO CONVERSATIONS

When Clara called Amos Thursday night, Liz said he was out in the pigeon coop. It seemed to take so long for him to come to the phone that Clara wondered if he was coming reluctantly or maybe didn't want to come at all, so that she was all the gladder when she finally heard his voice.

"Hi," he said.

And just like that, Clara knew something was wrong, and asked what.

"Nothing."

Clara took a deep breath. "Look, Amos, I know last night I was kind of creepy, but it was because I was mad, but now I'm not, not at all." She paused. "I played hooky today. I didn't know what I was going to do when I started out playing hooky this morning." She waited, and then she just went ahead and said it. "But it turned out that I spent most of the day thinking about you."

Amos didn't say anything.

"I guess you haven't been thinking about me, huh?" Clara said.

"No, it's not that." He waited. So did Clara. Then he said, "I doubt you'd remember, but there was a pigeon I really liked, a red one."

"Ruby," Clara said.

"Yeah."

"Why? Did something happen to her?"

"Yeah," Amos said, and explained what he knew. When he was done, Clara said, "What do you think killed her?"

"I don't know," Amos said. "That's what's so weird. I'd checked on all of them this morning before school. I *held* Ruby. She was fine."

"So you think some*body* did something to her?"

Amos didn't answer.

"You do, don't you?"

"Maybe."

A bad feeling moved through Clara. "No guesses?"

A second or two passed before Amos said, "No guesses."

After a long pause, Clara said, "You think Eddie, though, don't you?"

Silence, then, "I don't think anything, Clara." And then: "The truth is, I *don't* think Eddie. I mean, how could Eddie possibly know that Ruby was my favorite?"

This time it was Clara's turn to be quiet. Because she knew how Eddie might know. Only she couldn't say so to Amos.

It was just one more case of the truth being worse than the lies.

Third period Friday, Clara found Eddie out behind metal shop with two other boys, who vanished when Eddie gave them a get-lost look. "It's funny you're here," he said, turning back to Clara. "I was just thinking about you."

Clara brushed past this. She knew what she meant to say, and she meant to say it without any preparation. "Amos MacKenzie's favorite pigeon died yesterday," she said, and watched Eddie's face, but it registered nothing. His smile didn't change one iota. "Didn't even know the hero had pigeons," he said.

"Yeah, you did, Eddie. I told you about them. That day we went for a drive."

"How could that be," Eddie said, grinning, "when that drive didn't even exist?" His grin was set. "Isn't that what you told me? 'This never happened.'"

"C'mon, Eddie. I don't care what you tell me as long as it's the truth." To this, she added a lie that she thought might make it easier for him to confess. "I mean, I don't really care if you *did* do it. It was only a pigeon. But I just want to know."

Eddie's grin slowly dissolved. He looked serious. He looked directly into her eyes, just as he had that day in the halls before he smoothed his fingertip along her nose. "No," he said, "I didn't kill the hero's stupid pigeon."

She believed him. And the fact that she believed him changed things. There was a silence. From somewhere within the shop came the rhythmic *clink clink clink* of hammer to metal. It coincided roughly with Clara's heartbeat.

"I got some roses on Monday," she said.

"Oh, yeah, those," Eddie said. He ducked his head and rubbed his neck. "Well, those are another thing. When it comes to those, I don't have what they in presidential circles call deniability."

"The note said 'sorry.' Sorry for what?"

Again Eddie grew serious. He leaned close enough that Clara could smell the sweetness of the mint he was chewing. "For that little ride on Sunday that you never took," he said.

"I also found a note taped to my upstairs window," Clara said.

Eddie's face broke into a broad grin. "That was what I'd call fun."

Clara's heart was pounding. Eddie was no longer grinning. He was staring. His eyes seemed to go right through her. She wished he would do something, but she didn't know what.

"You doing anything tonight?" he said.

"No," she said, forgetting her arranged meeting with Amos, but then, remembering something else, she said, "But I can't do anything tonight."

"How about tomorrow night, then?"

She shook her head. "It's not that I have plans. It's my dad. He's gone on business till Tuesday."

A mistake. Clara felt at once it was a mistake to have said her father was gone, and as if to confirm this fear, a sudden flicker of recognition registered in Eddie's eyes. "So my aunt's staying with me," Clara said quickly. "My aunt Marie."

She felt her face flush with this lie, and she watched Eddie's serious expression relax into an odd, satisfied grin. "Sure," he said. "I understand."

40

A BLUES BROTHER'S BROTHER

Just before midnight, Amos had fallen into a deep dreamless sleep, and he had awakened before dawn Friday morning with a strange sense of focus. Take the bull by the horns. Turn and face the enemy. It's what his mother had done with their financial problems. It's what real people did. Amos turned on the light and dressed in his father's boxer shorts and V-necked undershirt. Then, while his mother was in the shower, he put on one of his father's shirts, which fit, and one of his father's thin dark ties. He decided to try a suit on for size, a dark somber suit. It fit with a loose baggy look that Amos liked, and he felt comfortable in it. He put on his black high-top basketball shoes. Then, while his mother was still in the bathroom and before his sister had even gotten out of bed, Amos stole out of the house.

In the cold bright sunlight, Amos walked and breathed deep. He already had his direction in mind, his destination, his course of action. He turned north on Walnut, avoiding Genesee, and walked uphill toward the expensive homes of Bandy Ridge. He leaned forward, into the grade, and kept up his pace until he turned into the long cobblestoned driveway of the house he'd decided to visit. Standing before the wide white door, Amos didn't pause before ringing the bell.

Though it turned out it was not a bell. There were chimes, a short melody of rich tones. From an unseen speaker, a woman's voice said, "Yes?"

Amos said, "I need to talk to Sands."

A moment passed. "May I tell Sandra who's calling?"

"Amos. Amos MacKenzie."

"Of course. Let me see if she's available."

Amos waited what seemed like a long time. Finally the enameled front door swung open. Warmth from within spread out. Sands stood there in shorts and a loose white T-shirt with some kind of fancy white-on-white embroidery at the neck. She broke into a smile. "God, with a hat and dark glasses, you'd look like a Blues Brother!" She broke into an easy laugh. "Or maybe a Blues Brother's brother!"

Amos didn't laugh. He waited patiently until Sands wasn't laughing, either. "I want to correct something," he said. "I just want to tell you that my mother *does* work at Bing's, and I'm sorry I didn't say so last night."

Sands smiled. "No need to apologize," she said.

"I'm not apologizing to you. If anyone deserves an apology, it's my mother."

Sands seemed to think he was suggesting that she apologize to his mother, because she said, "Hey, that's between you and your conscience. My rule is, Never apologize, never explain."

Amos gave her a somber stare. "I'm also here for my shirt."

Sands's eyes widened. "The one you gave to me?"

Amos nodded. "And the one you're now going to give back."

Sands seemed amused. "Why would I want to do that?"

Amos looked away for a moment, then redirected his gaze to Sands. Some of this technique, he realized, he'd learned from

Eddie. In a calm, steady voice, he said, "So as to avoid difficulty in your personal life."

Sands laughed, but not very hard. "Like what kind of difficulty?"

"I know stuff. For example, I know exactly how you and Sophie cheat in geometry."

Sands held his gaze for a few seconds, then all at once her eyes and smile seemed to give way. It was as if her whole aura collapsed. She opened her mouth as if to speak but didn't. She spun and walked away, leaving the door partly open behind her. He watched her disappear.

A few minutes later, a Hispanic woman appeared. "Miss Sandra sends this to you," the woman said, and in her extended hands, laundered and neatly folded, lay Amos's green shirt.

Amos stared at Clara's house from the bus stop across the street, standing in the shadows of a newly leafed elm. Clara's mother's dirty car was out front with the *For Sale* sign in the window. Her father's car was gone. As Amos watched, Ham ambled around the corner into the front yard, found a spot of sun on the front porch, circled tightly, and lay down.

Amos felt in his pockets and found a pencil and a business card from Long's lawn mower repair. THIS IS FOR YOU, he wrote in small block letters. SORRY ABOUT SANDS. AMOS. He stepped out of the shadows, opened the Wilsons' side gate, and latched it behind him. In the planting beds along the path, the soil was dark and chunky and gave off the rich pleasant smell of just-turned earth. Three terra-cotta rabbits sat in a row, as if waiting for the first tender shoots to appear. As Amos approached the front door, Ham's eyes snapped open and he let out a low growl. "Hey, Hambone," Amos said in a low, calming voice. "It's just me, Amos." He held out his hand, which Ham sniffed, then licked. Amos leaned the green shirt against the front door, tucked the note into its front pocket, and walked away.

There, Amos thought.

Maybe it would help, maybe it wouldn't. That didn't matter. What mattered was that he'd done something, and he was just getting started.

41

SETTING OFF IN THE DARK

Clara's skin ached. She was sitting in World Cultures thinking of Eddie Tripp. What had he meant when she'd said her father was away on business and something had flickered in his eyes and he'd grinned and said, "I understand"? *What* did he understand? Clara didn't know, but there was something in that look and those words that made her a little queasy.

Clara thought of how in this very class, she'd learned about communities in ancient cultures that would symbolically gather up all their sins and crimes and put them in a headdress and then put the headdress on a goat and drive the goat from the community, so they could get rid of the sins and crimes without really accounting for them, so that everybody could feel better about themselves and their neighbors. "This," Mrs. Templeton had said, "is known as a scapegoat."

Clara thought about her own neighborhood. Ever since she could remember, almost every strange thing that occurred and couldn't be explained was blamed on the Tripp brothers. Some government checks had disappeared from several mailboxes. Neighbors blamed the Tripps. A cat's head was found in someone's trash can. Blame the Tripps. Someone put sugar in the sixth-grade teacher's gas tank. Blame the Tripps. And when Amos MacKenzie's favorite pigeon died? Blame the Tripps. But nobody ever proved these things. So maybe Eddie and Charles didn't do them at all. Maybe Eddie and Charles were just the scapegoats.

Still, there was something creepy about the way Eddie had smiled and what he'd said. That was what was making her skin ache.

For the rest of the day Clara wasn't sure who she wanted to see in the halls, Eddie or Amos or neither or both. For a while, she saw neither.

She did see Bruce, however, coming out of study hall.

"Hey, did you check out Amos today?" Bruce said, and when Clara shook her head, Bruce said, "He's wearing this goofy suit with a tie and everything. You ask why and he goes, 'I've got an appointment.'"

"An appointment? Who with?"

"That's the funny part. He won't say. He just vagues out on you." Bruce grinned and shook his head as if in wonderment. "I don't know about our Amos. He used to be the dependable type, and now he's just as weird as the rest of us."

An hour later, when Clara finally did spy Amos in the halls, she was relieved at the way her spirits rose, the way her heartbeat quickened.

"Hey, it's Joe Friday," she said as they fell into close and easy proximity.

Amos grinned and glanced down at his clothes. "It's my father's suit. I tried it on for size this morning and kind of liked it, so I just left it on."

This seemed like the old Amos to Clara, the calm, quiet, friendly Amos. His eyes weren't nervous. He didn't mind standing in the halls talking with her. "Bruce said you said you had an appointment."

"Yeah, but I haven't had it yet."

"But who with?"

Amos shrugged. "It's kind of personal. I can explain better afterward."

"After *what*, though?"

Amos shrugged and smiled. "After the appointment."

This was exasperating, but before Clara could pose another question, Amos said, "I left you something by your front door at home."

Mild pleasure worked through Clara. "You did? What is it?"

Amos ignored this. The passing bell rang loudly. The clamor in the hall intensified. "So I'll see you tonight right after the play?" he said.

Clara nodded happily and began to backpedal. "C'mon," she called, "tell me what it is."

Amos stood fast, a rock around which other students streamed. "Well, it's not a new car," he said, grinning, "and it's not white roses."

The green shirt lay folded and propped against the front door. In the pocket, on the back of a business card, was a message. THIS IS FOR YOU, it said. SORRY ABOUT SANDS. AMOS.

Clara's pulse accelerated slightly. Her mood, already bright, brightened further. She suddenly realized her skin no longer ached.

She began to fold and band her newspapers, but her eyes kept floating off to the shirt, lying neatly on the front porch bench. Once or twice, she got up and moved it slightly, just to touch the soft flannel.

Clara nearly ran through her route, came home, made some Top Ramen, and still had some time to kill before walking to Melville for the play. She tried to read, but her gaze kept drifting toward the shirt, which sat now on top of her dresser. She was feeling too good about it, she decided, and whenever you felt too good about something, it was the same as inviting a come-uppance.

Clara jumped up, grabbed the shirt, and climbed through the ceiling of the hall closet to the attic, where her hope chest was stored. There wasn't much in it yet for a trousseau, only a brooch her grandmother had given her, a baby quilt, and a pair of em-broidered pillowcases. Otherwise, it held old artwork, old birth-day candles, and her old collection of Seneca arrowheads. Clara laid the shirt neatly on top and looked at it for a long moment.

Then Clara climbed down the ladder, brushed her teeth, combed her hair, and regarded her crooked nose for one last long moment before setting off in the dark for Melville.

42

THE WAITING ROOM

Amos hadn't seen Eddie all day, but he knew he would sooner or later, at the appointed time. He already felt better—not good exactly, but on the verge of feeling good. He'd liked standing and talking to Clara in the halls, almost willing Eddie to come around the corner. He liked telling her he'd left something on her doorstep. And he liked thinking of seeing her after the play.

He didn't change clothes after school. He wore the loose suit to *The Smiling Gumshoe* and, before curtain, kept scanning the audience for Eddie. He wasn't there. Except for one empty seat to the rear right, it was a full house. When a student started to take that last seat, an usher quickly appeared and explained something, and the student rose, leaving the single seat vacant again. Saved for somebody, Amos thought. The principal or somebody like that.

Presently the lights dimmed, the curtain rose, and Amos settled into the play. He'd seen it twice before, and the familiarity of the words and the dark warm auditorium induced Amos into a light but pleasant sleep, from which he was awakened by the explosion of the stage gun. He snapped open his eyes to see Clara falling forward with her mortal wound.

After the cigarette girls in their gold satin shorts had walked in front of the curtain with the banner that said END OF ACT I, after the audience had broken into applause and the houselights had come on, as various playgoers rose and stretched and drifted toward the lobby, a large form pushed his way into the auditorium against the current, his bald head rising above the crowd.

It was Charles Tripp.

Amos followed his direction to the single seat that had been kept vacant, but no longer was. Sitting there now was Eddie Tripp. He must've come in after the houselights were off, Amos thought. But it didn't matter. There he was. The guy he had the appointment with.

Charles was leaning close to Eddie, telling him something. When Eddie rose and he and Charles moved quickly for the exit, Amos stood and followed.

Okay, he thought. Here goes.

But outside, he lost sight of the Tripps. Amos lingered in the shadows. He wanted to see Eddie Tripp, not Charles. His appointment was with Eddie. Amos ventured further and further out. Then, suddenly, off to the left, he saw their half-sedan backing out of a parking space and beginning to move away.

Amos began to run, staying in the shadows of the tree-lined parking strip but losing ground on the vehicle until, fifty yards ahead, a green light dissolved into orange and then red. The half car, half truck pulled up to the light.

Okay, a voice within him said. *Do something. Just do it.*

Amos sprinted through the shadows. He drew close, closer.

The red light turned green.

As the half-sedan eased ahead, Amos lunged forward, caught hold of the back pickup rail, and was pulled awkwardly forward. He grabbed tight, retracted his feet, and felt his kneecaps swing hard into the bumper. A few terrifying seconds passed as the car moved along with Amos hanging only by his fingers, with his feet curled up behind him and rough asphalt sliding beneath him, but then he chinned himself up, and his feet found the bumpers. He rolled over the tailgate into the truck bed, hidden behind the lockbox. He took a deep breath. He was on board.

When the half-sedan slowed and turned off of Albany Avenue, a well-lighted four-lane street, and onto a dim residential street, Amos edged himself up and peered out over the lockbox. It was a tidy neighborhood that Amos recognized as the Kensington District, on the opposite side of Bandy Ridge from Clara's house. Older cottages sagged beside newer duplexes and a few home businesses.

As the Tripps' half-truck slowed further, Amos's body tightened. He slid over the tailgate and held himself in a crouching position on the rear bumper. To his right, a beauty shop was attached to a yellow stucco house. A spotlight shone on the word *Rae's*, painted in brilliant red.

Just beyond Rae's, the half-truck turned into a gravel driveway.

Amos leaped off the back, ducked into nearby shrubs, and lay perfectly still.

The Tripp brothers emerged laughing from the car.

"Well, when you're in the mood, you're in the mood," Charles said, and Eddie let out the cackling laugh that Amos remembered from that night in front of the Goddards' house.

Amos peered out from the bushes. At the end of the gravel driveway, sitting above an open and empty two-car garage, was an apartment with 2902A painted in ragged black on the white stucco wall. The front door and cantilevered front porch were reached by wooden stairs, which the Tripps were now ascending.

"'Course I'm *always* in the mood," Charles said, which brought more laughter from Eddie.

They didn't go through the front door. There were four windows running along the upstairs porch. Charles went to the third of these windows, slid it open, and with surprising agility slipped inside. Eddie followed behind. A moment later, one of them switched on the interior lights.

This, Amos realized with sudden clarity, was where the Tripp brothers lived.

Behind the apartment's windows, Eddie and Charles were moving about the lighted room, vanishing into other rooms, returning again. Both drank from tall glasses and talked in low voices, with Eddie's laughter carrying out into the night. At one point, to Amos's astonishment, Charles seemed to say, "Okay, then," and then lowered himself from view, which made no sense, because the garage below the apartment remained empty and dark.

And then, a few minutes later, Charles's shaved head and huge body rose again into the lighted room.

The lights went out, and the Tripps exited as they'd entered, through the third window, which they now closed after them. They were both wearing dark clothes.

"So we make her wait a few minutes," Charles said, and laughed. "I'll tell you what making her wait is. Making her wait is a freaking mood enhancer." He laughed thickly, and Eddie's cackle followed.

The tires spat gravel as Eddie backed the half-sedan quickly out of the driveway, and Amos lay flat, eyes down, while the headlights passed over him as the Tripps turned onto the street.

Amos stood and watched the taillights disappear. *Make who wait?* he wondered. He looked at the street, then at the apartment. He walked up the gravel, each step a loud crunching sound. The garage was empty except for empty oil cans, half-filled Hefty bags, and other trash. The walls were freshly painted, and the back wall was covered with sheetrock and hanging tools. Nothing was odd, except that it seemed shorter than most garages.

Amos went to the foot of the stairs and looked up. Don't hurry and don't sneak, he thought. Hurrying and sneaking attract attention. Amos took one step, then another. His heart felt like it had risen from his chest and wedged itself between his ears, where it pounded fiercely.

Don't sneak. Don't hurry. One step at a time.

When he reached the upstairs porch, Amos went straight to the third window and, without looking around, slid it open. He bent and stepped easily through.

Amos was inside, breathing again. The pounding in his ears softened a little.

He switched on a light. To his surprise, the place was tidy. Tidy and strange. It looked like a military dormitory. Instead of bureaus, there were two khaki-colored footlockers. The two twin beds were covered with army blankets and wrapped tight as wontons. Along one wall, an old khaki green door lay atop two stacks of milk crates to make a desktop, on which sat a newish wide-screen Sony, a neat stack of dirty magazines, a large, military-style flashlight, and a book called A *Teenager's Guide to the Legal System*.

There were three more doors in the room. One led to the kitchen, almost as tidy as the bedroom. The rinsed glasses in the sink still smelled of liquor. Within the refrigerator, besides Red

Dog beer, white tequila, and some red syrupy liquid in a tall bottle, there was Kix, Cap'n Crunch, sugar in a sack, Oreos, pork rinds, and barbecued potato chips. Stuff, Amos thought, you usually kept in cupboards, unless your cupboards had cockroaches. He swung open the freezer compartment. It was cold and frosty but contained no ice, no ice cream, and—half to Amos's disappointment, half to his relief—no frozen snakes.

The second door led to a bathroom, also spic-and-span, and the third door accessed a closet, with clothes hanging neatly on poles. But there was something else. Hanging from the interior side of this closet door was a fold-out photograph of a naked woman with tiny random holes punched through her. The photo had been used as a dartboard. Even now, three feathered metal darts protruded grotesquely from the punctured woman. It revolted Amos. He quickly pushed the door closed.

He looked around. So where had Charles lowered himself? And into what? Amos went over to the place at the rear of the room where Charles had seemed to be standing. There was nothing there but one of the heavy footlockers.

When Amos gave the locker a push, it and the rug beneath it slid aside and revealed something surprising. There, in the floor, was a flush-hinged trapdoor.

Amos gingerly lifted the small door and peered in. Nothing but darkness. He grabbed the flashlight from the desk and directed its beam into the hole. A slanted wooden ladder led down to a small room. Amos's heart again began to beat furiously. It was creepy. It was definitely creepy.

Okay. One step at a time.

He descended carefully, using the flashlight to illuminate

each spot where his foot would step next. When he was standing inside the small room, he scanned its contents with the light. It was filled with merchandise, all neatly sorted and stacked. Car stereos. Color televisions. Ornate silverware. Watches. Rings. It was like a modern version of a pirate's trove with glittery secret treasure. Except this trove had been stashed in a dark secret vault built at the back of a garage.

There was something else, too. Standing on one chest-high shelf was a typewriter, with a stack of clean paper beside it. Amos slid one of these sheets into the typewriter's roller. He picked out the letters from the keyboard one by one, *tap tap tap*. DEAR MR. AMOS. It was the same typewriting. Identical.

A noise. Amos thought he heard a noise. He switched off the flashlight, stood perfectly still, and heard only his heart pounding in his ears.

He pulled the paper from the typewriter, climbed the ladder, and was sliding the locker and rug back into place when he suddenly froze. A car was pulling up the graveled driveway. A car with loud music. Then the music stopped.

Amos went to the window and peeked out. Down below, a girl emerged from a dilapidated Honda Civic and headed toward the stairs. Amos spun around, looking wildly for another exit, but there wasn't one.

Down below, the Civic was driving away, but the girl's clicking footsteps could be heard on the stairs, approaching.

The closet? The kitchen? The bathroom? Amos listened to the girl's footsteps on the stairway. In a panic, he slid under one of the twin beds and hugged himself close to the wall. The front window opened.

"Chazbro? Eduardo?"

Amos held his breath.

From beneath the bed, he saw first one, then another black platform shoe step through the window. He watched them click across the linoleum.

"Charles? Eddie?" she called out. Then, under her breath, "You assholes."

She returned to the window and closed it. Then she went to the kitchen, opened a bottle, and walked into the bathroom, but without closing the door. Amos listened to the watery sounds of urination.

If he tried to escape, she might turn and see him. Probably she would hear him. But she couldn't really come running out at this moment.

Quickly Amos slipped off his shoes, slid from beneath the bed, and eased across the linoleum. He was nearly to the window when a pair of headlights turned into the driveway. It was the half car, half truck. The Tripps.

Behind him, the toilet flushed. Down below, the gravel crunched.

Cornered, frantic, Amos dropped back under the bed.

"Well, well," Charles said once he and Eddie were inside the apartment. "Here's our little wayward Brandykins."

"I'm here," the girl said, "but I'm not little, not wayward, and not yours."

Eddie let out a sharp cackling laugh. Charles, however, was silent. The Tripp brothers were wearing black Nikes. The smaller ones—Eddie's—went to the kitchen and came back with what sounded like iced drinks. "Tequila sunrises," he said.

"I'll stick to Red Dog," the girl said.

A tinkling of ice cubes, then Eddie went to the closet door, swung it open, and backed away from it. *Thunk. Thunk.* He was throwing darts at the fold-out. One of the darts bounced off the door and rattled to the ground, near the bed. Amos watched Eddie's hand pick it up. A thin straight scar ran across his forearm. It was so close Amos could've grabbed it. But this wasn't the appointment, he could feel it in his bones. This was more like the waiting room.

In a calm voice, Charles said, "And yet, Brandykins, now that I think of it, I believe I told you to wait."

"I *did* wait, you moron. I waited for something like forever."

Again, Eddie's cackling laugh.

Charles, however, was patient. "And then?"

"And then I got a ride."

"You got a ride," Charles repeated. "And who did you get a ride with?"

"Some guy who was nice enough to offer. Some guy who was *there* when the guy who was *supposed* to be there wasn't."

Thunk. Thunk. Then Eddie laughing and saying, "Now *that's* a delicate shot."

Charles ignored Eddie. His feet were still turned toward the girl's black platforms. "Some guy," Charles said. "What was some guy's name, Brandykins?"

"Why? What's it to you?"

Suddenly Charles's shoes moved closer to hers.

"Jason," the girl said quickly. "Jason somebody. He drove a little red Honda Civic." Something new had come into the girl's voice. It was fear.

Eddie, retrieving his darts, said, "Jason Tanner, probably." Eddie's voice had also changed—it was less casual, more apprehensive. Suddenly Amos understood that Eddie, like just about everybody else in the world, was a little afraid of Charles, too.

"What are you going to do?" the girl said.

"I didn't want to do anything, Brandykins," Charles said. "It's what you did, you and this Jason Tanner. You two have publicly put me into this position where, out of self-respect, I am *forced* to do something. And just when I have other business to attend to."

"What business?" the girl said to Charles, and when he didn't reply, she said, "You mean that business with Eddie's little itch?"

For the first time, Charles laughed, a great, full-throated laugh. Then, when he was done laughing, he spoke again in a quiet voice, almost to himself. "That's a good one. *Eddie's little itch.*"

"Well, you can count me out of that one," the girl said.

"But we'd like your assistance. We'll do a good-girl-bad-boys routine. You'll be the good girl. She'll trust you. It'll be fun. We're not going to do anything serious. Just enough to get the little itch's attention. So she'll be nicer to Eddie."

"Forget it," the girl said. "I mean it, Charles. I'm not interested in your sick fun and games."

For one still moment, none of the shoes moved. And then suddenly Charles's Nikes moved toward the girl. "What're you doing?" she said.

Charles didn't speak. He was on her, there was grunting and muffled sounds, and the girl's feet were lifted off the ground.

Charles carried her across the room and dumped her on the bed. For a moment, the bouncing mattress springs touched Amos's back.

"What're you doing?" she said again. Her voice was stretched thin with fear.

"Get the tape and rope," Charles said.

"Please, Charles," she whimpered. She'd begun to cry. "God, Charles, you're sick, really sick."

"C'mon, Charles," Eddie said in a small voice. "Cut her some slack, why don't you."

Charles's tone had turned steely. "Get the freaking tape and rope, Eddie."

After a second's hesitation, Eddie's Nikes moved to the foot-locker and came back.

"Hey, c'mon, that *hurts*," Brandy said, still crying. "That really hurts."

On each side of the bed, Amos could see one half of a pair of black Nikes. "God, Charles, that—" the girl started to say in a teary voice, and then was muffled. There was a ragged ripping sound of tearing tape, and then another.

A few seconds later, both pairs of Nikes were back on the floor. In his soft, crooning voice, Charles said, "Okay, we'll be back when we've taken care of Eddie's little itch. Will you wait for me this time? You will? Oh, that's sweet." A moment passed, and then Charles went back to his steely voice. "Laugh, Eddie."

Silence.

"I said something funny to Brandykins. When I say something funny, you need to laugh. Otherwise, you don't get my help with your little itch."

A moment passed. In a sulky voice, Eddie said, "Maybe I don't need your help."

Charles let out a crisp sarcastic laugh. "Oh, now *there's* a rich one. You took Miss Pubescence to Lookout Surefire Getting Plenty Point, and what did you get? Nada. Zero. Zip. And you know why that was? Because you're afraid to get a gal's attention. That's why you need me tonight. Because you're not what we in the getting-plenty business call a credible threat." He slipped into his sickening-sweet croon. "Isn't that right, Brandykins?"

Silence.

"She agrees," Charles crooned. "I can see it in her eyes." Then, in his steely voice, Charles said, "Funny. That was funny, Eddie."

Eddie forced a small croaky laugh.

"Okay," Charles was saying. "Supply check. Nylons. A bauble. Flashlight. Frankfurters and doggy debilitator." He made a soft malevolent laugh. "And of course Mr. Persuasion."

"We don't need that, Charles."

This time Charles's laugh was low and seething. "That's just one of your many deficiencies, Eddie. You go into battle unprepared."

"This isn't a freaking battle," Eddie murmured.

"One more deficiency. Failure to identify the enemy."

Charles's black shoes moved to the window. Eddie's stayed put.

"Let's go," Charles said in his cold voice.

Eddie still didn't move.

"Look, Eddie, I know how to handle this kind of thing. Nothing bad's going to happen to your little girly-poo. She just needs to see you in a little different light, and then her attitude will change all over the place. She'll make nice like you've never imagined."

After a moment, Eddie said, "No physical stuff?"

"None. I won't touch the girl."

"And none of your weird stuff?"

Charles laughed. "Not if you prefer a more conventional approach."

Eddie's feet shifted slightly. A moment later, he was following Charles through the window, and footsteps sounded along the porch, down the stairs.

When Amos heard the half-car roll out of the graveled driveway, he slid out from under the bed and stood up.

The girl on the bed looked wide-eyed at Amos, first at his face, then at his loose suit. It was the same girl he'd seen the night the Tripps had accosted him. She was wearing black platforms, Levi's, and a jacket. Her arms and legs were tied to the bed's head and footboard. Silver duct tape stretched tightly over her mouth.

Amos pulled the tape slowly at first, then quickly. The girl was crying. Black eyeliner streaked her cheeks. Spots of blood popped through her white lipstick.

"Where are they going?" Amos said.

"Who are you?" the girl said. The spots of blood were blurring on her lips.

"Where are they going?" Amos said again.

"I know who you are." She snuffled, but clear mucus covered her upper lip. "You're that guy we stopped on the street that night who nearly peed his pants."

"Where are they going?"

She snuffled again and said, "Untie me and I'll tell you."

Amos did. The girl wiped her nose. Then she said, "I can't tell you where they're going. Charles would kill me."

"Look," Amos said, "I think this involves someone I know."

The girl shrugged. She was no longer snuffling. Her composure had returned. She looked Amos in the eye. "She'll survive."

43

SOUNDS IN THE NIGHT

Before the play, Clara had peeked through the side curtain and, finding Amos sitting in one of the back rows, felt a warm thrill of both pleasure and safety. It was somehow reassuring, knowing Amos was there to escort her home.

But when she looked again following intermission, Amos was gone. Gone? Where would he go?

After the play, Clara dressed quickly and ran up to Mrs. Van Riper's office to store the stage gun in the safe, but was stopped short. The door was locked. She knocked. No one answered. She ran back to the auditorium and poked her head into the girls' dressing room. "Anyone seen Mrs. Van Riper?" she said, and one of the girls, without turning, said, "On multiple occasions."

"No, I mean in the last few minutes."

There was a vague negative murmuring, then Sands Mandeville, dressed in black pants and pink bra, turned and said, "I feel a draft."

Clara knocked at the boys' dressing room, and a boy standing near the door said, "She's definitely not here," and then a boy behind him, wearing only jockey shorts, said, "The Ripper left early. Had to get to the airport or something."

Clara, feeling rushed and desperate—how long would Amos wait?—tried Mrs. Van Riper's door one last time.

Locked. She felt the solid mass of the gun within the interior pocket of her long coat. It was safe there. And she could take it home and put it someplace safe. And then bring it to the play tomorrow night.

She ran out to the descending steps in front of the auditorium. Most of the people were gone. In the dim outside light, a few clusters of adults and students stood around talking. Amos wasn't there. Clara checked the stage entrance—nothing—and came back to the front steps. From one of the clusters of students, a large form broke off and came her way. It was Bruce. "Hey!" he said.

Clara smiled and said hello. Then, looking around, "Have you seen Amos?"

"Should I have?"

Clara explained.

Bruce, nodding, said, "That's what I was telling you. He used to be Mr. Dependable. Now he's scrambled eggs."

"You think he could've gone off to that appointment he was talking about?"

Bruce gave her a *maybe* look. "Seems kind of late for appointments, though."

Clara scanned the lawn and parking lot, which were growing quiet.

"Want me to walk with you?" Bruce said.

"Oh," Clara said, "you don't need to do that."

Bruce grinned amiably. "I've got nothing else to do."

Clara took one last look around before giving up on Amos. "Well, if you're sure you don't mind."

They walked quietly for the first couple of blocks, and then

Clara felt as if she ought to be more polite. "How goes the Barrineau Project?" she said.

"Who told you about that?"

"Oh. I guess Amos did. But I didn't tell anyone else."

They kept walking.

"So how's it going?" she said again.

"Not that great. I guess Amos told you I've been calling under an assumed name."

"Trent deMille," Clara said, chuckling.

"Right. So Trent and Anne Barrineau are talking tonight and I can tell right away something was different and finally she goes, 'There's this tall guy following me around. I think maybe he's been following me around for a while without my knowing it, but now that I'm aware of him, I see him everywhere.'"

Clara and Bruce kept walking. As they passed under an elm, a streetlight threw fitful shadows. "So what did you say?" Clara asked.

Bruce said, "I didn't know what to say, so I said, 'Well, why don't you just say something to this guy.' And in this supercalm voice, she goes, 'That's what I'm doing now.'"

"Oh, my gosh!"

"Yeah," Bruce mumbled.

"Then what?"

"I go, 'What do you mean?' and she says, 'I think you're the guy following me around. Are you the guy?' And I don't know what to do, so I go, 'Yeah. Yeah, I am.'"

"And?"

"She says, 'What's your real name?' and I tell her."

"And?"

"She goes, 'Well, I better get off now,' and then she says good-bye and hangs up."

"Oh, I'm sorry," Clara said.

"Yeah."

They turned silently onto Genesee. As they approached her house, Clara was relieved to see that it looked the way she left it—the one light on in the living room, the one light on in her room upstairs. "You want to come in for some hot chocolate or something?" Clara said, but Bruce shrugged. "Naw," he said. "Time for Trent deMille to go home and lick his wounds."

They said good-bye on the sidewalk. At the front door, Clara paused to watch Bruce's big silhouette dissolve into the darkness.

Clara went to the answering machine in hopes there would be a message from Amos. The light was blinking, but the only message was from her mother. "Hi, sweetie, it's me. I just tried you at Gerri's but got their machine, so maybe you're all at the play." Her mother faltered. "It's late over here." A pause. "It's just that I woke up thinking about you. So as soon as you get this message, will you please call me? I know it's expensive, but call just for a second to let me know you're okay." Another pause. "Okay. Bye, sweetie. I love you."

An old familiar softness opened within Clara. She thought about calling to put her mother's mind at ease, but knew it would involve a lot of complicated lying about how she'd gotten the message here at home when she was supposed to be staying the weekend with Gerri's family. So she didn't call. She thought about calling Amos to find out why he hadn't shown up but decided it would just be embarrassing for both of them.

Clara stuck her hand in her pocket and was surprised by the solid object it contained. The stage gun. Clara parted the clothes in the upstairs closet and climbed the ladder to the attic. She went to the hope chest and was glad to look again at the green shirt. She lifted it and nestled the gun into the baby quilt that lay beneath it, then latched the trunk.

But Clara was still edgy from the play and everything else, too edgy to sleep. She started the upstairs bath, heated milk for cocoa, let Ham out, then settled into a hot tub while sipping her chocolate. Outside, Ham barked sharply, but it tailed off. A cat, maybe, or a raccoon. That was part of what her father always called Ham's job description—keeping the backyard varmint-free.

Clara had tuned the bathroom radio to an oldies station and stacked several magazines on the tubside stool. She'd browsed an entire *Mirabella* and was on to *Seventeen* when, in the middle of an old Rolling Stones song, the radio and the bathroom light simultaneously went out, leaving the room suddenly dark and quiet.

"Ham?" she said, and then remembered he was still outside. Clara rose from the tub and, dripping wet, peered into the hallway. Dark there, too. She crossed the hall and switched on her bedroom light.

Nothing.

She peered out her window. Lights showed from the opposite houses. So it wasn't a general neighborhood blackout. Which meant a fuse was probably out downstairs. Clara told herself that was all the problem was. It was an old house, built before circuit breakers, built before microwaves and dishwashers. Her father had explained it a hundred times. Clara quickly toweled dry, threw on her nightgown, buttoned it up, and headed downstairs.

In the pantry, Clara lit a candle and opened the black metal fuse box. She looked and looked again. None were burned. She tightened them and wiggled them in hopes something would connect, but nothing did. Everything stayed dark.

There in the candlelit pantry, Clara suddenly felt afraid. It was an unreasonable feeling, she told herself, but that didn't make it go away.

Clara went to the front door. "Ham?" Clara called out. "C'mon in, Ham." While she was listening for the tinkling of his metal collar, Clara heard something else.

A creak from the rear of the house. She waited and it came again, and then from another direction another noise: a breaking twig from somewhere just beyond the front porch. Clara quickly closed the front door. She locked it tight. She couldn't look out through the front-door window. A strange numbness came over her, making her feel rubbery. She blew out her candle. She stepped back from the door and nearly tipped over. She held on to a table and grabbed for the phone. There was no dial tone, nothing. She looked down at her hands and thought, *These aren't my hands. I have no feeling.*

A creak from the kitchen, and another. The creak of floorboards beneath a moving person. Her father, maybe, home early from his trip.

"Dad?" Her voice seemed to come slowly up from under water. "Dad?"

No answer.

More creaking, to her left. With difficulty, Clara shifted her gaze. The front doorknob turned. She had locked the door, but now the doorknob was turning.

"Dad?"

Nothing.

Clara put her hands on the banister and pulled herself up step by step. This was like a nightmare. She tried to call for Ham, but nothing came out. The insides of her lips were so dry they stuck together. Finally, at the top, she sat back on her knees and looked down. There was no one there. But there were noises everywhere. And then low voices, thick low male voices.

"There?"

"Nup."

"Here neither."

A low male murmur. "Where now?"

"Up."

Clara wanted to cry out, or fall down and cry. She picked up the hall phone. Dead. She let it drop, *bang*. She looked around.

Down below, it became suddenly still.

Clara opened and closed the door to her room without going in, then dragged herself to the hall closet. She pushed aside the garment bags, began to pull herself up the wooden ladder. She had to take a breath between each rung. Finally at the top, she eased open the trapdoor and hauled herself through. She gasped and sucked for air. She couldn't get enough air. She could hardly keep her eyes open. She closed the trapdoor. She knew she should've pulled the garment bags together to cover the ladder, she'd known it all the time, so why hadn't she done it? Why couldn't she do it now?

It was dark in the attic. The only light came from the streetlight through a single gabled window. Clara thought of hiding among the boxes of Christmas stuff or behind the rack of Halloween costumes but knew she'd be found there. She thought of going to a window, trying to shout out. But what if she couldn't make sounds? Or what if *they* heard her before a neighbor did?

Clara closed her eyes and lay with her ear over the trapdoor. There was nothing to do. Just wait. Wait till they went away. Or wait till they found her.

She heard doors opening and doors closing. There were no voices now. Just footsteps. Footsteps into the bathroom. Into her parents' bedroom. Then into her own bedroom. A long time in her bedroom. Drawers opening but not closing. The little scream the last drawer makes, the drawer with her underthings. Then laughter. Low voices and muffled laughter.

Below, the footsteps grew dimmer. Footsteps on the stairs. Footsteps going away.

Then coming back. Going again slowly, so slowly, room to room. And finally coming to the hall closet. Coming to the hall closet and stopping.

"*Hey!*" A low tight whisper.

Heavy footsteps from behind. Them stopping, too.

Clara, on the other side of the trapdoor, couldn't swallow, couldn't speak. She just listened. It seemed like full minutes passed. Finally she heard the hangers move, heard a boot on the first rung.

They'd found her. They were coming up.

Clara stumbled for her hope chest and did a funny thing. She put on Amos's green shirt over her nightgown. She buttoned it all the way up to the throat.

A slow creak from behind her.

Clara turned.

The trapdoor lifted.

First the large one came through, then the small one.

44

BIG SUIT

Amos was running.

After leaving the Tripps' apartment, he'd run down the gravel driveway, across the street, and through the Kensington District, planning a route over Bandy Ridge through the business section into Clara's neighborhood to Clara's house. He turned uphill and ran steadily, a boy in a big suit. He charted the shortcuts he could take, the alleys he would use, and all the while, he ran steadily, sucking in the cold night air, his heart close to bursting, but running steadily, slanting across streets and yards, pounding along sidewalks, sweat streaming down his face. And yet the distances seemed to stretch, each block seemed to grow longer, and the harder he tried to run, the slower he seemed to go, so that the growing fear that he might be too late felt more and more like a fact, the kind of hopeless fact that made him want to stop, just stop and catch his breath.

On Walnut, he cut across a corner lot and saw a large, familiar form on the sidewalk in front of him. It was Bruce.

"Hey," Bruce said, stopping to let himself be approached.

Amos kept running. "Clara's," he panted, and then, over his shoulder as Bruce turned to watch him pass: "Something's wrong at Clara's."

"Everything's okay," Bruce yelled after him. "I just saw her a half hour ago. Everything's fine."

Amos knew in his bones this was wrong, but had no time to explain. His lungs ached for air, and his feet felt heavier and heavier. Each time they hit pavement, pain shot up through his calves. Threading across traffic on Albany, he glimpsed the Bank of Jemison clock tower: 11:37! Already 11:37 and he still had blocks and blocks to go. He was too late. He was way too late.

For one second, and then another, Amos slackened his pace, as if to slow to a walk and then just stop, but at that moment, a calm, steady, and familiar voice came into his ears. Amos knew whose voice it was. It was his father's. "Run, Amos," he said. "You can do it. You just need to put one foot in front of the other, and run."

And Amos, without quite realizing he'd begun, was running again.

45

IN CLARA'S ATTIC

It was dark, but as the two forms crawled up from the trapdoor and raised themselves to full height, one short and wiry, the other huge and hulking, a sudden terrible certainty came over Clara. It was the Tripps. She was certain it was Eddie and Charles Tripp. Eddie was one thing, but Charles...what was Charles doing here?

The small one—could it be anyone but Eddie?—switched on a flashlight and aimed it directly at Clara. She tried to stand, but sat back down, her back against her wooden hope chest. She wanted to cry, but nothing would come. She closed her eyes. She waited a long time and opened them again.

They were talking. One of them was talking. Charles was talking to her in a low, spooky, crooning voice. A question. "Didn't you want company? We thought you wanted company. That's why we're here. As an accommodation to you."

Eddie said nothing.

"Isn't that why you told people your father was gone this weekend?" Charles said in his oversweet croon. "Because you wanted some company?"

No. Clara tried to say no, but what came out was something strangled and dry and not human.

This seemed to encourage Charles.

He took several steps forward. Eddie kept the beam of light trained on her. They were looking at her, trying to see what she looked like. She knew what she looked like. Like something without bones. Like a bag with loose things in it. With effort, she tried to straighten her back, to stare hard into the beam of light. "What're you doing here?" she said in a dry, cracking voice.

"We're here to see you," Charles said. "We even brought you something. Show her, Eduardo. Show her what we brought."

Eddie brought out a necklace from his coat pocket and shined his light on it. It was a gold-colored necklace. "Twenty-four karat," Charles said in his sweet voice. "A token of our good intentions."

Eddie extended the necklace toward Clara and again flashed the beam of light glintingly across it, but the light caught something else, too. A fine crosswise scar across the forearm.

"Why're you doing this, Eddie?" she said in a small voice.

Eddie flinched slightly, pulled back his extended gift.

"His name is Eduardo," the big one said sweetly. "But if you like, you can call him crazy."

"I'll call him Eddie," Clara said in a sullen voice.

There was a long still moment, then Charles laughed. Eddie didn't. "Oh, Eduardo," Charles crooned. "This is a rabbit with spunk. This is a rabbit worth catching."

Clara breathed in and breathed out. "You're not supposed to be here," she said. "What you're doing is illegal."

Again Charles laughed, followed uneasily by Eddie. "The spunky rabbit has a sense of humor, Eduardo," Charles said. "She dispenses free legal advice."

"I know you," Clara said. "I know who you are."

Charles laughed casually. "Of course you do," he said, exuding sweetness. "We're all well acquainted. You invited us. That's why we're here."

Sullenly Clara said, "I didn't invite Eddie and I didn't invite you."

Again Charles issued an amused laugh. "Oh," he said in his calm, caressing voice, "that's what you can tell your father and your boyfriend Amos and maybe even yourself, but deep in your heart, you invited us. You wanted us to come. This is your own little dream. You made it up, and now we're here."

Clara hated this person, hated him with all her heart. She turned to Eddie. She didn't know what to say. She said, "I trusted you, Eddie."

This time Charles's laugh was harsher. "Trust? Trust is just another name for mental deficiency. Show me someone who trusts and I'll show you a village idiot."

Clara didn't look at Charles when he said this. She kept her eyes fixed on Eddie. "I did trust you, though. You told me you didn't kill Amos's pigeon and I believed you."

Again Charles's laugh was sharp. "He *didn't* kill the pigeon. He didn't have the *cojones* for that little task." Charles grinned. "He did, however, point out the treasured bird."

Clara's eyes were still on Eddie. "Is that right?"

Eddie didn't speak. In the dark, his face was just a dim, immobile mask.

"It was a simple matter of choices," Charles said. He was using his sweet voice again. "I told him he could either point out the milkboy's personal fave or I'd just kill them all."

Clara turned slowly to Charles. "How come you do this stuff?" she said. "How come you do all this stuff and make people hate you?"

"How come *who* does hateful stuff?" Charles said sweetly.

"You. You and Eddie. The Tripp brothers."

Charles grinned. "This is some weird case of mistaken identity. We are not the Tripp brothers. My name is...*Rico!* Yes, Rico. And my compadre's name is Eduardo. But we have heard of the Tripp brothers." He made a little laugh. "To be truthful, they scare us."

Charles waited a moment or two. He seemed to be enjoying himself. "I understand you're one of the really, really smart kids, Clara," he said in his crooning voice. "So let's have a review quiz. What is my name?"

Clara didn't answer. She felt her body going rubbery again.

In the same coaxing voice, Charles said, "What is my name, Clara?"

Again Clara said nothing. Her eyelids drooped. She didn't see Charles's hand fly out as much as feel it. But with sudden terrible quickness Charles was upon her, grabbing her shirt, jerking it tight around her throat.

"Hey!" Eddie said. "I thought you said—"

"Relax, Eduardo," Charles said in his sweet voice. "Your little itch and me are just getting up close and personal." He returned his gaze to Clara. "Okay, now. You understood the question, didn't you, Clara?" he said with exaggerated patience.

"Yes," Clara said in a small, tired voice.

A moment passed. In the dark, as Charles held her shirt front, she could smell his sour breath and the too-rich smell of his Right Guard deodorant. Abruptly Charles released his grip and leaned back. He pulled something from an interior pocket, a metal case, from which, with a quick decisive click, a blade flashed open.

"Clara Wilson," Charles crooned, "meet Mr. Persuasion." Charles's voice was still gentle, lilting, full of compassion. "Mr. Persuasion's here to help you see things from a different point of view. Now, what is my name?"

It was quiet in the room. From somewhere outside, a dog barked, but it wasn't Ham's bark. Clara looked through the dimness toward Eddie. He wasn't going to help. He wasn't going to do anything. He was just a silhouette. A silhouette of a statue. Something collapsed within Clara. "Rico," she said.

"Splendid!" Charles said with exaggerated pleasure. "And my compadre?"

"Eduardo."

"Excellent," Charles said, and he tilted his head down at the unsheathed blade, as if considering it. "Now, earlier in our lesson, we were talking about choices. Let's return to that. What I heard through the grapevine is that Eddie Tripp took you up to Lookout Surefire Getting Plenty Point." Charles's head lifted toward Clara. "Is that true, Clara?"

"He took me somewhere. I don't know what it was called."

"Oh, that's what it's called, all right. Lookout Surefire Getting Plenty Point."

Clara said nothing.

"So?"

"So what?"

"Did you get any at Getting Plenty?" Charles asked soothingly, and then rolled out a low rumble of laughter that reminded Clara of distant thunder.

"I don't know what you mean," she said.

Charles laughed again. "Oh, you can say that, Clara, but

don't insult us by expecting us to believe it." His shaved head turned. "Do you believe it, Eduardo?"

Eddie's head shook slowly: *no.*

After a moment or two, Charles said, "Okay. Back to our little lesson on choices. Now, when *I* take a gal up to Lookout Surefire Getting Plenty Point, I take the key out of the ignition and say, 'You have two choices, and one is to run.'" Charles's low laugh rumbled more fully this time.

"Hey, c'mon," Eddie said out of the dark in a low, pleading voice.

Suddenly Charles was leaning forward, and with a quick swiping motion, he cut first one button and then another from Amos's shirt. It happened so fast, Clara hardly knew what had happened, and then, as she peered down at the shirt, the knife sliced the other buttons free. She saw one hit the floor and roll into darkness. Was she about to be killed? The thought came to her that this was how murders occurred. One second you're talking to the killer, and the next second you're not.

In a low voice, Eddie said, "C'mon, you said no physical stuff."

Charles laughed. "I said I wouldn't touch her. You got to pay more attention, Eduardo. I haven't touched her. Mr. Persuasion has."

Charles tugged Clara's buttoned nightgown away from her chest and started cutting those buttons one by one. The tip of the blade nipped into her bare skin. *No,* she thought. *No, please, no.* And then she managed to say it: "No. Please, no."

Charles laughed a deep rich greedy laugh, was still laughing this laugh when something strange happened.

From behind Charles, looming as if from the mouth of a dark

cave, Eddie stepped forward and said, "No. No more. No freaking more."

Charles's laughter roared louder. He could hardly contain himself. "Oh, *yes,*" he said, and the knife worked through the last flannel-covered button.

"No," Eddie said, and laid a hand on Charles's shoulder, which made Charles recoil abruptly and swirl toward Eddie, flashing the knife now at his brother.

It took Clara a moment to understand she was free of Charles's grip. She clamped her nightgown together with both hands.

"Oh, Eduardo," Charles was saying with exaggerated disappointment. "I'd had such hopes for us tonight. This, after all, was your little itch. But then a funny thing happened, Eduardo. I got an itch for her, too, and as it turns out, mine is the bigger itch." Charles laughed, but there was something inside him lying in wait, Clara could feel it. "Now that I'm here and I see what I see, I begin to understand that I'm in one of my moods, and when I'm in the mood, Eduardo, I'm in the mood." Charles waited. "Your little Clara is *very* fetching."

All at once Eddie in wild rage charged into his giant brother. There were the heaves and grunts of furious contact, the sound of the flashlight pummeling flesh, and then something swift and silent, followed by a low, short *oof*ing sound. Eddie sat heavily down. He was gasping.

Charles was breathing normally. His voice held steadily to its exaggerated sweetness. "Sometimes you forget yourself, Eduardo." He beamed the flashlight toward Eddie, who held his hand over his face as if expecting another blow.

"You're lucky I'm a nice guy, Eduardo. A nastier character would've used the knife." Charles slid the point of the knife into Eddie's left nostril. "You understand, don't you, Eduardo?"

The only portion of Eddie's face that moved was his mouth. "Yeah," he said.

"Good." Charles's sweet voice had become reassuring, soothing, almost fatherlike. "I need you to go downstairs now, Eduardo. Don't worry about anything up here. Everything up here will be right as rain."

Eddie pulled his face back from the knife. Then, without a glance toward Clara, he slunk away and disappeared through the trapdoor, which he pulled closed behind him.

46

THE APPOINTMENT

Amos's body seemed about to explode as he turned finally up Genesee. He drew short sharp breaths and with each exhalation heard the word *run* in his mind. *Run, run, run.* When he drew up in front of Clara's house, it looked abandoned. It was completely dark. Amos, gasping, circled the house, peering in windows, hearing nothing, seeing nothing but darkness. In the front yard, off toward the bushes, he heard quick heavy breathing. He moved toward the sound, toward a breathing mass on the ground. It was Ham, lying on his side, taking rapid, shallow breaths. His eyes were wide and white. He stood uncertainly, then sat back down. "It's okay, Ham," Amos whispered, even though he didn't think it was.

As he was leaning over the dog, Amos heard a door open behind him. Into the dim light of the streetlamp walked Eddie Tripp.

Amos understood that this was the appointed time.

He stepped out of the shadow. "Where're you off to, Eddie?" he said, and was relieved his voice sounded steady and normal.

For a moment—because of Amos's suit?—Eddie seemed to think Amos was an adult, and looked ready to cut and run, but then, seeing who was actually wearing the suit, Eddie visibly relaxed. "Well, well. Our hero."

Amos stepped closer. "What did you do to the dog?"

Eddie laughed. "Dog?" he said innocently. "What dog?"

"And what were you doing inside the house?"

This time Eddie merely grinned. "Wasn't. I was just knocking on the door, and nobody answered. There a new law against knocking on a door?"

Amos didn't like the way this was going. It was as if Eddie kept sliding into a position just beyond him.

"And how about my pigeon?"

A false cackling laugh erupted from Eddie. "And maybe you'd like to finger me for killing JFK? Or how about Roger Rabbit? You want to finger me for killing Roger Rabbit?"

"No," Amos said, and a strange calmness came over him. "No, I'd just like to finger you for being such a lame human being."

Eddie's smile evaporated. A hardness came over him, but then softened again.

He held his hands up, fingers splayed, in a universal gesture of surrender. "You take things a little too serious, Hero," he said, and began moving toward Amos. "We don't have to agree on everything. In fact, we can agree to disagree. But we can do it with the mutual respect of warriors."

Amos didn't know how to respond to this. He had the feeling that the appointment was over before it really started. That Eddie-the-enemy had vanished and been replaced by Eddie-the-not-so-bad-guy. Amos lifted his head, straightened his back, and had relaxed for just an instant when from Eddie's small muscular body, a leg shot up and his shoe swung sharply into Amos's crotch.

By no more than an inch, Eddie's foot missed its target and lost itself in the loose material of the baggy trousers. Amos grabbed the foot with both hands and gave it a violent clockwise twist that sent Eddie over onto his stomach. He began to push himself upright.

The three terra-cotta rabbits stood on their hind legs in the flower bed beside the walk. Amos grabbed one of them, lifted it overhead, and struck Eddie a glancing blow. The figurine shattered. Eddie fell back, stunned. When he touched his scalp, his hand came away with blood. "Jesus," he said in a small voice.

Amos picked up another of the terra-cotta rabbits. "You want to go now, or you want to stay and keep chatting?"

Eddie got up unsteadily and, trying to keep his dignity, stopped rubbing his head. He tried to drill his eyes into Amos, but they had lost all influence over him. Still, Eddie kept talking. "You're a pretty sorry hero, Hero. I'm not Clara's real problem. Clara's *real problem* has got her cornered in the attic."

Amos glanced quickly at the house, then back at Eddie. "Charles?"

Eddie stared at Amos evenly.

Amos moved toward the front door, but looked back at Eddie. "Wanna help?"

Eddie shrugged and made a small, strangely contorted smile that Amos would always remember as regretful. "I tried," Eddie said. "Now it's your turn."

47

IN WHICH A SHOT IS FIRED

"Listen," Charles Tripp whispered.

He was standing over Clara in the darkened attic. The beam of his flashlight shone on Clara's face. Her eyes were wide with alarm. She couldn't run. She couldn't scream. She wished the attic window would open. She wanted to climb out onto the roof. She looked at Charles and looked away. He was huge. He was huge and bald and creepy. But she couldn't scream and she couldn't run and the window she wanted to climb out of wouldn't open. She would fight. But she somehow knew that her fighting would only heighten his appetites.

"Listen," Charles said again in a crooning whisper. "All we can hear are heartbeats. Your heartbeat. My heartbeat. There is something going on here, Clara, something beneath the surface, where things are important." He'd made his whisper soothing and low. "Can you hear it? Can you hear your heart go *bop bop bop?*"

In movies, at a moment like this, the heroine would sometimes spit into the villain's face, but Clara couldn't make any spit. Her throat was sticky and dry.

"Here," Charles said, kneeling close. He unbuttoned his shirt. He took Clara's hand and placed it over his left nipple. "Feel. Can you feel it pounding? Can you feel my heart going *bop bop bop?*"

Clara said nothing. She tried to pull her hand away, but he gripped it tighter.

"There," Charles said soothingly, resetting her hand. "What do you feel?"

Clara felt skin and hair and muscle and the sledgehammer throb of a pounding heart, either his heart or hers, she wasn't sure.

"There, Clara. Right there. What do you feel?"

"Nothing," she said in a hollow voice. "I'm dead. I'm already dead."

Charles laughed a low, pleased laugh. He touched a finger to her hand and ran it very slowly along her bare arm. Clara closed her eyes. She willed herself to stop feeling. She was somewhere else. It didn't matter where his hand was. She was somewhere else.

A low creaking noise, from behind them. Clara's eyes flew open. Charles twisted around. The trapdoor rose. Amos's head poked through, then his shoulders, his body rising, growing larger until he stood in the dim attic squinting into the beam of Charles's light.

"This is an attic," Charles said in his calm soothing voice. "It isn't a coffee shop. It's not designed for drop-in visits." Charles's voice was patient, but Clara sensed that he was annoyed, that he'd had all his preliminary fun and didn't like being interrupted now. He rose from his kneeling position.

Amos stood fast, waiting.

"Okay, okay," Charles said. His voice was no longer just patient. It was appeasing, almost contrite. He took a cautious first step toward Amos. "No harm, no foul, right? I mean, we're all human. You can't blame a guy for trying, right?"

Don't believe him, Clara thought. Whatever you do, Amos, don't believe him.

Charles set down his flashlight, beam on, so that a fan of light opened on the attic floor. "I was invited here," Charles said in his calm, sweet voice. "I was invited here by Clara." He turned in the dark toward Clara. "She might deny it, but it's undeniable. She invited us here. Me and my compadre. We came as an accommodation to her. We took nothing. We did nothing." Charles shrugged. "But now *you've* dropped in, and suddenly things are...too *congested*." Charles raised his hands, stretched wide his fingers. "So even though invited, I'll now excuse myself, if you'll just let me pass."

When he heard Charles's words and saw Charles raise his hands in surrender, Amos almost had to laugh. He'd seen this routine minutes before from Eddie. He knew what was coming, and this time he wouldn't have to trust to dumb luck. This time he'd be prepared. When Charles's leg swung up, Amos would slide back with his feet and lean forward with his arms to catch Charles's foot and twist him down, as he'd done with Eddie. And so, as Charles moved slowly toward him, hands raised, talking in a calm, soothing voice, Amos kept his eyes on Charles's feet.

Which was why Amos never saw coming the compact downward punch that Charles delivered with his fisted right hand to the center of Amos's face.

It was as if Amos's whole body gathered in and collapsed around his nose. As Amos was falling, Charles came up with his right foot to Amos's chin, snapping Amos's head back. For a long moment, Amos heard and saw nothing. Then he felt his body being shifted one way and another on the attic floor. He heard ripping sounds. He felt wide tape being wound around his arms, his legs, his mouth. "And your eyes," Charles whispered. "This is nothing for a hero's eyes to see."

Amos closed his eyes just before the wide silver tape stretched over them.

Clara was holding the gun.

She hardly knew she had it. But while Charles was wrapping Amos with tape, Clara, almost without thinking, had reached into her wooden hope chest, had slowly run her fingers across the baby quilt until she'd found what she hadn't really known she was looking for, the cool metal of the stage gun.

Charles, when he saw the gun, broke out in a low chuckle.

"You *are* a spunky little rabbit," he crooned, and took a slow step forward. He peeled back his shirt and pointed toward his heart. "Aim here, Clara," he crooned. "Where it's thinking of you and going *bop bop bop*." He took another step and another. "Where it's thinking of kissing your lips and kissing your earlobes and kissing your neck and going *bop bop bop*."

From outside, a deep, unamplified voice rose in the cold night air. It was Bruce, Clara could tell, using his huskiest register. "This is the Jemison city police," he called out. "We need all occupants to show themselves at the front door with hands raised. I repeat, we need all—"

Charles snickered. "If that's a cop, I'm Brad Pitt," he said.

Clara raised the stage gun until it was level with Charles's chest. He laughed and took another step. The gun was a bad idea. She shouldn't have brought it out. She wished she hadn't. Charles knew it was a fake or he knew she was a fake. He knew something. She wanted to cry but couldn't. She straightened and extended her arm, still pointing, and he kept coming, one slow step after another, saying things she willed herself not to hear.

What Clara did then wasn't planned. It was just some instinct, some divine shadowy instinct for self-preservation.

Very tiredly, Clara turned the gun away from Charles. She closed and opened her eyes in a long tired blink. Everything was happening in slow motion. Clara crooked her arm. She turned the hand with the gun inward. She pointed it at herself and stared with dead eyes at Charles Tripp. She pulled the trigger. The gun exploded and all at once she felt sharp pain and then a sticky wetness, and then she saw Charles draw up short, gazing down at her.

Charles Tripp stared at her with shock and disbelief. "You shot yourself," he said, and then said it again: "You shot yourself." There was something wild and scared in his gaze, which moved from her bloody wound to her vacant open eyes. She made a faint smile. Part of her was acting now, but part of her wasn't. She made turning the gun back toward Charles seem both wearying and unimportant. She knew what her eyes were saying. They were saying, *I just shot myself, so it doesn't much matter who in the big wide world I shoot next, but I think it ought to be you.*

Charles, taking two involuntary steps backward, stumbled over Amos. As he pushed himself up, he found himself near Amos's face. Amos's eyes and mouth were taped, but his ears were not. "You know what?" Charles whispered into Amos's ear. "You can have Clara Wilson. I wouldn't have her. I wouldn't have her with mayonnaise."

Then, while Clara watched with dead-alive eyes, Charles Tripp scuffled his way out of the attic and down the ladder.

He was gone. Charles Tripp was gone for good.

48

MOPPING UP

When Clara ripped the silver duct tape from Amos's clamped-tight eyes, she tore hair from his temples and lashes from his eyelids. The pain was startling. For a moment he kept his eyes tightly shut before opening them uncertainly. It took a second for shapes to form and come into focus.

Clara wasn't talking. Her hair was wet with sweat. She leaned forward and looked him in the eye for an instant and then without a word quickly ripped the tape from his lips. Amos clapped a hand over his mouth to keep from crying out in pain. He looked at Clara, who just kept unwinding the tape automatically. She was like someone who'd just been in a car wreck, Amos thought. "You okay?" he said.

She nodded. She didn't speak. When she'd untaped his hands and legs, she fumbled her way to the trapdoor and worked her way down. Amos followed. The lights were still off, but Clara leaned against a wall in the dark upstairs hallway. There was a funny clicking noise. When Amos came close, he realized it was her teeth. They were chattering as if from cold, even though the house wasn't cold. He took off his father's suit jacket and put it around her, and without any planning, they stood hugging, swaying slightly in each other's arms. "What did you do?" Amos said finally. "How come he left?"

"I shot myself with the stage gun. But it hurts a little bit when you do it point-blank."

Amos tried to look at her stomach, but there wasn't enough light. It was just a dark, gooey, frightening mess.

"I'm okay," Clara said. "Let's just get out of here before they come back."

"I don't think they're coming back," Amos said. "I saw Eddie as he was leaving." Amos paused. "Eddie was the one who sent me up to help you."

Clara looked blankly at Amos. She really did seem to be in shock. Amos was helping Clara down the stairs when Bruce's voice carried up from the front door. "Who's here?"

"Us," Amos yelled. "Everything's okay, I think. But check out Ham. He's in the front yard somewhere."

Amos helped Clara to the front yard, where Bruce was down on both knees beside Ham. The dog was trembling and panting and pressing forward into Bruce, who had to hold him up. Ham's legs shook uncontrollably, and his tail was clamped tight between his legs. Something was terribly wrong.

Clara bent down and wrapped her arms around the dog. "Oh, Ham, oh, Ham, it's okay, it'll be okay."

But it didn't look okay to Amos, as much as he could see from the streetlight. "Flashlight," he said. "Where's a flashlight?"

Without looking up, Clara said, "Top of fridge."

When Amos returned with the flashlight, he trained the beam on the dog. Ham's mouth was slack. He was drooling. His eyes were hugely white. They stared off into some other world.

"Hey." It was Bruce. He was holding a small vial he'd found lying on the patio. He shined the flashlight on it. *Strychnine*, it said. *Poison XXX*.

Clara began to cry.

Amos turned the flashlight back to the dog—panting, drooling, straining forward unsteadily into Clara—and then, when he saw a drop of blood fall on the pavement, he turned the beam toward Clara's stomach. He stared in horror. They all did.

The shot from the stage gun had frayed the flannel shirt and the nightgown underneath. There was blood everywhere. The more they looked at it, the less fake it seemed.

"Oh, man," Bruce said in a low, disconsolate voice.

"Ambulance," Amos said out loud to himself. "Ambulance." He ran to the kitchen, picked up the phone, and had already dialed 911 before he realized there was no dial tone. "Dead," he yelled.

"They're all dead," Clara said. "But I'm okay. I don't need an ambulance. It's Ham who does. It's Ham who's bad."

It was quiet for a moment except for Ham's rushed, shallow gasping.

Then Bruce said, "How about the keys for your mom's car?"

"Top drawer left of sink," Clara said.

"Okay, then," Bruce said, and within minutes, they were headed toward St. Stephen's Hospital, Clara lying on the backseat but scooched over to whisper to Ham, who lay on the floor, gasping. Amos sat sideways in back, watching Clara, watching Ham, and watching the road in front of them, all with equal nervousness. Bruce was up front, driving badly.

"Since when do you drive?" Amos said.

"Since Iowa. Farm kids drive young." He braked roughly for a merging car, then sped ahead. "'Course, in Iowa, you're about the only car on the road." Then he said, "How's the dog?"

"The same," Clara said.

Bruce increased speed, screamed around corners. Seven or eight blocks further west on Colonial, a police car appeared behind them, red lights swirling. Bruce pulled over and jumped out to meet the policeman.

"We've got a situation here, Officer. A girl's been shot and her dog's been poisoned. We're on our way to emergency."

The policeman beamed his flashlight into the backseat and held it on Clara's stomach for a long second, then shined the light on Ham. "Detective O'Hearn's on this case," Bruce said. "You might call Detective O'Hearn."

The policeman swept the light into Bruce's face, then snapped it off. "Okay, champ, we're gonna assume you've got a license. Just follow me."

The police car pulled out and led the way, siren blaring, the river of cars parting before them. The policeman had evidently radioed ahead, because when they got to the emergency door of the hospital, there was a nurse and attendant waiting with a gurney. And standing behind them, looking large and a little foolish in sweat clothes and jogging shoes, was Detective Lucian O'Hearn.

After they'd wheeled Clara into the emergency room, Amos went back for Ham. His breathing was labored, and he couldn't stand at all. Amos lifted him into his arms and walked into the emergency room.

"Her dog's been poisoned," he said to the nurse. "Her dog's dying."

"It's this," Bruce said, and handed the nurse the little vial he'd found on Clara's patio.

Detective O'Hearn walked over and without expression studied the vial and then the dog.

One of the emergency room doctors stepped out of a side door. His hair was matted, and his face had the pink, imprinted skin of someone who'd been napping. He looked quizzically at the nurse, who explained the situation.

"I'm sorry, but we don't take dogs," the doctor said.

"But where do we—" Amos said, and stopped. Ham's gasping had quickened. The dog's big body rocked and heaved.

"I don't know, but this is a hospital. For human beings. We don't take dogs."

Detective O'Hearn, who'd been staring fixedly at Ham, finally lifted his gaze. He presented his credentials and looked directly at the doctor. "You don't *normally* take dogs, Doctor." He smiled benignly. It was a smile that said, *I'm on your side.* "But you might on this one rare occasion."

The doctor studied Detective O'Hearn, then studied Ham, then turned to the nurse. "Well," the doctor said, "I guess if we can pump a human's stomach, we can try to pump a dog's."

49

THE LAST CHAPTER

The self-inflicted paint ball wound was a mild abrasion, according to Clara's doctor, and the episode as a whole had resulted in mild shock and dehydration.

"Which means?" Clara asked.

The doctor was an older woman. She smiled and peered down at Clara over her glasses. "It means that you're fine, but we're going to keep you overnight for observation." She nodded at the clear hanging bottle that dripped into a tube that led to her wrist. "We've got you on fluids. So all you have to do is sit back and rest." The doctor leaned forward. "Sleep is good," she said, smiling, and touched Clara's eyelids closed.

Clara left them closed. It felt nice, lying in this warm bed, being taken care of by this nice doctor and the nice nurses. It felt so nice she wondered if they'd put something in the fluids to make her feel this way.

"Hi, Polkadot."

Clara slowly opened her eyes. It was her father, turning through the door in a button-down shirt with cuff links and loosened tie, breathing heavily, as if he'd been running. He actually looked kind of dashing, Clara thought, if you applied a standard from, say, 1955. "Hi, Dad," she said in a slow voice.

He was holding her hands now and kissing her forehead.

When he drew back, his eyes looked wet, and all of a sudden Clara was crying, a full, complete, down-to-the-last-drop cry.

"You okay?" he said after a while.

"Yeah," Clara said, then realized with a start that she was almost asleep again. "I think they gave me a sedative or something," she said.

Her father nodded, and her eyes drooped closed again. She forced them back open. "How'd you get here so fast?"

Her father grinned. "Begged and pleaded with the airline."

Clara smiled and nodded. In a slow, slurred voice, she said, "Pretty good."

They sat for a minute, and then her father said, "I talked to Detective O'Hearn. He had me read your statement." Her father let his eyes meet Clara's, as if to let this sink in. "I read it all twice, and then I said that what you'd been through tonight was more than any little girl ever ought to go through. I know I shouldn't have said *little girl*, but it's what I think of you as. Then Detective O'Hearn said, 'That daughter of yours is one tough little monkey.'" Her father smiled and clasped Clara's hand. "I think it was about the highest compliment he knows how to pay."

Clara smiled weakly. She let her eyes fall closed, then with difficulty opened them again. She'd just remembered something important. "How's Ham?" she said.

Ham made the six o'clock news. Besides the crime element, it had novelty appeal. A Minicam wound through all the hospital entrances and doors, and there, amidst all the human beings, was St. Stephen's first-ever canine patient. They'd given him a muscle relaxant, the doctor in attendance said, then pumped his stomach and put him on IV fluids. "The patient," he said, "is doing beautifully." And here, on television screens all over the city and state, passed the image of Ham, his foreleg bandaged from the intravenous intrusion, but otherwise looking dazed and happy.

The Tripp brothers weren't together when they were arrested. Charles was apprehended around three A.M. in a 7-Eleven within a few blocks of the Tripp brothers' apartment. He was at the register, counting out money for the purchase of pork rinds and chocolate milk while a girl named Brandy Anderson waited for him in the front seat of the seduck. The Jemison police found Eddie at his mother's house. His mother wasn't at home, and Eddie didn't have a key, so he'd broken a window and climbed through. When the police arrived, they could see him through the living room window, asleep on an old sofa.

Back at the police substation, both Charles and Eddie pretended confusion about the questions Detective O'Hearn put to them and their attorney. Charles finally threw up his hands. "I find these questions baffling," he said in his calm, sweet voice. "I find our being here in this room baffling."

The Tripp brothers' attorney nodded in agreement. "It is a little baffling, isn't it, Mr. O'Hearn?"

"Look," the detective said amiably, "I've got so many charges here I can hardly hang on to them all. Animal poisoning. Breaking and entering." He leaned back in his swivel chair and folded his hands on his ample stomach. "This is not to mention criminal assault."

The Tripps' attorney had a bushy mustache, which he now combed with his fingers. "It's possible that the young woman was victimized. It's also possible that the perpetrators were not my clients."

O'Hearn didn't rise to the bait. "Look, kids," he said in a friendly voice, "Charles here made a rookie mistake. The victim saw his face. At close range."

"In the dark," the attorney said evenly, "while in a state of anxiety bordering on hysteria."

"She won't look too hysterical in court, Counselor. She's a sturdy number."

Charles Tripp leaned forward in his chair. In his low, sweet voice, he said, "If she tags us, it would be a terrible thing. She'd be tagging the wrong guys. It would be the kind of miscarriage of justice that can turn decent people bitter."

The name of the assigned county prosecutor was Thea Johnson-Hurlbut. "You really have to love a guy to marry into a name like Hurlbut," she said when she was introduced to Clara and her father, just to break the ice. Thea Johnson-Hurlbut said she had the authority to bring the case but frankly wondered about its merits. "This is no slam dunk," she said. "I'd say we go off at no better than even money." Clara's father said he'd leave it up to Clara. At that moment, Clara was looking at the prosecutor's briefcase. It was made of mahogany-colored leather, worn smooth. Clara loved the way it looked and what it represented, and in that moment, she knew that whatever profession she chose, it was going to have to involve a briefcase.

"Clara?" Her father's voice.

Clara nodded. Yes, she said. She wanted to go ahead with it.

The trial date was set for September. Meantime, the spring and summer passed in slow, sunlit perfection, though without horses. With her horse camp money, Clara opened a bank account for college or, as her father warily suggested, a trip to Spain. Amos had a morning job at Dusty's Oldtowne Market, which was fine because Clara was going to summer school every morning to make up for her bad grades in the second term. But this meant Amos and Clara could spend afternoons and evenings together. Sometimes Amos would help Clara with her paper route, and sometimes they'd just put the leash on Ham and start walking and wouldn't come home for hours. Sometimes they went to Monument Park to swim. Sometimes Clara would cut sweet peas or hydrangeas or whatever was blooming in her yard, and they would walk to the cemetery and put them in the sunken water vase above Mr. MacKenzie's grave. If they went to Bing's, Mrs. MacKenzie would give them free fries, and if they went to the Xavier Cinema, where Liz had taken a summer job, she would give them the employee discount.

One afternoon when they were in a listening booth at Bazooka Music, Amos and Clara caught sight of Bruce walking in with a girl. Amos and Clara exchanged looks and broke out laughing. Amos pushed open the door to their booth. "Hey, Crook, over here!"

Bruce and the girl approached. She wore a sleeveless top and a wraparound skirt that showed off her tanned, athletic legs. She was, Clara thought, achingly beautiful—it was no wonder she'd had half the guys at Melville drooling over her. She was Anne Barrineau. And she seemed happy to be in Bruce's company.

While Clara talked to her about what school was like at Eliot, Amos pulled Bruce aside. "What's the story, Crook?"

Bruce grinned and shrugged. "I hardly know. A couple days ago the phone rings and it's her and she's saying that she kind of missed our talking all the time, so we talked about four hours that night, and then yesterday we went ice skating and had a good time, so I don't know." He grinned. But there was something different about the grin. It was more adult, more self-composed. It was as if, for the first time since Amos could remember, his friend was truly happy to be himself, Bruce Crookshank.

One day in August, when Clara and Amos walked up to Sleeping Indian Rock, where water spilled into a series of deep pools, they lay on one of the flat rocks in the shade and ate Ritz crackers and little cubes of Laughing Cow cheese. Amos would lob every third or fourth cube of cheese to Ham, who sat attentively nearby.

"Question," Clara said.

"I'm listening," Amos said without looking up.

"What do you think of my nose?"

Amos seemed surprised by the question. He turned quickly. "I like your nose," he said. He tried to break the serious tone. "I like your nose and I like your toes."

A moment passed. The sound of riffling water rose pleasantly. A low *hoo-hoo*ing of mourning doves carried from the trees. "No," Clara said, "I'm serious. What do you think of my nose?"

"Okay," Amos said. "The truth is, at first I kind of thought it was different, not bad-different, but different. Then one day I realized it had just become a part of the larger you, and I knew I approved totally of the larger you. Except I just felt all this. I wasn't putting it into words or anything." He grinned. "Which is why it's sounding kind of weird to actually put it into words now."

"No," Clara said, "I think it's an okay way to put it." She thought about it. "I'm glad that's the way you think of it."

A few more moments passed. Then Amos said, "I don't know if you remember, but a long time ago, when my dad and I pulled alongside you after you'd come out of Banner Variety, my dad was talking about our old van, and he said that its value, like all things important to him, went way beyond surface beauty."

Clara didn't remember that. "I was so nervous I could hardly talk, let alone remember," she said.

Amos nodded. "Yeah, I don't know why I remembered it. At the time, it kind of embarrassed me. It was like he was trying to tell us how to think or something." He tossed Ham a cube of cheese. "But now I have a better feel for what he meant."

Clara made a low murmur. She wondered, painfully, if Amos was trying to say she wasn't beautiful but he liked her anyway.

"I mean, you're very pretty—you have surface beauty," he said, "but that's not why you're important."

Clara lay back in the shade and felt as light as the feathery white clouds that floated slowly east. The clouds were perfect. The sound of the water was perfect. Her face maybe wasn't perfect, but she decided to believe that Amos thought she was pretty. "Know what?" she said.

"What?"

"Always before," Clara said, "I wanted summer to end, to get back to school, but now I just want August to go on and on."

"August thirty-second," Amos said, laughing.

"August fifty-second," said Clara, who, it was true, did like getting the last word, whenever it was available.

50

EPILOGUE

In September, Clara missed just two days of school for the trial. On the witness stand, when Thea Johnson-Hurlbut asked her if she recognized her attackers, Clara said, "Yes."

"Are they in this room?"

Clara looked toward the Tripp brothers. "Yes."

"Will you point them out to us?"

Clara said, "That one, Charles Tripp, was the one with the knife and the one doing all the talking. He came very close to me, so I saw him clearly. The other one, Edward Tripp, refused to go along with Charles's cutting my clothes, and Charles threatened him with a knife." Clara had wanted to say more on Eddie's behalf but had been coached not to say anything more than was necessary.

The Tripp brothers' attorney asked a lot of questions meant to show that because it was so dark in the attic, and because Clara was in such a state of confusion, she couldn't identify anyone with certainty. "I can identify him," Clara said firmly, again looking at Charles Tripp.

Charles looked straight back at her. He had a complacent look in his eyes, and his lips were creased with a small, impenetrable smile. He'd let his hair grow into a brush cut, which camouflaged his veiny scalp.

* * *

Without telling Clara, Amos skipped school the day of the sentencing. *State v. Charles Clifford Tripp and Edward Abel Tripp* was listed on the court calendar along with seven or eight other cases. It was nearly eleven before the Tripp brothers were brought in. Amos knew that Thea Johnson-Hurlbut had asked for a sentence of four to five years and had told Clara that she was hopeful of getting it.

The judge was so slight a man that from Amos's angle, only his head showed above his enormous desk. Before the sentencing itself, the judge made a speech that Amos had a hard time following. "Given Edward's hitherto spotless record" was one thing the judge said. "And in regard to Charles, tempering justice with mercy" was another. Finally, when the judge was done with his talk, he sentenced Charles to six months in the state Youth Authority compound. Eddie would spend fourteen days in juvenile hall.

Amos was stunned. Six months? Fourteen days? Clara's attorney threw a protective arm around Clara and quickly escorted her out the far door of the courtroom. The Tripp brothers' attorney was grinning at his clients and shaking their hands. Charles Tripp seemed to be smirking. Before getting up from his chair, he took a second and jotted something on a piece of paper, but then, when he was done writing, he crumpled it into his fist. They were standing now, the bailiff leading Charles and Eddie off. Amos sat slumped watching, unobserved.

That, anyhow, was what Amos believed.

But as the prisoners were led across the front of the courtroom toward a side door, passing several rows in front of Amos, Charles Tripp flicked Amos a glance and then dropped the piece

of crumpled paper into a gray metal wastebasket standing just behind the rail that divided the spectators from the courtroom par-
ticipants. Amos waited until the Tripps were gone. He waited
until everyone having to do with the trial was gone. Then he
walked to the front, pushed open the gate in the dividing rail, and
picked the ball of paper out of the otherwise clean wastebasket.
He walked outside the courtroom and sat down on one of the
concrete benches that lined the wide, cavernous corridor. He
smoothed out the paper and stared at it. *It's not over till it's over,
Hero,* it said. *Our paths will cross again.*

Six weeks later, Clara hosted a Thanksgiving dinner. It should
have been the beginning of the good holidays—Thanksgiving,
then Christmas, when her mother was going to fly home from
Spain for a visit, and then her birthday—but it had a changed
feel to it. Clara couldn't find any of her mother's recipes and instead made things she found in magazines. Amos helped, as much
as he could. Clara's father was there, with Lydia, whom Clara, to
her surprise, couldn't help liking. Clara had invited Amos's
mother and sister, as well as Sylvia Harper, now Sylvia Harper
Onken, who arrived with her new husband, three mincemeat
pies, and a cranberry salad.

Everyone said they had a good time, but Clara thought it was
a failed Thanksgiving. Clara liked everyone there and had Amos
sitting right beside her, but it felt more like a stiff, polite party
than Thanksgiving. It was like everyone was trying too hard to
act happy. There was only one moment when it felt to Clara the
way Thanksgiving ought to feel. It was just before they started

passing the food. Amos's mother had broken into the various conversations by raising her voice just slightly. "I'd like to say a short prayer and…"

Amos grimaced exaggeratedly.

"…and I know my son would prefer I didn't, but if you'll allow me." She closed her eyes, and everyone else did, too, except Clara. She stared at the faces; they seemed to look intense and peaceful at the same time. "I want to thank God for this day he has provided us, and this food he has provided us, and these cooks he has provided us."

Clara watched the faces relax into murmuring laughter.

"I would also like to remember those who are absent from this table…" She paused, and Clara could tell that Mrs. MacKenzie was shaken and was trying to recompose herself, and then she went on with some words that sounded like a Psalm, but Clara was no longer listening. Clara was thinking of her mother alone in Spain, and of Mr. MacKenzie smiling at her from his old rusty Econoline in front of Banner Variety only a few months before. She even thought for a moment of Eddie Tripp, who had moved with his mother to someplace called Tarzana, California, and had written her two funny letters that both began, *Dear Dollface*. Clara put her hand under the table and closed her eyes. Before long, Amos's hand was there, too, and they were wound together, hers within his, or maybe it was his within hers—they felt so much like one that she could hardly tell the difference.